BOOKS BY NICHOLAS SANSBURY SMITH

HELL DIVERS V
CAPTIVES

NICHOLAS SANSBURY SMITH

BLACK
STONE
PUBLISHING

Copyright © 2019 by Nicholas Sansbury Smith
Published in 2019 by Blackstone Publishing
Cover illustration by K. Jones
Series design by Kathryn Galloway English

Printed in the United States of America
Originally published in hardcover by Blackstone Publishing
in 2019

First paperback edition: 2019
ISBN 978-1-9826-0417-2
Fiction / Science Fiction / Apocalyptic & Post-Apocalyptic

1 3 5 7 9 10 8 6 4 2

CIP data for this book is available
from the Library of Congress

Blackstone Publishing
31 Mistletoe Rd.
Ashland, OR 97520

www.BlackstonePublishing.com

To Robert Bray. Thank you for lending your legendary voice to the Hell Divers series and becoming the voice behind X. The series would not be what it is without you.

"Accept your past without regret, handle your present with confidence, and face your future without fear."
—UNKNOWN

PROLOGUE
THREE MONTHS AGO

Rodger Mintel awoke to the worst pain of his life. His whole body burned as if a swarm of mutant ants was eating him inch by inch.

He tried to scream but couldn't hear his voice, only the dull ringing. His eyes didn't seem to be working, either.

Maybe he wasn't awake, after all. He couldn't move his legs or arms, or his hands. All that seemed to be working were his nerves, and every fiber of his body was screaming at top volume.

He endured the torture for what felt like hours, but it could have been only minutes, or even seconds.

A few fragmented thoughts somehow got through the gauntlet of fire consuming his body. One of them was the memory of a rusted ship moored to a pier under a dark sky. Lightning forked through the flashing red vines that branched and twisted along the shore.

The pain again took hold, the images fading into bright flashes of red. He tried again to open his eyelids, but they wouldn't respond. He couldn't even grit his teeth.

Another memory surfaced in his mind's eye. He saw the ship's deck where he lay tethered. Someone lay next to him, unmoving.

A woman …

Mags!

The realization momentarily overshadowed the agony of his broken body. He couldn't remember anything beyond being strapped beside her to the deck, but he did remember getting ambushed by men in heavy armor back in the city.

He tried again to remember, but no matter how much he willed his brain to work, he couldn't focus. It was like being dog tired and drunk at the same time.

A new wave of hellfire took him, and this time he couldn't handle the torture. His mind gave up and shut off like a lightbulb.

When he woke again, he wasn't sure how much time had passed, but he did remember the pain. It had ceased, and he felt nothing but numbness.

"Am I dead?" he said aloud.

He could hear that, so maybe not.

Summoning what little strength he had, he managed to crack his eyelids open. A spot of dazzling brilliance made him squint, reminding him of the LEDs the Hell Divers had once salvaged from the surface and given his dad to use in the clock-and-wood workshop.

Hell Divers ... Dad ...

A flurry of memories tumbled through his brain. Thoughts of his family and working on the clocks and wood treasures brought him a fleeting moment of joy. So did the images of brightly painted passageways inside the *Hive*, the only home he had ever known.

He closed his eyes again, letting the memories come. They weren't all pictures of life in the sky. The next image transported him back to the rusting ship, where he was held with Magnolia. In his mind's eye, he saw Xavier Rodriguez carrying his dog, Miles. He climbed over the ship's rail, set the dog down, and cut Rodger and Magnolia free.

A sense of relief washed over him, only to shatter in the violent gun battle that followed in the recollection. Cazadores surrounded the three Hell Divers, but X stood his ground, slaying the barbarians.

Rodger remembered searching for a weapon to defend Magnolia and help X fight. Then he remembered the hulking shadow. A beast of a man towered over him. The thick, bony crests of Siren skulls rested on his armored shoulders.

El Pulpo, king of the Cazadores.

In the memory, Rodger recalled something hot ripping through his back, seizing his breath, both in the memory and now. Then came a blood-chilling scream that broke his heart and made him want to scream in reply.

The image of Magnolia, frozen on the deck and holding up her hands in shock, finally jerked Rodger into the present moment. His eyelids snapped open to a bright glow.

He was alive, after all.

His eyes slowly adjusted to the light and took in the narrow, blurred view of the room. It was a medical bay, its bulkheads fitted with machines and racks of supplies.

Across the space, two hazy figures stood next to a hatch, but he couldn't make out their features.

Was he back on the *Hive*? Had Magnolia and X managed to rescue him from the ship?

He struggled to move, but his body still wouldn't respond. Every inch of his skin felt numb, like the sensation of a foot falling asleep.

"Mags?" he stuttered. "Mom? Pops?"

If he was on the *Hive*, then surely his parents were here.

He blinked several times until the two figures came into focus.

"No," he whispered. "It can't be."

This wasn't the *Hive*. Militia soldiers didn't wear armor.

Through the numbness, a sensation emerged—a cold lump of fear in his gut. He also felt a slight swaying movement beneath him.

Realization sank in. He wasn't back in the sky. He was on the water.

The weight holding his eyelids down lifted, and he looked down at his half-naked body. Leather straps restrained his legs and arms. Another, over his neck, held his head down, limiting his field of vision. Liquid trickled through clear tubes, into the veins in his arms.

Was this why he felt numb?

The two armored sentries at the door spoke to each other, and metal shrieked as one of them opened the hatch. The larger man left the room, but the other guard stepped forward and spoke to Rodger in Spanish, in a voice muffled by his breathing apparatus.

Rodger fought the strap across his neck and lifted his head enough to glimpse the crudely sutured red gash in his lower chest.

For a moment, he just stared at the ugly wound. A horrible thought crossed his mind: maybe they had taken a piece of him and eaten it. But then, they wouldn't have bothered hooking him up to the tubes.

Someone was trying to save him, at least for now. The wound was fresh, which meant that only a few days had passed since his capture.

As he squirmed on the table, the burning came back.

Did it ever. He felt immersed in a universe of bright, searing pain.

His head fell back to the table, and he blinked over and over as the memories came crashing back over him. The fight on the deck of the ship between X and the Cazador soldiers. Miles barking, Magnolia screaming.

And then el Pulpo, grabbing him from behind.

He never saw what had impaled him through the back, but it had torn through his flesh and out his chest, which meant the red gash below his sternum wasn't the only wound.

Rodger looked away and tried to remember what had happened between then and now. But no matter how hard he tried, he couldn't recall a thing. He didn't know where Magnolia and X were, or the other divers, or what had happened to the *Hive*.

"Please," Rodger choked. "Please let me go."

The guard walked back to the hatch and opened it for the other soldier. This time, he had company.

Two men walked in. One was short and bald, with pale complexion, a brown robe, and a prodigious beard. He held his hands clasped behind his back. The other man had olive skin and glasses. A headlamp was pushed up over his untamed silver hair, and a white mask hung loosely around his neck.

Neither man looked like a soldier. If Rodger had to guess, the guy with the mask was some sort of physician.

Apparently, they weren't alone.

The clank of heavy boots came from the passage. In the dim light outside the room, Rodger glimpsed a hulking figure approaching the open hatch. He didn't need to see clearly to know that this was the Cazador king himself.

El Pulpo moved inside the room, scraping a Siren-skull shoulder pad on the frame of the hatch. Apparently unconcerned, he strode right over to Rodger's bedside, where his eye peered at the open wound.

Then he turned to the man with the mask, giving him orders in Spanish.

The man clicked on his headlamp, put on surgical gloves, and leaned over Rodger.

He remained there for several seconds, tilting his head slightly to play the light over the wound. Rodger had never felt so violated in his life.

"Please," he whispered. "Please, don't …"

El Pulpo sniffed the air and then wiped his bulbous nose. The man in the brown robe moved to the other side of his bed, hands still clasped behind his back.

"Do not fear, my friend," he said in a quiet, reassuring voice. "We have brought you back from the dead."

"Who are you?" Rodger croaked, blinking away the stars before his vision. The gray-bearded face had the wrinkled brow and kind eyes of a wise old man. This guy sure didn't look like one of the rough Cazador soldiers.

"My name is Imulah," he said with a warm smile that seemed a little forced. "I serve el Pulpo as a scribe."

Rodger was good at reading people, and something was off about this "scribe."

"Now that you're awake, why don't you tell me more about yourself," Imulah said. "El Pulpo has been waiting several days for the opportunity to speak to you."

Rodger's eyes flitted from the scribe to the Cazador warrior king. He didn't wear a patch to cover up the inflamed socket of the eye that X had destroyed.

"Don't be afraid," Imulah said. He brought his

hands out from behind his back and stepped closer to the bed. "Dr. Javan is taking very good care of you."

The man with the headlamp nodded at Rodger but still would not meet his gaze. The doctor and the scribe were both clearly tense, and Rodger suspected the presence of their king had something to do with it.

He couldn't help but wonder if these people followed him freely, or if they were enslaved, and what the barbaric leader had in mind for him.

Javan spoke in Spanish to Imulah, who translated.

"Do you feel any pain?" Imulah asked.

I have a freaking hole in me you could poke a rake handle through, so yeah, Rodger wanted to say, but he kept his mouth shut. His parents had always told him, "Least said, easiest mended," especially in situations like this.

"We do not want you to suffer, and we will provide more medicine to relieve your pain upon request." When Rodger still didn't answer, Imulah let out a short sigh.

El Pulpo didn't seem too pleased, either. He wiped away the sweat dripping off the octopus tattoo on his forehead and grunted through sharpened teeth.

"Let's start with something simple," Imulah said. "How about your name?"

After a moment of hesitation, Rodger decided there was no harm in telling him. "I'm Rodgeman."

"And you are from the sky, like your friends? We saw your aircraft, so please do not lie. Lying is very bad and will only result in more pain. You don't want that now, do you?" Imulah arched a brow.

Rodger caught himself before revealing anything about his friends in the sky. Not even to the nice one.

"Well?" Imulah said.

"I'm Rodgeman," he replied.

The kind smile on Imulah's face folded into a frown. "Do I need to remind you that we saved your life, and that we can—"

Rodger cut the man off. "Yeah, *after* this guy stabbed me in the back." An errant twinge of pain made him grit his teeth.

Imulah stiffened, correcting his slouched posture.

Sweat dripped down Rodger's face, and he closed his eyes to fight off the encroaching pain. Whatever they were pumping into his veins was starting to wear off.

Sensing his discomfort, Javan walked away from Rodger's bedside to check the fluids and medical machines. After a few seconds of monitoring the readings, he reported his findings to el Pulpo, and Imulah then translated for Rodger.

"Javan says you are healing nicely and there are no signs of infection. He's the one you can thank for saving your life."

Rodger looked at the doctor, who had stepped over to a sink to wash his hands with some sort of foam. Javan glanced over his shoulder and nodded at Rodger. But it wasn't a friendly gesture, just a blank robotic nod that told Rodger this man was just following orders.

"Why did you save me?" Rodger asked, his gaze returning to Imulah and finally to el Pulpo. "So you could *eat* me?" Rodger winced at a flash of pain. "That's what you people do, right?"

Javan walked back over and checked the line of fluids in his left arm. He said something to el Pulpo, who seemed to ponder this and then nodded.

The doctor returned to the wall of cabinets and pulled open a drawer.

"Why?" Rodger asked.

He wasn't sure he wanted to know the answer. The questions made him anxious, and one of the machines beeped in response.

Javan gave Imulah a worried glance, and the scribe moved over to the bedside.

"Calm down, my friend," Imulah said. "Your questions will be answered soon."

Javan pulled out a syringe and squirted out a bit of liquid through the needle.

"What … what is that?" Rodger asked, trying to move.

His heart pounded harder, and the machine beeped faster.

Javan gave an order in Spanish to the two Cazador soldiers, who moved over to help hold Rodger down as he squirmed beneath the straps.

"Lemme go!" he growled. "Let me *go*!"

He watched Javan insert the needle into a port in one of the tubes. A warm sensation of relief instantly washed through Rodger.

"Go to sleep, my friend," Imulah said.

Rodger fought against the drowsy euphoria.

"You will see your new home very soon," Imulah said as darkness took over.

New home?

He thought of the only home he had ever known, and his parents, Magnolia, and his other friends.

A final image appeared as his mind slipped away.

The flashback to the ship was the most vivid memory yet. They both had been by his side, talking to him and holding him after el Pulpo skewered him through the back and dropped him to the wet deck.

But then they had left him to die.

The memory made him heartsick. His friends had abandoned him to a life in captivity with these monsters.

ONE

PRESENT DAY

Xavier Rodriguez dunked the rag in the bucket of water, then placed it on his forehead. When he pulled it away, the cloth was stained red.

He was still bleeding.

Because you need stitches.

He needed more than stitches, though. He needed what humans had once called a vacation.

The worst part wasn't the open wounds; it was breathing. He knew what bruised ribs felt like, and this was worse. There wasn't much he could do if one of his ribs was cracked.

Looking down, he checked the nasty gash on the outer edge of his foot, where a bullet had dug a path. It still hurt like hell, and as if that weren't bad enough, he was still pissing needles.

But he had to admit, this wasn't the worst shape he had ever been in during his career as a Hell Diver. There were countless times on the surface when he had suffered far worse and would gladly have traded for his present condition.

He would heal. His body would regain strength.

And he would fight.

X spat a gob of phlegm on the floor of his prison cell and winced at the pain that shot up his sternum and across his ribs. When it passed, he moved over to the bars of his cell.

For three days now, he had called this place home. During that time, he had been in almost complete isolation, with no idea whether Miles, Magnolia, or Rodger were still alive.

"Let me …" His voice cracked, the words trailing off.

He rubbed his throat, scratchy now from hours of screaming. Screaming to let him out so he could kill el Pulpo and every Cazador soldier in the Metal Islands.

But the barbarians didn't seem to give much of a damn.

The only person to answer his shouts was a slave boy who brought him water and scraps of food twice a day. If his mental clock was working properly, then the kid would be returning very soon to change out the Cazador version of a shit can on the *Hive*—which happened to be a bucket that looked indistinguishable from the one they brought him water in.

He just hoped they washed it out first. The last thing he needed was dysentery, especially without access to any of the lifesaving medicines he had carried on the *Sea Wolf*.

X waited by the bars, eyes on the hatch at the end of the passageway, where the boy would enter. This brig had dozens of other cells but no other prisoners. For some reason, they were holding him in solitary confinement.

No, not *some* reason. It was a deliberate mindfuck. They wanted to make him desperate, so that by the time he saw the light of day again, he would honor his agreement to serve el Pulpo, like a weakwilled coward.

But what el Pulpo still didn't understand about X was that he had already endured solitary confinement for most of a decade in his trek across the surface wastes. Those years were the hard part. This? This was like taking a nap.

"I can handle isolation," he growled in his scratchy voice. "I *invented* isolation!"

Anyone who understood English would think him crazy, but that was the point. That was his game. Make them think he was crazy, so they'd let him out of here.

He turned to the small window in the cell—just a sliver no wider than a sword blade. All he could see was part of the oil rig, and a container ship that had docked there. A crane was unloading barrels from its deck while two men in dark suits and straw hats seemed to be tallying them. He still didn't know where the Cazadores were getting usable gasoline, but they had found a stash somewhere. After watching for a few more minutes, he sat back down on the floor of his cell and went on checking his wounds. When he had finished cleaning them the best he could, he lay back with his head cupped in his hands.

It was hard to relax knowing that Miles and his friends were out there, but he needed his mental and physical strength.

So X did what X did best: he shut out the rest of the world and focused on surviving.

Sometime later, the metal door squealed open.

He got up and moved back to the bars, squinting into the light that streamed down the passage. It took his eyes a few seconds to adjust to the brightness, and when they did, a man, not a boy, stood outside the bars.

Not a man, either, X realized, but a slave, a coward.

Imulah, the scribe who served el Pulpo.

"Hello, Xavier," he said in affable tones.

Two Cazador soldiers walked inside to stand guard in the open hatchway, holding spears in their armored hands. Helmetless, their eyes were full of rage and bloodlust, and they were fixed on X.

He didn't blame them for wanting revenge. After all, he had killed a pile of these cannibals single-handedly. For a warrior society, its "warriors" didn't hold up all that well against a seasoned Hell Diver.

When X didn't reply, Imulah moved closer to the bars and said, "How are you feeling?"

This time, he replied by spitting another wad of snot at the servant's feet.

Imulah took a step back and then sighed. "You and your lady friend are not as polite as Rodger. It's very disappointing."

"We aren't used to being slaves like you," X said.

Bending down, the bald, bearded man scrutinized X as if this were some wild creature behind the bars, and X glared back like that same wild beast.

"Normally, I speak with restraint when my handlers are listening," Imulah said. "But the two guards you see do not speak your tongue, and I'm going to be very honest with you, Xavier Rodriguez."

"Somehow, I doubt that."

Imulah glared at X. "You have no choice but to fight in el Pulpo's army. If you don't, he will torture Magnolia and Rodger and eat them in front of you, along with your dog." He paused and then finished his thought. "He said your dog will make a good *aperitivo*—'appetizer,' I believe, is the word you might understand—before the main course."

X grabbed the bars, baring his teeth much as Miles would.

Imulah, surprisingly, held his ground.

"I was once like you," he said quietly. His voice took on a melancholy tone. "I was once a warrior. My people fought the Cazadores when they found our small outpost on the island of Ascension. There weren't many of us, but those of us who could fight, fought."

X narrowed his eyes.

"El Pulpo and you are from the same place?"

"Indeed, we are," Imulah said. "We are descendants of the sky people that landed on the island and took shelter for over two hundred years in an ITC facility. Long before he became the king of the Cazadores, el Pulpo was just a boy named Maximus, the son of a man who died in the battle for our outpost. I, too, fought and lost that day. I was forced to endure the sight of most of my friends and family slaughtered, and I will never forget seeing Maximus …"

Imulah shook his head. "Even as a young boy of nine, he killed three Cazador warriors and bit the nose off the man who finally captured him. He was born to fight."

X had a hard time believing the story. Was this just a ploy to change his mind?

"Like me, Maximus became a slave when our people were conquered. He ended up thrown into the Cazador war machine, where he fought his way to power, climbing from spearman to king—over a mountain of dead warriors."

The story made sense, although X wasn't sure why el Pulpo didn't speak fluent English, unless he had forgotten what he knew as a child and grew up speaking Spanish.

"He led us to the greatest find of all," Imulah said. "To a place that held millions of gallons of gasoline, all preserved by an ITC additive that kept gasoline as fresh as the day it left the refinery."

"So you don't get your oil from the rigs?" X asked.

Imulah chuckled. "Of course not."

X looked again at the two men standing guard and giving him angry glares. The shorter of the two bared his teeth at X, and X gave him the middle finger, not knowing whether the guy even understood the gesture.

Imulah must have. "This is why el Pulpo respects you," he said. "He sees strength in you that he has seen in only a few men. He understands why Magnolia and your people call you 'the Immortal.'"

The scribe stood, wincing as his joints creaked.

"Perhaps, someday, you, too, will become king of the Cazadores," he said, clasping his hands behind his robe. Then he turned and left, stopping a few feet shy of the open hatch to let the servant boy inside.

The boy carried a bucket of water in one filthy paw, and an orange, a bread crust, and a few scraps of dried fish in the other.

"Better drink and eat up," Imulah said. He reached into his pocket and pulled out a small jar, then handed it to the boy to give to X.

"Use this on your wounds," Imulah said. "It will help them heal faster. You're going to need all the strength you can get. Your first fight at the sky arena is tomorrow night."

* * * * *

Captain Katrina DaVita stood alone on the bridge of the stealth warship USS *Zion*, staring out over a dark horizon. Lightning cleaved the clouds, leaving behind streaks of blue visual residue that faded long before the clap of thunder reached her ears. Waves continued to pummel the vessel.

The Metal Islands were out there, and so were her friends, somewhere beyond the soup of electromagnetic storms.

She resisted again the impulse to take the warship off autopilot and plow full steam ahead. But as captain, her responsibility was to the population of the *Hive* and *Deliverance* first, then to X, Magnolia, and Miles.

But knowing they were out there, imprisoned or perhaps worse, continued to haunt her and the rest of the team. For now, they had to find a way around the monster storm blocking the way and keep trying to make contact with the airships so they could firm up their battle plan.

Interference from the electrical storm had kept her from speaking to Chief Engineer Samson or her XO, Lieutenant Mitchells, for several days now. The storm was messing with everything, including their radar and instruments.

The panels in the cruiser's bridge beeped as she scanned the data. Normally, she liked the solitude of working alone, but too many things weighed on her mind tonight. The open water posed countless threats: mutant ocean denizens, AI defectors that were out there somewhere, potential Cazador pirate ships, and a monster storm that had a fifty-mile front and covered at least two thousand square miles.

The rain sheeted down on Trey Mitchells and Jaideep Abhaya as they patrolled on the deck below, the battery units giving their shapes a faint blue glow. The clouds flashed into view behind an intricate skein of lightning. The crack of thunder followed just seconds later, rattling the bulkheads.

She sent a message over the comms to pull Jaideep and Trey back inside. As the warship plowed into the oncoming waves, the blue-lit figures on the deck below changed direction, moving back toward the safety of the ship.

Katrina checked the radar next. The readings were still scrambled.

"Piece of crap," she muttered.

She picked up the radio and buzzed the Combat Information Center, where Eevi Corey and her husband, Alexander, were working up a weapons inventory.

"How are things coming down there?" Katrina asked.

"Good, almost done," Alexander replied.

"Meet me on the bridge in fifteen minutes."

"Aye, aye, ma'am."

Katrina considered calling the medical bay to check on Edgar Cervantes, who was still recovering from his injuries at Red Sphere, but she didn't want to wake him if he was resting.

The comm station beeped, and she moved over to pick up the call from Sandy Bloomberg and Jed Snow. The two youngest members of the crew were tasked with sweeping the compartments belowdecks for supplies.

"Captain, this is Sandy, do you copy?"

"Copy. Go ahead, Sandy."

"We're finishing the search of the locked compartments and have uncovered some dried food and a water-recycling system."

"Great work," Katrina said. "How about weapons?"

"Negative," Jed replied.

Katrina swore under her breath. She was hoping they would uncover more of the laser rifles the AI DEF-Nine units had used to such catastrophic effect at Red Sphere. Even a few of the advanced weapons would be a boon to the Hell Divers in the fight once they arrived at the Metal Islands. She prayed the Cazadores didn't have any of them.

"Report to the bridge in fifteen minutes," she told Sandy and Jed.

Several other beeps sounded, and Katrina hurried back through the bridge to check the reports. A ship of this size should be crewed by over a hundred people, but she had just eight, and most of them, including her, had no experience with an operations system this old.

Happily, the ship was advanced enough that it could run almost on autopilot, although she still preferred to have a human at the helm.

Maybe she shouldn't have sent Les and Layla back to the *Hive*.

She shook the doubt away. Second-guessing her decision wasn't going to do any good. Leading required her to stay confident in the wake of the tragic deaths they had suffered over the past few days.

Losing Erin Jenkins and Ramon Ochoa at Red Sphere had hit the team hard, and Michael Everhart's devastating injury compounded the loss. He would survive, but his diving days could be over. And how helpful could he really be in the coming war?

And although she really could have used Layla and Les, they were where they needed to be. She needed a fighting force, and Les was the only officer diplomatic enough to recruit one.

The hatch whisked open, and one by one, the greenhorn divers entered the bridge for their briefing.

She scrutinized the only Hell Diver team she had left. The youthful faces of Jed, Sandy, Vish, Jaideep, and Edgar reminded her of soldiers from the Old World. There was a reason that militaries wanted young people, and not just because they were faster and stronger. They also believed they were invincible.

The difference between a Hell Diver and an old-world soldier was the difference between a gladiator and a prize fighter—like the gladiator, anyone who joined a Hell Diver team knew that death was coming sooner or later.

She pushed the thoughts aside. They had a lot to cover.

"It's nasty out there," Trey said.

Jaideep shook his long hair and flopped into a chair.

"Trey, why don't you go see if you can reach the airships," Katrina said.

"Yes ma'am," he replied politely. Stepping through the maze of stations to a bank of communications equipment, he sat and placed his helmet on the deck.

Lightning outside the porthole windows flickered

through the bridge as the divers took a seat and more of the greenhorns stepped onto the bridge. Edgar Cervantes limped in after the others, doing his best to keep a straight back.

"You could have stayed in the med ward," she said.

"Doing fine, Cap."

Katrina could see the pain he was trying so hard to conceal.

"No dice," Trey said after fiddling with the equipment. "Samson still ain't answering. Can't get Lieutenant Mitchells, either."

"'Cause of that storm," Vish said.

Another round of beeps went off, and Eevi walked over to check the weather station. The former militia investigator glanced back at Katrina.

"This isn't good, Cap," Eevi said.

Katrina gave a nod and, in her command voice, said, "All right, everyone, have a seat and grab a bite. I have some updates to give and a decision to make."

All took seats around the metal table and dug into the fresh food they had brought down from *Deliverance*. The fruit was already starting to go bad, but the tomatoes were still firm and red and juicy. They also had some week-old bread and jerky left over, but that was it.

Once they finished this meal, they would be forced to use freeze-dried stuff and protein bars made in the bowels of the airships.

"Sandy, Jed, what did you find belowdecks?" Katrina asked, licking tomato juice from her fingers.

"Not much, really," Jed replied. "We have about two weeks of food that we brought down from *Deliverance*. But the new stuff ... not sure if it's any good. Freeze-dried, and packaged well, but it's dirt old."

Sandy nodded. "And the water-recycling system isn't working. Without it, we have two weeks of water, at best."

That was all Katrina had counted on needing, until the storm interfered. She followed an arc of lightning outside the port window, thinking about their odds. It could take a week or more to get around the storm, and she doubted X and Mags had that much time.

"What's the sitrep on the weapons systems?" Katrina asked. "We got those figured out yet?"

Eevi let Alexander explain. He let out a sigh, which told Katrina it wasn't going to be good.

"Like the food, these weapons are old. I'm guessing only about half the cruise missiles will even fire, and some might actually pose a danger to *us*. Four of the five .50-caliber machine guns are working, but only one of the MK-65 five-inch cannons is working. The one Layla used back at Red Sphere ..."

"I wouldn't say *working*," Eevi said.

Alexander sighed. "I believe it fires, but the turret won't respond to commands."

"Lovely," Katrina said. "I was hoping to use that gun to punch a nice hole in el Pulpo's palace."

"Let me see what I can do about that," Alexander said, grinning. "I'll keep working on it, Cap. Maybe I can get the other one working, too."

"We still have the laser rifle from Red Sphere; don't forget that," Eevi said.

Katrina nodded. She had sent one of the laser weapons up with Les for when *Deliverance* attacked the Metal Islands, and kept the other here aboard the USS *Zion*. The weapon's shoulder stock was sticking out of a bag a few feet from her chair.

"Anything else?" she asked.

"We have two old inflatable boats called Zodiacs," Eevi said. "The engines are battery powered, and I've charged them both. Only time will tell if they hold the charge."

The ship swayed, and Katrina reached out to steady herself on a station. She wasn't used to the violent roll and pitch of the open sea. She preferred the sky to this crap any day.

"Good job, everyone," Katrina said as she dug into her meal.

They ate quietly over the next few minutes. She listened to Jaideep and Vish joke around and share their food. Jed and Sandy were doing the same thing.

Their bond had strengthened in the past week. The two teenagers sat close together, arms touching— close enough to confirm Katrina's suspicions. The way they gazed at each other removed any doubt. She remembered the way she once looked at Xavier, and it wasn't much different from what she was seeing in the two young divers in front of her. Sandy smiled as Jed offered her the last chunk of bread from the *Hive*.

"Anyone wanna swap some bread for this savory guinea pig jerky?" Trey asked. He opened a tin and held it up.

"Sure," Vish said. He broke off a hunk of crust and tossed it to Trey, who tossed him a strip of jerky.

"So, when are the airships going to meet us at the Metal Islands?" Vish asked as he gnawed at the leathery meat. "And what happens when they do?"

"What the hell do you think is going to happen?" Jaideep said with a sideways glance.

"It depends on whether el Pulpo surrenders," Katrina said.

"I hope he does for his sake," Trey said, "or my dad's gonna rain missiles on him."

Katrina glanced at Edgar Cervantes, who picked at his food quietly. He looked up but didn't add his thoughts. He hadn't said much since losing his cousin, Ramon.

"How are you feeling?" she asked him.

"I'm ready to fight, Captain, but I hope we can get the Cazadores to surrender without damaging the oil rigs. Our people will need a place to go."

"I still can't believe this is real," Sandy said with a wide smile that showed off her crooked teeth. "I've always dreamed what the sun would look like."

"And the ocean," Jaideep said. "I can't wait to learn how to swim."

Vish said, "I'm going fishing and boating. Man, this is going to be—"

Katrina stood up and looked around her at all the

youthful gazes full of fear and hope. But she couldn't lie to them—having grand illusions about what they would find was dangerous.

"This is going to be hell," she said. "Don't forget, these people are our enemy, and they have our friends. We will have to fight, one way or another."

She moved over to the portholes. The billowing mass of clouds flashed from within, and tendrils of lightning licked the water on the horizon. She watched the raging storm like a soldier looking for a weakness in the enemy's defenses.

Right now, the storm was a bigger threat than all the cannibals in the Metal Islands.

But it was time to stop wishing the storm would weaken. It was time to make a decision.

"We have two options," she said to her team. "Keep looking for a way around this system to the Metal Islands, or just punch right through it."

She recalled Captain Maria Ash's words from when Katrina was still a novice diver.

"*Everything has a weakness,*" Ash had said to a group of Hell Divers. "*Even Mother Nature. Your job is to find it. Your life, and the lives of everyone you know, depends on you facing your fears.*"

Katrina had come up with a few of her own mottoes over the years, and one of them seemed to fit the moment.

"The way to paradise is through hell," Katrina said. "Eat up and get to your stations. We're sailing through the beast."

TWO

Michael Everhart sat on a bed in the *Hive*'s medical bay, looking down at the stump where his arm had been. Dr. Huff carefully peeled back the bandage.

"We have to let it breathe a bit," he said in his crackly old voice, "and I want to check for infection."

The oldest doctor on the ship—practically a fossil in Michael's eyes—sat on a stool and pressed a pair of spectacles down on his nose. After three days of heavy sedation, Michael was finally being weaned off the hard-core drugs. The pain was bad, but all he could think about were his friends.

X, Mags, and Miles were out there, and Michael was eager to get back into the fight. He was beginning to feel like a caged animal here.

Doc Huff muttered under his breath as he slowly scanned the reddened skin on the stump. He had already removed most of the burned skin, and scabs had formed around the open wounds.

Michael tried to gauge the doctor's reaction to it

all. He was ready to get the hell out of the medical ward and back to the quarters he shared with Layla.

"Hmmm, no sign of infection there, but …"

"But what?" Michael asked.

The doctor gently rotated the stump. "Well, that's … not …" he mumbled to himself, his dewlaps jiggling as he moved his head. "Everything seems to be healing nicely."

"Great! So when can I get back to work?"

Huff looked up, his goggles steamed from his warm breath. "You are kidding, right?"

"Uh, no."

The doc laughed nervously at that and continued looking over the injury. "We need to keep you on a schedule of cleaning this twice a day, Commander, and for the immediate future you're going to be on a daily dose of the gel your team brought back from the surface. Plus painkillers as needed. They will help stop the phantom pains from driving you even crazier than you already appear to be."

"I can handle them, Doc. I *need* to get back to work."

Huff stood in front of the table and folded his arms across his chest, looking at Michael as a disapproving parent might.

"You're clear of infection right now, but if you want to get one, then by all means, get back to work. It's your choice. I can't stop you."

"Just get me wrapped again, Doc."

Huff let out a sigh and picked up a vial of the

nanotechnology medicine Team Raptor had found in an ITC facility. Michael remembered the raid, two years ago, that had netted the precious meds, but he never thought he would be the one to use it.

The doctor squirted the gelatinous blue ointment and used his gloved fingers to massage it around the stump. After coating it, he applied a fresh bandage. Michael gritted his teeth while the doctor applied the ointment that burned like hell.

"All set," Huff said. "I'll check on you later today. If you have any phantom pains, let me know and I'll up your pain-med dosage."

As soon as the doctor left, Michael stood and grabbed his shirt off the chair. The hell with sitting here and waiting to heal. He didn't have the two weeks Dr. Huff had said it would take to heal completely.

Even with the applications of the nanotechnology, two weeks was way too long, and the gel did nothing to lessen the phantom pains.

He slipped his shirt over his head and his lean, muscular torso. Doing everything with one hand took some getting used to, but he was doing better on his own now.

It was time to get out of here and join Layla on the bridge, and then he was off to search the records for any information he could dig up on the AI defectors. After losing his arm to the machines, he wanted to learn everything he could about them.

He left the medical bay without drawing any

attention. The nurses on duty and Dr. Huff were with other patients, and even if they tried, they couldn't stop him from leaving.

He was down an arm, but he was still a Hell Diver.

What he hadn't expected were the stares and the comments as he made his way through the *Hive*, toward the tunnel connecting it to *Deliverance*. Everyone he passed stopped and stared, or else turned and followed him, calling out questions.

"Did the *Sea Wolf* really make it to the Metal Islands?"

"Is the Immortal fighting the cannibals?"

"Did they eat your arm?"

Michael let out a snort and pushed on, trying to jog. Lightheaded from the drugs, he quickly had to slow down to a fast walk through the freshly painted passages. He took comfort in the artwork. Captain Jordan's legacy was being purged from the ship, and everything he had destroyed was slowly being brought back: the records restored, new paintings gracing the bulkheads, and spirits lifted with hope.

In the skies, hope is a dangerous thing.

But this was the first time in his life that he felt it for more than a fleeting moment. X had indeed found the Metal Islands—a real place that could house the population of both airships.

A home for the future of humankind.

The question was, how much would it cost them to take it from the Cazadores? Or could these two very different groups find a way to coexist?

His gut told him that neither option would be easy and both would be costly.

More voices followed Michael down the passages, and he stopped when he saw Phyl Mitchells. The young girl carried a small chalkboard under her arm.

"Hi, Commander Everhart," she said politely.

"Hey, kiddo, how's school?" He leaned down to check the scribbles on the board. "Is that algebra?"

She nodded but still wouldn't meet his gaze. Her eyes were on his stump.

"What … what happened?"

"I got hurt, but I'm going to be okay."

"I'm glad you're okay," the girl said, "but do you know when Trey is coming home?"

"Soon. He's on a really important mission."

Curious eyes met his gaze. "Mission?"

"That's like a job to do."

"Oh."

"Don't worry about your big brother; he'll be okay."

"Okay," Phyl said. "I hope you feel better soon."

Michael watched her go until she was around the next corner. Like the rest of these people, the kid had no idea yet what was going on.

Michael jogged the rest of the way. By the time he got to the bridge of *Deliverance*, he was out of breath and sweating. His stump throbbed with every beat of his heart, and he cradled it in his good hand, gritting his teeth.

Ada Winslow, the young ensign, looked up from her station as he passed the two militia guards and walked through the open hatch. Her freckled face held a worried look.

"Commander Everhart. I wasn't expecting y—"

Layla cut her off with a shout across the room. "Tin! What in the wastes of Hades are you doing here?"

Michael smiled. "I got sick of sitting in that rat cage."

Ensigns Dave Connor and Bronson White both stood at their stations, studying him with empathy—especially Dave, who had lost a leg in an engineering accident years ago.

"Welcome back," Bronson said in his chalky voice.

"Good to see you, Commander," Dave said.

"Good to be here," Michael said. He walked through the circular open space. The stations surrounding the central island flashed with data and reports.

He still remembered the first time he was here in one of the comfortable leather chairs after Pipe and Commander Rick Weaver lost their lives at the Hilltop Bastion.

The sad losses played over in Michael's mind, and he winced at other painful memories. Erin Jenkins, Rodger Mintel, his own father … The list went on and on.

"Tin?" Layla said. "Are you okay?"

He nodded and sank into the chair beside the radar station she was monitoring.

"I've got something to tell you," he said. "But first, how about an update? Have we heard anything from the USS *Zion* yet?"

Her dimples framed a frown.

"I'm afraid not. Nothing from Timothy Pepper of the *Sea Wolf*, either."

"Damn …"

"The electrical storm separating the USS *Zion* from the Metal Islands is likely blocking the signals."

"Let's hope that's the reason," Michael said. He swiveled the chair over to the computer monitor and pecked one-handed at the display.

"What did you want to tell me?"

"Give me a second," Michael said as he kept typing.

Another voice entered the bridge, and they both looked up to see the tall frame of Les Mitchells duck beneath the hatch lintel.

"Commander Everhart!" Les said "It's great to see you up and about."

"Good to see you, Lieutenant," Michael replied.

Les walked through the bridge and joined Michael and Ensign Winslow at the radar station.

"How's the recruiting going?" Michael asked.

"Slowly," Les said. "Everyone wants to ask about the Metal Islands. When I tell them about it, they keep hearing sunshine and balmy ocean breezes and ignore any mention of cannibalistic barbarians that currently reside on the rigs."

"Yeah, tell me about it," Michael said. "I got harassed on my way here."

"Maybe it's time to tell them the truth," Layla said.

Les shoved his hands in his pockets. "I've been waiting for orders from Katrina before doing anything except recruiting."

"I also think it's time we sit down with Samson and talk about bringing Timothy Pepper back online on the *Hive*," Layla said. "I think we're going to need him."

Michael let his stump down, his eyes on the bandage. "Knowing now that Timothy Pepper of the *Sea Wolf* helped X get to the Metal Islands, I'm of a mind we can trust his counterpart on the *Hive*."

Les looked at Michael with uncertainty. "You lost your arm to an AI back at Red Sphere, but you're okay with bringing a different AI back online?"

Michael and Layla exchanged a glance.

"I'm with her," he said. "Pepper is not a defector, and I don't think we have any choice at this point. We're low on people and need the help."

Les pursed his lips to one side and then said, "Okay, I'll talk to Samson, and if he agrees, we'll bring Pepper back online."

* * * * *

Magnolia scanned the sky outside her window for any sign of the *Hive*, *Deliverance*, or the glowing blue battery units of Hell Divers falling through the clouds. In her mind's eye, she could picture the chutes blooming out, and the muzzle flashes of assault rifles flickering like mutant lightning bugs as the sky soldiers lowered to the rescue.

Where were they?

On the fourth day of her captivity, she was starting

to wonder whether the remaining divers were going to show up.

All she could see were the shiny, smooth edges of the airship above. She had studied it for several hours, looking for markings or anything else that might identify the craft as the ITC *Ashland*, commanded by Captain Marcus Bolter.

But what did it matter? Whoever had flown the ship here was long dead by now. Just bones or fragments, like most of the Old World.

Voices and a knock on the door pulled her away from the window. She hurried over to her bed, sat, and placed her hands on her lap.

The door to her small room opened onto a balcony outside, where two olive-skinned soldiers stood guard. The older of the two gestured with his spear.

"Come," he said.

The other soldier, no more than a teenager, looked at her chest as if trying to glimpse what was under her torn shirt.

Standing, she covered herself with her arms and followed the men outside. She raised one hand to shield her eyes from the sun. After being cooped up for four days in a dimly lit room, she wasn't prepared for natural light.

The older guard led her down the walkway, and the younger one followed. Both men wore faded dungarees, a machete, and a knife. Neither had a firearm, but she had no doubt they both were skilled spearmen.

She stayed close to the rail separating her from a

ten-story plunge to the sea. To the west, three boats curved through the water. One looked oddly familiar.

Magnolia stopped to squint at the view.

The *Sea Wolf.*

Two boats were pulling the twin-hulled vessel toward the tower where she had been held prisoner.

"*Rápido,*" said the man behind her, prodding her side with the wooden shaft of his spear.

She glared over her shoulder at the teenage warrior, who bared his sharp teeth. Magnolia returned the gesture, showing her own teeth.

He seemed to like that and chuckled, gesturing to his bearded cohort. They exchanged a few words in Spanish and then drew close, hemming her in between them.

"You like?" she said to the younger one. She let her hand fall away from her chest, giving him a peek. "How about you?" she said, eyes flitting to the other man.

His beard split open in a wide display of cracked brown teeth, and he reached out for her while his comrade goaded her with the butt of his spear. She slapped the weapon away, and the older guy shoved her backward into the railing.

When she regained her balance, she raised her right fist, then caught him square in the jaw with her left.

This got a chuckle from the younger guard.

Not wasting the moment, she put her full weight behind a kick to the injured man's solar plexus, which slammed him into the opposite rail and toppled him over the side.

A long scream rang out, cut off by a loud smack and splash. The remaining soldier darted over to the rail and looked over the edge. He turned, his grin replaced by a snarl, only to find Magnolia holding the fallen spear, leveled at his Adam's apple.

Now she was the one to grin ... until she heard the click of a hammer.

The young soldier showed his sharp teeth again, but Magnolia kept the spear point at his throat. A quick glance behind her revealed four rifles trained on her from the open hatch.

So much for her escape.

A shortish bald man in a brown robe stepped through the wall of armored bodies and weapons. He moved into the light, and she saw that it was the scribe, Imulah. He clasped his hands behind his back and shook his head at Magnolia.

"This is not a good start to your residence here," he said. Four armored soldiers followed him onto the balcony. They held their rifles and spears on her as the scribe stepped over to the railing for a look at the limp body below being hauled from the water into a boat.

"One of the first things I learned during Hell Diver training was, water won't save you if your chute doesn't open," Magnolia said. "In fact, if you fall far and fast enough, it's like hitting concrete."

Imulah tilted his head as if trying to figure out whether she was joking.

She wasn't.

"My instructor—the man who took el Pulpo's eye, by the way—said you're supposed to stiffen your legs and roll if your chute fails."

Magnolia jerked her chin at the railing. "Or if you fall over a balcony. Too bad bucko didn't take any Hell Diver courses."

"Drop the spear, Magnolia," Imulah said. "You don't want to anger King Pulpo again. He is a patient man, but his patience goes only so far."

"Screw that prick Pulpo!" she snapped. "Take me to my friends, or I'm going to feed this asshole's Adam's apple to the fish."

The frightened Cazador soldier glanced from her to Imulah.

"If you do that, your friend Rodger will become pig food," Imulah said. He arched a brow. "Do you have pigs on those airships? Did your instructor ever tell you what happens when you starve a pig and then offer it human flesh?"

He shook his head. "Not pretty, Magnolia. They pick the bones dry."

The scribe retreated into the throng of soldiers, and their boots clanked on the metal as they surrounded her.

"Drop the spear, and we will forget about this," Imulah said.

"And what about him?" she asked, looking down at the water.

"An unfortunate accident, but certainly not the first," Imulah said. "Come, we have a big day planned."

Magnolia considered her options. They might

just kill her the moment she dropped the spear. Then again, they could kill her now.

The other option was to obey the order and wait for a better opportunity. That would give her time to find out where Rodger, Miles, and X were being held. The legendary diver had fought brilliantly, but there wasn't much one man could do against such overwhelming force.

"That's good. Easy now," Imulah said as she finally lowered the spear.

She handed back the young soldier's spear and brushed off his shoulder. Then she smiled warmly and punched him in the diaphragm.

"That's for hitting me earlier," she said.

The gun barrels swung back up at her, but she knew now that the soldiers' orders were to keep her alive for their king—ideally, without any holes, bruises, or cuts.

While the soldier doubled over gasping, she stepped to the railing and looked down at the teal-blue water just as the *Sea Wolf* passed under the tower and into the storage marina.

For a fleeting second, she considered following the man she had killed into the water. If she followed X's teachings, she might live through the fall, but from this height, she was bound to break something.

No, this was not the moment to try an escape.

She took in a deep breath and strode past Imulah. "Which way?" she asked.

The soldiers lowered the weapons, and Imulah

led the way. He walked back to the open hatch and gestured for her to follow him into a windowless passage lit with sconces.

It still surprised her that these steel platforms had power, but then again, nothing really amazed her now that she had seen the sun for longer than a few seconds.

The soldiers continued through the narrow passageways. All the hatches were open, providing glimpses into the lives of the people who lived here. A few peeks were enough to see that the Metal Islands had a stratified society of haves and have-nots, like on the *Hive*.

This was definitely the upper decks.

Women wearing colorful dresses and jewelry attended to children playing with toy boats and seashells on the tile floors. In one room, a family ate dried fish at a wooden table. In another, a man in a gray jacket and matching pants sat at a table, tapping the keys on some old-world device with paper sticking out of it.

As she passed the living spaces, she noticed more men wearing the same gray suits and the same accessories, right down to the brown leather hats sporting a white feather. And they weren't the only ones dressed well. The women wore patterned frocks, seashell necklaces, and gold bracelets. They looked up as she passed, some of them shying away from her gaze, others smiling with unsharpened teeth spared from decay.

The people here were like those on the *Hive*, with a wide range of skin tones. But unlike on the *Hive*, she could hear several different languages begin spoken.

Were the Cazadores more civilized than she thought?

Imulah turned down another passage. In a big, open room to their right, dozens of servants were setting up several long tables. Goblets, plates, silverware, and bowls were arranged neatly in preparation for a feast. The scene reminded her of the sumptuous meals on the *Hive* the night before a dive.

The scribe continued past the room and opened a hatch to a stairwell that wound upward several floors.

"Where are we going?" Magnolia finally asked.

The scribe gave her an up-and-down look and said, "To find you something suitable to wear for tonight's festivities."

THREE

X watched the boy set fresh clothing outside the bars of his cage. The kid, no older than eight, was cute, with big, innocent brown eyes. At first, he had reminded X of Tin as a boy—until the little monster tried to bite him.

This was not an upright, smart youngster like Tin. The kid appeared to be practically feral.

Clicking his tongue, the boy stepped away from the cage while fingering the shark's tooth that hung from a thong around his skinny neck. He clicked his tongue again and pointed at the clothes.

"They want me to wear *that*? Hell no, kid." The loincloth looked like a leather diaper. "I'm an old man, but I'm not *that* old."

The two guards posted outside opened the hatch and walked into the passage, where they waved at the kid to scatter. He ran out of the brig, clicking his tongue.

"Little rat," X muttered. He still didn't know the

boy's name, only that he really didn't seem to like X. No one did, for that matter, especially the guards.

The two men made way for two half-naked soldiers who entered the passage, drawing their swords from sheaths on their belts. They wore little more than a leather loincloth like the one the kid had left for X: just that, leather shorts, and simple crossing leather straps that held a shield of animal hide over the back.

Both had beards and shaved heads.

"Put them on," one of them said in English. When X hesitated, he added, "You don't want us to beat you before your first fight, do you, Immortal?"

Bending down, X grabbed the clothes and pulled them through the gap between bars. He pulled off his shirt and turned his back to the boy and guards while he changed.

"Damn! You got more scars than an old whale," the soldier said.

X hardly noticed the scars on his body anymore. They were just a journal of sorts, a chronicle of fights, dives, and brushes with death. He had a feeling that by the end of the night, he would be adding another cut or two to the story.

But at least the recent wounds were healing. The bottle of gel Imulah had given him was high-quality medicine found in ITC facilities. He had discovered some on his trek across the surface years back, and it worked wonders.

All his cuts were already scabbed over, the bruises were fading, and he could breathe deeply now without his ribs aching. The only thing that still hurt was the gunshot wound along the outer edge of his foot, but even that was healing nicely.

Bending down, he applied the rest of the gel to the open wound. Then he pulled off his pants and tossed the filthy garments on the ground.

Naked, he picked up the leather loincloth and put it on, pulling the ends up through the waist thong in front and back. When it was secure, he put on his tattered boots and stepped up to the bars.

The two soldiers stood on both sides while the guards unlocked the gate. All four backed away as the door opened, allowing X to step out.

He raised his arms, stretching them and yawning.

All four men watched him closely, hands on their weapons.

"All right," X said, "so who am I fighting?"

The soldier that spoke English looked to his compadres and translated. Laughter followed.

"Hammerhead," the man replied after a good laugh. "And he's undefeated."

X chuckled and took a step forward, stopping just in front of the soldier's face. "So am I, asshole."

* * * * *

The USS *Zion* crested a forty-foot wave, giving Katrina a seemingly endless view of even larger waves, like dark dunes in a desert.

Katrina was really starting to hate the ocean.

She grabbed the armrest and braced herself as the warship nosed down and rolled slightly to starboard.

A warning beeper echoed through the bridge, and several voices called out with reports. Lightning speared the horizon, lighting up the cloud cover. For a fleeting moment, she thought she saw a giant beetle shape in the afterglow. The optical illusion faded away with the blue visual residue.

She looked back to the monitor, realizing she couldn't say with any accuracy where they were—only that they were holding a steady east-northeast bearing. Two hours into the storm now, and they were at the mercy of the beast.

The data on the screens was a scrambled mess.

"I'm not sure how much more of this we can take," Eevi said.

Katrina had flown *Deliverance* and the *Hive* through several storms, each one threatening the future of humanity. But the sky was different from the ocean. Down here, you didn't have just the lightning to worry about; you had to take the swells into account. Down here, you had no way to get above or below the storm, either; you had to plow right through it.

Another monster wave slammed the port bow. Katrina was going to be ill.

"If these readings are right, then the storm appears to be growing," said Alexander, who was serving as meteorologist. "I'm also detecting an increase in lightning strikes, but … I don't know if any of this data is correct."

Katrina looked back down at her monitor. The fifty-mile front appeared to have enlarged around them, but she still didn't know how long it would take to break through.

The waves had knocked them off the original course. It could easily take hours, even days, to find their way out, and they weren't going to last forever out here.

She had considered turning back, but they were too far in for that to be an option now, especially since the instruments were screwed.

I have no idea where we are.

The realization chilled her. Had she doomed her team by bringing them out here?

All she could do was hope that the warship, built for rough duty, would make it through. But the ship was ancient and had seen no maintenance in over two and a half centuries.

A lightning strike licked the bow, showering the foredeck with sparks.

"Holy Siren shit!" Vish yelled out.

"Everyone, stay calm," Katrina said, glancing over her shoulder.

Trey, Vish, Jaideep, Eevi, Alexander, Jed, Sandy, and Edgar were strapped into their various stations on the bridge, eyes glued to the cracked porthole windows letting in cascades of rain.

She turned back to her monitor. While she scanned the data and looked for a break in the storm, another voice called out.

"What's that?" Edgar said.

Glancing up, she scanned the swells. A flash of lightning illuminated a wall of water.

Not a wall. A mountain.

"Dear God," Katrina whispered as the wave grew in height.

It had to be near sixty feet tall.

She took the ship off autopilot and made her way over to the controls two stations over. The warship didn't have an oak steering wheel like the *Hive*'s, and she was glad for that at least. She hated that bulky thing and much preferred the cruiser's smaller black control sticks.

"Hold on," she ordered as she strapped herself in. "This is going to get pretty rocky."

Working the controls, she turned the ship as fast as it would move to meet the wave head-on. If they could avoid being hit from the side and ride over it, they might have a ...

Shit, we're not going to make it.

There wasn't enough time to orient the vessel to the wave. The colossal wall towered over them, and Katrina watched in horror as the crest began to descend on the ship.

She continued turning and managed to get them in a slightly better position. Several screams rang out across the bridge as the wave lifted the fifty-thousand-ton warship like a toy. The bow climbed at a dizzying pitch. Water sprayed the cracked windows; blocking her view of the crest the engines were powering them toward.

And then they were falling fast, like an airborne Siren on the attack.

She wasn't sure what happened next, but the USS *Zion* managed to stay upright when they went over the backside of the wave. The angle, though … It didn't feel right …

Katrina felt her stomach float upward inside her. Then the bow slammed into the trough of the next wave, the already cracked windows shattering from the force. Water flooded the bridge, and warning sensors and screams rang out on all sides.

She felt the sting of saltwater in her eyes, but the harness held her where she sat. Shielding her face from the spray, she looked out through the gap where the windows had been, expecting to see another monster wave about to swallow the vessel whole, like a whale sucking in a shoal of fish.

In the intermittent lightning bursts, she could see something out there. Not a rogue wave and not a sea monster—a landmass.

She steered the ship toward the island. Rain beat the inside of the now windowless bridge, adding to the inches of seawater sloshing on the deck. She tapped the monitor and closed the windows' steel hatches to protect the equipment. The shutters lowered, cutting off her view of the island.

She didn't know where they were, but it definitely wasn't the Metal Islands. There was no sign of the sun, only storm clouds.

A grinding and vibration shook the deck below

her boots, and the lights flickered. Her eyes flitted to the monitor, her heart quickening when she realized the source of the noise.

The ancient ship had taken too many hits, and now, finally, the lights were about to go out on the USS *Zion*. Power levels dropped rapidly as monitors flickered on and off. A grinding noise echoed through the bridge.

They were close to the lee shore now, and the storm waves were much smaller. Katrina unbuckled her harness and checked in with her crew.

"Is everyone okay?" she asked.

Several voices responded, barely intelligible over the *click click* of the shutters in the wind.

"Jaideep … He's hurt bad," someone said.

Katrina crossed the space, boots slapping in standing water, to find the young diver slumped in his chair beside his brother. Vish unbuckled his harness and went to do the same for Jaideep, but Katrina stopped him.

"No, don't move him," she said. "Might make things worse."

Vish looked up at her, fear in his eyes.

The other divers all circled around, and Katrina gave them orders one at a time.

"Jed, Sandy, give me a sitrep on all critical systems. Edgar, try and figure out where the hell we are. Trey and Alexander, gear up. I want you on patrol just in case that island is inhabited. Vish, Eevi, you help me with Jaideep here."

As the others went off on their appointed tasks, Katrina leaned back down to Jaideep. He had a bad gash on his forehead from hitting the bulkhead. Blood flowed freely from the nasty wound, but a touch to his neck confirmed he had a pulse. He was breathing, too.

Her main concern was a broken back or, heaven forbid, a broken neck. Especially after seeing that head wound. Despite the risk, they had to move him.

"Help me with him," she said to Vish and Eevi.

The three of them gently moved him onto the table where they had eaten earlier.

Thunder boomed overhead, rattling the steel shutters, and the ship continued to groan and shake as they pushed through the waves. The power levels were holding for now.

A crackling noise came over the comm station.

"Is someone trying to hail us?" Edgar said.

"We'll take care of Jaideep," Eevi said. "Go check that radio."

Katrina gave Eevi a nod and stepped carefully over to where Edgar sat. The water had drained through the scuppers, but the deck was still slick. She picked up the handset and hit the call button.

"USS *Zion*, this is Lieutenant Les Mitchells of *Deliverance*. Does anyone copy, over?"

Katrina almost smiled when she heard her XO's concerned voice. Finally, they were having some luck.

"Dad!" Trey said, rushing over.

"Copy, LT, this is Captain DaVita," Katrina said into the receiver. "What's your status?"

"Damn good to hear your voice, Captain," Les replied. "We docked with the *Hive* two days ago and have been awaiting orders." There was a short pause. "What is your situation, Captain?"

The lights flickered again, and several monitors blinked out.

"Not good," Katrina said. "We've broken through a storm and sustained some damage."

"What's your location?"

"I'm … not sure," Katrina said.

"Have you taken on water?"

"Not much, but we're not sure how bad the damage is yet. We're working on reports."

There was a pause, then the crackle of static.

"No, no, no," Katrina said as the radio fluttered.

The power held, and she quickly sent another message.

"How are the airships? How's recruitment going for that fighting force I requested?"

Another pause.

"Les, do you copy?"

"The ships are okay, but rumors are causing a problem," he replied. "Talk of the Metal Islands has spread like wildfire. I'm working with Sergeant Sloan to recruit your fighting force from the militia, but there aren't enough soldiers, and I don't feel right about recruiting from the passengers until we tell everyone the truth about the Cazadores."

Katrina had feared this all along, but the idea of telling everyone had her on edge. Doing so could create panic. But it sounded as though they didn't have a choice.

"You should also know, we sent a recommendation to Samson for reactivating Timothy Pepper on the *Hive*."

"What!" Katrina barked. "On what grounds?"

"We needed his help, and after learning that his counterpart helped X and Mags reach the Metal Islands, we think we can trust him."

"I'll leave it up to Samson, then," she said.

"Roger. So, what do you want me to do about the fighting force?" Les asked.

"What options do I have to pick from, Lieutenant?"

"I could cherry-pick individuals like I did for the Hell Divers, or I could tell people the truth and hope we can rally a small army to our cause …"

Static broke over the line.

"Les," she said. "Les, do you copy?"

More static crackled over the speakers.

Thunder boomed from a near strike outside. The electrical storm was messing with their comms again, and they were losing power. Katrina knew she didn't have long to make a decision.

Heaving a sigh, she brought the receiver back to her lips.

"Les, if you can hear this, your orders are to tell everyone on the *Hive* and *Deliverance* what's really down there. After that, put the word out, we need soldiers."

Keeping the passengers in the dark had been a policy of the captains before her, but she was finally going to break with those traditions. The people of the sky deserved to know the evil they would face on those oil rigs when the time came to fight for their new home.

FOUR

Les Mitchells slammed the radio down.

"Shit, we lost her."

After days of trying to get hold of the captain and the USS *Zion*, the conversation had been cut short, and Les had a dozen other things he needed to talk to Katrina about.

"Did she say what I thought I heard her say?" Layla asked.

The order had surprised them all, but at least he was now free to tell the truth and recruit on a wider scale.

"Someone already dropped the bombshell about the Metal Islands," Michael said. "Now it's just a matter of explaining what they really are—and what we're going to find there."

"Who would have done that?" Layla asked.

Les looked toward the small crew of Ensigns Dave Connor, Bronson White, and Ada Winslow. He trusted them and doubted that any of them were responsible.

Not many people knew that X and Magnolia had found the Metal Islands, and even fewer knew what the Metal Islands actually were and who lived there.

Chief Engineer Samson was one of those few. But there was always the possibility that a passenger with a radio could have intercepted a transmission.

It didn't matter now. The rumors were out, and they were growing and evolving like an electrical storm over a red zone. Even his wife and daughter were asking him for details.

A sudden thought made him cringe. Had Phyl or Katherine told a friend about the Metal Islands? That was all he had told them at this point, and he would give them the full truth before the announcement.

In a few hours, every soul on the airships would know the truth about the one habitable location they had discovered in over 260 years.

"I'll call a gathering tonight in the trading post and broadcast it over the comm systems," Les said. "In the meantime, I'll get with Sergeant Sloan again to see how many militia soldiers we have for the fighting force."

"This would be a really good time for some still-disgruntled lower-deckers to try something," Layla said, nervously brushing the end of a braid with her thumb.

"Maybe they'll save some of that anger for the Cazadores," Michael said, "and fight with us when the time comes."

"Maybe," Layla replied, clearly not convinced.

"Sergeant Sloan has assured me security on

the airships will remain her top priority," Les said, although he wasn't sure that was possible. They couldn't commit a force to the Metal Islands without leaving the airships' security team severely understaffed.

Michael stood, holding his stump in one hand. "Is there anything else, Lieutenant?"

Les shook his head. "Not unless you want to meet with Sergeant Sloan and me later."

"Michael should be resting," Layla said.

"That's all I've been doing. Besides, I have somewhere I need to go."

Layla shot him a wary glance. "Where?"

"To the archives. I want to see if the records have anything about Red Sphere."

Les had a feeling there was more to it than a little research.

"You're still healing," Layla said, "and it's probably about time for some more painkillers. Does Dr. Huff even know you left?"

"I don't take orders from the doc. I report only to the captain, and I'm certain she would appreciate more information on what we faced at Red Sphere. The Cazadores aren't the only enemy out there, you know."

Les wasn't used to seeing Michael argue with Layla, especially in front of others. There was something odd about his behavior, and not just because he lost his arm to one of the robots. They all wanted to avenge Erin's and Ramon's deaths at the hands of the AI defectors, but the only threat that mattered right now was the Cazadores.

The gravelly voice of Samson suddenly broke across the bridge. An unannounced visit from the chief engineer probably meant something was wrong. He rarely made the trip to *Deliverance* unless it was important.

"Lieutenant, you want to explain to me why I should be turning on that AI again?" he said.

Ah, yes, the discussion about trusting Timothy Pepper. He should have known this was coming.

Les sighed as the burly man made his way across the bridge, dabbing at his forehead with an oil-stained handkerchief.

"I'm going to be honest. I think it's a shit-can idea, especially after what happened at Red Sphere." Samson glanced at Michael but didn't address his injury.

"You've heard the reports of what Pepper did to help X and Mags reach the Metal Islands," Michael said. "For that reason alone, I think it's safe to say he isn't allied with the murder machines we encountered at Red Sphere."

"I agree," Les said. "But Katrina said this is your call."

"Don't you need his help?" Layla asked. "We're short-staffed, and Timothy can certainly fill in some of the gaps."

Samson shoved the hankie into the bib pocket of his coveralls. "Of course I could use his damn help. The *Hive* is falling apart like always, but I also don't like the idea of having him malfunction and kill us all in a fiery wreck … or worse."

"That's highly unlikely," Les said.

"But if there's even a ghost of a chance …" Samson's bloodshot eyes scanned each of them in turn. Then he made a sound somewhere between a snort and a sigh.

"Well?" Les asked.

Samson shrugged a shoulder. "I could use his help with some engineering issues, and we will need his assistance with Captain DaVita when we rendezvous at the Metal Islands … assuming we ever hear from her again."

"We just did," Les said.

Samson muttered, "No one tells me anything."

"We haven't had the chance—and already lost contact," Les said. He explained about the damage to the USS *Zion*, and Katrina's orders to call a meeting on the *Hive*, where they would discuss the Metal Islands and recruit fighters on a wider scale.

"She's lost her damn mind," Samson growled. "But I can't say as I blame her. Never thought I'd see the day when we found a habitable place on the surface."

"That makes two of us," Les said. "And that's why I agree this is worth the risk. That's why I let my boy stay down there."

The engineer stood there a moment, staring down at the patches on his boots. "All right, I'll give the order to turn Pepper back on, but the moment he acts up, I'll light him up like a Hell Diver in an electrical storm."

"Not funny!" Michael said.

"Ah, hell, we need a little humor around here," Samson said, clapping Michael on his good arm.

"When you reactivate Timothy, tell him I'd like to see him," Michael said.

"You got it, Commander."

Ada, Bronson, and Dave stood as Samson left. After all, he was acting captain of the *Hive*. When he was gone, Les took a seat again and massaged his temples.

"I sure hope Katrina knows what she's doing," he said, more to himself than to anyone else. His son was out there, on a warship in the middle of the ocean, and closing in on the Metal Islands.

The thought got Les to his feet. There was much work to be done.

He asked Michael, "You sure you don't want to come to my meeting with Sergeant Sloan, Commander?"

Michael shook his head, digging in, despite Layla's protests.

"Okay, but I would like—I *expect*—to have both of you by my side during the announcement tonight. It will be good for everyone to see some veteran Hell Divers up there with me."

"We'll be there," Layla said.

* * * * *

Magnolia had never worn a dress this fancy. She stood in front of a cracked mirror, turning from side to side to examine the loose-fitting white shift that came up just above her knees and fit snugly over her breasts.

"El Pulpo will like this *very* much," Imulah said.

The two Cazador women helping her with the dress and makeup nodded. Both were beautiful, and they spoke both English and Spanish. One, a slender freckled redhead, smiled warmly.

The other, olive skinned with a braid of black hair down her back, was even more stunning.

She focused her dark eyes on Magnolia and said, "Imulah is correct. El Pulpo will like you in this."

"Screw what he likes," Magnolia said, scowling.

Imulah ran a hand over his bald pate—the first time she had seen him flustered. She was getting on his nerves, but then, that was the point.

"What are your names?" Magnolia asked the women.

"Pardon me for not introducing them earlier," Imulah said. "This is Inge," he said, nodding at the redhead. "And Sofia."

"And they are who exactly?" Magnolia asked.

"El Pulpo's favorite wives, of course," Imulah said.

Magnolia almost gagged. Inge looked to be still in her teens, and Sofia didn't appear much older. It wasn't hard to imagine how terribly the barbarians treated them. Magnolia would teach them a thing or two about how to deal with men like el Pulpo.

For now, she just wanted out of this dress. She didn't even know why the hell she was wearing it.

"The blue streaks need to go," Sofia said, reaching out toward Magnolia with a pair of scissors.

She grabbed the girl's narrow wrist and squeezed. "No, they *don't*."

Sofia looked to Imulah, who sighed and nodded.
"*Lo siento*," she said. "Sorry."

Magnolia loosened her grip and turned back to
the mirror. She hardly recognized the woman standing
there. The dress fit her muscular body like a glove, and
the makeup Sofia and Inge had applied gave a glow to
her pale skin.

This wasn't the black-market crap she bought on
the *Hive*. This was the real stuff that women in the
picture books had once worn. It did a great job of
masking her bruises and cuts.

Imulah pulled out a pocket watch. "We must
hurry," he said, flipping the lid shut with his thumb.

Sofia and Inge remained in front of the mirror
while Magnolia walked out of the narrow quarters.
She stopped at the hatch and turned back to the two
young wives, feeling guilty for being so harsh.

"Sorry about your wrist," Magnolia said. "Hope-
fully, it won't cause a bruise, but if it does, you've got
that makeup."

The two women stared back at her. Inge seemed
frightened, but Sofia looked mad. Perhaps there was
some fire in this woman's belly after all.

"I was like you when I was a bit younger," Sofia
said. "Proud and aggressive. *This* is what happens
to people who resist. She turned away and dropped
her dress. Reaching over her shoulder, she pulled her
long braid away from her back to expose a network
of scars.

Magnolia gasped, but the lash marks didn't

surprise her. She knew the monster who had done this. It was the same monster she was scheduled to marry.

She had to get out of this hell.

"Let's go," Imulah said gently. He put a soft hand on her back, and Magnolia flinched at his cold touch.

"Don't touch me," she said.

Imulah lowered his hand and gestured toward a staircase where two Cazador soldiers waited. One of them started up the stairs, his sandals hardly making a sound on the metal rungs.

They climbed until she was out of breath, but she didn't stop to rest. When they finally reached the top of the tower, the two soldiers opened a hatch that led outside.

This time she didn't have to squint into the sun or shield her eyes. It would be dark soon—another day passed on the Metal Islands.

Birds soared overhead, and not the mutant vultures from the Turks and Caicos Islands. These birds weren't monsters, and the sun over the shimmering water in the distance wasn't an illusion.

How could hell be this beautiful?

She followed the two soldiers and Imulah down a dirt path inside what she now realized was the airship she had seen from the decks below. Along the outer rim grew a jungle of trees, rooted deeply in soil trekked in from who knew where.

Magnolia stopped when she saw their destination: an arena carved from the center of the airship's roof, with rows of seats surrounding a central pit of white sand. Hundreds of people were already in the seats or standing near the pit. Above the stands were several elevated booths with fans blowing on their occupants.

Imulah beckoned her toward a platform built over the dirt, surrounded by lush tropical plants and flowers. The two soldiers ahead stopped at the largest booth overlooking the arena and jammed their spear butts into the dirt. They stiffened and looked ahead, ready to protect their king, who sat inside on a throne overlooking the arena.

She could see el Pulpo, hunched over and enjoying a meal. He looked up at her approach, dropping a bone on the ground as he stood. The octopus tattoo on his forehead glistened with sweat. He mopped it with his sleeve and displayed his sharpened teeth in a stupid grin.

"Welcome," he said. "*Tú eres muy, muy bonita.*"

Magnolia stopped in the entrance with Imulah. The two soldiers behind her crossed their spears in an X, fencing her inside the booth.

"Let's go," Imulah said.

She walked into the booth and sat in a chair under a ceiling fan. The breeze felt good, but it blew her dress, exposing her legs. She pressed the material back down.

El Pulpo grinned and stepped over to the rail overlooking the sand pit. It took every bit of resistance to not stab him in the back of the head with the scissors she had taken from her quarters when the others weren't looking. But she had to play the long game now.

Cheers rang out from the stands as a wide hatch opened in the bulkhead of the hollowed-out airship. The cargo bay hatches looked a lot like the launch bay on *Deliverance*. Could this have been the same class of ship?

A middle-aged man in faded blue pants and a blood-red shirt strode out into the sand pit. He tipped back his spiked hair and raised a megaphone to his mouth. They all stood and cheered as he spoke in Spanish. When he finished, he repeated the words in English.

"Tonight, Hammerhead, with *ninety-nine* victories, returns to the Sky Arena." He raised his other arm into the air and clicked his tongue. "Never in the history of the Sky Arena has a warrior achieved one hundred kills. Will tonight be that night?"

He made a sweeping gesture as a huge warrior strode through the open gate. He walked over to the announcer, giving half the arena a view of the octopus tattoo covering the length of his back. The eight purple arms flexed and stretched with his muscular arms and thighs.

Hammerhead stopped, towering over the funny-looking man, and bellowed out a long, howling scream through the breathing apparatus over his mouth.

The crowd went wild, screaming enthusiastically as he raised two curved axes. He turned slowly, holding the weapons in the air until he faced the booth where Magnolia sat watching.

The warrior wasn't wearing much: just short black pants with a length of chain for a belt.

His thick pectoral muscles were adorned with a tattoo of a hammerhead shark.

El Pulpo smiled and looked over at her as if gauging her sense of awe. Both the announcer and the gladiator looked like clowns, but she kept this opinion to herself.

Another figure entered the arena, and she was not surprised to see the salt-and-pepper hair of Xavier Rodriguez. But she wasn't prepared to see him wearing only a leather loincloth and boots.

"What the hell did they make you wear?" she whispered.

Magnolia stood and watched X cross the arena. He held a hand up to shield his eyes from the lowering sun. Like his opponent, he, too, was covered with markings, but not of ink. His were the scars accrued over a lifetime of battles.

He pulled a chain that was wrapped around his waist and secured with a lock. But where was his weapon? Did they expect him to fight with his bare hands?

She didn't doubt his fighting skills, but this wasn't fair. Unless the chain was connected to a ball of spikes.

Armored Cazador soldiers streamed onto a platform that rimmed the fighting arena, about ten feet below the lowest seats. One of the warriors tossed a short sword to the dirt about twenty feet from X. It stuck in the ground.

A low growl came from the other side of the booth, and Magnolia stood as a Cazador soldier pulled Miles into the booth. The dog wore a collar with the spikes turned inward, and he yelped in pain when his handler yanked on the chain.

"Don't hurt him!" she snarled.

She jumped up from her seat, but el Pulpo blocked her way. He smelled of perspiration and barbecued meat.

"Sit," he commanded.

Magnolia held his gaze. This was her chance to stab him in his only eye, but she couldn't bring herself to do it. That would be a death sentence, not just for her but for Miles, X, and Rodger, too.

She sat back in the chair and crossed her legs, biding her time. When she looked back down at the sand, she saw that the chain X held wasn't connected to a ball of spikes, but to a half-naked man.

The crowded screamed with excitement as X pulled the chain.

Magnolia stood again and made her way to the railing. She squinted in the waning sunlight at another gladiator with a nasty scar on his chest, stumbling out into the pit. Rodger Mintel stopped a few paces from X, raised a hand to shield his eyes, and looked up at the booth, his big brown eyes meeting hers.

El Pulpo nudged Magnolia and grinned. "Time for blood, *mi amor*."

FIVE

"Stop looking at Mags and get out here!" X shouted. He pulled Rodger farther in from the gate. They were still three or four steps from the sword the Cazador soldier had thrown out. He needed the weapon if he was to have any chance of defeating the giant roaring at him from halfway across the stadium.

"Come on, man!" he yelled.

Rodger tugged back. "I can't … can't see …"

The crowd roared as the announcer introduced the two Hell Divers through his cone-shaped device.

"Entering the Sky Arena to face Hammerhead tonight is sky jumper Rodger Mintel, a.k.a. Rodger Dodger, and Xavier Rodri-i-i-igue-e-e-e-ez, known by his own people and his enemies alike as the *Immortal*."

This goofball reminded X of one of the old-world announcers from the fighting videos he had seen growing up. He loved watching the mixed-martial-arts fights, but he never thought he would be starring in one.

You won't be a star if you get whacked …

X slowly turned and scanned the hundreds of Cazadores looking down at them. Behind the warriors, citizens of the Metal Islands stood in front of their seats, screaming and clapping, showing off their pointed teeth.

People were chewing on strips of meat a kid was hawking from a box on a rope around his neck. Of all the strange and perilous situations X had found himself in over the years, this might be the weirdest.

"Kill him, X!" shouted a voice he knew.

X looked up at Magnolia, who had cupped her hands over her mouth. Then he turned to study his opponent, a huge man tattooed with images of an octopus and a shark. He lifted up two massive axes, his massive chest expanding as he sucked in air through his breathing apparatus.

He also wore some sort of optics that looked like old-world night-vision goggles. Hammerhead turned them on X and Rodger and let out another howling roar, pounding the tattoo of the octopus in the center of his chest.

X had fought all sorts of monsters on the surface, from Sirens and huge birds of prey to giant sea snakes and octopuses, to rock monsters. But he had never fought a man with monsters covering his skin. This was going to be interesting.

Shoving the announcer out of the way, Hammerhead started across the field. The little man hit the ground hard, and the crowd laughed as he scrambled away on all fours.

So much for a handshake first, X thought on his run to pick up the sword. Rodger let out a yelp as X tugged on the chain tethering them together.

"Stay behind me!" X yelled.

He grabbed the sword out of the dirt. Hammerhead was still about thirty feet away and running at them, snorting like one of the nightmare hogs back on the Turks and Caicos Islands.

As X backed away, he tried to cut the chain, but the dull blade only pushed the welded links down into the sand. He would have to fight this man while chained to Rodger.

At last, Rodger ran up and joined X, staying just behind as ordered.

"What … do we do?" he stammered.

"Help me bring this fucker down, and stop looking at Mags," X said. "Oh, and try not to get us killed." He raised the sword. It was solid, with a sturdy hilt, but the blade was rusty and dull. He would need to jam it into Hammerhead's face to kill him.

Rodger held up his fists, and X readied himself as their opponent came lumbering across the sand, roaring like a monster out of the wastes. Hammerhead stopped about ten feet from X, who waved Rodger farther behind him. The crowd screamed in delight as the gladiator raised and lowered his axes in a taunt.

"Stay clear of this asshole," X said, "and try and get this slack around his neck when I attack."

"Are you s-serious?"

X didn't have a chance to respond.

Hammerhead, done with his posing, strode toward them. X pushed Rodger away. He took off running, screaming like a small girl and holding the slack of the chain in both hands.

If X were just an observer in the stands, he would have laughed, but being part of the drama was far different. This was a fight to the death—nothing funny about that.

He followed Rodger as they tried to flank Hammerhead, but the guy was not just huge. He was also fast and ran diagonally to cut them off.

X held his ground and twirled the sword. "Over here, you ugly pile of shark shit."

Hammerhead roved his mechanical optics away from Rodger, the weak link, back to X. The sound that came from his breathing mask was a cross between a cough and a grunt. He pinwheeled his arms with the axes to confuse X on when and at what angle he would strike.

X backed away and waited for the opportune moment. He watched the blades carefully as they sliced the air. When Hammerhead got within striking distance, he swung the left axe, and X brought his sword up to meet the blade.

Steel met steel, and sparks flew.

X jumped backward to avoid a slice meant for his chest.

Hammerhead was even bigger than he looked from a distance, standing nearly a head taller than X and outweighing him by a hundred pounds.

He swung again and moved with the blow, slamming his chest into X and knocking him backward.

Grabbing the chain, Hammerhead yanked Rodger off his feet, knocking him to the ground with a thud and dragging him several feet.

X regained his balance instantly and sliced at his opponent's hand, missing by a finger width. Hammerhead dropped the chain and swung both axes from right to left in an effort to take off his head. The blades came close enough that X felt the wind of their passage through the air.

Hammerhead swung again, this time bringing the axe down as if splitting a round of wood. X rolled left to avoid being split in two and spotted Rodger, standing and holding two yards of slack chain.

But it wasn't his inept fighting partner that worried X. Behind Rodger, four Cazador soldiers ran in through another gate. Each was armed with a double-headed spear and dressed in heavy, clanking armor. X rolled up into a squat and spotted the leader, who held a shield with an octopus painted across it.

"Rodger, behind you!" X yelled. He sprang to his feet, wincing at the sharp twinge from the pressure on his wounded foot. Ignoring the pain, he ran toward Rodger, who finally turned.

The Cazador soldier carrying the shield moved in front of the others and lunged at Rodger with his spear. Seeing no other option, X stopped and threw his sword.

His aim was true, and the blade penetrated

the soldier's chest armor before he could raise his shield. X was almost surprised at the rusted sword's performance.

"His spear!" X shouted as the dead Cazador crumpled to the ground.

Rodger grabbed the weapon and tossed it to X. They came together as the other three spearmen closed in on the right and Hammerhead moved in from the left.

It was hard to hear anything over the screaming crowd, but X thought he heard Magnolia yell a warning. He looked over his shoulder in time to see the blur of an axe cartwheeling through the air. He had only an eyeblink in which to move his head aside. The weapon passed so close, he heard the blade whisper past his ear and smack into flesh behind him with a sickening crunch.

Rodger! X's heart sank at the muffled cry. But before he could turn to check on his partner, Hammerhead was on him. A kick in the chest sent him flying backward, and pain shot through ribs still tender from the battle in el Pulpo's throne room. He landed on his back, knocking the air from his lungs.

Through the pain, X managed to hold on to the spear, which he jabbed to keep Hammerhead at bay while he got to his feet, gasping for air.

The first thing he saw was Rodger, with all his limbs, and no blades jutting from his flesh. He was picking up the spear of a Cazador soldier. The axe that flew past X had planted square in the soldier's face, splitting it open like a watermelon. The dead man's feet jerked once, then went still.

Hammerhead screamed something in Spanish at the other two men, and they slowly backed away. It struck X then, the axe hadn't missed its mark. The behemoth gladiator wanted the glory of killing the Hell Divers all to himself.

"On me!" X yelled to Rodger.

They came together back to back, spears out. It was time to finish this big bastard.

Keeping low, X hurled the spear at the shark tattoo on Hammerhead's chest, but the gladiator parried with the flat of his remaining axe, knocking the shaft away. And on he came, swinging the blade before him.

X lunged out of the way, but the giant kicked him in the thigh and grabbed him by the arm. He yanked X back toward him and punched him in the side of the head.

Bees swarmed X's vision, and he tasted blood from the hole where a tooth had been. He spat it into the sand and drove an elbow up, catching his adversary under the chin. Hammerhead loosened his grip, and X managed to pull free before the giant could use the axe in his other hand to lop off a body part.

X scrambled away and heard the blade thump into the dirt where he had stood only a moment ago. He thrust his spear backward and was surprised to feel it connect.

Turning, he saw that the blade had severed the

breathing apparatus, exposing a missing cheek from an old battle. The opening gave him a view of jagged yellow teeth. Hammerhead let out a shriek of pain and stumbled backward, clutching his face.

The crowd was screaming so loud, X barely heard Rodger yelling for help. He returned his attention to the two Cazador soldiers, who were staring in disbelief at their injured champion.

"Down, Rodgeman!" he yelled.

Seizing the moment, X grasped his spear at midshaft, twirling it over his head. The spinning spearhead slit the throat of a shocked Cazador soldier, who dropped his weapon and clamped his hands over the spurting wound.

The other Cazador soldier jabbed his spear at Rodger, but Rodger and X both jabbed back. The man moved from left to right and ducked, but there was nowhere to go.

Rodger stuck him in the chest, penetrating the armor. The Cazador grabbed the shaft and fell back onto the sand, twisting in agony.

"I got him!" Rodger yelled with glee. He looked over at X, and his smile vanished as his eyes focused on the area directly over X's shoulder.

X turned as a shadow loomed over him.

Hammerhead grabbed him by the neck, lifting him off the ground.

Rodger lunged, but the gladiator shoved him away with his other hand. He hit the dirt and skidded on his back, the chain pulling taut between them.

The crowd roared and laughed, their noise filling the arena. The announcer spoke again in Spanish, bringing more laughter.

X squirmed in the grip of the beast holding him in the air. The insectoid optics peered at him as if he were a specimen being examined under a microscope. He gasped for air as Hammerhead tightened the grip around his neck. The stench of rotting teeth made X want to puke, but he had to suck in what air he could.

He battered Hammerhead in the ear, over and over, but it was like a gnat biting an elephant. Hammerhead screamed in fury, slinging spittle across X's face.

Vision narrowing, X could feel his life force draining away. He had only seconds before this guy broke either his windpipe or his neck. He swung his fist again, this time at the buglike optics over Hammerhead's eyes. The first blow didn't do much, but the second knocked them lose. Bulging, blood-shot eyes stared back at X. Hammerhead dropped him to the ground and brought up his hands to shield his eyes from the setting sun.

X lay in the sand for a moment, gasping.

"I'm coming!" Rodger yelled. Jumping on Hammerhead's back, he looped the chain around the thick neck and hung on. X felt the chain tugging, but he could do nothing except suck in air.

Hammerhead clawed at Rodger with his free hand, the other one still covering his eyes. He bucked and twisted, but Rodger clung tight with his legs.

X finally managed to push himself up on one

knee, but he was so light-headed, he fell back onto his belly. He couldn't get enough air, and he felt the slick of blood in his boot from the reopened bullet wound.

Get up, old man.

"Help me!" Rodger yelled.

X saw a double-headed spear half covered by sand. Grabbing it, he pushed himself to his feet. He staggered slightly, listening to the screams and wails of the fans. Everyone in the arena was on their feet— even el Pulpo, who watched from the balcony of his booth. Magnolia was by his side, and nestled beside her was a dog.

Miles, I'm coming for you, boy.

X broke the spear shaft over his knee and raised the two short spears.

Hammerhead had finally managed to get a hand on Rodger and had him by the beard.

"Hey, Smiley!" X yelled. "Got something for you!"

The broad, ugly face turned just as X jammed a spear blade into Hammerhead's gut and left it there. He howled in pain, letting go of Rodger, who kept doggedly pulling on the chain.

X plunged the second spear into Hammerhead's chest, just above the heart. The shark tattoo quickly disappeared beneath a spreading patch of crimson. The giant dropped to his knees and then onto his back, pinning Rodger to the ground.

Panting, X staggered over.

The crowd suddenly went silent, and X glanced up to see el Pulpo raise his hands in the air, grab the railing, and drop to the sand. The stadium filled with the clicking of ten thousand teeth.

Dozens of warriors ducked under opening gates and swarmed the field to surround their king. X plucked the two spears out of Hammerhead's limp body and turned to face the approaching warriors as they formed a cordon around him and the dead gladiator.

"X," said a muffled voice. "Get this guy off me."

Swords and spear tips bristled toward X, and one man drew a handgun. X hesitated and looked up at Magnolia. She nodded at him—confirmation that this wasn't the time and place to make their stand. After another moment's pause, he dropped the shafts. Then he bent down and pushed the gigantic corpse off Rodger.

"You okay?" he asked as Rodger tried to slither free.

The crowd went back to screaming, and a chant started to ring out. X ignored the din around him and reached down to help his friend. Rodger, flushed but apparently uninjured, sucked in a long breath and grabbed his outstretched hand.

The chants intensified, and X finally realized what these people were yelling.

"*¡Inmortal! ¡Inmortal! ¡Inmortal!*"

* * * * *

"Commander Everhart, I don't have you on the schedule for access," said Monk. The militia sentry stood with another guard, O'Toole, in front of the hatch to *Deliverance*'s launch bay and weapons lockers.

"I have my key card," Michael said, fishing it out of his pocket.

"Sorry, sir, but protocol has changed," said O'Toole. The fit, likable militia soldier had grown a beard since Michael saw him last.

"I'm not here for weapons," Michael said. "I just need access to the restricted archives again."

After clearing his throat, Monk said, "I'm sorry, sir, but you will need clearance from Sergeant Sloan or Lieutenant Mitchells. Our orders are to keep this area secure unless someone has specified clearance."

The two guards took their job of protecting the nuclear arsenal and weapons locker seriously, and while Michael respected that, he was losing his patience, especially when Monk glanced at his arm stump. He was really getting sick of all the staring.

"Go ahead and radio Lieutenant Mitchells," Michael said. "I just talked to him—didn't realize I would need clearance to get to the archives."

"Give us a minute, sir," O'Toole said.

Monk pulled out his walkie-talkie and put the order in, and after several minutes of pacing, they finally got a response from Ensign Ada Winslow that Les was now meeting with Sergeant Sloan.

Michael shook his head, frustrated. A phantom pain had set in, and he considered heading back to the medical ward for some pharmaceutical relief.

You can handle this, remember, Michael?

He gritted his teeth. Counting helped him focus

on something other than the agonizing pain, but it also reminded him that time was going by.

Since he could remember, there had always been a clock in his subconscious, ticking ever closer to doomsday. Right now, that clock was ticking for X, Mags, and Miles, and there was only one thing he could do for them right now.

"Let's just let him through," O'Toole said.

"What? We have specific orders," Monk replied quietly, turning his back to Michael.

"He's a Hell Diver."

The hatch clicked, and both men stepped away. A white glow emanated from the other side, coalescing into a human shape. The dark-skinned figure, dressed in creaseless pants and a suit jacket, stood inside the launch bay. He had a neat beard and short-cropped hair. The man—or hologram, to be precise—made Michael smile.

"What the hell!" Monk said. "I thought you were—"

"The captain ordered his reactivation," Michael said. "Good to have you back, Timothy."

"Thank you, Commander. It's good to see you. Samson said that you wanted to see me."

"Yes. Follow me." Now that the hatch had opened, Michael didn't wait for permission. He simply nodded at O'Toole and Monk, who stepped aside to let him into the launch bay. The hatch closed behind them, sealing with a loud click that echoed throughout the vaulted space.

"I'm only fifty-nine percent operational," Timothy

said, "but I should be one hundred percent within the hour and will have accessed the thousands of new files on the mainframe."

"That's what I wanted to talk to you about. What's the last communication you had with your counterpart on the *Sea Wolf*?"

"One moment while I scan for the transmissions."

Michael led them toward the Combat Information Center belowdecks, taking the staircase down to where he and Layla had their "date" a week ago. The click of his boots on the rungs reminded him of the final message from X.

By the time you hear this, we will likely be dead. But when you do come, prepare to face a brutal enemy— worse than the Sirens. Avenge Miles. Avenge Magnolia, and promise me that when you make this humanity's future, you won't resort to barbarism like the Cazadores. I dived so humanity would survive. I dived for this place. I love you, Tin. Be good, fight hard, and remember what you told me: Accept your past without regrets. Handle your present with confidence. Face your future without fear. I'll always be here for you in spirit, kid.

The message sent a chill of pride and dread through Michael. By the time they got down to the dashboard of computer equipment, Timothy had finished his scan.

"The last transmission we received from my counterpart was from three days ago," he said. "Shall I play it for you?"

Michael nodded.

"*This is Timothy Pepper of the* Sea Wolf. *I'm running on backup power and will be going idle soon. My vessel has been captured by the Cazadores and is being taken to a tower that appears to be the capitol of the Metal Islands. I have not heard from X or Magnolia for thirty-six hours now and suspect they are either captured or dead …*"

Michael sat down and slumped in the chair.

"*I've listened to the Cazadores on board for any information on their fate, but so far they have spoken only of a warrior who will not die. I've tried tapping into the radio transmissions, but there are very few. These people seem to communicate purely by word of mouth.*"

There was a pause. Then, "*The mechanics working on the ship continue to speak of a man from the sky—the same man that they say cannot die.*"

"X!" Michael said. "It's got to be X."

The hologram of Timothy Pepper on *Deliverance* scratched his beard. "That would be a logical assumption, Commander."

"Is that the last transmission?" Michael asked.

A nod from Timothy.

"Damn." Michael had hoped Timothy might be able to access something that Les and the other officers on the bridge couldn't.

He pulled out his key card and swiped it across the monitor, bringing the computer online.

"I need you to do some research for me," Michael said. "I need you to dig up every file you can find on the AI defectors and Red Sphere."

"One moment, sir." Timothy's hologram flickered

in and out as he worked, and Michael used the opportunity to open the hatches covering the portholes. Storm clouds churned outside *Deliverance*—the same dispiriting sight he was used to seeing. But it was the view of the *Hive* that gave him the chills.

Or perhaps that was from the pain firing up his shoulder and neck and into his temple. He closed his eyes and took a deep breath.

When he opened his eyes again, he saw hundreds of porthole windows covered by salvaged hatches on the side of the *Hive*. People had already painted most of them with fluffy clouds and blue skies. But a few hadn't been replaced.

Several portholes glowed from interior lamps and lights, providing a view inside the quarters where families dwelled on the upper decks. He was too far away to recognize any of them, but something about seeing the people inside their homes made him feel at home. He had been fighting to save this place his entire adult life.

Now he had a chance to create a new home—a home where the sun shone. Part of him still didn't believe it, but the Metal Islands were real, and Michael knew that they couldn't take the paradise from the Cazadores with the airships, a naval warship, the Hell Divers, and the militia soldiers. They needed something else, something that would involve a major risk. But if he could pull this off, it had the potential to change everything.

"I've finished my scan and have recovered one

hundred two files received from the *Sea Wolf* about Red Sphere and the defectors, otherwise known as model DEF-Nine," Timothy said. "What would you like to know?"

"I want to see their internal makeup and their programming."

"Let me pull those up. But, Commander, if I may, why are you asking this?"

Michael paused, recalling a memory of playing with a vacuum robot in his old quarters when X had come home with a bag of noodles, not long after his father perished on a dive.

"When I was a kid, while the other kids were playing with games, I played with robots," Michael said. "Building them, taking them apart."

"With all due respect, Commander, DEF-Nine units, or what you call defectors, aren't cleaning machines. They are killing machines."

"And like anything designed by humans, they will have a weakness or a glitch. Even you have them, Timothy."

"Touché, sir."

Michael twisted around in his seat and said, "I just have to find it, and if I'm right, then maybe, just maybe, I can find a way to control them."

SIX

"All hands report to the trading post in one hour," said the soothing voice of Ensign Ada Winslow over the comm system. "Lieutenant Les Mitchells will be making an announcement about the future of the airships."

Les stood in front of the hatch to his quarters and gave his wife a kiss on the cheek. His daughter, Phyl, held a doll in her hands, listening to the repeating transmission with her head tilted head as if she didn't understand what the ensign was saying.

"Fu-ture?" she said slowly.

"The new home you keep hearing about," Les said.

"You haven't told us everything, have you?" Katherine asked. There was anger in her voice—something he hadn't heard in a while. "You haven't told us what happened to X or the others."

"No, I haven't," he said. "I'm sorry, but I have … I *had* strict orders."

Katherine narrowed her gaze. "You promised you

wouldn't leave Trey. You promised you would stay with him."

She pulled away from his grip, giving him a moment to consider his words. When he was a young boy, his father had taught him never to make a promise he couldn't keep, and this one Les wasn't sure about.

Trey felt so far away …

He is *far away.*

They were practically a world apart, separated by a sea of electrical storms.

"Papa, I miss Trey," Phyl said. "Commander Everhart said he's on a mission and isn't sure when he'll be back."

Les looked from his wife to his daughter, wishing he could take their pain away, but he was frightened his words would only add more emotional agony.

His father had also told him never to lie, especially to two of the three people he loved unconditionally.

"When I dived last week with Trey, we found another ship at Red Sphere," Les said. "Not an airship. It's an old naval warship from the United States of America. Captain DaVita is sailing it to the Metal Islands, to help save X, Mags, and Miles from the Cazadores, and to …"

Les stopped as Phyl tilted her head. Maybe she wasn't old enough to hear the rest. It might just frighten her and make her worry about Trey.

But she deserved to know where her brother was going, and kids on the airship were resilient. They had been through more than any kid should.

"I've been tasked with putting together a fighting force to help Captain DaVita take the Metal Islands from the barbarians that live there. Trey is sailing to help on that mission."

Katherine put a hand over her mouth and arched her brows. "You sent our son to *war*?"

He hated how it sounded, but the hard reality was that humanity had been at war for the past 260 years.

A war for survival.

"Yes," Les said. "And if it comes down to it, I'll be joining him in the fight."

Katherine pulled Phyl close. "I … I don't believe this! I don't even know who you are right now!"

The stinging words took Les slightly by surprise. He wasn't used to balancing orders with what he told his family, but by not telling Katherine from the beginning, he had now lost her trust.

He suddenly missed his days as a simple electrician, when all he had to worry about were hot tunnels and live wires.

"I'm sorry, Katherine, I didn't mean to hurt you. I—"

She pulled back when he reached out for her. "I don't care what you meant to do. You sent our son to *war*, Les."

White noise crackled from the comm system, and the announcement from Ensign Winslow played again. Time was up, and he couldn't dawdle any longer.

"I have to go," he said. "I'm sorry. Please come to the trading post and listen to what I have to say."

Katherine didn't reply, and Les turned away so they wouldn't see the tears welling in his eyes. Opening the hatch, he left without looking at his wife or daughter again.

The passages were filled with people leaving their quarters and jobs to head to the trading post. Everyone wanted to hear what he was about to tell them, except for Katherine.

He jostled through the crowds, hurrying to the one stop he had to make before the announcement. Sergeant Sloan was standing outside the militia headquarters on the *Hive*, her back to the bulkhead, arms folded across her black armor.

"'Bout time, LT," she said.

"Sorry."

Sloan led him through a hatch into the militia HQ, which consisted of several offices, a locker room, a small armory, and a conference room, all empty.

They continued through a hatch that connected to the launch bay on the *Hive*. Inside the room stood thirty-odd militia soldiers in black fatigues. Some of them still had on body armor and helmets from their patrols. Batons hung from their duty belts.

Les ran a hand through his frizz of red hair. Most of these guys were retired from other jobs and now worked on guarding restricted facilities. They weren't seasoned warriors—hardly any of those were left. And there was no time to train people.

"This is everyone," Sloan said. "I know it's not much, but it's what we have to work with from the militia. Everyone else is either dead or with the captain on that warship. I've only got forty-two people under my command, and at least ten need to stay on the ships, to keep order if and when we decide to attack the Metal Islands."

Les tried to picture these people fighting the well-armed and well-trained Cazador soldiers that Timothy Pepper described in one of his last transmissions from the *Sea Wolf*.

In his mind's eye, Les saw the barbarians slaughtering the militia soldiers along with anyone else they sent down there.

"What, exactly, are we fighting?" asked Jack, a sixty-year-old former electrician who had trained Les when he was younger.

Les turned and whispered, "You haven't told them yet?"

Sloan shook her head. "Figured you'd want the honors."

"All right," Les said with a discreet sigh. "Follow me to the trading post. I'm going to explain everything there, and you can decide if you still want to fight with us."

The group of militia soldiers followed Les out of the launch bay and into the crowded passages.

"Out of the way," Sergeant Sloan said in her authoritative voice.

Fresh paint glistened on the bulkheads of the next passage—a scene of exotic animals drinking from a watering hole in a desert. Around the corner, another recent display of artwork had gone up on the overhead and bulkhead. Waves slapped the white beach of an island, and palm trees bent in the wind.

It was a dangerous image, Les realized. This was what most people would think of when they spoke of the Metal Islands. The flow of passengers moved through the colorful scene, but he knew the truth about the horrors they would find when they got to their destination.

The line continued around the next corner, where it bottlenecked in front of the trading post. Drifting scents from the food vendors mixed with body odor and the ever-present whiff from the nearest shit cans.

As Sergeant Sloan led the way into the room, Les tried to remember the last time he had seen the space this packed. All the vendor stalls had been moved back to the bulkheads. The tables normally reserved for eating were already occupied, and a small stage had been moved in front of them near the north bulkhead.

Les breathed in and out to quell his anxiety. He had never spoken in front of so many people. Layla and Michael were already on the stage, sitting in chairs next to a lectern. Ensigns Ada Winslow, Bronson White, and Dave Connor were standing behind them in their dress whites. A hologram glowed onto the stage and materialized into the form of Timothy Pepper.

"Hello, Lieutenant Mitchells," he said.

"Welcome back, Pepper."

Michael and Layla stood to greet Les as he stepped up onto the platform. He made his way right to the podium, stopping only to reach into his uniform and pull out his prepared notes.

Hundreds of people filed into the trading post, filling the space with conversations, sporadic coughs, and the cries of babies—the music of the *Hive*, the sounds of survival.

Les scanned the faces of the people he had spent his entire life with. He knew everyone by name, even the lower-deckers. But not everyone was here today. Missing were Katherine and Phyl. His heart broke at their absence, but he still had a job to do, a duty to these people.

Sergeant Sloan grabbed the microphone and tapped on the end, and a loud *thunk, thunk* erupted from the wall-mounted speakers across the space.

"Quiet, everyone," she growled. Her rough voice silenced the crowd, and she handed the microphone to Les. "Good luck, Giraffe."

More people squeezed into the room, and he waited for the final passengers. Sloan directed her people to fan out and hold security, and for that, Les was grateful. He had no idea how these people would receive his words—especially some of the less-stable folks who still weren't happy about the living conditions. There was some history of violence from lower-deckers at public gatherings this big.

As the final stragglers walked into the trading post, Les took a moment to scan the faces. In the very front stood Cole Mintel, his sleeves rolled up to reveal a new tattoo of the tree of life—a tribute to his dead son, Rodger. His wife, Bernie, stood on his right, and on the left were two farmers, Moon Lao and her husband, John. Dom, the curly-headed owner of the Dragon noodles stall, and Marv, proprietor of the Wingman, had also gotten in at the front.

Families with kids sat at the tables. Les saw the orphan siblings Chloe and Daniel amid other children and parents with tattered clothing and holes in their shoes.

It was the same sight he had been accustomed to his entire life. Even the officers and those civilians who held some of the more desirable jobs as engineers and farmers looked ragged and downbeat, worried about the announcement.

And he was about to ask for volunteers to fight a war?

Recruiting new Hell Divers was one thing, but recruiting people for the express purpose of killing other human beings was another thing altogether.

The room quieted, and all eyes were on Les.

He cleared his throat as he unfolded the sheet of paper. Then he folded it and stuck it back in his pocket. What he was about to say, he had memorized.

"As you all know," he said, "I'm Lieutenant Les Mitchells. Some of you may know me as Giraffe. I stand before you today as an officer and a citizen of the sky. For my entire life, I've lived among you, working by your side, raising my family as you raised yours, all in the hope that someday we could return to the surface. Until recently, I didn't believe it could happen in my lifetime and figured that only our grandchildren's children might be so lucky."

He paused, squinting to see several more people squeeze into the room, hoping it was Katherine and Phyl. It wasn't.

"As many of you may also know, Commander Xavier Rodriguez and Magnolia Katib have discovered a habitable place called the Metal Islands."

The room buzzed with murmurs and side conversations, just as he had predicted. Les looked over to Sloan, who pulled out a baton, strode over, and slammed it against the side of the podium.

"Let Lieutenant Mitchells speak!" she yelled.

Another smack of the baton, and the passengers finally quieted.

"The Metal Islands are located off the Virgin Islands, an old-world chain inhabited by humans. But they are not actual islands. They are oil rigs, and they are controlled by a warrior society called the Cazadores. These people have captured the crew of the *Sea Wolf*."

Les spoke faster before he could be interrupted again. "Captain DaVita is sailing there now in a naval warship, the USS *Zion*, which we found at another location …"

He let his words trail off as the trading post fell silent but for the sporadic coughs and a wailing baby. Les dreaded what he was about to say.

"Captain DaVita plans on offering the leader of the Cazadores a chance to give us our people back and let us share this habitable place with them, or suffer the consequences. But if they refuse this offer, we will be forced to go to war."

"War?" someone shouted.

More voices broke out, and Sloan slapped her baton against her hand, ready to crack heads.

Les swallowed, then explained why he was really here. "I've been tasked with recruiting a fighting force to help us take the Metal Islands if diplomacy fails. I know what I'm asking. For those of you who volunteer, make no mistake, this will be a brutal fight, but this is also the chance we've all been waiting for, and I, for one, am prepared to die for this new home."

Michael and Layla walked over to stand by his side.

"I'd like to say something," Michael said.

Les handed him the microphone. Static crackled over the speakers.

"We dive so humanity survives, and now we're asking you to fight under one banner to free our friends and to make the Metal Islands our home," Michael said.

He gritted his teeth, clearly in pain.

Layla reached out, but Michael shook his head. "I'm not done."

She pulled back, and he said, "No one has endured more pain and suffering over the years than X. After saving the *Hive* over a decade ago, he was left for dead by the tyrant Leon Jordan, even when Jordan knew he was down there, and forced to endure severe hardship on the poisoned surface for years and years. When we finally found X in Florida, he was a broken man. But he did not give up. He took to the seas, and he found the Metal Islands."

Michael paused again. "In Florida, I thought we were rescuing him, but he was really rescuing us. Now we have a chance to *actually* rescue X. To thank him for his service and sacrifices. I know that fighting in a war is a terrifying thing, but I'll be there on the front lines, and I hope some of you will join me."

He handed the microphone back to Les. Les squinted to make out two more people who had slipped into the back of the room. His heart leaped when he saw that it was Katherine and Phyl. They stood near the open doors, keeping back as if they were afraid.

"Lieutenant," Layla said.

"Thank you, Commander Everhart," Les said, snapping out of it and grabbing the sides of the lectern. "For those of you who are willing and able, we will have a briefing in the launch bay after this, to talk about the fight ahead."

Sloan motioned with her baton. "Step forward if you're volunteering."

At first, the entire room remained silent. The baby had even stopped crying. What felt like a minute passed before the first person stepped forward.

"These are the people who killed my boy?" said Cole Mintel.

Les nodded.

"I'm not much for fighting, but I can hold my own," Cole said.

"I'm in," said Marv. He grinned. "I'm getting sick of serving shine to all you drunks anyways."

Several nervous chuckles followed. A few more people stepped over to join the two men. Hushed conversations came from all directions, and the crowd began to move. Within a few minutes, fifty people had clustered at the front of the room.

It wasn't much, but it was a start.

Michael leaned over to Les as Sloan began organizing the group.

"I've got an idea, Lieutenant," Michael said. "One that might not require so many of these people to put their lives on the line if we do go to war."

Les gave him a searching look. "What do you mean?"

Michael motioned for Timothy.

"We go back to Red Sphere. Get more laser rifles and hack some of the defectors to help us take over the Metal Islands."

Les scrutinized Michael's face, looking for the joke, but the injured diver, who had lost a freaking arm at the facility, looked deadly serious.

"I'll lead the mission," Michael said. "Got some unfinished business there."

* * * * *

"I need that damage assessment, Eevi," Katrina said.

"Working on it, Captain." The former militia detective sat at a station, tapping at her keyboard.

Katrina knew she was being demanding, but she was anxious, and the way to keep things moving was to keep on her people. She needed them as sharp as a sword edge. There was some good news, though. Jaideep was going to be okay. He had a concussion and wouldn't be fighting anytime soon, but it beat a broken neck.

She tapped her monitor for a frontal view of the ocean. The water was deep here, assuming the readings were correct. But the island wasn't far away, and until she was sure of her instruments, she couldn't risk hitting a shoal.

The electrical storm continued to rage around them, scrambling all transmissions in or out. It was also messing with their equipment. Every life scan they had run on the island came back inconclusive.

"Jed, Sandy, have you figured out where we are yet?" Katrina asked.

The two teenagers looked up from the paper maps they had found stored in an officer's quarters. Since GPS wasn't working, Katrina had them try to figure things out the old-fashioned way.

"My best guess is, we're somewhere between the Dominican Republic and Puerto Rico," Jed said.

"If that's the case, then how far are we from the Virgin Islands?" Katrina asked.

"Somewhere around a hundred miles," Sandy said.

Not very far. And they were out of the worst of the storm. For now.

The rain kept coming down in sheets, hammering

the shutters. Katrina had lowered one and leaned over to look out the cracked panel—the only panel to survive the rogue wave. All the rest had blown out, leaving dangerous shards in the standing water on deck.

"Okay, looks like we got it," Eevi said, smiling in the glow of her monitor as she scanned the data. "The hull breach was limited to the bow—only two compartments flooded. Nothing serious, Captain."

"Power levels?" Katrina asked.

Eevi checked her monitor and said, "The new fuel cell we brought from *Deliverance* is still at ninety-eight percent, engines functioning at optimal levels."

"Good news," Katrina said. "Eevi, you have the bridge. Jed, Sandy, keep trying to figure out where we are. I'm heading topside."

The Hell Divers all went back to work.

A sharp sword, Katrina thought.

Katrina cautiously made her way through the broken glass and water to a ladder leading to the command center for flight operations. The rectangular windows gave her a view of the deck, the ocean, and the island.

She brought the binoculars up to her eyes and zoomed in, using the night vision to scan for hostiles. The bio scanners may not be working, but her eyes wouldn't lie.

The island definitely had flora. Beyond the rocky beaches, mutant jungles the color of blood and bruises covered the terrain. Surely there was some sort of fauna out there, but so far, they hadn't spotted anything.

Now that they had confirmed the ship was still seaworthy, she just had to wait until Sandy and Jed figured out which direction to sail.

Several more sweeps yielded nothing except for the stone foundation and walls of an old building along the shore. Vines had overtaken the walls and brought the roof down.

Farther down the beach, debris that looked like the remains of a ship caught her attention, and she zoomed in to find a barnacle-encrusted hull that could be as old as the *Hive*. Nothing she saw suggested recent human activity.

There were no Cazadores in this area.

She panned the binos over the *Zion*'s deck and spotted Alexander, working on the enclosed turret of the MK-65. Trey, with a rifle, was at the stern.

A voice called up from the ladder below.

"Captain, we're getting a transmission," Eevi said. "You better hear this."

Katrina hurried down to the bridge, where the comm system crackled with static and a voice.

"Does anyone … copy?" said a familiar voice.

She picked up the receiver. "This is Captain DaVita. Who am I speaking to?"

"Timothy Pepper."

Samson must have decided to bring him back on.

"Good to hear from you, Timothy. Where is Lieutenant Mitchells? I need to talk to him."

"I'm not sure where he is, Captain."

"What do you mean?"

"Captain, this is Timothy Pepper of the *Sea Wolf*."

Katrina almost dropped the receiver.

"The *Sea Wolf* has been relocated under the capitol tower of the Metal Islands, where X, Mags, and Miles are being held captive," Timothy said. "This is my fir—"

Static crackled over the system, drowning out his voice.

"Timothy," she said. "Timothy, do you copy?"

"Yes, I'm here, Captain."

"Listen, Timothy, do you know if X and the others are alive?"

"I've translated several conversations from my captors and can tell you that at this moment, X is definitely alive. Apparently, he just achieved a great victory in the Sky Arena."

"*Sky Arena?*" Eevi said with brows arched.

Gunshots snapped her attention away from the station. Everyone on the bridge hurried over for a view out the remaining window, to the MK-65 turret, where Alexander fired his assault rifle. She could see his muzzle flashes and the glow of his battery unit, but not what he was firing at. And she couldn't see Trey.

Eevi let out a scream and pointed at the sky, where a second blue glow seemed to be floating away.

Katrina brought her binoculars up and found the battery unit, attached to Trey, in the talons of a huge bird. A dozen others swooped toward the ship, and into the automatic fire from Alexander as he retreated.

For a second, Katrina stood in the flight-ops

command center, watching in horror as the bird flapped away. She thought of Les, and the pain he would feel if she didn't get his boy back.

Two seconds passed before she snapped to action.

"Grab your weapons!" she ordered. "We're going after him!"

SEVEN

Magnolia had never seen so much food in her life. She followed Imulah into a room of banquet tables decked in white cloths and gold runners, with old-world china dishes and glass goblets at each setting. Four chandeliers illuminated the bountiful feast being brought in by servants in clean white garments.

They carried all sorts of dishes: bowls overflowing with fruit, platters of meat and of fish, some of them with heads and eyeballs and fins.

The only thing from the ocean she had ever eaten was shark, and she wasn't eager to try anything that could look back at her. But her stomach did growl at the sight of plates stacked with strips of crispy bacon and hunks of ham coated in a clear glaze.

She had felt sick after the spectacle at the Sky Arena, where she had been forced to watch a dozen other matches after X and Rodger's bout with the giant.

In one contest, two male warriors were pitted against a woman with dreadlocks down to her lower back. She dispatched the first man quickly with her sword but let the other victim linger. After cutting his Achilles tendon, she straddled him and gouged out his eyeballs with her bare hands. That had the crowd standing, and it almost made Magnolia puke.

But that wasn't even the worst part. Before Magnolia even had time to look away, the female warrior had sliced off his testicles and held them in the air, letting out a howl like a wolf.

In the sky, life was precious. Every single soul was important. But not here, apparently. On the Metal Islands, fighting and killing were part of daily life. They glorified it. And from what she could see, these people didn't fear death.

After what she had just witnessed, Magnolia wasn't so sure she wanted her friends to come rescue her unless they sent a volley of missiles and bombs down first. There was no way the people on the *Hive* could win a fight against this warrior society.

"Tonight, you sit next to el Pulpo," Imulah said, gesturing toward a long banquet table at the head of the room. Dozens of chairs were set up along one side, most of them already occupied by el Pulpo's wives. Two large wingback chairs, both decorated in octopus engravings, remained empty.

"Let me guess: this is my seat," Magnolia said.

Imulah nodded politely. "Go ahead and have something to drink while we wait."

Magnolia pulled the chair back from the table, drawing the attention of the other nine women.

Sofia and Inge sat across from her, watching her every move as if she was a potential enemy, sizing her up with their youthful eyes. But they weren't the only ones.

An older woman with braided dark hair narrowed her gaze and stared at Magnolia. She licked her lips and clacked sharp teeth together as Magnolia sat down.

Why the hell would any of them ever want to sit where she was sitting? There was no way they actually loved el Pulpo, or even liked him.

Right?

Magnolia took a goblet and drank. The fruity liquid was surprisingly good. She set the glass down as helmetless Cazador soldiers in body armor filed into the room.

Next came a group of men wearing immaculate gray or dark-blue suits similar to the old-world suit that Timothy Pepper wore. Two of the men had slicked-back hair and neatly trimmed beards. One wore eyeglasses and carried a clipboard under his arm. It was the same guy she remembered at the dock when she arrived. He had stood there writing with a pencil, glancing up over his spectacles every few strokes as he tallied supplies and boats, or people, or whatever the hell he was doing.

The other men were bald and freshly shaved. She picked up voices in Spanish, English, and a language she didn't recognize. They all took their seats, but no one ate. Apparently, these people did have manners, after all.

Unable to resist, she finally took a piece of bacon and crunched it down, again drawing the attention of the wives. Inge clicked her tongue and looked away in disgust. Sofia cracked an amused half smile.

Magnolia shrugged and kept eating.

Servants continued bringing in more food and filling up glasses with the berry-colored liquid. The chandeliers were dimmed as a man brought in a torch and lit the sconces on the walls. An orange flicker of flames danced across the bulkheads.

Magnolia twisted in her chair to look out the porthole windows behind her. The glass provided a view to a jeweled sky, the most beautiful she had ever seen.

A shooting star ripped through the darkness.

For a moment, she felt a hint of joy. But she suppressed it, not allowing herself feel anything but anger. To buy into the pomp and pageantry was to betray her friends. Also, it was dangerous to let her guard down. She had to stay sharp and ready to seize the moment if the opportunity to escape should appear.

She turned back to the table just as a loud chanting began. The soldiers all stood and beat their chests as el Pulpo ducked through an open doorway and entered the room, with a smug grin on his scarred face. His eye roved from face to face until it locked on her, and his grin widened.

A dark-skinned warrior, one of the most massive men Magnolia had ever seen, followed the king into the room. The soldier held a chain with Miles tethered at the other end.

The dog trotted after his handler, head down, tail between his legs.

Everyone stood to greet King Pulpo, but Magnolia remained in her seat and took another drink. She wiped her mouth with her forearm and set the glass back down.

"Now is when you stand," said Imulah. He walked over and leaned down, whispering in her ear. "You'd better start showing some respect, or you will end up with a back worse than Sofia's."

Recalling the crosshatched scars hidden beneath the young woman's long hair, she finally did as he instructed.

El Pulpo made his way across the room wearing light armor—only plates on his forearms and shins. An open red silk shirt showed off his burly chest and a long seashell necklace. The strip of hair above the octopus tattoo on his forehead was slicked back with some sort of grease.

The warrior accompanying the king yanked Miles toward the table and made him sit beside the chair reserved for el Pulpo. The dog obeyed, going down on his haunches.

"It's okay, boy," Magnolia said.

Miles looked up and let out a soft whine.

I know. I miss X, too.

"Magnolia," el Pulpo said almost politely. Then he gestured toward the massive warrior looming behind him. "Meet Rhino," he said.

The man held out his hand to Magnolia. "Lieutenant Rhino," he said in a gruff voice.

She twisted to give the hulking bodyguard and,

apparently, officer, a once-over. He was by far the most muscular person she had ever seen. He had short-cropped dark hair and wore shiny silver octopus cuffs above his biceps, and hoops hung from his pierced ears and between his nostrils. His long goatee ended in a silver bead.

"Not very polite, are you?" Rhino said.

"Not to cannibals—even the ones that speak English."

He dropped his hand back to the pommel of the sword at his hip, and stiffened as el Pulpo took a seat.

The king held up his hands to silence his subjects. When the side conversations had died down, he raised his goblet. Imulah translated for Magnolia as el Pulpo spoke.

"Tonight, we make a very special offering to the Octopus Lord of the depths. Tonight, we will send the body of one of the fiercest warriors in the history of our people."

At first, Magnolia feared they were talking about dumping X into the ocean, but then she saw two soldiers dragging Hammerhead's corpse into the room.

They hauled the body to an open area left of the tables, right in front of a hatch, which Imulah opened to a balcony overlooking the ocean.

Moonlight streamed into the room, casting a white glow over Hammerhead's pale skin. Strips of flesh had been taken from his thigh and arms, leaving glistening wounds.

Magnolia dropped the piece of bacon in her hand

and gagged. She had seen the hog pens, but was she even eating pork?

Imulah returned to Magnolia's side and translated as el Pulpo spoke.

"Before we feast and prepare our offering, I want you all to meet the man known for killing Hammerhead. His sky people call him 'the Immortal,' and now I understand why."

Two more soldiers walked X into the room, holding swords to his back. His hands were cuffed and his feet shackled. He wore long pants and a ragged shirt that showed off the cuts and bruises from the fight.

X shuffled inside, stopping near the corpse of the gladiator he had killed with Rodger's help. All voices in the room fell silent as all eyes focused on the legendary Hell Diver.

"Fuck y'all lookin' at?" he growled. Seeing Magnolia and Miles, he softened and smiled, revealing the gap from the tooth he lost in the arena. The smile, while warm, was also sad, and Magnolia nearly broke down at the sight of her friend in chains.

El Pulpo turned to Rhino and gave him instructions in Spanish.

"*Sí, su Majestad.*" The lieutenant walked over to the corpse and pulled a long knife from his belt. Bending down, he cut a strip of meat away from the body. Then he stood and faced X.

"El Pulpo said you have once again proved your worth as a Cazador warrior, but the final test before your first mission is to become one of us." He held out the flesh.

X reared back. "Oh, hell no," he said.

"To become one of us, you must eat the flesh of a fallen Cazador." Rhino continued holding the flesh out and looked over to el Pulpo.

The king said something to the two soldiers who had brought X into the room. They grabbed him under the arms, and one of them kicked him in the back of the knee, forcing him down.

"No!" X shouted. "I won't!"

Miles growled, but el Pulpo snapped his fingers, and the dog cowered and looked away.

"Don't you touch him, you sack of shit!" X shouted.

Rhino grabbed his jaw and got a round peg of wood between his teeth. X snorted and fought, but it was just a matter of time before the huge warrior would stuff the meat down his gullet.

"Leave him alone!" Magnolia shouted, jumping up from her chair.

El Pulpo also stood, towering over her.

"Sit," he said.

She watched in horror as Rhino finally forced X's jaw open, but he continued to struggle, squirming and fighting in the grip of the two soldiers. One of them punched him in the kidney. He arched his back and grimaced.

"Stop!" Magnolia shouted.

El Pulpo grabbed her by the wrist, just as she

had grabbed Sofia earlier in the day, only his grip was much stronger. He could break her arm if he wanted.

"*Vas a aprender*," he said. "You … learn."

He shoved her back into the chair and then set off across the room. The men in suits and the women stayed put, but the armored soldiers got up from their seats and followed el Pulpo to the area in front of the open hatch. One by one, they bent down with their knives and each took a piece of flesh.

Imulah whispered to Magnolia, "I told you to do as you're told. Next time, he won't be so forgiving."

She shivered in rage and horror.

"They believe the flesh of a fallen warrior gives them strength," Imulah said, "and that if they eat it, they absorb some of his skills and courage. I need not partake in this tradition, because I'm not a warrior, but if you are asked, I would advise you follow the order. It's a huge sign of disrespect to do what X is doing."

When the men had finished eating the dead hero's flesh, el Pulpo grabbed the cadaver and, with Rhino's help, hoisted it out onto the balcony. Another servant wrapped a long rope around his ankles and tied the other end to the railing. Once it was secure, they heaved the body over the edge, and it splashed into the water below.

When they came back inside, X was still squirming in the grip of the other warriors.

"You will eat eventually, Immortal," Rhino said. "Or perhaps, someday soon we will feast on *your* flesh. First, though, we have a mission for you."

"No," Magnolia cried as he was taken out of the room. Miles got up and barked, and this time a soldier kicked him.

Magnolia bolted from her chair and kicked the soldier, knocking him to the ground. Then she grabbed a knife off the table.

"You touch him again, and I'll cut your tiny nuts off and feed them to your Octopus Lords from the depths," she snapped.

Miles growled as a shadow flickered on the bulkheads. When she turned, she saw el Pulpo looming behind her. He backhanded her in the face, knocking her onto the table.

"Don't touch them!" X yelled from the open doorway. "I'll fucking kill you! I'll kill you all!"

The soldiers punched and kicked him into submission, but he continued to yell as they dragged him away.

"I'm going to kill you, el Pulpo! Bet on it!"

* * * * *

X expected to be led back to his quarters and given another beating, but instead, Rhino and the other two Cazador soldiers took him down an outer stairway toward the docks.

"You aren't very smart, are you?" Rhino asked.

X used his shoulder to wipe the blood from his cracked lip. His entire body hurt from the kicks and punches. Several of the soldiers had gotten in some licks back in the banquet hall, but he would return them in kind soon.

The bastards were all going to die.

He just had to hope his friends would survive long enough to give him a chance to free them. Knowing Magnolia and her attitude, it was only a matter of time before el Pulpo lost his temper with her again, and next time, he might do more than smack her.

Halfway down the forty-floor tower, they stopped, and Rhino went inside an exterior hatch, leaving X with the guards.

If his wrists and ankles weren't shackled, he would have killed them both and jumped into the water below. But this wasn't his chance, and Rhino returned a moment later with another man.

Rodger stepped into the moonlight and staggered over, shirtless and shoeless. "Damn, X, your lip is all—"

"Get going," Rhino said, shoving Rodger.

"Hey, easy!" Rodger protested.

"Where are you taking us?" X asked.

"You'll find out soon enough," replied Rhino.

As they descended the stairs, X scanned the skyline. Where the hell was Katrina? Surely, they would be on their way now, so what were they waiting for? He was starting to wonder whether they were even going to come.

Of course they'll come. As far as we know, this is the only habitable place in the world.

Michael and the others would be here. The question was not *whether* but *when*. Until then, he would just keep trying to survive. But he wasn't sure how many more Hammerheads he could take on.

One thing was for certain: he wasn't immortal, just very lucky. Having a high pain tolerance also helped.

Rodger, on the other hand, could hardly handle a slap on the back. He bitched and moaned behind X, grumbling about this and that.

"I told you to do as they say, X," he said. "It's easier on all of us if you do."

A whistling came from the banquet room, where el Pulpo stood at one of the windows. He blew into the white shell necklace.

The two guards ahead suddenly moved to the outer rail of the staircase to look over at the water.

Rhino remained behind X and Rodger, watching both Hell Divers closely.

"What's going on?" Rodger asked.

"The Octopus Lords have come for their offering," Rhino said.

"Holy shit!" Rodger gasped. "Those things are *real?*"

Spotlights from different platforms on the tower were pointed down to where Hammerhead's corpse hung by the rope, half in and half out of the water.

The whistling continued as el Pulpo blew into his necklace. He lowered it a moment later as the beams picked up motion beneath the calm ocean.

All at once, several arms lined with suction cups broke through the water, wrapping around Hammerhead's mutilated corpse. A soldier cut the rope and dropped it to the water as the beast pulled its meal into the depths. Bubbles floated to the surface and then calmed.

"Holy shit," X murmured.

"The whistle from hell," Rodger said. "They worship the octopuses like they're gods."

X laughed at the notion. "Pretty half-assed gods. I killed one on the way here."

Rhino narrowed his eyes and reached for the hilt of his sword. "Blasphemy!"

X heard anger in the man's words and backed up a step. "Just kidding. But I did kill a shark. You guys don't worship those ..." He cringed, remembering the tattoo on the dead gladiator's chest.

These guys worshipped all sorts of monsters, it seemed.

Rhino kept his hand on the sword hilt. "Move."

"Okay, okay," Rodger said.

He walked in front of X, taking the lead down the winding stairway, and X got his first glance at the docks below—the same ones he had passed when he docked the WaveRunner and sneaked into the tower.

This time, dozens of boats were moored there. Dockhands in shorts and sandals loaded boxes and crates into the vessels. They were going somewhere.

He wanted to scream. Without that hoard of ITC-preserved gasoline, el Pulpo would be running a ragtag little band of foragers, doing whatever they could to scrape by. He never would have enslaved X, Rodger, and Magnolia.

But then, X never would have found his way to the Metal Isles and, just maybe, a home for his people.

Not that such a gift would stop him from killing the bastard.

When they reached the bottom of the stairs, X stopped and turned to Rhino.

"I'm not leaving without my dog and Magnolia."

The warrior pulled the long, curved sword from its sheath and raised it above his head. "You will go where you're told, or I'll prove to all these sheep that you aren't immortal … by slicing you in two."

The blade glistened in the moonlight. Despite the threat, X took a step closer. He came up only to Rhino's jawline, and he had to look up to meet the warrior's gaze. The hoop between Rhino's nostrils quivered with a loud snort.

"Don't fucking try me," Rhino said. "I could have ripped Hammerhead's heart out in half the time it took you two idiots to kill him."

"I want to see my dog and Magnolia," X said. "If we're going somewhere else, I want to say goodbye."

"You just saw them when you failed—again—to follow el Pulpo's orders."

X grunted. "You don't get it. I'm not a Cazador and never will be."

"I said the same thing once. Look at me now. You can have a good life here if you obey."

X noted a certain hesitation in his voice—just the slightest pause, but there it was.

X said, "You're not like the others, I can see that. So why do you serve them?"

"Because, like you, I have no choice. And, unlike you, I have come to grips with that fact."

X took a step backward. He couldn't get a read on this guy. Was he a servant? A loyal soldier? Or maybe something else?

"Your dog and Magnolia will be fine as long as *you* do as you're told," Rhino said. "Now, keep moving and follow me. The ship sails soon."

He waited for X to back away before resheathing his sword. Some of the dockhands looked up from their work as X and Rodger continued across the piers. Soldiers patrolled the area, holding spears and rifles along the water's edge.

Hearing a cranking noise behind them, X looked over his shoulder and up the side of the tower, to where the elevator descended from the upper decks. The glow from a torch illuminated a man wearing a brown robe.

As soon as the gate opened, Imulah hurried toward X and Rodger, but Rhino kept walking. He didn't stop until they got to the boats.

Two Cazador soldiers holding submachine guns stood by the stern. Another three worked on a large engine. Rhino spoke to them all and then motioned for X and Rodger.

"Get in," he said.

Rodger balked. "Where are we going?"

"Wait!" Imulah called out.

"What now, old man?" Rhino said.

Imulah stopped, panting. He held up the torch and looked from X to Rodger.

"El Pulpo wants this one to stay. He said he can't fight and is a liability to the mission."

"I can, too, fight," Rodger said.

"Good, keep him," X said. Wherever this boat was going, it was better that he travel alone. El Pulpo was actually right about Rodger being a liability.

"It's okay, Rodge," X said. "Go with Imulah. Look after Magnolia and Miles. Okay?"

Rodger thought on it a moment and then nodded.

X reached out his hand. "I'm sorry I left you on that ship in Florida. I swear on Miles I thought you were dead."

"It's okay." Rodger shook his hand. "I know you tried to save me, but this time you need to worry about saving yourself, Xavier. Do what they tell you. Survive. Rhino is right about obeying."

X narrowed his eyes at a man who had accepted his fate as a slave. He didn't exactly blame Rodger or like him any less, but slavery wasn't for X. After all he had been through, he couldn't bring himself to follow another's orders.

Rhino climbed into the boat, and X got in after him. The mechanics finished working on the engines. One of them gave a nod to Rhino, who gave orders to the Cazador soldier standing at the helm.

The engine grumbled to life, and as soon as the mooring lines were free, the pilot peeled away from the dock, kicking up a wake. Several other boats followed, laden with supplies.

X sat on a crate and watched the wake snaking back to the piers and the tower. The elevator was already rising back up the tower, the glow of the torch illuminating the faces of Rodger and Imulah inside.

Watch after them, X whispered to himself.

He forced his gaze away from the structure and back to the water. The light from oil rigs dazzled. The solar panels and gas-powered generators created a nearly endless supply of energy here. X found himself wondering what Samson would think of this place.

The old bastard will love it.

X ran his tongue over the gap where his tooth had been. Between his new injuries and the old ones, he felt exhausted, old, and beat-up.

But he still had fight left in him, and he still held on to hope that the airships would show up. In the meantime, he would complete this mission, whatever it was.

Maybe el Pulpo needed someone killed on one of the other oil rigs, or maybe X was being sent to another arena, to battle another gladiator. Whatever the task, he would do what he needed to do in order to survive.

The boat picked up speed as they sailed farther away from the capitol tower. A half hour into the ride, they had curved away from all the eastern oil rigs.

On the dark horizon, something else glowed. Long and low. This wasn't a rig. It was a ship.

As they drew closer, he could see that it was a warship like the one he had discovered in Florida. Harpoon guns were mounted in the bow and stern. Flamethrowers and machine guns pointed skyward from armored turrets manned by Cazador soldiers.

This ship was equipped to fight a war. They had even added barbed wire to the deck rails, as X had done on the *Sea Wolf*.

But these warriors had taken their planning a step further. They had added turrets with flamethrowers and harpoon guns, and, hanging over the side of the ship, a spear the length of a rowboat. X had never seen the like.

The memory of the ship in Florida sent a tingle through his old bones. Then he saw the empty cages stacked in the bow, and another memory surfaced in his mind.

No … Oh, no, God damn it.

The boat wasn't sailing for one of the other rigs. He wasn't going to duel another gladiator or assassinate someone who had disobeyed el Pulpo.

Xavier Rodriguez was being sent back to the wastes to fight the demons.

EIGHT

Katrina couldn't will her heart to slow down. It thumped like the small inflatable boat now banging over the wave tops, speeding away from the USS *Zion*. She kept her rifle pointed up at the sky, where the monster birds circled.

At first, she had thought they were Sirens, but they seemed to be the vultures that X, Magnolia, and Miles had encountered back at the Turks and Caicos Islands.

In the green field of her night-vision goggles, she counted only six of them now. The others had returned to the island, one of them with Trey in its talons.

Over an hour had passed since the beast snatched him off the deck, and it took that long to get this boat in the water.

A glance at her HUD confirmed he was still alive. Thank all the gods he had been wearing his armor on deck. Finding him without it would have been like looking for a specific apple in a grove of apple trees—to say nothing of what the bird's talons would have done to him without the armor. Even with it, he could be mortally wounded.

She had to find him fast, without losing anyone else. Despite the warnings from most of her crew, this was exactly what she planned to do.

There was no way in hell she would leave him out here. Captain Jordan had done that to X—left him out there all those years. Never again would a Hell Diver be left to die alone in the wastes.

The beacon on her HUD blinked. He was still breathing, and his heart was still beating.

I'm coming, Trey. Just hold tight …

She looked around at her small team. Behind her at the steering console sat Alexander, and Vish and Jed were in the stern, their blue battery units illuminating their armor and weapons.

They all were packing heavy—each carrying an assault rifle, blaster, and pistol. Extra magazines protruded from vests on the outside of their armor, and bandoliers around their arms and thighs held extra shells. She had the same setup but had decided to clip on the captain's sword, which was supposed to be just ceremonial.

They needed the weapons and ammunition against the Cazadores. That was why she hadn't brought the laser gun. She could afford to expend some lead, but not the precious battery of laser bolts.

The Zodiac's battery-powered motor was surprisingly quiet. Otherwise, she might not have heard the loud caw from above as one of the more intrepid birds decided to take a dive at the boat. She brought up the rifle scope and waited until the creature folded its wings to swoop down. Getting her target in the crosshairs, she fired a three-round burst into its breast.

An otherworldly screech followed as the thing cartwheeled down and down, splashing into the ocean left of the boat.

"Faster!" she yelled back at Alexander.

He gave it more throttle, and the boat thumped over another wave. The batteries showed 70 percent— already nearly a third down from the charge they received overnight. She prayed they would hold out long enough to get through the mission.

The silhouette of the USS *Zion* faded in the darkness behind them. Eevi, Sandy, Jaideep, and Edgar were on their own for now.

"Eevi, do you copy? Over," Katrina said into the comm.

The response came a few seconds later. "Copy, Captain."

"Make sure you keep those things off the ship," Katrina said.

"Roger that, Captain. We've already got the fifty-cals tracking any hostiles in the area. Good news, too. The storm appears to be weakening. We should be able to send long-range transmissions and use the GPS shortly."

Katrina sighed with relief at this small bit of good tidings. But there was no time to celebrate.

"Reef ahead!" Jed shouted.

Alexander curved around a cluster of sharp rocks jutting out of the water ahead and brought the boat toward the beach. The remains of the building she had spotted from the command center wasn't far, and she could also make out the hull of the wrecked ship.

A burst of machine-gun fire came from the USS *Zion* as the .50-cals poured tracer rounds into the sky, taking out a vulture that had ventured too close. Having the weapons system back online was another bit of luck that Katrina welcomed.

She turned back to the stern of the Zodiac, energized and ready for the mission. They jolted over the last of the waves and rode the surf in to the beach, where they hit with a grinding slide.

Katrina hopped over the side and grabbed a handle, and the other three divers helped her pull the boat up above the high-tide mark. They dropped it near the edge of the jungle, and Katrina took a moment to get her bearings. Trey was somewhere to the north—not far, judging from the beacon on her map. Maybe not even a mile. Another stroke of luck.

"On me, and watch your step," Katrina said.

Alexander marched right up, but Vish and Jed both hesitated.

"We're really going in there?" Vish asked. He tilted his helmet at the fortress of treetops reaching toward the storm clouds. Thunder boomed in the distance as if warning them away.

"You're welcome to stay and guard our ride out of here," Alexander said.

Jed cradled his rifle and walked over to Katrina and Alexander. Vish looked over his shoulder at the water, cursed under his breath, and joined them.

Katrina wasted no time setting off into the jungle, stepping over vines that snaked across the dirt. A beetle the size of a rabbit perched on a rock ahead, its chitinous shell reminiscent of the *Hive*.

The raucous calls of the birds rang out in the distance, but she didn't spot any in the canopy ahead or perched on the branches around them—perhaps due to the spikes covering the branches. The unwelcoming limbs swayed in the hot breeze.

Her HUD gave a reading of eighty-four degrees. If not for the radiation warnings, she would have taken off her helmet by now.

A bush glowed ahead, and she bumped off her NVGs for a moment to see the diamond-white sparkle with her own eyes.

"Stay away from that one," she said. "The crystal petals contain a poison that's lethal from a single scratch."

"Lovely," Vish said. "Just lovely."

Katrina bumped the goggles back on, slung her rifle, and pulled out her sword as they approached an area blocked off by a curtain of vines. This was flora unlike any she had come across on the surface, and there seemed to be no way around it. She tried to slice through the middle, but the edge caught in the sticky material. Several more chops finally hewed a doorway through the red and purple mat.

Trees loomed in the path, their leafless branches reaching out like skeletal fingers. Another bug skittered across the dirt and vanished into the spiky underbrush. The foliage to the right glowed as she approached, and the purple flower petals began to open.

"Keep away from those, too," Katrina said. "In fact, don't touch anything."

"Wasn't planning on it," Vish said.

Bearing left, she continued along the narrow trail. The chirr of insects and the croaking of some other unknown creature ceased as they pushed into another open glade. She stepped carefully between the red vines sprawling across the jungle floor.

After a half hour of hiking, the path ended at the base of a rock-studded hill. To the north, dark trees crested the top of the mountain she had seen from the command center.

Sheathing the sword, she unslung her rifle and checked the beacon on her HUD again. It didn't appear to be coming from the other side of the hill or from the jungle surrounding the hill, but from *inside* the hill.

Was there a nest at the top?

"Stay here," she told the others.

After making a quick scan of the sky, Katrina started up the hill, rifle up and ready. Her heart pounded at the thought of what she might find at the crest.

But when she got there, she saw nothing but more rocks, a pile of dung, and scattered bones. Beetle shells and fish heads were strewn on the ground. The wind whistled over her armor, and the cries of the birds on the hunt rang out in the distance.

"Trey, do you copy?" Katrina whispered. She had tried several times to raise him, but there was no response, which told her he was either unconscious or …

She turned, taking in the view. To the north, the jungle continued, and to the south, the ocean slapped against rocky coastline. The USS *Zion* was still out there waiting, guns silent.

Perplexed, she checked the beacon. It told her Trey was right beneath her boots.

Cradling her rifle, she went back down the hill. Loose rocks moved underfoot, and Vish moved out of the way as a fist-size cobble hit the dirt beside him.

"Find anything, Cap?" Alexander asked.

"No, but I think I have an idea." Flashing a hand signal, she directed the team to the right. They followed the tree line around the base of the hill until they came to a small ravine on the north side.

Flicking on the tactical light of her rifle, she raked the beam over the rocks below, where she found just what she had expected. The cave entrance was recessed, and she had to bend down to get a look.

"Trey, do you copy?" Katrina asked.

She waited several seconds, listening to the static, making sure she wasn't mistaking his raspy breathing for the crackle.

No ... not him.

"Vish, Jed, stand watch. I want to check this out." She motioned for Alexander to follow her into the cave.

After bumping off her NVGs and switching to her tactical light, Katrina ducked under a slanting rock overhang into a damp chamber, where she stopped to scan for threats.

With her finger on the trigger guard, she played the light over the surrounding rock and found nothing but a spongy red moss covering the jagged walls and underfoot. Alexander moved in behind her, and they started across a squishy floor.

The chamber narrowed to a passageway that snaked downward, opening into another chamber. Her boot crunched over something beneath the carpet of moss. Bending down, she found the shapes of bones covered by the soft growth. She swept the light again and gulped at the realization: they were standing in a boneyard.

Rising to her feet, she shined her beam down the passage, which appeared to end at a wall of whitish vines like those she had cut through in the jungle.

"You think that thing took him down *here*?" Alexander whispered.

It did sound crazy for a bird to live in a cave, but this was where the beacon was transmitting from.

Alexander pointed to another passage, which forked off about twenty feet ahead. Katrina motioned him to follow. Ducking under jagged limestone ceilings, they moved into another tunnel. The passage narrowed even more as they went deeper.

Her eyes flitted between the passage and her HUD.

A few minutes later, they entered another chamber, where she stopped to listen to a dripping sound. Then she continued into a tunnel.

Alexander stopped and held up a fist. "What the hell ..."

Katrina almost fired a burst into the huge bird splayed out across the white wall at the end of the passage. Its wings were spread, head to one side. The torso and legs were gone—nothing but strings of meat and sinew leaking blood onto the mossy floor.

The source of the dripping sound ...

She slowly moved the light to her left—and gasped. Bound to the same wall was a human figure.

"Trey," Katrina whispered.

When she started forward, Alexander held her back.

"Something's not right," he said. "If that bird is what captured him, then what captured *it*?"

Katrina paused to study the carcass. Something had torn the creature in half. Something big.

As if in answer, the crack of gunfire broke the silence.

Alexander looked back the way they had come.

"I think we're about to find out what did this," he whispered.

"Vish, Jed, do you copy?" Katrina said over the comms.

Static.

More faint gunfire.

And then a screech unlike any Katrina had heard in her days as a Hell Diver—a cross between the squealing of an injured pig, and the cries of a human baby.

"Hurry, let's get him down," she said.

Alexander shouldered his rifle and backed across the room, covering Katrina as she approached the wall. She swung her sword, hacking at the white strands that held Trey in place. On the third swing, the blade stuck, and she had to yank it free.

"Trey," she said. "It's me, Katrina."

His eyelids fluttered, and he tried to turn his head, but his helmet was stuck fast. And then it hit her: the wall wasn't a wall, but a spider's web.

The gunshots continued outside the cave, but she and Alexander were too deep to send or receive intelligible transmissions, which was probably why Trey hadn't answered earlier.

Another rage-filled shriek echoed through the tunnel as she worked to free Trey. Alexander had joined Katrina, hacking with his knife at the tough fibers, when the rocky floor trembled. A crunching noise echoed, and she felt more vibrations under her boots. The mountain above them seemed to be shaking.

They pulled Trey away just as one of the other divers emerged. He jumped through the entrance of the narrow passage and seemed to hover midair. Blue light pulsated as he floated toward them.

Alexander shouldered his rifle and pulled the trigger before Katrina could stop him. Then she saw the curved black thorn protruding from Jed's battery unit. The disruption of the circuitry created a strobe-like effect that made it difficult to see what had impaled him, but she could see enough to know it was some sort of spider.

The beast had to be three times a man's girth and just as tall. Bulky enough that it was struggling to get into the chamber.

She unslung her rifle and aimed its light at the creature as hairy legs swiped the air.

"Kill it!" Alexander shouted. He shouldered his rifle and fired at the misshapen eyes, spattering the ceiling with green goo. The beast roared and tried to advance into the chamber, its clawed appendages scraping the rocky floor and throwing up divots of moss.

When her rifle clicked dry, Katrina drew her sword. She waited a second for Alexander to change his magazine, then set off across the tunnel.

Jed's body slumped off, and the creature finally managed to get through the entrance, scuttling toward her. She raised the sword, flicking off the headlamp and bumping on her NVGs for a more complete view of the monster.

Two arms with pincer claws swiped at the air as it set off to meet her in combat. This nightmare arachnid was also part scorpion, with only four legs, the two clawed arms, and a spiked tail ending in the curved spike that had skewered Jed.

"Watch out!" Alexander yelled.

She brought her sword up and parried one of the clacking pincer arms. Then she ducked as Alexander unloaded another magazine, exploding several of the eyeballs on the front and near side of the creature's head.

The beast now had a blind spot, and she used the opportunity to hack at a leg, severing the horny exoskeleton and the fragile flesh beneath with a single swing.

It fell to the ground, pushed itself back up, and darted its spiked tail at her. She moved to the left, and the pointed tip hit the floor, catching in the springy moss. Then she swung the sword in an uppercut, taking the last foot of tail off before the beast could retract it.

A spray of green blood showered Katrina. She rolled away from the thrashing tail, got back up, and sliced off another leg, bringing the beast down onto its belly. Down to the two legs and the arms, the creature tried to snag her with the scissor claws. A single wrong move, and it would snap her in half as it had done to the bird.

The next swipe came close, but Katrina ducked, swinging overhead. The blade chipped the armored appendage, but before she could react, the other claw snatched her sword and sent it skidding across the cave floor.

The abomination pushed itself forward on the two remaining hind legs and brought both arms up, claws open. She staggered backward and fell, holding up an arm to shield herself as the creature moved in to finish her off.

"Captain!" Alexander yelled. He fired from the side into the clawed arms and the head.

More gunshots sounded from the entrance of the passage, and the creature reared and twisted toward the gunfire. Katrina didn't waste the opportunity to scramble upright and run for the sword.

By the time she grabbed it and turned, the monster had collapsed to the ground, its remaining eyeballs staring at the Hell Divers who had brought it down.

"Guys!" shouted a voice. "Guys, I think I killed it!"

Panting, Katrina staggered over to the fallen beast. She jabbed the sword into the last forward eyeball and leaned into it, pushing the blade so deep that she had to put her boot against the carapace to pull it out.

The pincers clacked together once and fell open as the monster finally went limp.

Katrina wiped her visor clear of goo and staggered away, trying to compose herself and catch her breath. She hurried over to Alexander, who was kneeling beside Jed. The reading on her HUD told her he was already dead, but to be sure, she pulled off a glove and felt for a pulse.

She bowed her head at what she already knew. He was gone, and there was nothing they could do to help him.

"Captain," Alexander said. He put a hand on her shoulder, and she stood to go check on Trey.

"My God, it just came out of nowhere!" Vish said. His rifle shook in his hands. He hugged the wall, inching his way around the dead horror. "Ew-w-w, that thing is really gross …"

Vish stopped, his words trailing off at the sight of Jed on the ground.

Trey stirred and put a hand on his helmet.

"You okay?" Katrina asked.

"I … I think so."

Katrina gave him a minute to get his bearings and gestured toward Jed. "Vish, Alexander, help me pick him up."

"You want to take him with us?" Alexander asked.

Katrina hadn't realized it needed to be said. "We never leave a diver behind."

* * * * *

"X is still alive," Katrina said over the comms.

Michael would have pumped his right fist if he still had it—and if bad news hadn't followed so quickly. But that was how things seemed to go these days, and he had a feeling the news was going to keep getting worse.

"Jed?" Michael asked.

"Yes. I'm sorry, Michael," Katrina said. "I know he was your friend. He really respected you."

Michael clenched his jaw at a fresh wave of phantom pain. "He was a good kid," he said. "Always looked after his mom."

The crew of *Deliverance* huddled around the comms station, holding a moment of silence for the lost diver. Every officer was present: Les, Layla, Michael, Dave, Bronson, and Ada. Despite the bad news, they all were eager to hear what Katrina had planned and what Timothy Pepper had transmitted from the *Sea Wolf*.

"I'm going to play the last transmission for you all to hear," Katrina said.

The voice of Timothy Pepper on the *Sea Wolf* crackled over the channel. Michael leaned closer to listen to the replay.

"I've translated several conversations from my captors and can tell you that at this moment, X is definitely alive. Apparently, he just achieved a great victory in a place known as the Sky Arena."

"The transmission was interrupted when the vulture snatched Trey off the *Zion*'s deck," Katrina said. "But there's more …"

She played the next message from Timothy Pepper of the *Sea Wolf*.

"If my translation is correct, the sky princess is slated to marry el Pulpo, and the sky beast has become his personal pet."

"Sky princess?" Layla said.

"Sky beast?" Les added.

"Has to be Magnolia and Miles," Michael said. "They *are* still alive."

"Yes," said Katrina, "and it also means we have time to keep planning, which is a good thing. Listen to this."

Another old transmission came over the speakers.

"From my calculation, there are hundreds of Cazador soldiers, and probably closer to a thousand. They have dozens of oil rigs and hundreds of boats, and that's just at this location. There could be more I am not aware of . . ."

"Let me talk to her," Les said. He moved in front of Michael, who backed up to let him through to the comms.

"Captain, I've been able to recruit only thirty militia soldiers, and fifty civilians ranging from farmers to shopkeepers. How the hell are we supposed to win against those kinds of numbers?"

A pause came on the other end.

"We can't," Katrina finally said. "We will have to use our weapons and hope el Pulpo surrenders."

"And if he doesn't?" Les asked.

"Then we start destroying his home until he does."

Her words sounded sharper than normal, and Michael exchanged a glance with her XO. Les had been in a somber mood since learning that his son had been carried off by a vulture. Although Trey was safe now, the close call had brought home just how dangerous this mission was.

"I'm going to share my idea with her, okay?" Michael said to Les.

He scratched the tuft of red hair at his temple, frowned, and then nodded.

Michael closed his eyes to fight off another jolt of phantom pain. It felt real, as if his arm were still there and burning—not just the flesh, but the bones, too, even the marrow.

"Commander," Ada said.

"Sorry," Michael said. He moved back to the comms. "Captain, I have an idea that might help us avoid using our own people in this fight, or any bombs or missiles."

"I'm all ears," Katrina replied.

"I've had nothing to do over the past few days but sit around and heal, so I spent some time researching Red Sphere and the AI defectors. After a detailed conversation with Timothy Pepper, I discovered they have a weakness."

"I'm not sure I understand what that has to do with anything," Katrina replied. "Why do I care about the defectors?"

"I'll let Timothy explain," Michael said.

The holographic form of the AI flickered to life in front of the communications equipment. Timothy folded his hands together in a triangle in front of his lips, almost as if praying.

"Captain, this is Timothy Pepper," he said. "The defectors are some of the most advanced AI ever built by Industrial Tech Corporation. They were designed to be dropped into a hot zone, dispatch an enemy, and leave after inflicting mass casualties. This typically meant that civilians were destroyed in the process."

"So I've heard," Katrina said.

"During the war, the defectors hunted down human survivors at places like Red Sphere."

"So why didn't they leave?" Katrina said.

"Because they completed their final mission," Michael said. "Until we showed up."

"Go on."

"Captain, Timothy believes we can drop an EMP bomb from *Deliverance* at Red Sphere to shut down the defectors. After we disable them, we'll reprogram them to use at the Metal Islands, as part of our army."

Layla gave Michael another incredulous side glance. She had already given her opinion: she hated the idea.

"Return to the place you almost died?" she had said. "Your quest to save X is going to get you killed. Maybe get us *all* killed."

Michael cleared his throat. "Captain, I'm requesting permission to take *Deliverance* back to Red Sphere, deploy the EMP bomb, and bring Timothy Pepper to the surface with us to reprogram the defectors and to collect all the laser rifles we can find."

"You're injured, Commander," said Katrina. "How can you expect to fight if you can't aim a rifle?"

"X fought in far worse shape than I'm in, Captain."

"Indeed, he did. I'll give you that."

There was a long pause while Katrina discussed the idea with her crew aboard the USS *Zion*.

"You need to rest, not fight," Layla said. She laid a hand gently on his back and whispered, "Tin, I'm really worried about you."

The comms crackled again.

"All right," Katrina said. "Bring only a skeleton

crew with you to Red Sphere, but be careful with that ship. I need it fully functional."

"Understood, ma'am," Les said.

"You have four days, Lieutenant. On the night of the fifth, we're meeting at the Metal Islands at dark. We will offer el Pulpo the terms of surrender then. If he doesn't accept, then God have mercy on our souls."

NINE

Two days had passed since X boarded the freighter with the Cazador crew. At least, that was how much time he thought had slipped by. But on the surface, time had a way of vanishing without so much as a memory, leaving him wondering.

He had never thought he would feel that way again.

Clenching his fist, he wanted to pound the metal wall of his closet-size cell, but he didn't need another injury now that everything was healing.

Lifting his leg, he checked the bullet wound on his foot. The gel had worked wonders, and the scab was the only one left on his body. He put a tattered sock back on and brought his knees up to his chest, trying to get comfortable in a room so small he couldn't even lie down.

The hull groaned as the ship cut through the water. They had hit a patch of rough seas earlier that had him worried they might capsize. X hugged his body for warmth and closed his eyes.

He awoke to footsteps in the passage outside his cell. He put his feet back on the deck and stood, expecting to see the same three-toothed Cazador man who brought him his meals.

Instead, Rhino opened the hatch and ducked down to look at him. Form-fitting armor accentuating his muscular body covered him from boots to neck. He carried a helmet under his arm.

"Get ready," Rhino said. "We're almost there."

X didn't bother asking where they were. "I'm ready now."

"Then follow me." X stepped out into the narrow passage between rusted bulkheads. Several dangling lights flickered, casting shadows and revealing another Cazador soldier in front of an open hatch. He looked at X through a helmet with almond-shaped mirrored lenses.

"In there," Rhino said.

A breathing apparatus built into the guard's helmet crackled as the man threw up a hand salute. Rhino gave a nod, then jabbed X in the back, pushing him into an armory.

Racks of weapons secured by ropes covered the right wall. Over a row of lockers hung banners and flags representing different types of fish and, of course, a giant octopus.

On a bench sat two muscular men, putting on armor over tight-fitting black radiation suits. Another guy, already suited up, watched X as he stepped into the room.

"Immortal," said one of the men sitting on the bench. He finished putting on his armor, stood, and beat a fist against his chest. The other guy followed suit, but the man across the way just stood there like a statue.

"Don't confuse that with liking you," Rhino said.

"Got it," X replied.

Rhino pointed to the two men by the benches. "This is Luke, and Ricardo." He gestured toward the guy across the way. "That's Wendig. Cousin of Hammerhead."

X scratched at the thick stubble on his jaw and resisted the urge to say something snide. There were too many guns in this place to start mouthing off.

"*Lo siento,*" X said instead, remembering the words for "I'm sorry."

Wendig strode over, armored chest puffed out like a rooster's. X could hear the huffing of his breath inside his helmet.

Rhino stepped between them.

"Take it easy," X said.

Wendig's helmet turned from Rhino to X, then back to Rhino. He backed away and punched a metal locker, denting it.

"These are three of the soldiers you will be fighting with," Rhino said. "I will be leading this expedition. You listen to my orders and do what I say, or I promise you, things will not be good when we get back to the Metal Islands."

X went back to scratching his salt-and-pepper beard.

"Your armor is in the locker over there," Rhino said, pointing.

X walked over and opened it to find his Hell Diver armor. They must have found it on the WaveRunner.

Rhino gave a proud nod. "Every man should go into battle with the armor he feels comfortable in."

"So why did you guys make me wear that leather jock strap back at the Sky Arena?" X said, unable to resist.

Rhino cracked a wide grin and then let out a bellowing laugh—the first time X had seen the man show any sort of emotion.

"That was just a test."

"And this isn't?" X asked.

"This is a mission. And a test. Now, get dressed."

X quickly got into the clothing laid out for him and then put on his armor. When he had finished, he laced up his boots, keeping the left one loose over his injured foot.

"You got my weapons, too?" X asked.

Rhino laughed again, more lightly this time. "You think we're giving you guns so you can shoot us in the back?"

He moved over to a bulkhead with a rack of spears, swords, knives, and the electrical prods that X had seen back in Florida.

Rhino lifted a spear shaft off the rack and broke it in half as if it were an herb stick. He tossed the short shaft to X.

"Just in case you feel like stabbing any of us in

the back," Rhino said. "This way you will have to get very close."

"If I stab you, it'll be through the eye, like I did el Pulpo," X said.

Rhino's pierced nose flared. He lifted a sword off the rack, but instead of splitting X's skull with it, he twirled the blade and looked down it to check the edge.

"This should do," he said. "It's a solid blade and will split flesh and bone if wielded properly."

X reached out with his other hand and took the weapon. Rhino tossed him a leather sheath with a strap that he slung over his shoulder.

The other three soldiers, all fully dressed now, turned their helmets toward him, hands on the grips of their carbines. Wendig angled the barrel of a rifle at the deck, not far from X.

"Watch it there, fella," X said.

Rhino put his helmet on and grabbed his small round shield. An engraving of a long ray-finned fish with gaping jaws and fang-like teeth was engraved in the center.

The other men had the same fish etched into their armor. It had to be some sort of team symbol, like Raptor.

Rhino threw the shield over his shoulder, grabbed a double-bladed spear, and ducked out of the room. The other three soldiers fell in line behind X.

They walked up a ladder to another level, then took a second ladder to an open hatch. Black skies had replaced the bright sun, and X looked out at a sight he had known his entire life.

Lightning pierced the darkness as he climbed out onto the weather deck. Part of him felt that he deserved this, that the sunshine wasn't supposed to last. He had broken too many promises over the years and failed to save too many people he loved.

He let out a sigh and prepared to do what he did best: fight.

Lieutenant Rhino walked toward a maze of large rectangular crates that blocked the view over the starboard and port sides. A command center rose above the boxes in the center of the ship. Through its filthy windows, X saw the pilot and several other men. Above the bow rose enclosed turrets, manned by Cazador soldiers with flamethrowers and harpoon guns, scanning for hostiles.

In the respite between thunderclaps, X heard the clank of armor, the thud of boots on the deck, and the crash of waves against the bow. He checked his wrist computer and thumbed the monitor. It showed a 51 percent battery level.

Next, he checked his HUD. The temperature was a balmy eighty-five degrees, and radiation levels were in the yellow zone. Luckily, his suit was sealed and all systems appeared to be working.

Raised voices sounded as they entered an open space on deck.

Around the next crate, X saw the source. Standing on the bow between rows of empty cages were a hundred Cazador soldiers, all of them armored and heavily armed. One man held a Minigun with an ammunition belt feeding from a backpack that also had an axe hanging from the side. His armored gloves were fitted with brass knuckles. Another man carried a flamethrower with a tank of fuel on his back.

Behind them, X saw the battlefield: an old-world city, tucked against a sheltered bay. Buildings, including some just shy of what his people would call a scraper, rose toward the storm clouds. Lightning illuminated the ruined structures and the shapes cutting through the sky overhead.

Were these vultures, like those he had seen in the Turks and Caicos Islands? Or something more familiar?

Rhino gestured for X to join him at the helm in front of the small army of soldiers. X did as ordered and stood by the lieutenant's side. The man carrying a flamethrower and the one with the Minigun stepped up to flank Rhino and X.

Every helmet seemed to focus on the blue glow of his battery unit.

Rhino held up both hands and yelled in Spanish.

He repeated the message in English and then another language that X didn't recognize, and the Cazador warriors beat their fists against their chest armor.

"Today we embark on a great hunt of the deformed ones, the first in many months. We will bring our trophies back to the Metal Islands, where their flesh will continue to bring our people great strength."

What a great fucking honor.

Over the mechanical din came the unmistakable electronic wail of a beast that had hunted X all his years on the surface. The male Sirens screeched as they took to the sky, their leathery wings beating the air.

"Those who take the most trophies will bring home the bounty when we return to the Metal Islands," Rhino continued. "This time, el Pulpo is offering his oldest wife to the winner, to make way for his new bride."

The soldiers went wild at the offer, and Rhino looked over at X. "The king has only so much room, and he's got to clear some for his new bride, the sky queen."

X glared through his visor at Rhino but didn't take the bait. When he didn't reply, Rhino added, "Maybe you will win his old wife, Immortal."

"Or maybe you will die and be eaten and shat out by the deformed ones," said the man with the flamethrower.

The soldier with the Minigun heaved a laugh that crackled from his breathing apparatus.

X couldn't see their faces behind the almond-shaped mirror lenses, but he had a feeling they both looked a good deal uglier underneath the helmets. One thing was certain, they didn't lack for protein in their diets. Both men were giants, almost the size of Rhino.

Maybe that was what you got when you ate humans.

The laughter died down, and Rhino turned to his small army. He raised his hands in the air and, in his booming voice, yelled, "Go! Take your trophies!"

The roar that followed seemed to shake the deck of the ship. Several sailors, dressed in military green, tossed ropes down to the water, where rowboats had already been lowered.

X remained standing beside Rhino while the grunt soldiers moved to the starboard side, eager to begin the hunt.

It was hard for X to imagine men being excited to hunt the beasts that had hunted, terrorized, and killed so many Hell Divers over the years.

He looked up at their prey, soaring over the city, screaming in their electronic discords as they searched for prey of their own.

A light flashed on the horizon, illuminating a silo-shaped building on the coastline. The Sirens changed course, flapping toward what looked like a lighthouse. The Cazadores had activated the beacon.

The hunt was on.

In these wastes, the monsters were no longer the hunters. The humans were, and X was about to see why they called themselves the Cazadores.

* * * * *

"We are above our target," announced Timothy Pepper. The hologram stood at the helm of the bridge on *Deliverance*, hands at his sides. "Skies are clear of any major disturbances, sir."

"Good. Hold us steady," Michael said.

"Aye, aye, sir."

Les checked the porthole windows. Storm clouds swelled across the horizon, but the lightning looked sporadic, and *Deliverance*'s advanced sensors detected a friendly drop zone, according to the AI.

"You're sure, Timothy?" Les asked. "Last time we were here, this was a sea of lightning."

"The storm has weakened and moved westward, according to these readings," Timothy said. "But I will perform several more scans before I lower us over the target."

"At least, we won't have to dive this time," Michael said.

Les looked out the windows toward the ocean below but couldn't see anything through the darkness. The thought of returning to the place where both Erin and Ramon had lost their lives made him nervous. And his nerves were already taut from other worries.

For the first time in decades, he was away from every member of his family. Katherine had hardly kissed him goodbye when he left, and even Phyl's hug had felt lighter than normal.

You're just being paranoid, Les. They love you, and they know you love them.

Soon, they would be reunited, as long as Commander Everhart's crazy plan worked. For a moment, he tried to picture what life would be like if all the stars aligned and they managed to take the Metal Islands.

Would the losses required to get there be worth it?

Would he sacrifice himself so his family could live out its days on the surface?

Living in the sunshine, on the crystal-clear water, breathing fresh air. It seemed like a dream. And to get there, he would have to fight his way through a nightmare.

You can't think that way. Failure starts with doubt. Trey and you will survive. You have to survive, for the fate of humanity.

"Lieutenant, come take a look at this one last time," Michael said.

Les crossed the bridge, glad for the interruption. He hovered behind a station where Layla and Michael studied the blueprints of the defectors that Timothy had downloaded. Michael believed that the three of them could reprogram the machines after shutting them down, but Les wasn't so sure. He had a background in electrical engineering, not artificial intelligence.

That's what Timothy is here for, I guess.

"This is their central nervous system," Layla said, looking at the display.

Les took a seat and examined the layout. The humanoid machines had hard, flexible spines, just like humans, and a network of wires analogous to human veins.

"We built them to look like us," he said.

"But they aren't anything like us," Layla said. "They are programmed for one thing only: killing."

"Right, which is why we need them." Michael clicked on the screen to pull up an inside view of the metal-encased brain. "The question is, how do we program them to kill only Cazador soldiers."

"That's where Timothy comes in," Layla said.

"I will program them to destroy only those humans who pose a threat and are carrying weapons."

"And if some kid picks up a gun?" Michael asked.

"I can stipulate that they don't target anyone below a certain age group," Timothy replied, "but there is no guarantee."

No one spoke until Michael broke the silence by tapping the screen. "The defectors have a super-computer the size of a fingernail, encased in a titanium-alloy skull. The rest of the endoskeleton is a lab-created hyperalloy metal."

"That explains why our bullets didn't do shit at Red Sphere," Layla said. "Good thing we have the laser rifle."

"With luck, we won't need it," Michael said. He closed his eyes, no doubt feeling another wave of pain in an arm that wasn't there.

Layla had been by his side the entire time. "You sure you're up for this?" she asked.

Michael nodded with a slight grimace. "The arm is almost fully healed thanks to the nanotechnology. It's just these damn phantom pains." He looked down at the stump, then back to Les and Layla. "You guys ready?"

Layla nodded.

"Ready as I'm going to be," Les replied. "But I do have a question for Timothy about that EMP bomb.

I'm an electrician by trade, so please explain how we'll be able to bring the machines back online after we fry them."

"Good question, Lieutenant," Timothy said. "The exoskeleton protects their interior parts from EMP weapons, but their batteries are vulnerable. Theoretically, the EMP bomb should shut them down, and before restarting them, we will reprogram them."

"It's a good plan," Michael said.

Les wasn't sure whether Michael was seeking agreement or trying to convince himself. And while Les didn't like a mission with such a theoretical outcome, he couldn't see any better options. If the defectors could save human soldiers from going into battle, then so be it.

"Timothy, prepare to drop the EMP bomb on my order," Michael said. "We're headed out."

"Roger, sir. And good luck."

Michael moved over to the comms station. "All hands, this is Commander Everhart. We are preparing to descend over the target. Please get to your designated stations."

The three divers left Timothy standing in the center of the bridge. Their first stop was the armory, where they prepared their gear and suited up.

Unlike on other dives, they weren't sending down any supply crates. Everything they needed was going down attached to them. Most of it was electrical equipment and weapons, although Les doubted that bullets would have any more effect on the defectors than last time, should they encounter any that withstood the EMP blast.

Suiting up took longer than normal, with Layla helping Michael get into his armor. She finished by giving him two painkillers. He swallowed them with a gulp of water.

"I'm good," Michael said confidently when he saw Les scrutinizing him.

The commander tucked his ponytail into the back of his armor, grabbed his bag, and led them back into the passageway to the cargo bay. Timothy's white glow illuminated the dim space.

"The most recent weather scan has revealed only a slight electrical disturbance in the drop zone," he said. "In other words, we should be fine to descend."

Famous last words, Les thought. He walked through the hatch of the cargo bay, recalling the time Timothy had malfunctioned here upon seeing his dead family.

The memory only added to Les' anxiety, and he hesitated as he approached the launch bay doors. Michael and Layla were already there, waiting with their gear bags on the platform.

Les slung his carbine over his shoulder and carried his packs out.

You dive so your family survives, he reminded himself.

"System checks," Michael said.

"Raptor Two online," Layla replied.

Les checked his HUD and systems one last time. "Raptor Four online."

Timothy joined the divers by the door and looked down at the lift gate they were standing on. His shape flickered, and for a second Les tensed up, worried that Timothy might have another episode.

The AI's form solidified, and he pulled at the cuffs of his suit jacket. "The EMP bomb is prepped and ready to drop, Commander."

"Execute," Michael replied.

A distant clank sounded, but no explosion or blast followed—only the dull vibration of the ship's engines under their boots.

"How long until we know if it worked?" Layla asked.

"Only a few minutes for my infrared sensors to scan," Timothy said.

"Weren't these models designed with stealth technology aimed at reducing infrared signatures?" Michael asked.

"Good question, Commander. And yes, they were, but I've reprogrammed the sensors on *Deliverance* to look for the faint exhaust plume that the battery on the DEF-Nine units produces. It's one of their only flaws."

It didn't sound foolproof to Les, but it did make him feel a little better.

They waited in silence, listening to the hum of mechanical systems and the distant roll of thunder. As Les stood there, a memory from his last trip to Red Sphere surfaced, but he pushed it aside.

"I'm detecting a complete blackout on and below

the surface of Red Sphere," Timothy said. "The EMP bomb successfully fried the grid and shut down the defectors. There is no trace of an exhaust plume from any of my scans, which means the machines still down there are, as you say, toast."

"You're sure?" Layla asked.

"One hundred percent positive. However, if it makes you feel better, I will scan one more time once we descend to the piers."

"Okay, take us down," Michael said.

The three divers moved over to the bulkhead, where they secured their gear bags and strapped into the bucket seats.

For the next few minutes, Les watched the porthole windows. Lightning traced the skyline, leaving behind its residual blue image on his retinas. The deck groaned as they lowered over Red Sphere. Les watched their altitude tick down and down.

At a thousand feet, Timothy held the ship steady. "Performing a final infrared scan," he said.

Les flinched as light flashed outside the cargo bay. Thunder followed, easing his fears of a bolt from a laser rifle.

"All clear, Commander Everhart," Timothy said.

Michael unclicked his harness, and Layla helped him sling his backpack. They cradled their weapons and moved over to the cargo bay door. It clanked open, revealing black clouds and a dark ocean.

Les stepped up to the ledge and looked at the piers surrounding Red Sphere. Several ships remained docked. Debris from an explosion surrounded the central structure.

Deliverance continued to lower over the landing zone. The draft of air from the turbofans hit the concrete docks, whipping up dust and debris. Les stepped closer to the edge, feeling a lead weight in his gut.

Layla grabbed his armor and pulled him back.

"Easy there, Lieutenant," she said over the comms.

He stepped back to look at the derelict concrete, checking the green field of his night vision for movement. The front of the facility had collapsed, scattering chunks of concrete out across one of the piers.

They would have to find another way in.

"Extending the platform," Timothy said. "Please proceed with caution."

Les walked down the ramp with an injured, overzealous Hell Diver; a woman young enough be his daughter; and an AI that had gone crazy at least once. Their mission: to infiltrate a dark facility that housed killer machines, and then reprogram those machines to kill Cazadores.

What could possibly go wrong?

TEN

Magnolia woke to the sound of laughter in the hallway outside her room. For the past three hours, she had tossed and turned. But it wasn't the feather-stuffed mattress or warm air that kept her from dozing off. She couldn't stop thinking about X and Rodger.

Where had the Cazadores taken them?

Moonlight streamed in through the open windows, and the shutters clicked in the breeze. The noise irritated her. She swung her feet over the side of the bed and walked across the cold floor for a look outside.

Even at this late hour, several people were lounging out on their balconies. A man in an immaculate dark suit, and a woman in a thin black dress sat on metal chairs drinking and smoking brown sticks.

Magnolia remembered them as cigarettes from old films and books. The smoke sticks, as her people called them, were outlawed on the airships due to the risk of fire, but it didn't surprise her that they would have them here. It also meant they grew tobacco somewhere on their many farms. The Cazadores had the resources to keep many old-world traditions.

She gazed at the sky and breathed in the sweet-smelling smoke. The starry dome ended in the distance, where the storm clouds still raged. The view made her wonder how electrical storms worked and why they didn't pass over this area. It also made her wonder whether more places like this existed out there. If anyone knew, it would be the Imulah. But for now, she would keep the questions to herself.

After shutting the windows, she walked back over to the side table and poured a glass of water. The laughter she heard a few minutes earlier had ceased, replaced by approaching footfalls.

Magnolia quickly made her way back into bed. She pulled the blanket up to her neck and turned toward the wall. A key turned, the lock clicked, and the door opened.

"Magnolia," said a familiar voice.

She turned to see Rodger standing in the doorway.

"Rodge?" she said, sitting up slowly.

"Yeah, it's me," he said, holding out his arms.

She rushed to embrace him, careful not to squeeze too hard. Having her arms wrapped around the friend she had thought dead nearly broke her, and she choked up at his warm touch.

"How … how did you get here?" she asked.

Pulling away, he interlaced his fingers with hers. "I don't have a lot of time, Mags, but there's something we have to do."

For a fleeting second, she thought this was it: their chance to escape.

"Something *you* have to do, rather," Rodger said.

"Anything," Magnolia said. "I just hope you know I thought you were dead ..."

He let go with one hand and held it to her face, running his fingers over her cheek. "I believe you. X already explained."

She hugged him again. "I'm so sorry."

"It's okay, Mags."

She pulled back and searched his eyes. "So what can I do? Anything, Rodge, just tell me. I'm ready to fight. Ready to escape."

Rodger seemed disappointed at her enthusiasm. "No," he whispered, shaking his head. "We can't. You can't. You have to marry el Pulpo."

She pulled away from his grip. "What!"

Rodger moved forward, but she backed away again, her legs hitting the bed frame. The moonlight accentuated his features, and her heart melted at the broken man standing in the glow.

This was no longer the jokester, strong Hell Diver, and talented woodsmith in front of her. He was a shell of his former self: bearded, gaunt, with bags rimming his dark eyes.

"What have they done to you, Rodger?" she said softly.

"They saved my life, and now I'm going to save yours."

Magnolia narrowed her gaze. The old Rodger

would never have said that. The old Rodger loved his family, loved the *Hive*, and had loved her.

Or so she thought.

"El Pulpo killed you, then brought you back so you could be a slave," Magnolia said. "I'd rather die than marry that monster."

"Mags, you're not listening to me," Rodger said. "You have no choice."

She froze when she glimpsed a figure in the hallway. Imulah stood in the shadows, hands clasped behind his back, watching.

Now she understood. Rodger hadn't sneaked here on his own; he was escorted by the scribe, to persuade her to stop being such a hostile bitch.

I'll never stop being hostile, or a bitch, especially to that asshole el Pulpo.

"Please, Mags," Rodger pleaded, grabbing her by the arm. "They'll kill you—and me, and Miles, and—"

She yanked free of his weak grip. "X is out there," she growled, "right now, fighting for me, and …" She tapped Rodger on the chest with her finger. "He will never give up, and we can't, either."

"It doesn't matter. He can't save us. Chances are, where he's going, he won't even be able to save himself."

She moved away from the bed, closer to him. "What do you mean?"

Rodger glanced over his shoulder at Imulah, who finally entered the room.

"He means X is on a mission that he probably won't come back from," Imulah said. "Many soldiers will die, but those who return will be hailed and glorified in the halls of the Octopus Lords."

Magnolia almost rolled her eyes. *Halls of the Octopus Lords? Please.*

"You still don't know X like I do," she said. "That's fine, though; I'd rather you underestimate him."

"We underestimate nothing," Imulah said. "You may think he will free you or that the sky gods will come and save you, but if they do come, we will destroy them, as we did the others."

Rodger looked at the floor.

"What do you mean, the others?" Magnolia asked.

Imulah made his way over to the window and stuck his head outside. He looked up, and suddenly Magnolia understood. She joined him there and felt a chill at the sight of the airship above them—the location of the Sky Arena.

"You weren't the first that found us," Imulah said. "And you probably won't be the last. We knew about the *Hive* and *Ares* for many years. We listened to your transmissions, but we never responded. But now you see what happens to those who try to take this place from el Pulpo."

Magnolia stepped away from the window, suddenly feeling that she was going to be sick. The journey here on the *Sea Wolf* was supposed to save her people. It was supposed to be a fresh start—a place where humanity could rebuild and live in peace without the fear of crashing to a poisoned earth.

But when they set off for the Metal Islands, they

had no idea what kind of evil dwelled here. Maybe X had, but Magnolia had expected only some pirate ships.

Now she knew the truth.

While humanity had continued to advance in the sky, on the surface it seemed to have devolved, back to a more primitive state. Where the sword ruled over the law. Where violence and pain were glorified, and the people worshipped a sea creature.

Imulah moved closer. "Magnolia, I've told you many times, but you don't listen, so I thought I would bring Rodger to talk some sense into you. Time is running out for you to get your mind in the right place."

"Time is always running out," Magnolia replied. "I'm used to the feeling, and you can't scare me with threats, in case you haven't figured that out already."

Imulah raised a hand and pinched his fingers together, then opened them as if he were dropping something on the ground. "The sands of time have almost run out. Tomorrow night, you will be dining with el Pulpo in the gardens, and I fear he will lose patience with your strong spirit and no longer be enamored of it."

The old scribe stepped between Rodger and Magnolia.

"El Pulpo has enjoyed your presence thus far. Make sure that lasts, for your sake and your friends'." He patted Rodger on the shoulder and turned to leave. "And don't forget about that dog. I've heard el Pulpo mention how delicious he looks."

She glared at Imulah's robed back, holding back

what she really wanted to say. Before she could react, Rodger leaned forward and hugged her. She didn't embrace him, but she did hear what he whispered in her ear when Imulah moved away with his back to them.

"I haven't given up, Mags, but you have to play the game like me, so when we do get a chance, we can escape."

Then he was gone. The door locked with a click that echoed through the empty room. Magnolia slumped on the bed, heart thumping and a tear racing down her cheek.

* * * * *

The rain had stopped, but the open cargo bay of the USS *Zion* was still slick. Interior lights shone on a fallen Hell Diver. The body of Jed Snow was wrapped in white blankets and chains to take him down once they pushed him over the side to his final resting place.

The ship rocked gently in the rough water. They had anchored here for three days, within view of another island. Unlike the mountainous place where Jed died, this landmass was mostly flat, and while there seemed to be some flora, most of the terrain appeared to consist of black rock. For this was a relatively new island in geological terms, born of a volcano beneath the sea. Near one end, a red ribbon of lava glowed.

Katrina had watched in awe for the past two days, seeing Mother Nature at its most primordial for the first time in her life. When she wasn't looking out over the awesome sight, she was planning for the rendezvous at the Metal Islands and getting the weapons in operational shape.

In two days, they would meet the airships at their new home. First, though, Michael, Les, and Layla had to complete their mission at Red Sphere, and Katrina was starting to get anxious for news. She brought up the wrist computer that allowed her to stay connected to the command center of the USS *Zion* and receive any incoming transmissions.

The last time she talked to Les, they had just reached Red Sphere and were preparing to drop the EMP bomb. It had to work. She was sick of waiting around and hoping. She wanted to take action.

Her eyes flitted back to the reason the divers were in the cargo bay. The white sheets covering Jed rippled in the wind. She had considered taking his body to the island to bury him, but despite the clear weather and lack of radiation, it was still too dangerous. She wouldn't risk another attack by some mutant beast.

Instead, they had decided to do Jed's send-off in the water. It was no different from in the sky, really. When someone passed away on the *Hive*, they would drop the body from the launch tubes, sending it back to the earth, the way it was always supposed to be.

"We're all here now," said Trey.

She turned to see the other divers present in the cargo hold. Trey, Sandy, Eevi, Alexander, Vish, Jaideep, and Edgar joined her in the enclosed space, out of the wind and rain. Katrina laid her gloved hand on Sandy's shoulder.

The teenage girl had suffered greatly on the journey, seeing her blossoming love destroyed by aberrant evolution in the wastes. Katrina feared she had lost two divers to that hybrid monster on that island. She wasn't sure Sandy would be of much use when they reached the Metal Islands. Since Jed's death, the girl had mostly slept.

"I'm not very good at this," Katrina said. "But I'd like to say a few words about Jed before his send-off. First, though, does anyone else want to say anything?"

"I do." Sandy wiped away a tear and stepped closer to the body.

"I didn't know Jed very well when we were younger," she said. "He was the shy kid in school. Kept to himself. Helped his mom after classes and was pretty much by her side until her last breath. I never heard him talk about his father, who died as a Hell Diver not long after he was born."

She drew in a breath and let it out. "I don't know if you guys know this, but he told me something about Michael and Layla when he first volunteered to join the Hell Divers. A memory from when he was a kid."

"What memory?" Katrina asked.

Sandy cracked a half smile. "He said they approached him and his mom in the trading post when he was about six or so, and they gave him a cookie to eat."

Katrina grinned. "Sounds just like Michael and Layla."

Sandy wiped away another tear. "Jed never forgot that. He said it taught him how to treat people. He used that kindness in his own life, and he treated me like he treated his mom. Always looking out for us and making sure we were okay. Giving us the last drink of water or the last bite of food or making sure we were comfortable. I think that's when I knew I was falling in love with him, when I woke up at night and he was covering my feet."

Katrina felt the tears welling up in her own eyes. The emotions she had suppressed were boiling back up with the memories of a good man. There weren't many left in this world, and each loss hurt.

"Jed told me he volunteered to become a Hell Diver because of Michael and Layla, but also because he always liked me and wanted to protect me," Sandy continued. "And now he's gone because of me."

"It's not your fault," Trey said. "It's mine. He would never have been out there if I hadn't let my guard down on the deck."

"It's no one's fault," Katrina said. "We're here because of the Cazadores. All we can do now is avenge him when we get to the Metal Islands."

"I *will* avenge him," Sandy said.

There was anger in her voice. Good. Anger, when managed properly, could be a powerful motivator. At least, that was how Katrina used hers, and she had plenty stored away in the tank.

"He was a good man," Edgar added. "Ramon and Jed used to run laps in the launch bay. He said Jed was the only one who could beat him in a sprint."

"I knew his mom," Eevi said. "She worked as a seamstress. Chances are, everyone here has worn something she made."

Thunder boomed in the distance, and rain pattered down on the weather deck. The storm was back.

Sandy bent down to the body and tucked a hand-written note inside the sheets. Then she put her hand on Jed's chest.

"Be at peace," she said.

Katrina nodded to Alexander and then to Trey, and together, the three of them picked up Jed and carried him to the starboard rail. The cold rain hit them at a slant, and Katrina tucked her exposed face against her chest. None of them were wearing their armor, and now she wished she had at least thrown on a poncho.

Sandy followed them to the rail and helped them lift Jed's body.

"On three," Katrina said.

She counted down, and on three, they eased him over the side. All four of them looked down to watch the ocean swallow the body. Bubbles gurgled to the top as the white spot below the surface dimmed and then disappeared.

"Bye, Jed," Sandy said.

Katrina put a hand on her shoulder again and guided her away from the railing and back into the protection of the cargo bay. Eevi hit the button to close the hatch, and all the other divers but Trey walked with Sandy to the ladder for the upper decks.

He waited for Katrina as the door clanked shut.

"Captain, may I talk to you?" he said.

"Of course, Trey. What's on your mind?"

He turned to make sure everyone was gone. When the last footfalls faded away, he said, "I'm sorry for letting you down, Captain. Jed's death is on me, not the Cazadores. That's why I want permission to take a Zodiac and scout out the Metal Islands before we meet the airships there. We have two days before—"

"No," Katrina said, cutting him off. "It's too dangerous, and your old man would kill me."

Trey stiffened. He stood a good foot taller than she. "Captain, I was actually hoping you would come with me on this recon mission."

She backed up slightly so she could meet his gaze and confirm that he was serious.

"It would be a great honor for me," he added.

Katrina had actually considered doing some reconnaissance before the airships arrived, but dismissed the idea as too dangerous.

"I want to surprise the Cazadores when we do show up," she said, "and getting spotted beforehand is too risky to the overall mission."

"Ma'am, all due respect, but don't you think el Pulpo *expects* us to come? He isn't stupid, and he's likely interrogated X and Magnolia, right? He has to know they weren't out here all on their own."

She had considered that, too.

Before she could respond, her wrist monitor beeped. She held it up just as a message played over the comms system.

"Captain, please report to the bridge immediately," Eevi said over the channel. "I've picked up something on radar, and it's heading this way."

Trey and Katrina looked at each other. He was probably wondering the same thing: Had the Cazadores already spotted them?

ELEVEN

"Take this, and be careful," Michael said. He lifted the weapon by its curved grip and handed it to Layla.

She exchanged her AK-47, loaded with armor-piercing rounds, for the laser rifle and pressed her helmet shield against his before stepping over to the ladder.

"I'll look after her, don't worry," Les said. He followed her up the metal rungs.

Michael watched from the front of the central structure, standing by a massive steel door warped and pitted from a powerful blast. The concrete walls had collapsed into a mountain of debris that now formed a jumbled apron to the main building.

Rain blew sideways through the translucent hologram standing beside him. Michael couldn't see *Deliverance* or hear the whir of the turbofans, but the airship was up there, hovering two thousand feet above Red Sphere and ready to descend at a moment's notice.

"According to these blueprints, this facility had only three entrances and three exits," Timothy said, gesturing toward the ruined doors. "This was one of them."

Michael recalled the blast from the USS *Zion* that had saved his life and, apparently, destroyed the main access into Red Sphere.

"What's the other way besides the rooftop?" he asked.

"I'd rather not say, Commander, because it would be highly dangerous. But if you must know, it's underwater."

"Well, that's out," Michael said. He turned away from the AI and bent down to get his first look at one of the defectors.

The humanoid machine was buried under the mountain of concrete rubble and steel. The "skull" was crushed, and half the chest and torso were also flattened, but an undamaged arm stuck out of the pile, metal fingers reaching toward the sky.

Under the chunks of rock, he glimpsed a laser rifle.

"Oh, hell yes!" he murmured, slinging his rifle across his back. He got down and began pulling away rocks until it was free. Then, holding his new laser rifle, he stood and walked back a few steps to get a better look at the rooftop.

Layla and Les were nearing the top now, but that ladder was in bad shape. Several rusted rungs didn't look as if they could support much weight without snapping like a calorie-infused herb stick.

"Be careful, Layla," Michael said over the comms. "Three points of contact at all times."

She looked down. "You found a laser rifle?"

"Yeah. It was buried, but it looks operational." His breath caught when she stepped through a decaying rung and fell down a step. Les reached up with a long arm and grabbed her ankle.

"I'm good," she said.

The two divers kept moving, and Michael let out the air in his lungs, clouding his visor. When it cleared, Layla had reached the top of the ladder. She swung her legs over a parapet wall and brought up the laser rifle.

Les followed suit, and both divers disappeared from view.

"See anything?" Michael asked over the comms.

He heard crackling, then a reply from Layla. "All clear up here. We're headed toward the hatch."

Michael went back to scanning the piers for contacts. The ship where Erin died was docked to the left. More debris littered the pier. Erin's blood had long since washed away in the rain and the surf that pounded the edges of the docks.

Michael blinked at the view, remembering the young diver's courage. She had saved him that day by laying down supporting fire, paying for his life with hers.

Standing there, waiting, Michael realized how lucky he was to be here, even without his arm. So many divers had perished over the years, trying to keep the airships in the sky, and now he just might have a chance to see something none of them had ever seen: habitable land.

He brought the laser rifle up in his left hand, as ready to fight as a one-armed diver could be. It wasn't just the killer robots that had him on edge. Sea monsters lived in those cold, dark depths.

Holding the weapon one-handed, he felt its weight. Within a few minutes, his arm was shaking. But it was the phantom pain that finally made him sling the laser rifle and grab the stump under his shoulder pad.

"Commander, are you okay?" Timothy asked.

It was so bad, Michael could only grit his teeth in reply.

"We got the hatch open," Layla said over the comms. "I'm taking a look to see if the entrance is blocked here, too."

"Layla …" Michael groaned. "Wait …"

"Tin?" she replied. "Tin, is everything okay down there?"

He closed his eyes as a drop of sweat raced down his forehead.

"Long, deep breaths may help," Timothy said.

Tell me something I don't know.

Dr. Huff had given Michael several pain-managing techniques, and he really didn't need the AI to repeat them now.

"Timothy, what's going on down there?" Les asked.

"Michael is experiencing some phantom pains and has asked you two to wait before going inside."

"Roger that," Les said. "Standing by."

Lightning bloomed inside the line of bulging

clouds to the west as Michael opened his eyelids. The pain finally faded with the blue residue of light.

"Sorry," he said. "Layla, I want you to send in the drone before you go down. Okay?"

"Two steps ahead of you," she said. "I'll run the feed through our wrist monitors."

Michael held his wrist monitor up as it connected to the feed. A fuzzy display came online as a remote-controlled drone whirred into the opening and down another rusted ladder.

The small aerial robot's light captured the concrete passageway and steps. It didn't go far before hitting a blockage of debris.

"Damn," Layla said. "You see this, Tin?"

"Yeah."

Michael cursed under his breath and pivoted to Timothy. "Where's the other entrance?"

"I'll show you," he said.

Layla and Les climbed down from the ladder and rejoined Michael and the AI. He waved a translucent arm, and the divers filed in behind him, weapons up, and moved around the main structure.

Wind and rain slammed into them as they made their way out onto one of the piers stretching away from the central platform.

"Where are we going?" Layla asked.

Timothy walked past the rusted hull of a fishing boat. "To the other entrance—or exit, rather," he said, pointing with his hand.

Layla looked over her shoulder at Michael, who

shrugged back at her. Les had his rifle shouldered again. The barrel wasn't pointed at the pier or even the boats, but at the water.

"I have a bad feeling about this," he said over the comm.

Timothy stopped at the end of the pier, his hologram standing at the edge. Water slurped against the side, splashing through his legs.

"Beneath each of the piers is a hatch," Timothy said. "They were meant to be exits in case of an emergency. They were designed to be escape only, and not an entrance."

"But you just said a few minutes ago it was an entrance," Michael said.

"This one is." Timothy looked down into the water. "The hatch was used in one of the videos I downloaded from Dr. Julio Diaz's team. Check your wrist computer and I will play it for you."

The feed came online. In it, a man crawled through a tunnel.

Flashlight beams flickered through the space, hitting the feet and legs of the man ahead. A trail of blood streaked across the floor from his tattered boot. He turned, wearing a mask of horror. Despite the blood smeared on his cheeks, Michael recognized Dr. Julio Diaz, who had once run the labs at Red Sphere.

"Hurry," Julio said. "We're almost there."

"They're inside," said a female voice.

The same person who apparently was taking the shaky video turned and looked behind her. An orange glow flickered at the end of the passage, and an electronic wail echoed.

The woman turned back to Julio, who had stopped ahead. He punched at a keypad on the wall, then bent over a large spoked wheel. Grabbing the sides, he tried to spin the hatch open.

"Dana, it's stuck," Julio said. "I can't get it."

She squeezed beside him to help, and the camera angle went awry, providing a jerky view of the floors, ceiling, and then the tunnel, where the orange light brightened. In the glow, a defector moved on all fours like a dog, its hyperalloy exoskeleton clanking.

"Hurry!" Dana said.

A cracking noise sounded, and she pivoted back to Julio, who finally managed to unseal the hatch.

"You go first," he said, backing away.

She went to move when a bolt flashed by her, hitting the ceiling. Hunks of shrapnel rained to the floor. Another bolt cracked, and blood spattered the wall.

Julio let out a scream. The camera dropped to the ground, the angle giving Michael a perfect view of Dana, or what remained of her. The female face, identifiable only by the long hair, had a sizzling hole where the nose and eyes had been.

"Dana," Julio stuttered. "Dana, no ..." He crossed his chest and whispered something about God, then dived through the open hatch. Water splashed up into the blood-stained passage.

The clanking of metal limbs followed, and a moment later the machine reached Dana, grabbing her by the leg and pulling her away from the camera that continued shooting the ancient feed.

It lapsed into white noise on their displays, and the divers all looked up, their visors turning to one another.

"That was the last transmission Dr. Diaz ever made," Timothy said. "I have no idea what happened to him, but apparently he was able to open the hatch right below us."

Michael stepped over to the edge of the water.

"Be careful, Commander," said the AI. "There's no telling what kind of beasts lurk down there."

"Can you do a scan from *Deliverance*?" Layla asked.

"I can, but the ship will need to descend into range."

Michael looked up at the sky and then gave the AI a nod. The turbofans whined overhead, and the thrusters fired, purple flames streaking through the dark clouds.

"Here she comes," Les said.

The airship's belly and turbofans broke through the bottom of the bowl of clouds.

"Scanning now," Timothy said.

Using his night-vision goggles, Michael searched the water for fins or any movement along the dock but saw nothing.

"I am not detecting any organic life-forms, or anything to suggest the defectors have come back online," Timothy reported.

"You're sure?" Layla asked.

"One hundred percent."

"Never heard that one before," Michael muttered, stepping back to the edge.

Les reached out again but then lowered his hand.

"I'll go first," Michael said. He looked back down at the dark water, but before he could jump in, Layla moved in front of him with a rope.

"You crazy, Tin?" She clipped the rope to a carabiner on her waist and started taking off her gear. "You can't just jump in, or you'll sink like a rock."

He backed away. She was right, of course. He was going to get himself killed if he didn't get his mind right. The cardinal rule of Hell Diving was to be cautious and patient.

When Layla had peeled away most of her armor, she pulled her hair back into a ponytail.

"Three-sixty awareness," Michael said, grabbing the uncoiled rope. "Tug if you run into any problems, and we'll be right there to help."

She smiled, then dived into the water.

* * * * *

Rhino gestured to the guy with a flamethrower, then to the one with the Minigun. They stood with their backs leaning against the bow of the skiff.

"This is Fuego, and Whale," Rhino said.

Fuego dipped his helmet, and Whale thumped his armored chest with the brass knuckles he wore. The boat crested a wave and slid down into the trough, and both monstrous warriors bobbed up and down.

X didn't respond. He pulled his oar through the water, staying in rhythm with the other three oarsmen.

"You already met Luke, Ricardo, and Wendig," Rhino said. He stood in the center of the boat and moved from man to man, yelling something in Spanish.

"*¡Mas rápido, Barracudas!*"

Now he knew what the toothy fish symbol on their armor represented.

"The only team I'll ever be is Team Raptor," X muttered under his breath.

The men pulled harder on the oars, upping the tempo. There was a motor on the back, but X guessed they were either conserving gasoline or trying not to make noise.

X was on the fourth oar and was barely keeping up with the others. Water leaked around the patch-work of repairs on the wooden hull and was already sloshing around his ankles.

"Faster, Immortal," Rhino said.

X pulled harder while keeping his boot on the biggest leak.

A wave slammed the side of the boat, splashing more inside. Rhino yelled again to row faster.

He wasn't the only one. An army of Cazadores stormed the beaches of the old-world coastal city, yelling at the top of their lungs, each eager to claim the first kill and add a Siren skull to his armor.

But oddly, they kept their rifles and handguns slung or holstered and advanced toward the city with spears and swords out.

They were either crazy or trying to conserve ammunition, X decided. Probably both. What sane person would come out here to hunt for the mutant humans? Especially in this area. A check of his HUD showed the radiation still in the red.

X had spent his ten years on the surface trying to avoid the monsters, but when he did find them, it usually meant there was an Industrial Tech Corporation facility nearby. And, of course, that was where the real loot was. All his life, the end-of-the-world facilities had kept him, and everyone else in the sky, alive with their supplies.

He wondered whether raiding an ITC facility was another part of this mission. Or were they really here just to kill and capture Sirens?

No matter, he would soon find out.

The Barracudas were the last to the beach. Fuego and Whale clambered over the bow and stood guard while the others jumped onto the sand.

Wendig, Luke, and Ricardo grabbed rope handles on the side of the boat, and X helped them drag the vessel up.

He followed the team up the beach, his boots sinking in the wet sand. Rhino, with his shield still over his back, took point, carrying a long spear with a sawtooth head on either end.

He stopped while the other Barracudas gathered behind him. Then he pulled from his duty belt a black bar that looked like soap, and rubbed it over the spearheads. After placing the bar back in the pouch, he pulled out a lighter and lit the blades, creating metal torches that he twirled once, then twice.

He then pulled his shield from his back, and with the shield in one hand and the flaming spear in the other, he set off. Wendig, Luke, and Ricardo moved out with their single-headed spears, but X kept his shortened spear slung over his shoulder and unsheathed his sword.

They moved up the beach, away from the lighthouse still blinking in the distance and attracting the Sirens like bugs to light. In the past, X would have taken out his battery unit to avoid them, but not today. He was with a small army now, and he needed the battery to power his suit and night-vision goggles.

In the green hue, he scanned the remains of yet another postapocalyptic city. This place had probably been a tourist destination at one point, attracting people to its sunny beaches and tiki bars.

Now it was just another wasteland. The largest tower, once standing at least thirty stories, had broken in half, its top falling and crushing two other buildings. Scree surrounded the impact zone.

Some of the buildings, with their exteriors and foundations intact, looked much as they may have looked 260 years ago. But there wasn't much left of the old-world vehicles that stood rusting with their tires rotted out, windows gone, and interiors nothing but dust and metal bones.

Several Cazador teams were already thronging the first of the roads, heading into the city of brown and gray structures. Vines blocked their route, stretching across the cracked and crumbling asphalt roads. The first of the men hacked through the foliage to clear a path for the bulk of the army.

The Barracudas continued up the beach. A sunken boat ramp led away from the sand to a sagging concrete retaining wall.

Most of the Cazador warriors had taken the ramp, but Rhino selected a different route. He jogged toward a stone stairway, with several broken steps and a twisted handrail, that led up a hill.

Thick tropical trees towered overhead, their red fronds swaying in the breeze. Red pulp from what looked like bite marks oozed down the bark.

It seemed the Sirens had eaten every moving thing. X didn't see so much as a cockroach. As he set off into the dense vegetation, the first gunshot sounded. Rhino held up a fist, and the Barracudas stopped in the radioactive dirt to look to the east.

The vantage gave them a view of the city, and the army moving through the streets and around broken-down buildings. Another gunshot cracked, and a Siren rose above the sunken roof of a rectangular building, a Cazador warrior hanging from its talons. The man struggled in its grip, firing a handgun at the creature.

It finally dropped him from two hundred feet, and he plummeted back to the surface, his armor and bones crunching audibly on the pavement of a vine-infested road.

The noise brought back to X the painful memory

of losing his best friend and Michael's father, Aaron. And just as before, the female Sirens nesting in the buildings darted out and descended on the dead man, tearing him into manageable pieces before skittering away with meals for their young.

The soldiers on point made it to the street a moment later and charged with their spears, spilling Siren blood on the asphalt. One of the Cazadores skewered a female and hoisted the body into the air—the first trophy.

"And so it begins," X said.

Rhino twirled his flaming spear and set off down the other the side of the hill. "The rest of the Barracudas don't think you will live out the day, Immortal," he called out, "but I give you at least two."

His bellowing laugh crackled from his breathing apparatus.

"Try ten years, asshole," X muttered.

The other soldiers moved past him, Wendig reaching out and shoving X so hard he hit the dirt.

"*Puto*," Wendig said, looking over his shoulder.

X pushed himself up and grabbed his sword from the dirt. When he rose to his feet, he saw the flashing lighthouse where the Sirens circled, their huge wings beating the air audibly as they flapped around the structure.

"*¡Vámonos!*" Rhino shouted. Ricardo, Fuego, and Whale vanished over the north side of the hill, and Wendig and Luke double-timed it to catch up.

In the streets to the east, the army of Cazadores

battled the Siren hordes. It took only a few minutes for the monsters to grow in number from a few dozen to hundreds, filling the streets with flesh the color of corpses.

The beasts had been busy here over the past two and a half centuries, breeding and growing in numbers. Even children joined the horde, anxious for fresh meat.

X jogged after the other men, suddenly realizing the Barracudas weren't going on the same mission as the rest of the army. The warriors in the city, fueled by the promise of trophies, prestige, and perhaps a wife, were a decoy to keep the beasts away from Rhino's small unit.

Their mission was something else entirely.

An electronic wail rang out from the west, and X brought up his sword as three of the eyeless monsters scrambled over the edge and bolted out across the hilltop toward Wendig and Luke.

A shout came in Spanish, but X was too busy throwing his sword to see where it came from. The blade sailed past Wendig and struck the front Siren, knocking it off its feet.

X pulled the short spear from his shoulder and ran to meet the other two Sirens, which barreled into Luke. Wendig went down a moment later, unable to move in time to avoid the fleet-footed predators.

Adrenaline rushed through X at the sight of another group of Sirens pulling their way over the rocks to his left. Long limbs covered in leathery, wrinkled skin hit the ground at a dead run. Ropy muscles glistened with water.

They had come from the ocean, flanking the Barracudas.

So much for a decoy, X thought.

Maybe the Cazadores weren't the hunters after all.

He thrust his spear through the gut of one of the beasts straddling Wendig and pulled it out with a strand of intestine hooked on the serrated edge. The beast gripped the wound as Wendig pushed the screeching creature into the dirt. He then pulled out his handgun, twisting to fire at the beast clawing Luke's armor a few feet away.

Dust rose around the warriors in the chaos, but through it, X glimpsed a dropped full-length spear and picked it up. He pivoted to face a pack of six female beasts, and for a moment he considered abandoning these men to fend for themselves. They were his enemy as much as the monsters were.

But where would he go? If he fled and was captured, he would be killed for desertion, and the thought of being stranded out here again filled him with enough dread to keep him in the fight.

An ethereal wail made him look up at a massive male beast flanking from the sky. More Sirens flapped away from the city to storm the hill, heading for Rhino and the other men, who had already moved down onto the other side.

At the hilltop, X went to work with the spear, stabbing, slicing, and swinging the sharp blade at the cadaverous-looking flesh. Blood streamed from the gashes as he inflicted mortal wounds.

A human scream followed the alien cries of pain, and X saw Luke squirming under the weight of another Siren. The beast impaled his eye with a talon and twisted it as the Cazador wailed in agony.

The beast retracted the claw from the bleeding socket. Wendig turned and fired three shots that punched neat holes into its eyeless skull.

It slumped onto Luke's limp body.

X moved to Wendig's side as the man reloaded. Holding up his spear, he prepared to jab at the team of Sirens surrounding them. Saliva dripped from open maws, the beasts tilting their heads as they seemed to study their prey.

They moved in all at once to overrun the two men.

A wave of fire suddenly blasted through the air, slamming into three of the beasts. Flames coated their flesh, and they dropped to the ground, flopping and howling.

X thrust the longer spear into the eyeless face of a fourth beast, which had avoided the fire. The blade caught it in the side of the head, puncturing skull and brain.

The whine of an automatic weapon came over the electronic cries, blowing limbs off the other two beasts.

X yanked his blade free and backed away as Rhino, Fuego, Ricardo, and Whale traversed the hill. They easily dispatched the remaining Sirens that had flanked them, and then turned their attention to the fliers.

Rhino jabbed his flame-tipped spear into a swooping beast, and it caught fire. He pulled the spear out and sliced off a wing with the next stroke.

The creature crashed in flames.

Whale let the Minigun hang from its strap and pulled the axe from the loops on his backpack. He brought it down on another beast, splitting its head like a round of wood.

He laughed as he moved on to the next beast, lobbing off an arm and then a leg before opening the chest cavity with the third swing. Reaching down, he pulled out a handful of viscera and held it dripping in the air.

The other men cheered, but X just looked on in amazement. Some carcasses still burned, the flesh sizzling as it melted off the bones.

Rhino pierced the heart of a Siren crawling away and then knelt beside Luke. He put a finger between the gap in his helmet and neck armor, feeling for a pulse. Then he stood and gestured for the other men to gather around.

They bowed their heads as Rhino spoke several words in Spanish. Then they pounded their chests and stripped Luke of his weapons. Whale tossed the fistful of Siren guts at X's feet.

"*Cómelo*," he said. "*Te pondrá pelo en los testículos.*"

The other men laughed.

"What did he say?" X asked Rhino.

"He said, 'Eat this. It will put hair on your balls.'"

"You're a seriously sick fuck," X replied. He used the breather to check his HUD while the other soldiers gathered their weapons. His suit hadn't been compromised, but his old injuries were aching again, and he felt fresh blood inside his boot.

"So you want to let me in on the real mission now?" X asked Rhino, who was already walking away from their fallen comrade and the gore-spattered ground.

"You will see soon enough," Rhino said. "Now, keep moving, and maybe you will earn a spot on the Barracudas."

Wendig walked past X, but this time, instead of pushing X to the ground, he clapped him on the shoulder, then hurried after the others.

TWELVE

Magnolia sat with the other wives in the gardens. The platform jutted from the capitol tower, providing a view of the ocean, and plenty of sun.

She folded her arms across her see-through blouse. Never in her life had she dressed in anything so seductive and downright silly. A floppy straw hat shielded her fair skin from the baking afternoon sun, and she made sure she was directly under the canopy of a tamarind tree. The other women lounged about, some of them dipping their legs in the limpid pool.

Flowers bloomed around the edges of the sparkling water. In the grove of fruit trees just beyond, servants picked oranges into wicker baskets.

For several minutes, she watched them work, wondering what their lives were like here on the Metal Islands. Every morning, the workers would come from other oil rigs like those she had seen on her ride to the main tower, from which el Pulpo ruled his domain.

One thing was certain: the servants did not live

like his wives. The wives lived like royalty, lying on folded chairs on the deck, drinking goblets full of the berry drinks they called wine.

Another servant brought pieces of sweet candy and plates of berries. He made his way over to Magnolia, offering her some, but she grabbed a glass of water instead and thanked him with a smile.

But for the soldiers standing guard, one might think this was an old-world resort where tourists came to vacation, and the man was just a worker.

But he wasn't a worker; he was a slave.

The man gave Magnolia a toothless smile and moved over to Inge, who greedily snatched a handful of candy without a single word or gesture of thanks. Sofia kindly accepted a glass of wine. She also took a hand towel and dabbed her forehead. Then she lifted her sun hat and looked at Magnolia.

"You will get used to the brightness," she said. "I was born in a bunker and didn't see the sun until I was brought here."

She grabbed a bottle off the table and tossed it to Magnolia.

"Put this on. It will help protect you from the sun."

The other women were already slathered with the ointment or whatever it was. Magnolia declined the bottle and stayed in the shade.

It felt like a betrayal. Why should she be enjoying the sunshine and a cold drink while X was out there fighting and Rodger and Miles were in chains?

She was in this position merely because she was

beautiful in the eyes of the Cazador king. Her looks had never gotten her anywhere on the *Hive* except into trouble. But in this society, a woman's looks seemed to be prized above all else.

She took a sip of water and got up from the chair. Sitting around promoted boredom, and boredom made her want to do things she might later regret.

Pulling her sun hat down, she walked toward the rail overlooking the ocean. One of the women sat up and glared at her, baring her sharp teeth like a wild animal as Magnolia passed by. She was Alicia, the oldest of el Pulpo's wives, the woman who had taunted her at the banquet several nights ago.

Magnolia returned the smile and kept walking toward the railing. Gray clouds crossed the horizon, their bellies full of rain. For the first time since she arrived at the Metal Islands, she hoped one of them would block out the sun for a while.

She gripped the steel pipe balustrade and looked down at the docks below. A group of men in jackets and matching trousers were there, overseeing a shipment of crates being unloaded from several boats. She still didn't know exactly what they did, but they seemed to be some sort of clerks, helping run a complex barter economy based on currency of tobacco and wine.

Magnolia leaned back against the parapet railing and looked up. Colorful paintings covered the exterior walls that had been built onto the ancient oil rig. They were far more beautiful and sophisticated than those on the *Hive*.

"They didn't make those, you know," said a voice.

Sofia stepped up to the rail, taking a drink of her wine and then offering it to Magnolia, who decided to accept it out of courtesy. After a decorous sip, she handed the goblet back.

"What do you mean?" Magnolia asked.

"The only one el Pulpo has ever ordered is that one." Sofia turned and looked at the metal octopus sculpture bolted over the empty throne.

Magnolia thought of Captain Jordan. It seemed that human monsters had a way of rising to power, even in a paradise like this.

"Those paintings were made by people before us," Sofia added, looking out at the sparkling sea.

"Before us?" Magnolia asked.

"Things weren't always like this," Sofia whispered. "They weren't ever peaceful, but they weren't this bad until el Pulpo came to power. After being captured at birth, he rose through the ranks to become the most ruthless and feared warrior of the Cazador army."

"And?"

"To get to where he is now, he went on a rampage, killing the general of the army and all the loyal lieutenants, until no one was left who dared to challenge him."

This, too, reminded Magnolia of Captain Jordan.

Sofia glanced over her shoulder again, as if fearful of eavesdroppers. Satisfied the guards couldn't hear her, she said, "Once he had control, he started a campaign to find remaining bunkers and survivors on the surface, to help fill the ranks of his armies and build this empire."

"We always looked for survivors but never found any," Magnolia said. "I don't understand—"

"There aren't many left. That's what el Pulpo realized when he set out in the ships and used the lighthouses to try and find survivors. Instead, his ships mostly came home loaded with the deformed beasts."

Magnolia shuddered, thinking of the Sirens in Florida. She still couldn't believe these people *ate* the monsters, but then, they had a lot of traditions that made little sense.

"That's why el Pulpo turned to cannibalism," Sofia said, sipping her wine. "It was the only way to feed his army. There wasn't enough protein from what we grew, so he started feeding his men ... other men."

Magnolia didn't want to believe what she was hearing, but it wasn't all that great a shock. The potential for cannibalism had been a genuine concern on the *Hive* for many years.

She turned to look up at the tower wall—a welcome distraction from the grisly topic. The mural showed a large white ship with hundreds of windows and balconies. In the archived magazines of the Old World, such vessels were known as cruise ships. Had one of them survived the apocalypse and come here?

"Who was here before el Pulpo?" Magnolia asked.

"The people who worked on the oil rigs. Then came boats that fled the devastation of the war. I'm not really sure, honestly. Most of the history has been lost over the years."

"And you? Where were you born?"

Sofia's expression grew sad. "In an ITC bunker, in a place called Texas. There were thirty of us then, but only a few of us are still alive."

"I'm sorry."

She gave a shrug of resignation. "This life is hard, but it's better than living underground. I don't know what it was like in the sky, but I'm guessing it wasn't as good as this." She looked at the deck as if she didn't want to finish the thought.

"I wasn't a slave up there, and you weren't one underground. And I'm guessing you weren't beaten or raped there."

"No, but we didn't have this, either," Sofia said. She raised the glass. "It helps numb the pain."

With that, she took another drink and walked away, leaving Magnolia to contemplate the past and her future.

* * * * *

Katrina counted her blessings. The Cazadores hadn't spotted their stealth ship. She had steered the USS *Zion* around the north side of the island and tucked it into a bay to hide.

Standing in the crow's nest, she used her night-vision binoculars to watch the two vessels. One was a long container ship, the other a fishing boat with an octopus symbol painted on the side, leaving no doubt in her mind that it, too, was part of el Pulpo's fleet.

She felt a shiver even though the air was warm. Never in her life had she beheld another human being who did not live on the airships. These were the first surface dwellers she had seen, but instead of wanting to embrace them and ask them questions, she could think of one thing only: killing them.

Moving the binos, she dialed in the fishing boat on the ship's starboard flank. The sails were down, and they were using engines to plow through the sloppy seas. Several people moved on the deck, but none wore armor or carried weapons. These men appeared to be fishermen and nothing more, hauling in a net from the water. It was a reminder that the Cazadores weren't all soldiers.

But they're cannibals.

"What do you see?" Trey asked.

"Two Cazador vessels," she replied, handing the binos back to him. Alexander stood to her left, squinting into the darkness.

"I don't think they spotted us," Katrina said. "At least, not yet. I'm going to pull us back farther around the island."

"But this is our chance, ma'am," Trey said.

Alexander brushed a curtain of wavy hair out of his face. "Chance for what?"

"To capture the ships and add them to our fleet," Trey said excitedly. "Think about it, Captain. If we can take it over, we could dress in their gear and surprise the Cazadores completely when we get to the Metal Islands."

"What if they have radios?" Katrina said. "None of us can speak in their tongue."

Trey shrugged. "So we go dark and don't respond to any transmissions."

Katrina smiled at his enthusiasm. "You know what you sound like?"

Trey shook his head.

"You sound like a younger version of me."

Trey grinned.

"We don't know how many Cazadores are on board," Alexander said. "They could outnumber us ten to one, or even more. And if we do capture them and they send an SOS, we're screwed."

Katrina took the binos from Alexander and focused them on the main ship. Several figures patrolled the deck, where containers were stacked three high.

She could only guess at their contents, but she had a feeling it was loot worth taking. Several armed and armored guards patrolled the deck.

"How have we never discovered these ships before?" she whispered.

The answer was simple. The *Hive* had never come this far before, and radio transmissions from the surface would likely have been blocked by the electrical storms anyway. It staggered her that people had been living down here all this time. She just wished they were a nicer sort of people.

Using the binoculars, she continued scanning the decks and counted ten soldiers. Another two stood in an operations tower with glass windows.

Her team was definitely outnumbered, but she had weapons to even the playing field if she decided to attack.

"We can take them, Captain," Trey said.

She turned to look at the youth. Did he know the sort of violence he was suggesting?

"You've never killed a man, Trey," she said. "It's not as easy as you think, even when you have hate burning in your soul."

"All due respect, Captain, but it's us or them, and I'm ready to make sure it's them."

Alexander massaged the stubble on his chin. "I was an enforcer in the militia for the past two decades, and the most dangerous times were when I didn't know what I was up against." He pointed to the ships. "We have no idea what's below those decks."

"He's right," Katrina said. "There could be a hundred soldiers down there. We can't just board and try to take them out."

Trey backed off the idea, then brightened. "Why not just sink the damn thing, then, and salvage whatever doesn't sink? The fewer Cazadores, the better."

Before Katrina had a chance to respond, Eevi called out from the bridge.

"Captain, there are two smaller vessels moving around the south side of the island, coming this way. Just picked them up on radar."

"Get on those weapons," Katrina said to Alexander. "Trey, follow me. Everyone else, stay off the comms."

They scurried down the ladder to the bridge, where Sandy and Edgar stood at separate stations, monitoring screens of data.

"Are those really Cazadores?" Sandy asked.

There was no fear in her voice, but something else that Katrina knew well: anger.

"Yes, get battle ready just in case they spot us," Katrina said. "I want everyone in armor and carrying a rifle."

She grabbed her helmet from the captain's chair and strapped it on, then took the laser rifle from her pack and followed Eevi out onto the weather deck.

The rain had stopped, but lightning flashed across the horizon. As her optics came online, she detected movement to the south. Two smaller vessels, carrying mounted riders, sped over the water. She had seen these little open boats in an old-world magazine. Called WaveRunners, they were fast and agile.

Katrina ran along the rail toward the ship's bow. The enclosed MK-65 turret and two of the .50-caliber machine guns were already trained on the oncoming boats.

She brought the binos back up to her visor and centered them on the enemy. The riders hugged the WaveRunners as they curved around the peninsula. In a few moments, they would be able to see the dark bulk of the USS *Zion* in the bay, if they hadn't already.

Her binoculars showed the small craft and the

riders in detail now. Both men were fully armored and wore large backpacks. They had weapons and other gear strapped to their boats.

Katrina caught herself holding her breath as the scouts navigated a shallow area where jagged rocks stuck up like teeth through the waves. The riders appeared to be experts, weaving in and around the minefield.

Instead of taking a right into the bay, they kept their heading, speeding away from the peninsula and out into open water. Neither man took a backward glance. If they weren't wearing night-vision goggles, it was quite possible they hadn't seen the stealth warship sitting in the bay.

She lowered the binos and relaxed a degree.

The comms crackled, and she flinched at the break in radio silence.

"Captain, we have two more contacts to the north," Eevi said.

Katrina ran to the starboard side of the ship and looked out over the bay. Two more WaveRunners had flanked the USS *Zion*, and these riders had definitely spotted it. They sat on their vessels, bobbing in the water, binoculars pushed up to their goggles.

The .50-caliber machine gun mounted to her right swung toward the two WaveRunners.

"Alexander, hold your fire," she said over the comms.

The riders began to turn their vessels. She shouldered her laser rifle, lining up the iron sights. Before the WaveRunners could pick up speed, she pulled the trigger. A bolt flashed over the water and hit the back of the first vessel.

The explosion blasted the rider straight up, his body flaming. The second WaveRunner skimmed away over the waves at full throttle.

The blast had likely given away their location, so Katrina decided not to waste another precious bolt from the laser rifle.

"Take him out, Alexander," she ordered over the comm.

She stepped back as the .50-caliber rattled to life, raining brass on the deck. The WaveRunner jolted over the surface, picking up speed as the rider tried to escape. He swerved left, then jerked to the right before the little craft exploded in flames.

"Nice shooting," she said.

Smoke trailed away from the destroyed boats. Katrina brought the binos back up to check the first two WaveRunners. They had changed course and were already two-thirds of the way back to the container ship, which continued to sail away, leaving a long wake. The fishing boat didn't seem to be slowing down, either.

Maybe they hadn't heard the gunshots.

Katrina moved back to the bridge, where most of her crew remained at their stations. She checked the radar for any sign of other boats leaving the container ship. It appeared they had lucked out for now. But the cannibal warriors would likely turn around when they realized they were missing two WaveRunners. And when that happened, the Hell Divers would be ready for them.

THIRTEEN

Les stared at the dark water. This wasn't his first dip in the ocean at Red Sphere. But the other time was to save Michael, and he really, *really* didn't want to dive into that murk again.

Most of the Hell Divers had learned to swim in a small decommissioned pool in the *Hive*'s water treatment facility. It was part of the training since some missions required a diver to swim. But he didn't have the hours under his belt and was one of the weakest swimmers of the group.

Layla, on the other hand, was a strong swimmer, and he was glad she had the lead on this mission. The rope clipped to her belt had allowed them to pull her back to the pier when she discovered that the tunnel Dr. Julio Diaz used to escape Red Sphere was flooded.

She emerged from her fourth dive ten minutes after vanishing into the ocean. This time, she was wearing her armor and helmet so she could breathe inside the tunnel.

Working together, Les and Michael pulled her back toward the surface. It was tough work, especially for Michael, who had only one hand to lend, but after several minutes of hauling on what felt like a massive anchor, her helmet finally broke the choppy surface.

She climbed onto the pier and sat there while all three of them caught their breath.

"You okay?" Michael asked.

A nod.

"It's a twenty-minute journey through that tunnel, to a hatch that leads into the facility," she said. "I fixed the second rope to guide us."

Les cringed at the thought of swimming down the long, narrow passage, even with a rope to guide him, but he didn't protest.

"Tin's going to take longer," she said, "but the hour of reserve oxygen in our helmets should give us plenty of time. The hard part will be right after you jump in, which is the other reason I rigged that rope."

"Is this our only way in, Timothy?" Michael asked.

The AI's hologram flickered to life. "According to the knowledge I have gleaned from records accessed, this is the only entrance into the facility."

"Say we manage to activate the defectors," Layla said. "How do we get them out?"

"They can function underwater," Timothy said. "You just have to tell them where to go and give them a way to climb out, which shouldn't be a problem now."

Les shuddered at the thought. This plan was

looking bleaker by the minute. To Layla, he said, "You definitely found a way inside?"

"Yes." She wiped her wet visor. "The hatch into the facility is in the tunnel ceiling, and it's also open. I surfaced and found a chamber. There's an open door inside."

"Okay," Michael said, "let's stop lollygagging and get this done."

Les reinventoried his gear for the dive. Almost everything was stowed, but his obsessive-compulsive tendencies had him worried about some of his electronics in the dry bag, especially his second minicomputer, which he had used to hack into old facilities just like this one and would soon be using to reprogram the defectors. After making sure it was watertight, he got in line behind Michael.

Les tied two butterfly knots in the rope, at twenty-foot intervals from the end that was clipped to Layla. He clipped his waist carabiner to one loop, and Michael clipped into the other. The far end was already in the water, tied to something inside the open hatch below.

"You sure it's tied tight?" Les asked.

"On my life," Layla replied. "I'll lead the way just to make sure. You help Michael. Timothy, we'll see you once we get inside, okay?"

"Roger," the AI replied. "And good luck."

His form dissolved in the night.

"Let's dive," Michael said.

Layla stepped back to the edge and jumped into

the water. Michael went in right after her. Les hesitated until the slack between Michael and him played out, and then said "screw it" and jumped in.

He sank ten feet before he started kicking, and fear gripped him as the world turned pitch black. His armor, the bag, and the gun over his shoulder pulled down on him. Struggling, he kicked and used his arms to pull him upward. Once he was right under Michael, he grabbed the fixed rope.

All he had to do now was kick and pull his way up to the open hatch. Layla was already through.

As Les waited his turn, he glanced down at the gray pillars, like gigantic spider legs, that held up the pier. He couldn't see the bottom where the pillars were buried, but he could imagine what dwelled down there. In his mind's eye, he saw giant crabs, squids, sharks, and glowing beasts.

A flash of movement past his helmet made him flinch and grip the rope tighter, but it was only a large bubble that had escaped his vest. In a way, this reminded him of his first dive from the *Hive*. But jumping through the clouds, you didn't have monsters that could swim up and bite your leg off or swallow you whole.

Kicking harder, he pulled himself up toward Michael, who was struggling. An arm reached down from inside the tunnel. Layla grabbed Michael's left hand, and Les pushed up on his butt to give him a boost.

She pulled him up into the passage and then moved out of the way for Les. Sometimes, he really hated being so tall.

By the time he pulled himself in through the hatch, his legs and feet tingled from the adrenaline. The hard part was over now, and his heartbeat gradually slowed to normal.

White noise filled the speakers in his helmet, and Michael came online. "Helmet lights on," he said.

Les reached up and turned his lamp on, then directed it back down through the open hatch. The beam penetrated perhaps fifteen feet into the depths. Beyond that range, anything could be lurking.

Seeing nothing, he moved back into the submerged tunnel, where Michael and Layla crouched. She shined her light on the end of the rope she had tied to the spin wheel on the hatch. They unclipped from their butterfly loops and set off down the tunnel.

Moving was difficult inside the cramped passage, and Les felt as if he was fighting a current. The weight of his gear didn't help. His rifle barrel bumped and scratched against the ceiling, so he just tried to keep low, pushing his boots against the cylinder wall to move forward.

He ran his helmet light over the walls, stopping on a long gash from a laser bolt a defector had fired two hundred fifty-some years earlier. Another chunk of ceiling was missing where the second shot had punched a hole through Dana's skull.

The violent images in the video had him on edge again, but he shook them away and pulled himself through the water.

They were ten minutes into the journey, and he was already feeling the burn in his fatigued muscles.

Michael and Layla stopped ahead to rest.

"You okay back there, Giraffe?" Layla said, her voice crackling.

"I'm …" He took in a breath. "Good."

The next stretch of tunnel showed more evidence of the defectors. Grooves from hyperalloy fingernails streaked across the floor. Here was something else, too, which Michael and Layla had missed.

Les worked a small black object out of the crack between two panels of the tunnel floor and held it up to his beam. There wasn't much left of whatever it was, but he had a feeling it had probably belonged to Julio or Dana.

He dropped the artifact and swam on.

The team moved for the next fifteen minutes without stopping until they reached the hatch in the tunnel's ceiling.

Another transmission crackled over the comms channel. "I'll go first," Michael said. He climbed through the opening into the chamber and then pulled the short laser rifle from his holster.

Les followed Layla into a round room with a vaulted ceiling. Their lights revealed walls stained with some sort of green and red moss, the same kind he remembered seeing in one of the ships docked at the piers, where they had found the strange pile of bones and machines.

He put his backpack down and pulled three magazines from his dry bag, stuffing them into his vest.

Michael was already walking toward the exit. The steel door lay on the concrete floor where it had fallen.

"I'm bringing Timothy back online," Layla said. She pulled out a tablet from *Deliverance* that allowed the AI to travel with them beneath the surface. A few taps to the screen, and his hologram emerged like a ghost.

A fourth beacon flickered on their HUDs as the AI took form.

"Everything working properly?" Layla asked him.

Timothy flashed several times and then let his hands fall to the sides of his suit jacket. "I'm one hundred percent functional and—remarkably, if I do say so myself—still connected to the airship."

"Good. So you've already scanned these levels with the airship's infrared sensors?" Les asked.

"Working on it, Lieutenant. Give me a minute." The AI vanished, almost as if he was annoyed.

Michael jerked his helmet toward the door. "Let's move, guys."

"You don't think we should wait?" Layla asked.

"We don't have time, and Timothy already cleared the facility once. Now, let's hit it."

Layla slung her bag and pulled out her laser rifle. The team moved into another hallway, which had power conduits snaking along the walls. The lines connected to a bank of electrical boxes. Beyond this, several chunks of ceiling had broken away and fallen to the floor.

Laser rifle up, Michael navigated the debris. The three helmet beams flicked back and forth over another scene of violence. Bullet holes pocked the walls, and broken glass crunched under his boots. Les froze, gritting his teeth at the noise. The other two divers glanced back at him.

"Careful," Layla said. "There's more debris up here."

Les checked his HUD again. The radiation levels inside Red Sphere were too low to register, but he still didn't want to tear his suit or a boot on a snag. He brought his gun back up and kept moving toward an intersecting corridor.

"Take a left," Timothy said.

Michael walked around the corner, then waved his laser rifle at a translucent web blocking the passage.

"Shit. I'm ...," he said, struggling.

Layla pulled the knife from her duty belt and cut through what appeared to be a spider's web Michael had stepped into. While he was getting free of the sticky strands, the others all looked for the creature that had spun the web.

"Not detecting any life-forms," Timothy said.

"So this is hundreds of years old?" Michael held up his left hand, the glove still covered in the white substance.

"I doubt that," Layla said.

Michael wiped his hand on the bulkhead and started walking. Layla looked over at Les, shrugged, and followed Michael.

Their next turn was at a stairwell. Every step Les took, his mind raced with questions. How could a spider live here all this time unless there was an ecosystem they didn't know about?

Timothy coalesced in front of the team, looking

up from two stairs below Michael. "Commander, I'm not getting any electrical outputs down here, but I am seeing something quite unusual. Aside from your three heat signatures, *Deliverance* is now detecting a faint heat signature three levels below us, but it is not from the exhaust plume of a defector."

"Maybe it's the spider," Michael said.

"Doubtful, Commander," Timothy replied. "This entity is the size of a person."

Layla stopped on the stairs. "Maybe a *really big* spider?"

"Perhaps," Timothy said. "Or it could be a false positive, since the chances of finding anything alive down here are, for all practical purposes, nil."

"I think we need to check this out," Michael said. "You good with that, Lieutenant?"

Les took in a deep breath. He really didn't like the idea of looking for some mutated bug the size of a human, but his scientific side itched to find out what was causing the anomalous reading.

"LT?" Michael entreated.

In answer, Les walked past Michael and Layla.

"I'll take point this time," he said.

* * * * *

The battle for the coastal city raged in the distance. X and the Barracudas moved silently along the remains of a three-story brick mansion with a tile roof that was mostly intact.

A brick-and-stone pathway meandered across a courtyard. Fountains and upended sculptures of lions and other old-world creatures marked the terrain.

Rhino held up a fist, then motioned for the team to get down.

A pair of Sirens sailed over the rooftop and flapped away, their eyeless faces scanning the ground with echolocation or whatever they used to hunt their prey.

The electronic wail that followed told X they had been spotted. Rhino, apparently realizing the same thing, flashed a hand signal toward a brick building on the eastern edge of the property.

The roof, once glass to support an indoor greenhouse, was gone but for a few jagged shards attached to the metal support beams.

This wasn't the first time X had walked into a building that reminded him of some prehistoric monster's rib cage. The curved metal bones rose overhead, some of them broken and hanging loose—daggers that could impale a man.

Rhino directed the team to fan out, away from the broken-out windows that provided an aerial view inside the building. X pulled out his battery unit, powering down so the beasts couldn't detect his energy signature.

He kept close to the western wall, on the left side of an isle framed by hundreds of concrete and stone planters. Most of the pots were cracked and broken.

Only one plant remained.

A flashing orange stem supported a barbed ball of closed petals from a planter two rows down.

X approached cautiously, using the glow from the plant and the sporadic flashes of lightning to guide him through the destroyed greenhouse. He had seen one of these creatures on the surface before and knew that getting too close could result in a nasty bite, injecting venom that would make for an even nastier death.

Rhino, Wendig, and Whale moved down the other aisles, but Fuego lumbered down the aisle of broken pots with Ricardo, both of them oblivious to the threat. As they approached, the stem began to move, creating a strobe-like effect of orange light.

The petals opened, exposing a circular jaw and fangs the length of a finger, each of them dripping purple fluid. The barbed petals shot forward and latched on to Fuego's left arm. He gave a muffled cry of surprise that echoed in the broad open space.

X drew his sword and brought the blade down on the extended stem, severing it. Green fluid shot across the floor, spattering Fuego's armor.

Ricardo laughed uproariously, the noise crackling through the ruined greenhouse, but Rhino didn't find it amusing. He hurried over, grabbed the spiked ball of petals still attached to Fuego's armor, and tore them off.

X would have laughed if not for the flicker of movement across the room. All at once, a dozen of the bizarre flowers rose up on thick stems.

Fuego ignited his flamethrower and engulfed the mutant flora in a wave of fire before Rhino could stop him. The plants shook as the flames consumed them, and it took only a few seconds for the fragile stems and petals to wither and die, filling the pots with ash.

"*¡Imbécil!*" Rhino growled. He looked skyward at a Siren swooping down toward the flames. The rise and fall of the ethereal screech receded above them as the beast sailed away to alert its cohorts.

X secured the battery unit back in its chest slot to bring his HUD and NVGs back online. Reaching over his shoulder, he drew the short spear and waited with the sword in one hand, and the spear in the other.

The Barracudas moved out into combat intervals as a second electronic wail answered the first.

Rhino pointed his double-headed spear toward the exit at the other end of the greenhouse.

The men cautiously made their way down the aisles, helmets turned skyward. Lightning forked through the clouds, and in its glow, a missile came shooting down.

Tucking its wings, the Siren smashed into the metal bones of the ceiling, breaking them like so many twigs and hitting the floor, where it wrapped its body with its wings and crashed into a planter near Whale.

Still wrapped up, it barrel-rolled through several pots, crushing them and the smoldering remains of the poisonous plants. Whale jumped clear, dropping the Minigun as he hit the ground.

The Barracudas all moved to help him dispatch the beast, but it was just a distraction. By the time Whale was on his feet with his axe in hand, three more dirty-white torpedoes crashed through the metal framework.

A draft of air hit X, and he looked up as a beast lowered through the gaping hole, flapping its wings to slow its descent. The long, spiked tail whipped, and a pasty, wrinkled face opened to let out a raucous whine.

X hurled his spear into its gut, then ran for cover. Concrete and stone shattered all around as other beasts bolted away from the first gunshots.

Rhino stabbed at one of the creatures and retreated with Wendig toward Whale, who was pinned down by a massive Siren. He punched the beast with his brass knuckles, breaking its jaw, and then pushed it off him.

In less than thirty seconds, the team had been divided: X was cut off with Ricardo and Fuego on one side of the greenhouse, and Whale, Wendig, and Rhino were on the other.

Another Siren crashed through the ceiling and twisted to scan the room, baring jagged teeth.

"Behind you!" X yelled.

Fuego turned the flamethrower on a beast running at him on all fours, but it slammed into him as he pulled the trigger. The gout of flames shot toward X, who dived for cover in the nick of time.

A human scream followed, and X scrambled to his feet to find Ricardo doused in flames. He crashed into a metal shelving unit and collapsed to the floor, rolling and screaming as the armor melted and fused to his skin.

X raised his sword and moved toward a creature bolting toward him on all fours. He planted his left leg and brought his right leg forward as if about to throw a punch, but instead brought his sword down in the center of the eyeless forehead.

Rhino was right about the sword: wielded properly, it did indeed split flesh and bone.

The monster slumped to the floor. X put a boot on its neck and yanked the weapon free, catching a spray of blood on his visor.

He didn't bother wiping it. There wasn't time. Another Siren folded its wings and scampered toward him.

Time seemed to slow, giving X a fleeting moment to take in the scene. Grunts and screams, muffled by breathing masks, blended with the electronic rise and fall of what sounded like miniature alarm sirens as the Cazadores fought the mutant abominations hand to claw.

A screech snapped him back to the moment, and he brought up the sword. The point was missing, apparently still lodged in the Siren skull at his feet.

He tried to jab at the creature leaping toward him, but the broken end of the sword only slowed the Siren down as it slammed into him. He hit the ground hard.

The male Siren had at least a hundred pounds on X. The sword's hilt stuck out of its muscular chest, the jagged end buried deep in the flesh. If he could just get a hand around the hilt and twist it, maybe he could get the creature off him, but the damn thing had his arms pinned to his sides.

A foot clamped around his ankle, another around his knee. Wings flapped upward, rising above the creature's spiked back. In another moment, the leathery wings would envelop him. The Siren loosened its grip on his hand for an instant, and he jerked free, grabbing the sword hilt and twisting it back and forth.

The beast roared in pain, and X bashed it in the jaw, breaking out several teeth. But that just enraged it even more, and it head-butted his helmet with the bony crest of its skull. Before X could throw another punch, it grabbed his free arm and put its full weight on him.

He squirmed against the massive beast—a futile attempt that wasted his energy. He was pinned like a mouse under a cat and was about to become a meal.

The Siren's weight forced his helmet to the side, giving him a view of the room.

The other men weren't faring much better. Ricardo's body lay smoldering a few paces away. Fuego was on the ground, with two Sirens chewing at the armor on his leg and arm while he struggled to regain his footing.

Wendig and Rhino were out of sight. Only Whale was still on his feet. He threw his axe at a beast, missed, and grabbed it by the neck as it sprang at him.

The huge man held the creature in the air in his left hand. Using the brass knuckles on his armored right fist, he pummeled the eyeless features to pulp before dropping the carcass to the floor.

A sudden lessening of the weight on X gave him another opportunity to face the creature on top of him. Saliva dripped, mixing with the Siren blood on his helmet visor. Looking through the gore, he watched in horror as wormlike lips parted to expose a maw of barbed teeth.

It let out a wail and brought its head down toward his neck just as he brought his helmet up and smashed it in the face. X scrambled for the broken sword on the floor, grabbed it, and ran to gain some distance and catch his breath. Before he could escape, a talon grabbed his boot, tripping him.

Armored boots came pounding toward him as the beast dragged him backward. He flailed with the sword, groping with his other hand for something to grab, finding nothing but broken planters.

He heard the juicy crunch of impaled flesh. The grip on his boot loosened, and X rolled onto his back to see Rhino, pulling his spear out of the Siren's torso.

"That's another for me, Immortal!" he yelled.

Another Siren hurdled a pile of broken pots and grabbed Wendig by the arm, twisting and breaking it. The human scream filled the room. Before the aberration could finish Wendig, Rhino thrust his spear through its ugly head.

X took a moment to check his HUD, praying that the suit's integrity wasn't compromised. A quick glance revealed he was still at 100 percent. He wiped the blood and flecks of gore from his visor and staggered to his feet.

Whale helped Wendig up while Fuego and Rhino stood back to back, jabbing at the Sirens testing their defenses.

"Give me a weapon," X said.

Rhino thrust his spear at another Siren, clipping its neck. The beast skittered away and took to the air, where Fuego turned it into a blazing meteor.

The last two Sirens made a dash to escape, and Rhino held up a fist to stop his men from firing. He moved over to check Ricardo, but it was obvious he wouldn't be getting up again. Half his helmet had melted, and hot goo bubbled out.

X caught his breath as the other men recovered their weapons. There was no time for the thumping of chests or words spoken to honor Ricardo before the next threat sounded.

A vibration rumbled through the floor, and a guttural roar rang out somewhere outside the building. It was a noise X had heard only once before in the wastes and had hoped never to hear again—a noise he had immediately known to run from without ever even seeing the source.

Whale and Rhino spoke in hushed voices. Even through the breathing apparatus and despite the language barrier, X could hear the fear in their deep voices.

Only then did he realize that the departing Sirens were fleeing not from the Barracudas, but from a whole different order of enemy—the true apex predator on this island.

"Time to see why we came here, Immortal," Rhino said. He grabbed the submachine gun Ricardo had dropped, and held it out to X. He held on as X grabbed it.

"You're going to need this for what comes next on this hunt, but do not make me regret giving it to you. You got it?"

X nodded and took the weapon as the same deep roar sounded again in the distance. Whatever made it was a monster unlike any X had seen before, and he had a feeling he would need more than a rifle to bring it down.

FOURTEEN

The sun dipped below the horizon, leaving gashes of purple in the orange glow. Magnolia couldn't see the edge of the barrier between blue sky and eternal darkness, but she could picture in her mind the endless stretch of storm clouds on the other side, and the airship she had always called home.

Another day had passed on the Metal Islands, and the *Hive* and *Deliverance* still hadn't shown up to rain destruction down on el Pulpo and his people. She was starting to wonder whether Katrina was even coming.

But tonight, darker thoughts occupied her mind. Was it possible something had happened to the two airships? Had they been destroyed in the electrical storms, or taken down by sabotage within?

"You ready?" Sofia asked, holding up a palette of makeup.

Magnolia turned from the window and moved back to the wooden desk positioned in front of a long mirror. Inge pulled the chair out and motioned for her to sit.

She looked at her naked reflection. The bruises across her light skin continued to fade, and the deeper cuts had turned to scars. El Pulpo's youngest wives, Inge and Sofia, used makeup to cover the worst of them. But it didn't hide all her wounds accrued from years of diving.

"Where do you get this shit?" Magnolia asked.

"A woman on one of the rigs makes it," Sofia said. "Don't ask me how, though."

She leaned in and powdered Magnolia's nose while Inge worked on her neck.

"I heard Alicia will be given away to one of the warriors from the hunt," Inge said. "You remember her from the banquet, yes?"

"No wonder she keeps clacking her teeth at me," Magnolia said.

"I'd prefer to stay with el Pulpo at this point," Sofia said. "Some of the younger warriors have been known to kill their wives for the slightest infraction."

"*Kill* them?" Magnolia asked, twisting in her chair.

"Close your eyelids so we can finish," Sofia said.

"You sure you don't have anything in black? Magnolia said. "This isn't really my style."

"Style?" Inge asked.

Magnolia sighed. "Never mind."

A knock came on the door and she opened one eye as Imulah's bald head poked into the room.

"Hold on!" Magnolia said, covering her breasts with her arms.

"She's not quite ready yet," Inge said.

Imulah backed away but left the door ajar. "Hurry up. We don't want to keep the king waiting."

"We will be done shortly," Sofia said. She walked over to the bed to examine the two dresses laid out on the mattress. A long strapless green dress and a short peach-colored one.

"I think this one will look the best," Inge said of the second option. Sofia picked it up and handed it to Magnolia.

Slipping into the light, tight-fitting dress, she pulled the straps up and turned toward Inge, who held up a white shell necklace and earrings. Sofia tied delicate sandals to her feet while Inge helped her with the jewelry before stepping back to look her over.

Both wives smiled, admiring the product of their labors, but Magnolia didn't even stop to look in the mirror. She didn't care what she looked like; she just wanted to get this over with.

"Thank you," Magnolia said on her way out. Imulah led her quickly through the halls, into the gardens, and over to the elevator cage, where two soldiers stood sentry. They opened the gate to allow her and the scribe inside. The cage then lowered, clanking toward the docks below.

The last glow of sunset faded in the distance. Imulah watched intently, as if searching for something.

"I always look for the green flash," he said.

Magnolia studied his silhouette as the light inside the elevator flicked on. The tip of his gray beard moved in the breeze. Sweat trickled down his wrinkled forehead, toward his pale gray eyes. She couldn't help but wonder what those eyes had seen over the years.

"What is this flash?" she asked after a pause.

He pointed toward the horizon. "I'm told that sometimes, when the sun goes down, there is a very brief green flash. It occurs in just a split second, hardly visible to the naked eye. I've always looked for it but have yet to see it."

Magnolia followed his finger, but movement in one of the tower windows distracted her. A girl no older than eight, half hidden by a drape, watched the slow-moving cage as it passed.

"I'm not sure that it's real," Imulah said. "But if it is, someday I would like to see it."

"I never thought I would ever see a *sunset*," Magnolia said.

Imulah turned slightly and smiled. But the smile quickly faded and his features darkened.

"You must not fail tonight, Magnolia, or I fear your visit to the Metal Islands will be cut short in a most unpleasant way."

The cage continued to lower, and she realized they weren't heading to another level for this dinner. They were heading to the docks. Several soldiers and dock-hands were preparing a long white speedboat below. No other boats were moored there.

A few minutes later, they were boarding the vessel. A single dockhand jumped in, followed by two Cazador warriors. Neither of these men wore armor, but they were armed with automatic rifles and machetes. Belts of bullets crossed over the chest of the man on the right, almost concealing a long scar from his naval to his pectoral muscles. Tattoos marked his arms, and his chin sported a beaded goatee. The other soldier was also covered in tattoos and had a red Mohawk.

They didn't look like the type to put up with any crap, and she wasn't sure she could take them if the opportunity arose.

Imulah climbed into the boat and gestured for her to take one of the padded seats in the stern. The two soldiers sat in the bow, their weapons cradled.

The dockhand was an older man with a shorn head. He wore a white shirt, seashell necklace, and tan shorts. After firing up the boat, he turned to look at Imulah, who gave him a nod.

The vessel pulled away from the docks and headed out across the water. On the horizon, one by one, the other oil rigs lit up, but one remained dark.

To her surprise, the dark structure seemed to be their destination. She tensed as the boat banged over the wave tops, the engine groaning. Both soldiers kept their eyes on her during the ride. She flashed them a smirk, though she wasn't feeling especially sassy tonight.

On the decks of the first oil rig they passed, hundreds of tarps and tents were strung up between shacks of metal and wood. On every level, families sat around kettles cooking over small open flames. Magnolia caught the scent of barbecue, which almost made her sick. She tried not to think about the sort of meat they were eating.

How could they? They had the resources to create makeup and seashell necklaces, so why did they need to eat human flesh? Because of some sick idea that it made them stronger, or because they really didn't have a choice?

She felt nauseated at the thought, and the jolting of the boat didn't help.

Folding her arms across her chest, she closed her eyes and tried to fill her mind with positive thoughts. What she needed right now was hope—hope that the airships would descend and save her or that X would come back and help her escape.

But with each passing hour, those scenarios seemed less and less likely.

When she opened her eyes again, she wasn't sure how much time had passed. She turned to see how far they had traveled, and could hardly even spot the airship on the top level of the capitol tower.

"Almost there," Imulah said. She didn't remember ever seeing the big, dark structure before, and at a glance, it looked unoccupied.

There were no farms, slaughterhouses, or tent cities—just a few sparks, and lights set up on the metal platforms. On the top level was construction equipment, including a crane.

As they got closer, she could see that this place was inhabited after all. Hundreds of figures were working on the decks. Sparks from welders rained down, going out before they reached the water.

She took a longer look. Were those *cages*?

Two of the platforms looked as if they were being turned into a massive prison. She stood and turned as the boat curved away and headed toward a hodge-podge armada of vessels, bobbing in the chop with their running lights on. Long ropes tethered them to the pillars of the oil rig several hundred feet away.

She braced herself, holding on to the gunwale as the speedboat slowed and her sandals skidded on the slick deck. She was surprised to find the *Sea Wolf* among the boats. The mainmast was gone, and three large motors had been added to the back.

"We're here," Imulah said.

The speedboat pulled alongside her former vessel, and men on the deck threw over a rope. The driver turned off the engine and lashed the vessels together. Once they were secure, Imulah motioned for Magnolia to make her way over to the *Sea Wolf.*

She climbed aboard a very different boat from the one she had sailed with X and Miles. The Cazador mechanics hadn't just fitted it with new engines; they had given it a fresh paint job. And they hadn't stopped there. The image of the wolf was gone, replaced by a glistening image of an octopus.

Sitting in a wingback chair at a table amidships was el Pulpo. Miles sat on his haunches, the collar's reversed spikes digging into his fur and skin. He let out a whine at Magnolia but did not get up to greet her.

El Pulpo did, though, spreading his muscular arms in welcome.

"*¿Te gusta?*" he asked.

She wanted to spit on the image painted on the deck but thought better of it. The king walked over and grabbed a lock of her short hair, leaning down to sniff it. Then he kissed her cheek and led her over to the table, where he pulled out a chair.

Imulah followed them over and stood with his hands cupped behind his back while the other two soldiers took up spots near the railing festooned in barbed wire, their rifles cradled across their tattooed chests.

Instead of sitting back down, el Pulpo turned to look at the oil rig. He wore the same open-faced red silk shirt and shell-whistle necklace from the banquet. Plates of armor covered his forearms and shins. A gold hoop hung between his nostrils, and the strip of hair on his head was spiked up over the octopus tattoo.

He said a few words in Spanish to Imulah and finally took his seat across from Magnolia.

"Our king knows how difficult this journey has been for you," Imulah said. "He understands how much you love the sky gods. For that reason, he has decided to let them live here if they come. It is a great honor."

Magnolia's gut clenched at the words. *An honor?*

"Your friend Rodger has already accepted his fate. He has volunteered his skills as a woodsmith to help build new homes for your people on the tower the Immortal tried to destroy."

"What?" Magnolia choked out. She abandoned her chair and stepped to the rail, to scan the construction crews on the oil rig. It took her only a moment to spot Rodger's thin frame and bearded face among the muscular workers. He was looking out at the boat when a Cazador soldier flicked a whip against his back.

"No," she whispered. "No, this can't be real …"

Imulah joined her at the rail. "Be happy that el Pulpo has decided to let your people live if they come here," he said. "You can ensure they don't die, by marrying him. I think this is a very generous offer, considering what your people have already done to offend the Octopus Lord. Letting them live out their lives here is a gift."

He jerked his goatee at the oil rig.

"In chains?" she said with a snort. "I give myself to him, and my people get to live in a *prison*?"

"It's better than death. Trust me. I know this."

She turned toward the old scribe, her lip curled in a snarl. She was sick of his fake empathy, sick of his words. He was just as bad as his bosses.

A tear ran down her face, but she wiped it away. Then she looked at the dinner table, where two covered plates were set out. She wasn't interested in the food; she was looking for a knife, a fork, or even a spoon to pluck out el Pulpo's other eye.

He followed her gaze, smiled, and gestured for her to sit.

"Choose wisely," Imulah murmured.

She considered her options. Die right now, right here, or marry the octopus king and give her body to him while Rodger and the other slaves built a prison for her people to live out their lives.

Her heart sank at the prospect of what she had never thought she would wish for: that the airships would stay away and her friends would continue living in the skies.

* * * * *

Just as Katrina had suspected, the Cazador container ship slowed, and the fishing vessel turned around to look for the missing WaveRunner scouts. She had watched them from the crow's nest of the USS *Zion* while coming up with a plan to ambush the two vessels—a plan that required getting very close. Fortunately, the enemy ship's long, slow turning radius gave her some time.

She loaded an EMP grenade into the launcher mounted on the bottom of her rifle. Shutting down the enemy's electronics so they couldn't transmit any messages to the Metal Islands was her first objective. But to do it, she must get within hailing distance, which meant leaving the relative safety of the USS *Zion*.

So far, Eevi hadn't detected anything over the radio channels. They weren't even sure the Cazadores used radio, but Katrina wasn't taking any chances.

"Won't that thing fry our systems, too?" Trey asked as they prepared to board the Zodiac.

"The USS *Zion* is EMP resistant," she said, "but the Zodiac isn't. That's why we have *those*."

Trey looked down at the three paddles in the bottom of the boat, grinned, and put his helmet on.

Then he palmed a magazine into his rifle and slung it over his back. Alexander dropped the rope ladder down to the Zodiac.

A few minutes later, the fire team boarded the inflatable craft and sped away from the stealth warship, leaving it in the hands of Eevi, Sandy, Edgar, and the Abhaya brothers.

The plan was simple: lure the Cazador ship and fishing boat into the bay, where the USS *Zion* waited. Katrina would take the Zodiac to flank the enemy vessels and then use the EMP grenades to fry their electronics.

Alexander twisted the throttle, and the Zodiac surged forward. Pushing around the north side of the island, they took the waves at an angle off the port bow, rocking sideways over them instead of meeting them head-on. The Cazador ship was coming in from the south.

Katrina kept her rifle at the ready as they started around the northern shore. A bright river of lava cascaded into the ocean ahead, raising a cloud of steam off the water.

"Give it a wide berth," Katrina said.

Alexander turned the boat, arcing around the glow. As soon as they cleared the lava flow, he gunned the engine and steered them closer to the eastern shoreline of black volcanic rock.

Katrina pulled out her night-vision binoculars. The Cazador ship had almost completed its 180-degree turn, and it and the trawler stopped about a half mile from the southern peninsula.

"Slow down," she said.

Alexander eased off the throttle, and they coasted, rocking side to side while she scanned the ship and the trawler. There could be only one reason to stop: because they had spotted the USS *Zion*.

Just as Katrina planned, the container ship's davits were lowering dozens of smaller boats and WaveRunners over the side, and at least fifty Cazador soldiers were waiting to climb down ladders and board the rides.

"Oh, shit," Katrina whispered when she saw several soldiers carrying shoulder-fired rocket launchers. The USS *Zion* had thick armor, but it wasn't invincible. She wasn't sure how many direct hits the ship could take.

No matter, they won't get the chance …

She didn't open the channel to Eevi, because Eevi was seeing the same thing they were, which meant the machine guns on the *Zion*'s deck were lining up on the enemy boats.

"Let's go," she said to Alexander. He hesitated, and she raised her voice. "Punch it!"

The Zodiac surged forward across the rough waters, hugging the shore for concealment. She brought the EMP-loaded rifle up to her shoulder. She would get only three shots at this.

Cazador soldiers climbed down the ladders to their vessels, and a few WaveRunners zipped away. If any of the riders were wearing night vision, it wouldn't be long before they spotted the Zodiac moving against the dark backdrop of the island. Or an inopportune lightning flash could give them away.

Katrina suddenly felt completely exposed as they rounded the peninsula and shot out into open water.

Trey moved up to the bow with her, holding the laser rifle.

"We can't let them get close to *Zion*," he said.

"They'll have to paddle or swim," Katrina said. She pulled the trigger, and the first EMP grenade thumped away, sailing over the container ship and hitting the water on the far side. Muttering a curse, she loaded another grenade.

Half the boats had already taken off and were headed toward the bay, where the USS *Zion* sat waiting.

"Pick your targets carefully," Katrina said to Alexander and Trey.

The flotilla of WaveRunners and small boats fanned out. Nearly all of them were now away from the mother ship. They had definitely spotted the *Zion*. In a few minutes, they would be within firing range.

Katrina needed just one lucky shot. She raised the rifle again and waited for her opportunity as the Zodiac bobbed in the chop.

The cargo ship was no more than three thousand feet away. She could hear shouting on deck. She was close enough that the EMP blast would also knock out the Zodiac's motor.

Now she could see the source of the shouting. A Cazador stood on the deck, pointing in the Zodiac's direction and yelling at the top of his lungs.

Drawing in a breath, she imagined the EMP

grenade smacking into the deck of the container ship. Then she pulled the trigger and watched it shoot away. It landed on the weather deck and rolled behind an old-world vehicle that had tracks instead of tires.

Alexander turned the boat parallel to the container ship to get a better firing position. The armada of small craft racing toward the bay suddenly stopped dead in the water. But the invisible EMP blast didn't stop the Cazadores' guns.

A flash burst from one of the WaveRunners as a missile streaked away.

"Open fire!" Katrina yelled to her team.

She gritted her teeth as the missile vanished behind a wall of rock that blocked her view of the bay. She waited, dreading the sound of the explosion to follow. Instead, she heard the beautiful crack of the .50-cals. Green tracer rounds lanced across the ocean, riddling the disabled Cazador boats.

Soldiers jumped off their boats to avoid the hail of lead, but for most, it was too late. Explosions boomed all across the rough waters, throwing flames and body parts into the air.

Return fire from the container ship hit the water around the Zodiac, snapping Katrina's attention away from the slaughter. She aimed her rifle at the muzzle flashes on the container ship. There were five different shooters, maybe more.

"Take down the hostiles on the deck!" she yelled.

Alexander and Trey both went to work, firing laser bolts and bullets at the men shooting at the Zodiac.

Bullets punched through the rubberized canvas compartments, and air hissed out.

"Engine's fried!" Alexander shouted.

Katrina bumped her chin pad to open a line to Eevi. "Don't hit the fishing boat, and come pick us up. You have our beacon locations."

In less than the time it took to blink, Katrina saw a red streak coming right toward her. There was no time to move or return fire. The bullet hit her upper chest, knocking her backward onto the boat's soft floor.

The air broke from her lungs, and tiny stars burst across her vision. More rounds punched into the Zodiac, and water poured in over a deflating section of pontoon.

"Abandon …" she choked. Reaching up, she took Trey's hand. As he helped her sit up, an explosion rocked the deck of the container ship, obliterating the hostiles.

Two entire stacks of containers burst apart, raining a loud clatter of steel chunks onto the deck. A container slid over the side into the water in a massive splash.

Alexander bent down and helped Trey keep Katrina up as the boat floor sank beneath them. She blinked away the stars and saw one of the most beautiful sights of her life. It wasn't the sun or a sandy beach with palm trees—it was the USS *Zion*, barreling out of the bay at full speed, .50-cals firing at anything that moved on the container ship, and the MK-65 pounding the deck with explosive rounds.

Trey and Alexander got a life vest under Katrina's

head and torso. She sucked in air, but no matter how hard she tried, she couldn't get enough. Beneath her armor, she could feel wet warmth moving down her ribs, confirming her fear that the bullet had penetrated.

Through blurry eyes, she watched people jumping from the deck of the container ship, some of them on fire, others trying to avoid the flames. They didn't all look like soldiers, and she knew they were probably engineers, electricians, cooks, and servants.

As she maneuvered to keep the life vest under her, she recalled what Trey had said about attacking the ship. *The fewer Cazadores, the better.*

But what about the innocent men and women who *weren't* soldiers? How were they any different from the men and women on the airships?

In war, there are no innocents. Everyone is the enemy.

Those words had come from a history book, probably the same one Trey had read in school. Still, as the weapons on the USS *Zion* slaughtered the Cazadores, she couldn't help but feel a rising dread.

It's us against them, she thought. *Your job as captain is to ensure the survival of your people.*

She hadn't started this war, but if she survived this wound, she would damn well finish it.

FIFTEEN

The divers at Red Sphere had spent the past hour trying to open the steel door into the labs. Somewhere on the other side was an organic life-form that Timothy Pepper continued to detect in his scans.

Michael had a feeling the AI was right about it not being a spider. Their scans were picking up something else, something bigger, and he had to figure out what before they moved any deeper into the facility to find the defectors.

Les disconnected his minicomputer from the control manual and shook his head. "I can't hack it, man."

Michael swore under his breath. He was starting to lose patience. Nothing was going right. The pain meds had already worn off, and his bandage needed changed. On top of that, he was due for another round of ghost pains.

Think positive. You're going to be just fine. Not an easy thing to do here in the very place he had lost his arm. But too much was at stake to let anxiety and pain mess with his head. X had suffered far worse than this, for far longer.

It was time to get serious about this shit.

Michael held up plan C: the laser rifle. "Everyone back," he said.

"You're kidding, right?" Les asked.

"You got a better idea?" Michael asked. "Come on, get behind the wall."

The team moved back down the passage and around the corner. Even Timothy vanished and then rejoined them behind the barrier.

"Commander, all due respect, but I have more experience with that weapon," Les said. "If we're going to do this, best to let me."

"Be my guest," Michael said, handing it over.

"Try this one," Layla said. "Just so we know it works."

Les took the new rifle from her and moved around the corner to check the target. "If the laser bolts cut through, I'll try and make us a smaller door, but make sure you guys stay back."

"Be careful, Giraffe," Layla said. "And make it big enough for you to get through."

That got a weak chuckle, which ended in silence as Les crouched with half his body behind the corner, and half in the hallway. Then he lined up the iron sights and pulled the trigger. The brilliant line hit the door, bathing the corridor in a red glow.

"It's working!" Les said.

A minute later, the door came crashing down on

the concrete, shaking the floor and echoing through the space. Michael cringed at the noise.

"If any of those things are still ticking, they know we're here now," Layla said.

Timothy reappeared, and his voice came over the comms. "Still not detecting any exhaust plumes. But the organic signal is stronger."

While the other divers listened and scanned their HUDs for movement, Michael moved around the corner to see the glowing red outline of a doorway inside the door.

Les handed the laser rifle back to Layla as Michael sucked water from the straw in his helmet and waited for a wave of dizziness to pass. Then, taking point, he approached the opening cautiously, flitting his helmet beam across the dark lab.

Dust particles, stirred by the crashing steel door, danced like snowflakes in their headlamp beams as they entered what appeared to be an undisturbed space. Four separate rooms, all blocked off by glass walls and secure doors, made up the labs.

As they progressed deeper, Michael saw that the four sections were just half the space. Through another glass wall, he could see two more walled-off sections. In both rooms, white suits hung from hooks on the racks, and coiled red cords dangled from the ceiling.

He checked the room on his right, which contained white lab tables and several chairs. But there were no cobwebs—or evidence of any other living thing, for that matter. The high-tech lab appeared to have done exactly what it was designed to do: keep even the most microscopic particles out—or in.

The thought made him shiver as he brought up his hand and signaled the team to check out the first four sections. He went left, directing his helmet beam at the enclosed glass space filled with several dozen three-foot-tall stasis chambers.

Each of these glass cylinders contained murky green liquid. Skeletal remains rested on the bottom of one of them, but the water was too clouded for him to make out the species.

"Over here," Michael said over the comms.

Layla and Les joined him outside the glass wall.

"Gross," Layla said.

Les shined his beam inside. "What are those?"

"No idea," Michael replied. "Timothy, where is that signal coming from?"

"I can't get an exact location, but it should be somewhere inside this room."

Michael moved to the next glass enclosure, where eight metal vats were lined up against a gray wall. The lids were closed, and thick electrical cables ran up to a bank of boxes that once fed them power.

"This must be where Dr. Julio Diaz worked," Les said quietly.

"Maybe we'll finally learn what that work was," Layla replied.

Michael really didn't give a damn what the doctor did. He just wanted to figure out what was making the signal, then find the machines so they could get the hell out of here.

He moved past several lab stations. On the long tables were microscopes, computers, and trays of vials. Several robotic machines with spiderlike arms were huddled in the corner of the room.

"Looks like an operation area," Layla said. "Maybe they used it for experiments."

They moved on to the final walled-off area, their headlamps shooting through the glass and illuminating a clean room where scientists had once prepped to enter the lab.

A faint clanking noise pulled Michael back the way they had come. His beam hit the opening Les had cut in the door.

"Did you hear something?" Michael asked.

Layla and Les shook their heads. He motioned for them to return to the first section of labs, where the stasis chambers were sealed off.

"See if you can hack this door," Michael said to Les.

Les hooked up his patch cords and began the process while Michael and Layla walked around the glass walls, shining their lights into the chambers beyond. Cables ran up from the floor to the chambers they had once powered to keep the contents alive.

There were twenty chambers, all filled with the same murky fluid that kept him from seeing what else they contained. He went back to the one with the bones that could be a small human skeleton.

"A child," he whispered.

A click sounded.

"Got it," Les said.

The divers met Timothy outside, where his hologram spread a bright glow through the open room.

"Stay sharp," Michael said.

They fanned out down the aisles of stasis chambers, their light beams flitting back and forth. Michael headed straight for the cylinder with the child-size remains. He used his gloved hand to wipe off the glass, but that didn't help any.

There was only one way to see what was inside.

"Everyone out of the room," Michael said.

"Why?" Layla asked. "What are you going to do?"

He raised his laser rifle, prompting Les to gently pull Layla away. Michael waited until they were outside the glass walls. Then, back-stepping a few feet, he aimed the laser rifle and pulled the trigger.

Glass exploded, and fluid sloshed onto the floor, pushing Michael back a few more steps. All that remained on the floor of the stasis chamber was the skeleton.

He had stepped around the puddle to examine the remains when he again heard the mysterious clanking noise. He glanced over his shoulder at Les and Layla, who both nodded. They had heard it this time.

It came again a few beats later, louder this time—a mechanical noise, not something an organic life-form would make.

"Timothy," Michael whispered over the comm channel. "Are you picking up any exhaust plumes?"

"Negative, Commander."

Stepping back from the bones inside the destroyed chamber, Michael walked carefully around the skirt of broken glass and green fluid.

The laser bolt had bored through another cylinder and the metal wall behind it, where a red hole glowed. He stopped a few feet away and bent down to direct his light at the opening. The beam penetrated into what appeared to be another room.

"Check this out," Michael said. He made his way around the final two chambers and found a door he had missed earlier, hidden in the shadows in the corner, behind several other vats.

"That signature is getting stronger," Timothy said.

Layla and Les stopped outside the new door.

"I didn't see this earlier," Layla said quietly.

"Me, either," Michael replied. "Les, see if you can get it open."

While Les again unpacked his minicomputer and patch cords, Michael moved over to the still red-hot opening in the wall and looked through it.

The helmet beam illuminated another lab, full of larger stasis chambers, but unlike the smaller ones, the liquid inside these cylinders wasn't green, and the remains weren't skeletal.

"Mother of God," Michael whispered.

Inside each chamber was suspended a naked man or woman. Cords were attached to their extremities.

The door to the lab clicked, unlocked, and Les stepped away.

"What?" he asked, oblivious to what Michael was seeing through the hole.

Layla stepped up to the open doorway. "Holy wastes!" she gasped. "What in the apocalypse are those?"

Michael moved over to examine the stasis chambers inside the room. The new angle gave him a view of several bodies that didn't appear totally human after all. Some had mechanical limbs and even heads that looked … robotic.

"Guess we finally know what Dr. Diaz was doing here," Layla whispered.

Les stared for a moment and then shook his head. "I had a bad feeling about coming back here. Looks like I was right."

Timothy reappeared in the entryway of the room, his glow spreading outward and illuminating more of the chambers.

"Commander, I have a theory on what we're seeing here," the AI said.

"What's that?"

"Hybrids."

"Hybrids?" Layla asked.

"Yes, and I believe most of them were still alive and hooked up to backup power before we dropped the EMP bomb."

Layla shook her head. "No, that can't be."

"You're saying we killed them?" Les asked.

"Not all of them," Timothy replied. "I've pinpointed the location of the organic life-form."

"Show us," Michael said.

The three divers followed the AI, weapons up, beams playing over the chambers containing the human-machine hybrids.

Timothy moved down the center aisle and stopped beside one of the vats. The man inside was so wrinkled from age and immersion that his skin looked like a dried piece of fruit. His bald head had slumped against his chest, exposing a smooth metal crown. Most of this man was now machine. Only the arms, chest, and head remained human.

Unlike the other bodies, this ancient man wasn't wearing a breathing apparatus—probably because he didn't have lungs, Michael realized.

"So where is it?" Layla asked as she walked around the other chambers. "I don't see any live ones."

"Right here," Timothy said. He turned his hologram toward the man in the chamber in front of Michael.

Layla stared. "He's still …?"

The hybrid slowly opened his eyelids, looking out with one human eye and one mechanical eye that roved from Les to Michael. When it focused on the holographic shape of Timothy, the human eye widened, and the robotic eye glowed orange.

"Holy shit," Les said, backing away. "What the heck is this thing?"

Michael stayed where he was, watching the old man squirm inside the vat, his wrinkled skin like plastic. He tried to speak, bubbles bursting from his mouth. The terror in his features and movements was difficult to watch.

This man had suffered for God knew how long.

The hybrid's lips continued to move, trying to speak to the divers. He squirmed against the restraints holding him in the vat.

"This is wrong," Les said. "I really think we should get out of here."

The hybrid managed to raise a hand, putting his palm against the glass. A stream of bubbles burst out of his mouth as his lips moved and the robotic eye flashed an angry orange.

"Timothy, can you make out what he's saying?" Michael asked.

There was a long pause from the AI before he replied.

"Yes, Commander," Timothy replied. "He's repeating, 'Destroy me ... destroy me ... before I kill you all.'"

* * * * *

Throughout dinner, the clanking of hammers and the whine of electrical equipment played like some undisciplined, atonal band. And it appeared to be music to el Pulpo's ears. He watched the construction crews as he mowed through his three courses of fish, ham, and chicken. He was plainly delighted at the work being done on the rig.

To Magnolia, the noise was grating and unpleasant, but at least it distracted el Pulpo's attention from her. She picked at her food as the crews worked into the night on the prison that would hold her people captive.

Under the table, Miles whined as if he knew what it meant for his friends. She could tell he was itching to rip his handler's throat out, but there was nothing he could do against the spiked collar.

By the time the moon was high in the open bowl of sky above them, el Pulpo had downed his sixth goblet of wine. He got up from the table, the feet of his chair shrieking on the metal deck.

Then he lumbered over to the hatch leading belowdecks—to relieve himself, Magnolia assumed. She remained at the table, looking at the dead fish that stared back from her plate. The past few hours had been torture, but at least, thanks to the distractions, she wasn't forced to carry on much of a conversation with the bastard.

He didn't seem interested in what she had to say, anyway. Imulah had translated the few things el Pulpo said to her. Simple questions about her former life on the *Hive*, which she answered in the fewest words possible while the king stared at her breasts.

She glanced back at the scribe, who remained standing near the rail of the boat, flanked on either side by the two Cazador guards. They hadn't taken their eyes off her the entire night. Behind them, beyond the barbed wire that spiraled above the rail, the pilot of the speedboat that had ferried Magnolia here watched from his vessel.

There was nowhere to run.

She looked at the oil rig. Sparks showered into the water from a metal gate two men were welding out of pipe. Rodger was up there somewhere, helping build the cages.

The sight sucked the spirit out of her. She felt numb, weak.

The will to fight had drained away. Years ago, when she had gone to the brig on the *Hive* for stealing, she had felt trapped. That dreadful feeling had returned. Her heart ached, and her stomach churned with anxiety.

She had joined the Hell Divers to get out of prison, even though it meant she would probably die on a dive. But she hadn't. She had survived by fighting tooth and nail, only to end up a prisoner once more.

This time, however, she feared what would happen if she didn't cooperate with the Cazadores, more than she ever feared dying on a dive. Back then she didn't have anyone to care about. No one would have mourned her if she splattered on the surface, and she wouldn't have lost any sleep over the death of anyone around her.

But now she had Rodger, X, Miles, Tin, Layla, Katrina, and Les. They were all counting on her. They were more than friends. They had become her family.

Cooperating with her captors could help them, maybe even save them. But it also meant betraying what she was: a fighter.

The hatch to the *Sea Wolf* opened, and for a moment she pictured X stepping out onto the deck. But it was just el Pulpo ducking under the hatch frame, his unbuttoned shirt blowing in the breeze, his muscles glistening with sweat.

He returned to the table holding something under his arm. When he sat in his chair, he pulled a knife from the sheath on his belt and used the tip to pick food from between his sharp yellowed teeth. He flicked a bit of meat down at Miles, who licked it off the deck.

Sick bastard.

She hadn't seen them feed the husky at all since she arrived. No wonder he was so hungry. Before anyone could stop her, she grabbed the hunk of fish off her plate and tossed it down to him.

This earned her a glare from el Pulpo, and then a laugh. He took the black object from under his arm and set it on the table. It looked like a hard drive. He pushed it over to Magnolia, and she leaned closer for a better look.

"Our lord wants you to know that we found your friend yesterday," Imulah said.

"Friend?" she said quietly. Staring at the hard drive, she realized that the friend was Timothy. The AI's consciousness and programming were stored on this drive, which was effectively his brain.

Before she could pull it away, el Pulpo stabbed the hard drive with his knife, then tossed it overboard.

"No!" Magnolia shouted.

The assemblage of digital programming and memory that had been Timothy sank into the water. A tear welled in her eye, but she forced it back, not wanting to give this filth the satisfaction.

"Our lord now wants to know if you're ready for

the final course," Imulah said. "I believe your people would call it *dessert*."

"No," she snapped. "I'm not feeling very well."

The scribe translated her words, much to el Pulpo's annoyance. He frowned and fixed his eye on her as if trying to look into her guts for a lie.

Magnolia turned away.

"You should drink more wine before you go to the room downstairs that has been prepared for your first night together," Imulah said. These were his words, she realized—not something el Pulpo had told him to say.

"It will make you feel much better," the scribe added.

Magnolia nearly gagged.

Did you see that, you repulsive lump of Siren scat?

El Pulpo picked up his goblet. Chugging down the remaining wine, he slammed the glass on the table and continued watching her. This time, Magnolia followed Imulah's advice, hoping it would make her rape by the cannibal king less awful.

Sofia was right about the wine: it did help numb the senses.

"I'll be back with his final course in a moment," Imulah said. He left them at the table and made his way belowdecks.

"*¿Estás enferma?*" el Pulpo said.

Magnolia glanced across the table and was surprised to see his features soften. She wasn't sure what he was trying to say, but he almost seemed concerned for her welfare.

She wasn't buying it.

"*¿Estás enferma?*" he asked again, patting his belly.

She shook her head, not understanding.

A few minutes later, the scribe returned carrying a tray with a covered dish. He placed it in front of el Pulpo, who plucked the lid off a plate full of slimy fish eyes. They all seemed to be staring at Magnolia.

"You sure you don't want some?" Imulah asked. "It's a delicacy."

Magnolia forced herself to look away as el Pulpo slurped one down without chewing. He continued popping eyeballs into his mouth as if they were candy jam from the *Hive*, while she sat and waited, her guts cramping with anxiety.

The minutes ticked by, drawing her ever closer to the dreaded consummation of her "marriage" to the cannibal king.

The rumble of a boat motor snapped her out of her doom-ridden thoughts. She twisted in her chair as the soldiers moved away from the railing back to the stern. The beams of two WaveRunners flickered over the water as they sped toward the armada of small craft.

The lights hit the *Sea Wolf*, and both soldiers leveled their weapons. El Pulpo grunted, clearly not happy about being interrupted just before taking his bride belowdecks.

She eyed the fork beside her plate and once again considered driving it through his remaining eye, deep into that demented brain.

The two WaveRunners slowed, and the soldiers

guarding the king relaxed when they saw it was just more Cazadores. They slung their rifles and threw ropes to the riders.

Both men got off their WaveRunners and jumped onto the landing pad, where they raised goggles from their filthy faces and boarded the *Sea Wolf*. El Pulpo belched and walked over, his arms folded across his muscular chest.

"*¿Qué pasa?*" he asked.

They spoke fast in Spanish, making it impossible for Magnolia to make out any of the words except one: "*Inmortal.*"

Whatever they said next made El Pulpo furious. He pulled his knife from the sheath on his belt and threw it across the boat, sinking it deep into the cabin behind Magnolia.

He turned back to her, giving her the elevator eye. Then he snorted and pushed one of the soldiers out of the way. The man fell onto the deck as his lord stepped to the landing and jumped onto one of the WaveRunners.

The driver of the speedboat started his engines. One of the Cazador soldiers from the *Sea Wolf* jumped on, and the other man returned to his WaveRunner.

The third soldier remained standing next to Imulah, both of them looking at Magnolia. She watched as the vessels sped away after el Pulpo.

Delighted though she was at the reprieve, she couldn't help wondering what was so urgent that he would leave her and the fish eyes he so loved.

"What's going on?" she asked.

The scribe walked over to the table but didn't take a seat. He picked up a large eyeball and chewed it slowly before spitting out the hard round lens, which bounced like a marble on the deck.

"Two of our vessels have gone missing," he said. "It could have been a storm, but there was no SOS. They just went dark."

"What about X? They mentioned him, I think."

Imulah stroked his beard. "You are starting to pick up our language, I see."

"Tell me what el Pulpo said." Magnolia paused, then added, "Please."

"The Cazador warriors have finished their hunt, but apparently the Barracudas haven't returned. The Immortal was with that team."

The scribe took another fish eye and gestured toward the hatch with it still in his hand. "Since you're not feeling well, you can go lie down belowdecks to rest. I'm not sure when our lord will be back."

She looked out over the waves, the guilt of her complacency eating her insides. Timothy was gone now, and whether or not he had been able to communicate with the airships before, he certainly couldn't share any intel now. On top of that, X was out there fighting, or possibly even dead, and she had all but given up her own fight.

No more, she thought. *When he gets back—and he will come back—I will fight for humanity. I will fight for our people.*

SIXTEEN

An ethereal shriek pierced the night. X waited for a gunshot to follow, but he hadn't heard any for a while. Even though the Barracudas were miles away from the main Cazador army, they should be hearing *something*. The battle couldn't be over already unless … Could the Sirens really have killed close to a hundred men?

A sporadic burst of gunfire finally came. The chatter hardly pierced the din of wails that sounded like a malfunctioning alarm on one of the airships. He had trouble believing that the mutant beasts could stand against such a large, well-armed tactical force. But they were cunning and strong creatures, evolved to survive in the wastes, and to fight.

The Barracudas, in fully armored suits and carrying heavy weapons, weren't faring so well, either. Ricardo and Luke were dead, and Wendig had a broken arm. Whale, Fuego, and Rhino didn't seem deterred, however. They took a steep trail up into the jungle that bordered the coastal city.

The team crested the hill and set off under the dense canopy. The electronic whines of the monsters faded away, replaced by the chirping of insects and the creaking of branches in the wind.

A light rain pattered the ground, turning the poisoned earth to a fine slurry. X kept his rifle up and ready, his finger on the trigger guard.

Ten minutes into the trek, they came across more ruined buildings. Several rooftops protruded from the purple canopy of trees four and five stories high. One had grown right up through a building, its red branches bursting through the now collapsed ceiling like an explosion frozen in time.

Farther north, several acres of jungle were burned, perhaps from a lightning strike that started a fire. The storms had mostly passed, but sporadic flashes forked through the clouds every few minutes.

Rhino crouched down to look at tracks in the mud. Then he stood and continued up an overgrown trail that had once been a road. Very little of the fragmented asphalt remained, and the jungle closed in as the path narrowed ahead. Branches covered in thorns reached out like sharp fingers.

X had avoided places like this back in the wastes of the former United States, where more than once he had narrowly avoided becoming plant food. Rhino kept his distance from the branches by moving to the center of the road. The Barracudas seemed as wary of the trees as he was.

But the trees weren't the only threat. A vine

undulated like a snake across the ground. Rhino sliced it in half with his double-headed spear, and the vine retracted, oozing violet sap onto the fractured asphalt as it recoiled back into the jungle.

Fuego walked behind Rhino with his flame-thrower, ready to blast through anything too thick for the lieutenant's blades.

Around the next corner, a lattice of thorny vines crisscrossed the path. Rhino waved Fuego back and used his serrated spear blades to carve a doorway in the spiny mat.

Fuego walked closely behind, followed by X and then Wendig. Whale held rear guard with the Minigun, watching and listening.

X wasn't sure that even it would stop what they were hunting. The tracks in the mud were three times the size of Rhino's. He eyed the path the creature had taken to get around the vines. Branches thicker than his arm were snapped off at seven feet above the ground.

The submachine gun that X carried suddenly felt no more substantial than a slingshot, and the spear may as well be a mop handle.

He missed Ty, and thinking of him brought back a swarm of memories of the other friends he had lost over the years. But there wasn't time to think about those people now. He had to get the hell off this island and back to the living. Magnolia, Rodger, and Miles still needed his help.

A distant cracking sound snapped him alert, and he slowly scanned the green landscape of his night vision for the source. To the left of the road, several ruined houses, mostly just foundations and the bones of walls, stood between the trees.

Another cracking sound came from behind X, and a scorpion almost the size of Miles came skittering out of a pile of concrete. Whale split the creature in half with his axe, and the pincers clicked feebly as a pool of green blood spread outward.

Rhino ordered the team ahead, pointing with his spear. The tracks continued beside the road but jeered off on the right to avoid a section blocked by a fence of waist-high plants.

Spiked branches with suction-cup tentacles hung limp, looking almost harmless, but X knew better. Five years earlier, he had watched a pack of Sirens get tangled in them.

The barbs carried a venom that paralyzed their prey; then the tentacles sucked the victim dry. Days later, he had come across the dead Sirens. Their milky-white skin had shriveled over the bones, the flesh sucked out.

"Hold up," X said. "We need to find a way around those."

Rhino stopped and scanned the structures left of the road. Then he checked the tracks that diverged to the right.

Fuego raised his flamethrower and looked to Rhino.

"Wait," X said, holding up his hand. "You want to tell every beast where we are?"

Ignoring X, Rhino gave Fuego a nod and stepped

back. A jet of flames shot out of the barrel, engulfing the spiny black thicket. The tentacles came alive, squirming in the intense heat, before beginning to wither and turn to ash.

The men followed Rhino through the now-cleared path off the left side of the road, into a lightly vegetated area outside a two-story building. The concrete walls, probably built to withstand a hurricane, had withstood the test of time, and it still had part of a roof.

Framing the house on both sides were the remains of less resistant structures, now little more than foundations and basements full of dark water. X saw a V-shaped ripple cross the pool on his right and moved closer to the team.

He bumped off his night-vision goggles, relying on the glow of the burning thorn bushes behind him as he followed the others through the concrete building's open front doorway.

Columns held up a sagging roof over the entrance. Inside, a rusted metal stairwell led to a second floor. The team cautiously made its way up the stairs and across the creaky floorboards.

Rhino motioned X into one of the bedrooms. The only furnishings that had survived were the frames of metal chairs, and the rusted springs of a mattress. A tapestry of moss and mold covered the black walls.

Wendig's raspy breathing told X the man was in a lot of pain. He doubted they could count on him to help when they did find their target.

A roar snapped X from his thoughts.

He moved over to an empty window frame and watched the flames. Smoke rose from the smoldering plants, which continued to squirm and writhe like the giant octopus he had killed on the *Sea Wolf*.

Rhino moved beside X. "Hold your fire until it gets close," he said. "Aim for the eyes."

"Eyes?" X muttered, picturing a beast with eyes the size of a human. He watched the flames, realization setting in. The lieutenant wanted the beast to see the fire.

This was a trap. So why did X feel like bait?

Through the cracked wall between the two rooms, he could see Fuego and Whale, their weapons pointed out the windows.

X brought up his submachine gun and looked back to the flames. They were spreading into the forest across the road now, licking their way up a tree trunk to the limbs.

His eyes roved back and forth, searching the canopy and the terrain for any movement. Tree branches cracked, and X centered the barrel on a palm that jerked and then swayed from side to side. Its lavender fronds shook violently before the entire thing crashed to the ground. There came another cracking sound, like a bone being snapped.

"Get ready," Rhino said to X. He said something in Spanish to Wendig, who moved into the other room to tell Whale and Fuego.

Rhino's almond eye slots turned to X.

"You're about to meet the devil," he said. "If you

can take its head, you might impress el Pulpo. He's one of only a few men ever to kill one of these beasts."

Though X couldn't see his features, he picked up on the excitement in the Cazador lieutenant's voice. It made him wonder, did these people actually *enjoy* fighting monsters?

Wendig came back into the room, taking the window next to X's. Using the ledge as a bench rest, he got down on one knee and shouldered the rifle with his good arm.

The fire continued to spread into the jungle, hiding the trees and undergrowth behind a dense wall of flame. X moved his gun barrel from left to right, then back again. All at once, the foliage across the road came alive as hundreds of rodent-size insects skittered out of their lairs. The creatures were fleeing something besides the fire.

X flinched as the upper half of a flaming tree came flying across the road and through the open window in the other room. He turned just as the projectile smashed into Whale, in a shower of sparks. The biggest man X had ever seen flew backward like a straw doll.

Rhino shouted something in Spanish, then said, "I'm going to flank it."

Before X could react, the lieutenant was running out of the room and down the stairs.

X looked back to the road just as a walking nightmare burst out through the wall of fire. Swollen muscles flashed orange across a body as thick as one of the tree trunks. The thing opened a bony jaw and let out a roar louder than thunder.

Wendig and X answered the cry with automatic gunfire. In the other room, Fuego directed his flame nozzle onto the road, coating the beast as it lumbered toward the building.

Looking through the iron sights, X hardly believed what he was seeing. Unlike the Sirens, the monster didn't have a skin covering. And yet, the muscles didn't appear to be unprotected, and the head was almost all bone.

The burning beast brought up black-taloned hands to protect its eyes from the gunfire and flames. X had never seen one of these before, but Tin and Magnolia had described something similar that they'd encountered at the Hilltop Bastion.

Was this the type of beast that killed Commander Rick Weaver?

The thick pectorals rhythmically flashed orange, as if in time with its thumping heart, as it reached over its back. When the creature brought its arm back down, the claws held a bony dart the length of a man's forearm.

It threw the projectile, but X ducked just in time to avoid it. A long, sharp bone thudded into the wall and stuck like an arrow, quivering.

X rose back to his feet and waited to get a shot at the creature's eyes, as Rhino had instructed. The monster hunched down as it ran toward the house. For such a large beast, it moved surprisingly fast, darting from tree to tree for cover.

As it moved, X saw it kept the bone shard darts stowed in the flesh of its own body, in the meaty part just above the shoulder. From this angle, they appeared to fan out around its neck like some kind of morbid spiky collar.

About fifty feet away now, it flexed its muscles and let out a deafening guttural roar. The noise was louder than a dozen Sirens at close range, and the upgraded speakers he had installed in his helmet amplified the noise even more.

The echo continued even after the monster stopped screaming. Ears ringing, X peeked above the window frame to see the beast pulling another bony dart.

He brought up his gun and held the trigger down, riddling the monster with bullets. It stumbled back but then threw the projectile, this time at Fuego, who unleashed another rope of flame at the same moment.

X looked over into the next room as the bony missile hit the tank over Fuego's shoulder, punching right through the thick steel. The soldier screamed at the top of his lungs and continued hurling flames at the beast.

"No!" X yelled, diving away. But it was too late. Fuego exploded in a massive fireball that burst through the opening in the wall and slammed into X and Wendig.

Flaming shrapnel punched into the walls, ceiling, and floor. X felt the burn of something in his leg and then his arm, then all across his back. He rolled on the floor to put out the fire.

His optics winked off, shrouding him in darkness for a moment. The flames provided enough light to show Wendig, lying in a fetal position and groaning.

X couldn't hear much, just the dull ringing and then a clanking sound and, finally, a human scream—not of pain but of anger.

He pushed himself up to the window to see Rhino standing in front of the structure. A wave of dizziness dropped X back to the floor, where he took several deep breaths. He felt no loyalty to the Cazador lieutenant, but he had to help before the abomination killed them all.

Come on, Xavier. Get up or get cooked …

X pushed up from the floor a second time and then crashed back down again. He rolled onto his back to find a hunk of shrapnel in his thigh armor. Another piece had stuck in his shoulder pad, and a third was lodged in the side of his helmet, just above the visor. He wasn't sure any of them had penetrated, but he couldn't swear that the warm wetness in his suit was just sweat. *Could be piss …*

I hope it's just piss.

The floor of the room to his left suddenly collapsed, crashing to the first floor. X had a feeling the floor under his boots was next. He managed to get up, holding steady during a wave of dizziness. His vision cleared to see Wendig reaching up.

Fuck you.

X grabbed his rifle and walked away, but hesitated when he reached the doorway. He had killed this guy's cousin, and now he was leaving him to burn alive?

He would leave you to burn.

Right?

"Don't make me regret this, you prick," X said. He stumbled back over and grabbed Wendig's hand. Planting his boots against the uneven floor, moving inches at a time, he dragged Wendig out of the room. Then he helped him up, pulled the good arm over one shoulder, and got him down the stairs.

Outside the building, the grunting and roaring continued as Rhino fought the beast with his double-headed spear.

X began to cough as he staggered down the steps with Wendig. The smoke had started to infiltrate his helmet now that his battery wasn't working to power the filter. He stopped to fiddle with the battery, which had been knocked loose from its socket, but even when he clicked it back into position, it didn't activate.

It was just another way for him to die, he thought as they reached the bottom of the stairwell—cooked alive in this formfitting armor oven.

Most of the lower room was on fire when X spotted Whale lying beneath the half a tree that the beast had hurled through the window.

He and Wendig moved over to help, but it took only a glance to see that the big guy wasn't getting back up. The log had crushed Whale's chest plate, and a branch had sheared off the bottom of his helmet and unhinged his jaw.

And yet, somehow, he was still breathing.

Wendig reached down with his good hand. He yelled in Spanish, gesturing for X to help.

"You fucking serious, man?" X said. It didn't take a genius to see that Whale was done.

But to X's astonishment, Whale grabbed his axe off the ground and then used the haft to push himself to his feet. Blood leaked out of his cracked chest armor and trickled from his broken jaw.

He brought the axe up, and for a fleeting moment, X backed away, thinking Whale was going to swing on him. Instead, he stumbled through the burning room and led the way outside, where Rhino and the beast dueled.

The fires in the forest and the building gave X his first close-up view of their enemy. It stood seven feet tall and had a muscular frame wider than two men.

Its taloned hands parried Rhino's double-headed spear, deflecting the blow with a loud clang. The beast took several steps backward, turning a gray armored back with the collar of spikes.

It brought a fist down toward the top of Rhino's helmet. Rhino raised the spear, but the shaft snapped in two, and a talon shrieked down his chest armor.

Whale staggered forward and swung his axe down on the back of the beast, lodging the blade between two of the bony spikes. It let out a roar and turned on its attacker.

"No!" Wendig shouted. He fired the handgun in his good hand, and X pointed his submachine gun at the eyes, but the weapon clicked on a jammed round.

Rhino jabbed one end of his broken spear into the monster's neck from the side, earning himself a backhand that sent him crashing to the ground. Whale punched the monster in the face with his brass knuckles, with an audible cracking of bone. Doubling over in pain, he fell to his knees in front of the beast as it reared backward, one hand to its face.

Letting out an enraged scream, it grabbed Whale by the helmet in both hands and popped his head off like a cork from a bottle. Then it tossed the head at X as the body slumped over, squirting twin jets of blood into the air.

Wendig struggled to change the magazine in his pistol, and X grabbed the sheathed blade off his duty belt as the monster lumbered toward them.

Behind it, Rhino was getting back to his feet. He picked up one of the broken spear shafts and made a run for the creature as X and Wendig backed away.

A boom and crack sounded behind them as the house collapsed in a billowing cloud of glowing embers. Sirens, spectators to the violence, circled overhead, waiting for a chance at fresh-killed meat.

When X turned back to the monster, it had stopped to sniff the air. Rhino used the opportunity to grab the haft of the axe still jammed in its back, and wrenched it free. When it turned toward him, he jammed the other half of his broken spear into its eye.

X moved to flank the thing while Rhino brought the axe down on its chest, sinking the blade deep in its muscle. Blood welled out, covering Rhino in carmine.

The shriek that followed sent all three men reeling backward. The noise was unbearable, even now that X's speakers were offline. He fell to his knees, gripping his helmet where his ears were to no avail.

In its rage, the creature turned and kicked Wendig, sending him skidding across the dirt and into the flooded basement of a neighboring house.

X stood and turned away from the beast, making it a few feet before it picked him up by one leg, and flung him through the air. He landed on his back near Rhino. The impact knocked the air from his lungs, but it also saved his life. If he had landed facedown, the shards of shrapnel would have been driven through his armor, suit, and flesh.

Another roar sounded as X rolled up to a sitting position. He blinked and blinked, trying to get a view of Rhino. The lieutenant, weaponless, was back on his feet now with his fists up as the creature approached.

He jumped back to avoid a swipe of curved talons. Then he threw a punch at the jaw, which did little more than fuel the creature's rage. It reached out and grabbed Rhino by the neck, lifting him off the ground, as X finally got to his feet.

He staggered the first few steps but then managed a trot. The creature lifted Rhino higher until his boots were a good three feet off the ground. X looked for something to fight with, and his eyes narrowed in on the spiky apparitions on the beast's back. He grabbed one and pulled with all his strength.

The beast dropped Rhino's limp body to the

ground and whirled toward X, hunching down and screeching. X jabbed the spike at its remaining eye but missed, and talons slashed his chest armor.

He smacked down on his back again as the monster towered over him. Reaching down, it plucked him off the ground and raised him into the air. The huge hand clamped down on his throat, cutting off the air and threatening to crush his windpipe.

He flailed with his arm, trying to find something to grab—something to fight back with. Over the years, he had survived because he always left himself an out, but this time, he didn't have any.

The beast pulled him closer to its face. As X's vision faded in and out, he looked into the soulless gaze of a monster straight from the pits of hell. And in the reflection from that baleful eye, he saw the triangle of shrapnel sticking out of his helmet, just above the visor. Leaving the pointed shard lodged where it was, he rammed his head into the monster's eye.

The mutant howled in agony and dropped X to the dirt, where he scrambled away.

X filled his lungs with air, and as his vision cleared, he watched a dripping wet man limp across the dirt with a broken spear in his hand. He approached the monster, waited, and then jammed the blade into the roof of its open mouth.

The ground shook as if a tree had fallen.

X also collapsed, allowing himself a breather.

He felt a hand on his shoulder a moment later and glanced up at Wendig. Reaching down with his good hand, the warrior helped X to his feet. They staggered over to Rhino, who was slowing coming to.

"You okay?" X asked.

Rhino pushed himself up and looked at the dead monster. All three of them stared for several seconds, catching their breath.

"Impressive, Immortal," Rhino finally said. "Only one thing left to do now: take the head."

"I wasn't the one to bring it down." X nodded to Wendig, who had already grabbed Whale's axe. Using his good hand, the injured Barracuda hacked at the neck, in the flicker of the raging fires.

SEVENTEEN

"Timothy Pepper of the *Sea Wolf* is not responding to any messages," Sandy said from the bridge.

Katrina swore under her breath. Losing the AI had severed their one connection to the Metal Islands. She had just left the medical ward, where Eevi had wrapped a bandage around her chest.

Pain from the bruised rib stopped her halfway up the ladder. The dent in her armor could be pounded back into place, but it would take weeks to recover from the injury.

Wincing, she took in a shallow breath and let it out. She was lucky. The bullet could easily have pierced her armor and killed her. But it didn't. She was still alive, and she was about to have an enemy ship and a trawler in her possession. Aside from the news about Timothy, today was shaping up to be a good day.

But before she could celebrate over the two captured craft, she had to make sure she had neutralized the threats on them. She continued up to the ops command center for a better view. Trey and Alexander were here, scanning the waters for any Cazador soldiers who may have escaped the slaughter.

The USS *Zion* was a good distance away from the two main enemy ships and the expanse of sea where the .50-cals had chewed apart the smaller vessels, but the Hell Divers were not to take any chances.

The other divers were belowdecks in the combat information center or on the bridge, monitoring the weapons and scanning the water for heat signatures.

"Captain," Trey said.

Alexander nodded and handed her a pair of binoculars. She aimed them at the bay, where smoke rose off the smoldering flotsam, and corpses wearing life jackets floated amid the debris.

"Captain, we have the MK-65 turret aimed at the container ship," Alexander said, "but so far we haven't seen much movement."

Katrina centered the binos on the ship. Fire still burned in the operations tower, whose metal skin splayed outward like a crown.

On the deck, several stacks of containers had toppled onto their sides. Others floated low in the water. The starboard hull had gaping holes from several shell impacts, some of them still billowing smoke.

The devastation made her wonder whether the vessel could be salvaged. She was honestly surprised it wasn't on the bottom of the bay.

"What should we do with the live ones?" Alexander asked.

"I say let 'em drown," Trey replied.

She moved the binos back to the water between the *Zion* and the Cazador container ship. Clicking a button, she turned on the infrared function. Multiple heat signatures lit up.

Several soldiers hung on to their damaged vessels. Of the original warriors, only about ten to fifteen were still alive, and many of them had to be mortally wounded.

"We could always run 'em over," Trey said.

Katrina lowered the binos to look at the young diver. "Your father would not be proud of that suggestion."

"Why have mercy on them?" Trey asked. "There's no way in hell they would do the same for us."

"If I may," Alexander said. "We used almost thirty percent of the working ammunition, so whatever we do, it shouldn't involve any more of our reserves."

"I do agree with that," Katrina replied. She looked back out over the flaming junkyard strewn across the water. She didn't have enough personnel to take these people captive, or the medical supplies to treat them for their injuries.

The other divers looked at her, waiting for her decision.

"We leave them," Katrina said firmly.

Alexander and Trey both nodded, awaiting her next orders. She considered them carefully and decided to move forward with the salvage operation.

"I want a fire team ready to board the container ship as soon as possible," she said. "I'll take lead again."

"What!" Alexander said. "All due respect, Captain, but you're injured, and needed here. Let me take lead."

"I agree with Alexander," Trey said. "You need to rest."

Katrina put a hand to the bandage wrapped around her chest. They were right; she just didn't want to admit it. She was used to leading by example, but this time she was in no condition. If anything, she would just be a liability to the other divers.

"Okay, fine, but take Vish with you," she said.

Alexander forced a smile. "Don't worry, I got this."

"What do we do with the live ones on that ship?" Trey asked.

"Depends on who they are," she said. "If you discover civilians, then we'll take them captive, but if they're soldiers, you shoot to kill."

"Understood, ma'am," Trey said. He turned, but Katrina thought she saw him crack a half grin.

"Be careful, Trey. You, too, Alexander."

They both nodded and walked down the ladder to the bridge, where Eevi and Sandy were busy monitoring their stations.

"Weigh anchor," Katrina ordered. She pulled the receiver off the comm station and connected to the CIC. "Vish, report to the cargo bay ASAP. Jaideep, Edgar, you stay on those weapons and fire on anything that comes close to us. We're leaving the bay."

"Aye, aye, Captain," Edgar replied.

Katrina turned to see Alexander and Eevi embrace. They held each other for several seconds in a tight hug. The stolen moment gave her time to question her own orders. What if more enemy sailors were hiding on the boat?

"Captain, how are you feeling?" Sandy asked.

Katrina decided to let her orders stand. She limped over to Sandy.

"I'm fine—just a bruised rib," she said. "How are you holding up?"

Sandy lifted a shoulder. "I thought killing Cazadores would make me feel better, but I don't know. I almost feel … guilty."

Katrina pondered the words. Part of her felt the same way.

"This is war, Sandy," she said. "We have to be strong. It's only going to get harder from here on out."

A beep sounded—a welcome distraction.

"Anchors up, Captain," Sandy said.

Katrina bit the inside of her lip and moved over to her station. She tapped the touch screen, and brought up the controls, plotting a course around the bay to flank the container ship and the fishing vessel.

A message from the cargo bay played over the comms as she worked.

"We're ready to move out," Alexander said.

"Stand by for my order," Katrina said. She hit another button to raise the hatches over the broken porthole windows, giving her a view of the burning container ship.

Her eyes flitted from the view outside to her screen. The scanners continued to search the waters for hostiles. Eevi had manually adjusted the sensors to pick up anything the size of a human. They had tried it on the container ship, but the fires were messing with the infrared sensors.

Katrina steered the warship out of the bay, providing a new view of the fishing vessel in the distance. She cursed when she saw that it was moving.

A flash of lightning confirmed what she thought she had seen in the darkness. Now that the trawler's engines were out, the Cazadores aboard were trying to escape under sail.

She picked up the receiver to connect back to the CIC. "Edgar, I want you to target that fishing boat with the MK-65, but hold your fire until I give the order."

"Roger that, Captain."

She put the receiver back down and kept the heading toward the container ship. Smoke dissipated from the bridge as a light rain suffocated the fires. The drops pattered inside the porthole frames on the *Zion*, but Katrina kept the hatches open to give her a view of their target.

She used the manual controls to guide the warship around the two Cazador vessels. The MK-65's enclosed turret rotated toward the fishing ship. Her plan was to board the container ship first, clear it, and then go after the trawler.

"Alexander, Trey, Vish, you're clear to launch," she said.

The team left the ship in a second Zodiac.

It wasn't long before they came into view. Blue battery units ascended a ladder to the davits from which the Cazadores had lowered their boats.

Eevi and Sandy moved over to the porthole windows with Katrina to watch. They were close enough that Katrina could see dead bodies with her NVGs. The blue glow of the Hell Divers faded away, melting into the interior passages.

"We're in," Alexander said over the comms.

A beeping sound issued from the radar station, and Katrina motioned for Sandy to check the monitor. Eevi remained beside Katrina, chewing on a fingernail as her husband moved deeper into the ship.

"They will be okay," Katrina said, trying to reassure Eevi.

"Uh, Captain," Sandy said, "looks like those sensors have picked up multiple heat signatures in the bay, moving fast."

"Is it possible one of the boats came back online?" Katrina asked.

"I'm not sure," Sandy said.

Katrina moved back to the ladder. "Eevi, you have the bridge. I'm headed back to the command center."

"Got it, Captain."

Katrina stopped halfway up to catch her breath and hold her aching chest. Then she continued to the top and centered her binos on the bay. The green hue of the night-vision optics didn't reveal any moving vessels.

Distant gunshots rang out from the container

ship, and a voice came over the comms. "Captain, we're engaging a group of four Cazadores," Alexander said. "Two are down, two more on the run."

Be careful, God damn it.

She trained the binos on the ship, but a quick scan revealed nothing. She turned them back to the bay and switched to infrared. Sure enough, a pair of red heat signatures moved through the water.

Katrina switched to night vision, expecting to see Cazadores using oars or paddles to escape in boats. But these weren't boats, and they weren't Cazadores.

"My God," she whispered. The two sharks were fifty feet long, almost double anything from the books she had read growing up.

Dorsal fins cut the surface as they navigated the debris field and searched for food. She zoomed in to see one of the beasts swallow a flailing survivor in a single bite.

The other men tried to climb onto the destroyed boats. One of them made it onto a WaveRunner just as a shark grabbed his leg, severing it with razor-sharp teeth. The soldier slumped into the water, where the second shark inhaled the rest of him.

In a matter of minutes, the two monsters had picked the bay clean of bodies, living or dead. Katrina stared in horror, holding the binos to her eyes as the sharks turned and swam toward the USS *Zion*.

Another message crackled from the comm system. "Captain, this is Alexander, do you copy?"

"Go ahead, Alexander, I copy," she replied, trying to mask her fear.

"We have neutralized all hostiles so far, and ... we found something, Captain."

"Found what?"

"You're going to have to see this to believe it."

* * * * *

The hybrid human lay unconscious on the metal table, water dripping off its wrinkled flesh. Layla had pumped the guy full of morphine after taking him out of the chamber, but Les wasn't convinced that would keep him from getting back up and doing what he warned them of: killing them all.

He checked the straps on the man's wrists and metal ankles. They seemed secure, but metal limbs were powerful, even though they were attached to a body that looked over a hundred years old.

Michael checked the restraints over his legs. "He's secure. Go ahead and hook him up to the computer."

Les reluctantly uncoiled a cable from his gear and connected the nodes to the man's neck. Then he plugged in his wrist monitor and raised his arm to check the vitals.

This couldn't be right.

"How is this guy still alive?" Les asked. "I'm not getting a heart rate, and he doesn't look like he's breathing."

"That is because he has no heart and no lungs,"

Timothy said. "But if you take a closer look at your monitor, I'm sure you will see electrical activity in the brain, which is actually a computer the size of a fly—a fruit fly."

Les did a double take as he saw what looked like brain waves on his screen.

"I don't like this," he repeated for the fifth time. "What's the point of talking to this … guy. Especially after what he said when he was still in the tank."

The words repeated in his mind.

Destroy me before I kill you all.

"I want to ask him a few questions," Michael said. "Maybe he can help us."

Les tried not to snap, but this was crazy. "Commander, he just said he would kill us all if he got the chance. Did you not hear that?"

Timothy folded his arms across his translucent suit jacket. "That's why I suggested hooking him up to a monitor. I should be able to hack into his brain while he is unconscious. There is little risk to you all from doing this."

"Little risk?" Les asked. "The guy is basically a defector with skin. Remember? The machines that nearly killed us the last time we came to this hell hole?"

"He's asleep, Lieutenant," Michael said. "And we have him secured to the table. I say we let Timothy do this."

Layla looked over at Les. "Before we leave, I personally want to know what work was being conducted here. We may never have the opportunity again."

"The answers reside in his skull," Timothy said. "He may also know where the defectors are."

"You guys are nuts," Les said. "You, too, Pepper."

"I do take slight offense at that," the AI replied.

Les heaved a breath, fogging the inside of his visor. "Well, if you're going to hack in, hurry up. I want to find what we came here for and get out of this underwater dungeon."

"What else do you need from us?" Michael asked Timothy.

The AI moved over to the head of the table, where the hybrid's metal crown rested. "Hook up the electrical nodes to Layla's computer, and I will get started."

They worked quickly, Layla doing most of the prep. After she had finished hooking up the cords to the additional computer, she took out her tablet.

"You're up," she said to Timothy.

The AI flickered several times and closed his eyelids. "Tapping into the network … working on getting past the firewall …"

Les directed his flashlight through the other labs as they waited, growing increasingly uneasy. They had been down here over eight hours already, and he wanted to get moving.

"This firewall is tricky," Timothy said.

Les paced as they waited, and checked his submachine gun several times. He had a round chambered, and he knew that the magazine was full, but he was nervous, and fidgeting with the gun took his mind off the reality of his situation—at least, for a few moments. But it wasn't long before he focused back on the situation.

Trey was sailing across the dangerous seas for the Metal Islands, and more than Cazadores were out there waiting. He needed to get back to his boy.

"We're in," Timothy finally said.

Les moved back to Michael and Layla, who hovered behind her tablet. She placed it on a lab table, using the kickstand to keep it upright.

"I'm scanning millions of documents, downloads, and memories," the AI said. "But I'm narrowing the search to anything that may contain … Ah, here we go."

A video feed came on.

"This will give Layla a good idea of the work they were performing here," Timothy added.

The familiar face of an olive-skinned man wearing a surgical mask around his neck came online. He smiled at the camera.

"This is Dr. Julio Diaz, recording on February fifteenth, 2041. We are now operational and beginning our tests on the first subject."

The camera panned from the young doctor to a white calf with black spots. Cables led away from the plastic skin protecting the animal, and four mechanical legs.

"This is Spade," Julio said. "As you can see, we've removed all four of his limbs and replaced them with robotic limbs. These vacuum-sealed biostasis vats will accelerate the healing process. Once that's done, we will begin the tough part of my work: replacing parts of the brain with our new microchips."

Les looked over at the man lying on the table. Had he been one of Julio's patients 260 years ago?

Not possible.

Les remembered the boneyard he and Michael had found on one of the ships docked outside. Bones from humans and animals. The defectors had worn some of them as decorations. A memory of a machine sporting a cow skull surfaced in his mind as he looked back at the calf on the video.

What sort of macabre experiment was going on here?

Timothy brought up a new video dated seven days later. The calf was standing, using the new mechanical limbs to walk around the white lab. It stumbled, fell, and pushed itself back up.

"Today, we will begin the process of removing Spade's brain and replacing it with a microchip," Julio said. "Once this process is complete, we should be able to control the animal—much like operating a remote-control drone."

Another video popped online, showing the surgery. Julio and several members of his team were dressed in white surgical gowns, but they weren't performing the surgery themselves. They were sitting at consoles and supervising as a surgical robot with six white limbs worked on removing the top of the calf's skull.

"Is that an ITC spider?" Layla asked. She wasn't

looking at the screen, but at the machines in the corner of the room.

"Yes," Timothy said.

"I mean *those*," Layla said, pointing.

The AI turned from the table. "Oh, yes, those are the same machines that performed the surgery you're watching now. I believe we have one on *Deliverance*."

Les didn't know much about it—only that it used similar technology to the early da Vinci surgical systems that were discontinued and taken over by ITC, like most technology in the twenty-first century.

"I'm excited to begin the final stage of our little friend's journey," Julio said. "Once we complete the transition to mechanical parts, we will then begin the most important part of our research: to make Spade the longest-living cow in the history of his species."

"Did I miss something?" Layla asked.

Timothy paused the video. "Yes, I believe we did. Let me see if I can go further back."

Les scanned the labs again and locked his headlamp on the medical machines in the corner. The spiders were really starting to freak him out.

"Relax, Lieutenant," Michael said, although Les could hear the edge to his voice, too. "Aside from this guy, we're alone down here."

"I just want to get this mission over with," said Les. "We still don't even know where the defectors are." He looked at the mission clock. "We're going on nine hours down here."

"I know, I know," Michael said.

"Here we go," Timothy said.

The divers turned back to the tablet. Dr. Diaz and his team clinked glasses on the deck of a villa overlooking the ocean. Clouds crossed the blue sky as they celebrated, and a breeze rustled the fronds of palm trees on the beach.

"Good evening," Julio said. "Today, I want to thank every one of you. We have come a long way in a short time. That the United States Navy commissioned us for biostasis research just five years ago is hard enough to believe. And now we have secured our biggest contract yet, with Industrial Tech Corporation's biomedical division. This will allow us to take our research a step further, using animal-machine hybrids that will help us in our goal of increasing the quality and length of human life."

He raised his glass again, and the rest of the team followed suit.

"Interesting," Timothy said as soon as the video ended. "I have just completed a scan of some other files and discovered that Dr. Diaz's team was using tardigrades and wood frogs in its research on stabilizing cells to survive harsh conditions such as freezing."

"ITC was working to extend biological life spans," Layla said.

"Yeah," Michael said. "Like, trying for immortality."

Les shook his helmet in dismay as he looked at the wizened old half man, half machine on the table. "If you call the singularity 'immortality.' I don't call that living if you take away what it means to be human. I mean, come on, this guy doesn't even have a *heart*."

"It's just more evidence that humans created the world we live in," Michael said. "We created these things, the defectors, and the virus that caused the blackout during World War Three."

Silence settled over the divers. Even Timothy remained quiet. He unfolded his arms and let them hang, as if he didn't know what to do with them.

"Is there anything else?" Layla asked. "Do we know who this guy is?"

Les put his machine gun in the other hand. "How about where the defectors are?"

Timothy scratched his meticulously trimmed jawline. "One moment, please."

The tablet screen glowed again, and this time a video came online of one of the defectors dragging a man into the lab by his shredded legs. Blood streaked across the trail behind them.

He squirmed and screamed in the machine's grip. "Stop, please! I beg you! I will destroy all my research. I promise!"

The orange visor of the defector dragging the man flashed.

"So is that Dr. Diaz?" Layla asked, leaning closer to the tablet.

Another machine reached down and grabbed the man by the arm, helping the first one lift him onto a table.

"This was recorded in the same lab we're in now," Timothy said.

The video feed moved over a row of tables beside Julio. A woman lay on her back, her features erased by a gaping hole in her face.

"That must be what's left of Dana," Michael said.

"So Julio never escaped after diving into the ocean," Les said.

Before anyone could answer, a recorded scream made the three of them start.

The two defectors raised their long arms, their exoskeletons opened, and mechanical saws extended. The blades came to life, the whine rising over the doctor's screams as they lowered to his flesh.

The machines started on his legs and then worked their way up to remove his arms, each time searing the wound to stem the blood loss.

He was still conscious when they moved to his head, but Les had to look away when they started on his chest. The grotesque scene was too much even for him.

As the surgery scene played on the tablet, the man on the table in front of the Hell Divers began to quiver. His body convulsed, and the robotic limbs rattled against their metal restraints.

Les went to get morphine from the medical pack. They had to get him sedated again. Apparently, the memory was stirring this man awake.

But why? Unless …

"Holy shit," Les gasped. "Is this guy Dr. Diaz?"

The thin, wrinkled lips of the man on the table opened. "No," he croaked. "No, stop. Ple-e-e-e-ease!"

"Unplug those cords," Michael said to Layla. She quickly pulled the sensor nodes away from the head, but it was already too late. The man-machine broke one of his restraints with ease. The eyelids snapped open, both the human eye and the mechanical one homing in on Les. The freed metal arm reached toward him, and Les jumped back just before the robotic fingers could grab his wrist.

The divers all backed away as the hybrid doctor snapped all the other restraints. It sat up and tilted its wrinkled face at them. Layla reached out to grab the electrical cords, but the hybrid was faster. He smacked her with his robotic arm, knocking her backward into a table.

Michael fired a laser bolt at the machine as it moved. The blue flash took off its right arm at the shoulder. Les aimed his rifle at the head and fired a burst that missed, punching into the wall.

The hybrid got up on all fours, directing its gaze at Les. But this wasn't the same soulless gaze he had seen in the other machines. Part of Dr. Julio Diaz was in there—the same part that had begged the divers to destroy him when they found him in the stasis chamber.

Michael squeezed off another bolt, this one sizzling through the chest and bringing the hybrid to the ground, where it landed on its back, twitching.

"Hold your fire," Michael said to Les. He looked over at Layla. "You okay?"

She was already getting back up but had her hand on her belly. "I … I think so."

Timothy held up a hand to stop Michael from shooting again. "We still don't know where the defectors are," he said. "Before you destroy Dr. Diaz, perhaps we should ask him."

Michael kept the laser rifle aimed at the downed machine. Its chest smoked and sparked, and blood leaked from the shoulder of the severed arm. The hybrid continued twitching. "Defectors …" it said in a cracking voice.

Timothy bent down and said, "Doctor, please tell us where the DEF-Nine units are."

The hybrid rotated his head toward the AI. "Gone. They left after an … attack … There is only one left now."

The words chilled Les, but they didn't stop him from stepping closer to the hybrid. "Where did they go?"

The hybrid looked up at him. "Intercepted a … signal, but I do not know their destination." The wrinkled forehead creased in anguish. "Please … you must destroy me."

"You achieved your goal of immortality," Layla said as she limped over.

"No," Michael said. "No one lives forever. Not even X."

He fired a bolt through Julio's skull, ending his suffering. Michael lowered the weapon and walked over to the robotic arm he had blown off. Picking it up, he looked over at the spider machines in the corner.

"No," Les said. "You can't be serious, Commander."

"We came here for defectors, and I'm not leaving without something that will help us when we get to the Metal Islands," Michael said. "Besides, now you guys can call me 'Tin' again."

They didn't quite laugh, but the words helped ease the tension.

"Timothy, do you think you can get that spider on *Deliverance* up and running?" Michael asked.

"Certainly, sir."

EIGHTEEN

The dirty yellow glow of the lighthouse beacon shone through the mist, providing a beacon for the two surviving members of the Barracudas and Hell Diver Xavier Rodriguez. They had hiked for hours through the mutated jungle. X was slogging along on fumes. By the time they got back to the outskirts of the city, he had reached the point of exhaustion that would make most men collapse.

Rhino moved by his side. The Cazador lieutenant hadn't spoken of his injuries, but it was obvious he had taken a severe beating from the bizarre creature back in the jungle. Despite the pain, he marched on until Wendig finally raised a hand and sat down on a boulder to rest.

"*Un minuto*," Rhino said to Wendig. "Take a minute, Immortal."

X sat on the ground, using the time to catch his breath and do a systems check of his armor and suit. Blood and ash covered him from head to toe, as if he had taken a bath in gore and then rolled in a fire pit. But at least he'd been able to get his suit back online and operating.

He took a sip from the straw, sucking mostly air. The lonely shriek of a Siren made him reach for the sword they had retrieved from the debris pile. Rhino yielded the axe Whale had dropped, and Wendig raised a handgun, scanning the skies.

Seeing the two remaining members in their sorry state reminded X of just how much the Barracudas had suffered on this mission. And for what? The trophy head slung over Wendig's shoulder?

What a waste of life, X thought.

In a way, these men reminded him of Hell Divers on a mission gone awry, like the one that killed his entire team ten years ago thanks to a faulty weather sensor. The day that his best friend, Aaron, died.

No, he realized. These men were nothing like Hell Divers.

X cursed himself for even making a comparison. Hell Divers risked their lives to save humanity. The Barracudas hunted for personal honor and privilege.

The shriek of the Siren faded away, and the team pressed ahead. Over the next ridge, X noticed that the glow from the lighthouse beacon had stopped.

"Why'd they turn it off?" he asked.

"Because they are getting ready to leave," Rhino said. He said something in Spanish and reached out to help Wendig. After watching the beast kick him into the water-filled basement, X was surprised he could walk at all.

"Got to move faster," X said.

Rhino simply nodded, and Wendig looked over but didn't reply. His arm was in a sling, and he was having a hard time walking.

They pushed onward as thunder boomed above them. A light rain pattered on their armor, but it wasn't a cooling rain—acidic, according to the readings on his HUD.

X wiped his visor clean and helped Rhino cut away vegetation growing on the path. They worked together for several minutes, but there was no good way forward.

The vines and spiny bushes grew in deep thickets around the foundations of ruined buildings. X stumbled as he swung his sword, nearly falling into a tangle of the carnivorous vines.

Keep it together, old man.

An exhausting hour later, they could finally see the beach. The boats still waited on the sand. He breathed a sigh of relief. The Cazadores hadn't left without them.

Almost back … Keep moving.

X was going to reward himself with a long nap on the voyage back to the Metal Islands.

Rhino put an arm under Wendig as they moved down a steep incline to the debris-filled street below. Closing in on the lighthouse, X saw the first sign of the battle that had raged against the Siren hordes.

Several of the beasts littered the road in a circle around a single Cazador soldier. The man had killed five of the creatures before their talons opened his armor and strung his entrails away from his corpse.

The grisly sight reminded X of Hades, but he pushed the memory away and followed Rhino and Wendig around the corner. A group of four men on sentry duty brought up their rifles.

"Easy," X said, raising his hands in the air. Covered in gore and dirt as they were, the team probably looked a lot like the monsters they had been fighting.

Instead of putting up his hands, Rhino yelled at the grunt soldiers, who quickly lowered their weapons and backed away from the makeshift barrier to let the group through.

All four helmets turned to Wendig and the bony head slung over his armored shoulder as he limped past.

"*El rey demonio,*" one of them said.

The four grunts all pounded the octopus logo on their chests.

"What did they say?" X asked Rhino.

"'The demon king.'"

"That's what you call that thing we took down?"

Rhino nodded. "But I call it the 'bone beast.' There aren't many of them left."

"What was it? I mean, what did it evolve from?"

Rhino shrugged his massive shoulders. "A bear, maybe? Who knows?"

"There weren't bears out here, I don't think."

"Does it matter?" Rhino asked.

X shook his head. "Not especially."

Rhino called out over his shoulder at the four soldiers.

"*Somos todo lo que queda.*"

The men all grabbed their gear and fell in line.

Rhino walked by X. "They thought there would be more of us," he said. "Come on, let's get back to the boats."

The small group set off down another street, where they had to climb over a pile of rubble that blocked the way. At the crest, Rhino raised his hand to several soldiers on the other side. The men all looked up from their work of checking bodies and salvaging weapons and gear. Armored heaps lay on the asphalt—soldiers who had died of their wounds.

The thick of the battle appeared to have been right here.

Siren carcasses lay among the dead, their eggshell-white bodies hacked to pieces. Limbs, heads, and torsos littered the road while other bodies were still strangely intact, their charred flesh still smoking.

But they weren't all dead.

The clank of metal rang out from the road ahead. X stopped to watch wagons laden with cages. The convoy crossed through the intersection. A boxy metal vehicle moved slowly on tracks over the broken concrete, pulling the wagons behind it.

An octopus symbol marked the hull of the ancient

war machine, which reminded X of a vehicle he had taken refuge in years ago with Miles.

Rhino kept walking, but X stood staring at the wagons. Inside the cages, Sirens were chained to the floor, unable to move. Gags covered their mouths to prevent them from shrieking and biting.

X had captured a few of the beasts back in Florida, but he always killed them. He still couldn't believe the Cazadores ate these things, but seeing their warrior culture, he now understood why. They believed that the meat of a worthy foe made them more powerful.

Rhino quickened his pace as the wagons began to move around another corner. The vehicle pulling them crunched over a pile of broken concrete, crushing it beneath the tracks.

A group of about forty soldiers marched alongside the wagons. Was this all that remained of the fighting force that landed on this beach only hours ago?

Catching up with the group, X saw the answer on the beach just below the lighthouse. The support crew of sailors in the green military uniforms had come up from the beaches and were stripping dead Cazadores brought down from the city.

Some of the men had already completed their tasks and arranged the corpses neatly in the sand. They made four rows, ten deep. Adding the other losses in his mind, X counted fifty to sixty dead soldiers.

On the *Hive*, such a loss would have been a disaster, but unlike in the sky, the Metal Islands seemed to have no shortage of warriors.

Still, he couldn't believe how costly this mission had been for el Pulpo.

He walked up along behind the wagons. The very last cart carried Siren children. These weren't chained like the adults, but their mouths were covered in gags and masks.

"For the sky arena," Rhino said, jerking his helmet at the kids. "Whale used to fight them with his brass knuckles. I'm going to miss that."

X picked up some sadness in his rough voice and had a feeling that it wasn't just the breathing apparatus of his helmet. He didn't exactly have empathy for Rhino, but he did know what it was like to lose close friends.

A crunch sounded as the tracked vehicle pulling the wagons ran over a dead Siren. The head imploded, painting the broken asphalt with blood and brains. The vehicle continued at a crawl and began turning toward the boat ramp.

Voices called out, and the final preparations began on the beach. The remaining soldiers moved to the rowboats while green-uniformed sailors loaded gear and weapons.

X scanned the ocean for their ship and saw it still anchored about a mile out.

"Immortal, come here," Rhino said. He climbed onto a boulder and raised his arms, attracting the attention of the men. The soldiers and sailors abandoned their tasks to form a circle around him.

Most of these men were covered in blood and moved sluggishly. A few had severe injuries and cracks in their armor, which would end up killing them if they didn't get back to the ships soon.

But whatever Rhino had to say was apparently more important.

"Today we have achieved victory," he yelled. "Today we came and conquered the demon king."

He repeated the message in Spanish to great applause. The soldiers raised blades and fists in the air as Wendig held up the head of *el rey demonio*, or, as Rhino called it, the bone beast.

The men beat their chests, riling up the Sirens, which struggled against their chains in the cages. The soldiers and sailors stood there for several minutes while Rhino continued his victory speech.

X turned away, unable to take part in what would have been a solemn gathering on the *Hive*. Most of the time, when Hell Divers didn't come back, there were tears, not shouts of triumph.

As he looked out over the waves, he felt a hand on his shoulder.

X turned, expecting to see Rhino, but it was Wendig.

Rhino finished his speech and jumped down off the boulder. The other men dispersed, and he joined X and Wendig. "You did good today, Immortal," he said. "Wendig agrees and would be proud to fight with you another day."

X snorted. "Just because I helped you fight those monsters doesn't mean I don't think you guys are assholes."

Rhino laughed, and Wendig tilted his helmet slightly in confusion as Rhino explained.

"We still think you're an asshole, too," Rhino said. "Now, come on, let's get back to the ship."

The Barracudas walked to their boat, and X helped them drag it back down to the water. It didn't take long to load the boats and push them out into the surf, but several were left behind on the beaches—another reminder of the great losses the Cazadores had suffered here—wherever this was. To X, the island was just another nameless wasteland full of things that wanted to kill him.

He helped Rhino launch the boat through the surf and then pulled himself in to join Wendig and several other soldiers who would help row back to the main vessel.

A lone Siren's shriek pierced the air as X pulled the oars through the rough water. The Cazadores had conquered this place, but if X knew anything about the wastes, it was that life would find a way.

* * * * *

Katrina climbed the ladder into the container ship, wincing with each step. Her eyes were on the water below. The sharks were still out there, but they were the least of her worries now.

Vish waited at the top of the ladder and bent down to help her up.

"Are you okay, Captain?" he asked.

She nodded and unslung the laser rifle. With her injuries, it was easier to handle than an assault rifle, and it didn't need reloading.

Turning on a flashlight, she followed Vish across the cargo hold of the Cazador vessel. She felt naked without her armor and helmet, but she couldn't get the chest piece on without cutting off her breath, and she didn't need her helmet here in this green zone.

The clean air filled her lungs as she walked through the open space. She swept the light over rusted barrels, plastic crates, and several old-world vehicles. Vish, holding a submachine gun, was waiting for her near an open hatch.

"This way," he said.

She followed him into a passage where several bodies lay, their naked flesh covered in tattoos. The beam from her flashlight confirmed they were Cazador soldiers.

A laser bolt had opened a hole the size of an apple in the chest of a male, melting his insides away. She stepped over him and saw the dead eyes staring at the ceiling. Her heart pounded at her first up-close view of another human being who wasn't from the sky— something she had never thought she would see.

"You okay, Cap?" Vish asked.

She nodded and pushed on, trying to keep her breathing and heart rate under control.

As she took a ladder down to the next level, she couldn't help noticing an eerie similarity. Just like the *Hive*, this area reeked of despair. The stink of shit cans, body odor, and the scent of cooking meat filled her nostrils.

Open hatches provided glimpses into quarters previously occupied by the Cazador warriors. Trays with half-eaten meals sat on tables, and mugs of liquid sat where they were abandoned.

The Hell Divers had caught the enemy in the middle of the last meal they would ever eat.

"Almost there," Vish said.

Katrina readied her blaster as they made their way deeper into the bowels of the ship. Playing cards were spread out across a metal table in the next quarters, the chairs all pulled away, one of them on its side. The common area even had a flat-screen television mounted on the rusted bulkhead.

In the next space, hundreds of boxes were stacked, all of them marked with symbols that appeared to be painted on by the Cazadores. Vish opened a hatch and gestured for Katrina to go inside. She stepped out onto a metal vestibule overlooking a long room that smelled of moldy fruit and decaying flesh. She covered her nose with her sleeve. Boxes, crates, and two massive containers rested on the deck below.

"Down the ladder, ma'am," Vish said.

She led the way, her boots clanking on the metal. One of the rungs near the bottom was missing. She stepped carefully past it and raked her flashlight over the deck.

"Let me go first, Cap," Vish said. He moved out in front, his rifle cradled across his blue battery unit.

The young diver continued to impress Katrina. So did his brother. Maybe they would live up to the standard of divers after all.

They walked through a maze of boxes ten feet high, and more stacks of crates marked with faded letters.

"Alexander, you over here?" Vish asked.

"Yeah."

Coughing followed, and then what sounded like sobbing. Katrina hurried around the large brown container, where Alexander and Trey guarded a group of ten Cazadores.

The men and women wore black suits and didn't appear to be soldiers, but they didn't look friendly.

Grease covered the features of a heavyset male who reminded her of Chief Engineer Samson. She walked over and looked down at the guy. He avoided her gaze, keeping his head down.

"We cleared the ship and took these people prisoner," Alexander said. "But when we were finishing our sweep, we found this ..."

He motioned away from the group of prisoners, toward the open doors of a long storage unit. Katrina made her way around one of the doors to find bars covering the entrance. She brought up her flashlight, and the filthy faces of over a dozen men, women, and children looked back at her.

Blankets, sleeping bags, and other filthy garments were spread out across the deck. Her light illuminated metal dishes and a row of buckets near the bars.

Now she knew where the shit-can stench was coming from.

"They don't speak Spanish," Alexander said. "Or English."

Katrina held her light on the prisoners. One of the men moved away from the huddled group at the far end and approached the buckets as if immune to the smell.

He held his hand up to shield his eyes as she moved the beam over his dark skin. Salt-and-pepper black hair and a mostly gray beard clung to his emaciated features. A torn shirt hung from his bony frame.

The man tried to speak, but all that came out were noises. When the other divers directed their beams at his mouth, she saw why.

Someone had cut his tongue from his mouth.

Katrina swallowed hard at the gruesome sight. She moved the light to check the other people, focusing it on several young girls and a middle-aged woman, all with dark complexions. They all were rail thin and looked as if they hadn't eaten in weeks. Both girls looked away, but the woman glared back at her.

Katrina could only imagine what these people had gone through. She holstered the blaster in an effort to seem less threatening. No need to terrorize these people any further.

"We're not going to hurt you," she said, holding up a hand. "We're going to get you out of there."

Several voices responded, all in the same foreign tongue. Nothing she recognized.

"Ma'am, there's something else you should see," Trey said quietly, as if he didn't want to show her.

She stepped away from the barred gate and ordered Vish to stand guard. What could they possibly have found that was any worse than the sorry state of these prisoners?

"Steel yourself," Alexander said. "This ain't pretty." He walked to another container, and with a shriek of metal, Trey opened one of the doors.

The sleeve over Katrina's nostrils did nothing to keep out the rancid smell coming from the container. She shined her beam inside. On a table lay a rusty saw and a bloody hatchet right next to a hunk of …

She almost turned away from the grisly sight of a corpse, both legs sheared off and cauterized at the knee. Straps held down the dead man's wrists. A carpet of dried blood surrounded the table.

Now she knew what was on the trays she had seen in the cabins earlier. The Cazadores' final meal had been a feast of human flesh.

She walked back to the Cazador prisoners, fury building inside her. She wanted a closer look at the people capable of such an atrocity. Several of them looked away, but one man broke out in laughter.

She ended his mirth with a kick that broke out several teeth. The other prisoners began to squirm in their restraints, but Trey stilled them by firing a shot into the overhead. The round ricocheted off a wall.

Crying came from the container, but it wasn't until something wet rolled down her face that Katrina realized she, too, was weeping. She forced her gaze away from the cannibals, back over to the bars of the container.

The man in tattered clothing pointed at the Cazador prisoners and then clenched his fists.

"Is he saying what I think he's saying?" Trey asked.

"Hell if I know," Vish replied. "Dude has no freaking tongue. How gross is that?"

Another man emerged from the back of the container and gently helped the old man to the side. This man wasn't as thin, but Katrina could still count his ribs through his T-shirt.

He opened his mouth and tapped his chest.

"Victor," he said.

"Captain Katrina DaVita," she replied.

The man spoke again, pointing at the guy with no tongue. "Ton."

Katrina nodded and said, "Nice to meet you, Ton."

The man tried to speak again, but he could make no intelligible sound.

"Victor. Ton. Fight," Victor said, raising his fists. He pointed at the Cazadores. Then he grabbed the lock in the bars and glared at Katrina.

"Victor. Ton. Fight."

Alexander stepped up beside her.

"I think he's saying, if we let them out they'll help us fight," she said.

"Ma'am, I'd highly advise against that," Alexander said quietly. "We don't know if these people are any better than the Cazadores."

Katrina took a moment to scrutinize the other captives inside the container. It struck her then that she could just as easily have been staring into the lower decks of the *Hive*.

These people weren't murderers. They weren't cannibals. They just wanted to survive.

"Get them out of there and fed," she said to Alexander. "I saw boxes of food on the way in."

"What about the Cazadores?" Trey asked.

Katrina looked over her shoulder at the savages. She had no empathy left for these people. Snorting in disgust, she said, "Maybe those sharks are still hungry."

NINETEEN

"What do you mean, they attacked Cazador ships?" Michael asked. He was winded, tired, and dealing with the phantom pains again, but the news of Katrina's battle on the open seas had him and the other two divers stunned.

They were finally back on *Deliverance* after their fruitless mission to Red Sphere. Apparently, a lot had happened since they entered the facility.

"Is Trey okay?" Les asked.

Ada Winslow, the freckle-faced young ensign, rose from her chair. Her eyes were dull with fatigue, but she still managed to smile politely.

"Everyone on the USS *Zion* is fine," Ada said. "Last I talked to Captain DaVita, they were boarding the container ship to search for supplies and neutralize any remaining hostiles. From what she said, it was a slaughter."

Michael wasn't sure whether to celebrate or worry. He set his backpack on the deck. A metallic robotic hand stuck out the top. The arm he had brought back from Red Sphere was lighter than it looked.

The backpack slumped over, and the hand clanked on the deck, drawing the eyes of Dave and Bronson.

"The hell is that?" Bronson asked in his gravelly voice.

"That's all that's left of the defectors," Michael replied. "They left Red Sphere before we got there."

"Where did they go?" Ada asked.

"Good question," Layla replied.

"Get the captain on the horn," Michael said. "And get us the hell out of here."

He looked at the main monitor across the room, which showed an aerial view of Red Sphere. From the sky, it looked a lot like a virus shell and the spikes surrounding it.

The airship vibrated as they began to move. Michael stared at the screen and then held up his hand.

"Hold on," he said.

"Holding," Bronson replied.

"Timothy, do we have any shots of what Red Sphere looked like the last time we were here?" Michael asked.

The AI appeared in holographic form.

"Yes, I do, Commander. Bringing it online now."

Michael got up from his chair and stepped closer to the monitor. "Bring it up side by side with the current image."

Layla joined him in front of the monitor, and the

other officers huddled up behind them. The pictures came online a moment later. It took only a second to see that one of the ships was missing.

Why didn't I think of this earlier, Michael thought.

"Well, I'll be dipped in shit," Les said.

"Is there a way to track that ship?" Michael asked, turning to Timothy.

The AI shook his head. "I'm sorry, Commander, but that is beyond the technology we possess. We don't even know which direction they sailed."

"Shit," Michael muttered. Having the DEF-Nine units out there and hunting down remaining humans was the last thing they needed right now, but he couldn't focus on that when the Metal Islands were so close. He could only hope the machines weren't heading there. Although it would neutralize the threat from the Cazadores, it would also destroy the oil rigs and kill his friends.

"Get us out of here," he said.

The officers went back to their stations, and he moved over to the comms system. Ada smiled politely at him and brought the receiver to her mouth.

"Captain DaVita, this is Ensign Winslow, do you copy? Over."

Familiar static hissed through the bridge. Michael looked at the mission clock on his wrist computer. They were thirty-six hours and forty minutes out from the rendezvous, which didn't allow much of a window for surgical attachment of the robotic arm, and almost zero recovery time. But that was where the rapid-healing nanotechnology came in. If it worked, he would be okay to dive. Theoretically …

"How long until we get back to the *Hive*?" he asked.

Bronson looked over from his monitor. "I've plotted several courses, and depending on the weather, the fastest we can get there is five hours."

Before Michael could reply, a voice came from the comm speakers.

"Ensign Winslow, this is Eevi Corey," said the voice. "I will patch you through to the captain. She is currently on the Cazador container ship with Alexander, Vish, and Trey."

Les motioned for the receiver, and Ada handed it back to him.

"Ensign Winslow, good to hear from you," came a strained voice. "How is everyone on *Deliverance*?"

"Captain, this is actually Lieutenant Mitchells," he said. "We're well and have returned from Red Sphere. Unfortunately, the defectors were gone."

"Gone …"

"Yes ma'am. They left before we got there, and we have no idea where they are sailing."

"So the mission was a failure?"

"Not entirely," Les said, looking over at the robotic arm. "We did manage to find a working laser rifle and something else that might come in handy."

"That's good news, Lieutenant."

"Yes, how about you? We heard you encountered some Cazador vessels."

"We discovered something terrible on board," Katrina said. "These cannibalistic bastards were returning from a trip where they found a bunker of survivors."

More survivors? Michael thought. After all the years in the sky, never finding anyone on the surface, it had seemed almost unthinkable that the Cazadores were out there. And now there were even *more* people?

"The Cazadores are worse than I thought," Katrina said, speaking faster, clearly more agitated. "They have been eating these people, piece by piece."

Layla put a hand to her mouth, covering her lips to hold back a gasp.

The rest of the crew remained silent, taking in the gruesome news better than Michael had expected.

"We did find supplies on this ship to help nurse the survivors back to health," Katrina said. "Some are even in good enough shape to help us."

"Help us do what, exactly?" Les asked.

"Fight." Katrina paused. "I've made a decision."

Michael braced himself for the rest.

"After seeing what I have here, I've decided we aren't going to give el Pulpo a chance to surrender. We will attack him and end his miserable, murdering existence."

Layla looked over at Michael, clearly concerned. But he actually liked the idea. If they attacked the Cazadores without warning, it could give them a chance to save lives.

"Cut the head off the snake, and the body will die," he said.

"I'm also changing the rendezvous point," Katrina

said. "I want the *Hive* and *Deliverance* to come to our location. It's a green zone."

"What's your plan once we get there?" Les asked.

"We'll transfer all noncritical personnel to the container ship. Then we will fly the *Hive* and *Deliverance* to the Metal Islands. Militia soldiers, dressed in Cazador armor, will sail on a fishing trawler we have captured, and I will attack in the USS *Zion*."

Michael liked that idea, too. It gave them more options and the element of surprise.

"We don't have the defectors," Katrina said, "but we have more ships and more people than before. I'll send the coordinates over shortly. Until I see you all again, good luck and Godspeed."

"You, too, Captain," Les said.

"Ensign White, plot a new course," Michael said. "And make sure you've got the radar searching the ocean for any other ships—just in case we stumble upon the defectors."

"You got it, Commander."

Michael watched the team go to work and then drew in a breath, preparing himself for what came next.

"If anyone needs me, I'll be in the medical bay," he said. "Timothy, I'll need your help. You, too, Layla."

"Hold up," Les said.

Michael walked with the lieutenant to the front of the bridge. Layla joined them near the main monitor, which still showed a view of Red Sphere below.

"There's something I think we should do before leaving," Les said.

"And what's that?" Michael asked.

Les jerked his head at the screen. "I think we should take it out."

"Take it out?" Layla asked.

"Nuke it from above," Les replied. "There's nothing left down there that is not evil."

"I'm good with that," Michael said.

Layla thought on it and then nodded. "Me, too."

Michael walked off the bridge, contemplating the orders. He had never liked having the nukes on board and hated what they represented. But dropping one on Red Sphere seemed the right thing to do.

He grabbed Layla's hand as they walked down the passage toward the medical ward, leaving the officers to carry out the task.

The battle for the Metal Islands was quickly approaching, and without question there would be blood. He needed to be ready to fight.

* * * * *

Magnolia hadn't slept since arriving back at the capitol tower. She waited at her window, breathing the salty breeze, searching the sky for airships, and whispering something she had never thought she would say.

"Please, don't come."

She could barely believe she was saying this, but life in the sky was better than life in cages, and there was no telling what el Pulpo would do to her people.

Myriad lights flickered across the surface of the

ocean, like the reflection of the star-filled sky. Only these weren't stars. They were boats. More of them on the open water than usual. Some looked like fishing vessels; others were larger yachts. All of them seemed to be heading toward an armada forming in the distance.

A horn pierced the quiet, and bells chimed in the distance, shattering the stillness and waking people below and above her in the tower. Lights in the rooms flicked on, and residents opened their windows to see what was happening.

One by one, torches flickered to life on the docks below. There were people down there. More than normal. In the glow of the flames, she saw that these weren't just servants and dockhands. There were soldiers—dozens of them, wearing armor and carrying weapons.

Something was afoot.

She tried to get a better view by leaning out of the window. The *Sea Wolf* was docked below, right where they had moored it after her journey earlier in the evening. But it wasn't alone.

The entrance to the underwater marina had opened to release a black boat with a long, narrow platform and planing hull. A spike the length of a man jutted like a spear off the pointed bow.

The long, sleek hull was unlike that of any other vessel she had seen in her captivity. Even from above, she could see the gleaming surface and the image of a purple octopus painted on the bow. Some sort of machine gun was mounted just over the image.

Aft of the bow was an enclosed turret with two

gun barrels pointed skyward. Amidships, a glass windscreen surrounded the single cabin and several seats.

Two men stood at the helm, carefully guiding the craft out of the marina. Equipped with three powerful engines and a row of exhaust mufflers on the back, the boat looked as if it were heading out to a race.

But Magnolia knew better. This was no race boat; it was a war boat.

She looked closer, not wanting to believe what she was seeing. From each side of the bow hung nets filled with human bones, and two skulls rode proudly atop the windshield posts.

It was obvious this vessel belonged to Lord Pulpo. The sick bastard was parading the remains of his enemies, for all to see.

Smoke coughed from the twin stacks as the boat maneuvered alongside the torch-lit dock. The soldiers standing there cheered and beat their chests.

Three more black vessels left the storage marina, and the warriors threw up their fists, chanting "¡El Pulpo!" over and over.

Each of the new boats was also fitted with a machine-gun turret and had a sharp ram jutting from the prow. But unlike the first vessel, these didn't have fancy paint jobs. Rusted armor covered the hulls, and the gunwales were festooned with razor wire.

All across the tower, people opened their windows or came out on their balconies. Unlike the soldiers, these Cazadores weren't cheering. They watched the ships in silence.

The dockhands worked quickly to fill the vessels with supplies. The light from the torches captured several scribes waiting with their hands clasped behind their robes. They brought their hands out and formed a pyramid as a group of soldiers knelt before them, their armored helmets bowed. Were they *praying*?

These men were preparing for battle, and it wasn't hard to guess who the enemy was. Her friends were coming.

She suddenly felt sick to her stomach, but before she could sit down, she heard a knock at her door. She hurried over to open it, expecting to find Imulah.

Standing in the hallway were the same two goons who had escorted her out to the *Sea Wolf* earlier that night.

"Get dressed," said a familiar voice. Imulah was there after all, standing in the shadows, his arms hidden in the long sleeves of his brown robe.

"Where am I going?" she asked.

The scribe avoided the question. "Get dressed, and hurry."

"Not until I know where I'm going."

Imulah let out a sigh and nodded at one of the soldiers. He yanked on her arm, and instead of resisting, she let him pull her knee into his groin.

The second guy threw a punch that grazed her cheek as she moved her head sideways. Ducking back into the room, she grabbed the lamp off the bedside table. When he came at her again, she smashed him in the face, shattering the glass bulb in his eye.

His friend came at Magnolia fast, but she was nimbler and sidestepped, tripping him as he lunged. He fell on his face and slid across the floor.

Pivoting, she kicked him in the jaw. The ball of her bare foot hurt from the impact, but the teeth that rattled across the floor told her he had gotten the worst of it.

Before he could get up, she went down on one knee and slammed her elbow into the base of his skull, cracking his nose against the floor. Then she whipped her arm around his neck, grabbed the wrist with the other hand, and jerked sideways.

A satisfying crack filled the room.

"NO!" yelled the other goon.

Magnolia pulled the knife from the dead Cazador's belt and turned to the second guy, who had managed to stand, one hand to his injured eye, and was staring at his dead friend.

She threw the blade, hitting him with a thump square in his muscular chest. He sank to his knees and slumped over on his side.

Imulah took off as Magnolia pulled the knife out of the dying guard.

"Get back here you little prick!" she shouted.

As he reached to open the door at the end of the next hallway, the knife hit him in the hand, pinning it to the doorjamb. He let out a scream, which Magnolia ended with a swift elbow up under the chin. He slumped down, and she yanked the knife out, freeing his hand before his weight could rip the flesh.

Imulah gripped his bleeding hand, whimpering in pain.

She slapped him across his face to get his attention. "Listen very carefully," she said, "because I'm only going to ask you this once."

He held her stare, lips quivering.

"Where are those boats going?" she asked.

"I …"

She slapped him again, cracking his lower lip. He whimpered again, and she held the blade to his throat.

"Tell me."

"The sky gods," Imulah choked out. "El Pulpo thinks they are coming here." Magnolia pulled the knife back from his throat, letting him breathe.

"How does he know this?"

Imulah clutched his injured hand. "I don't know, I swear. I just know he knows."

"Get up," she said.

Imulah pushed his back against the wall and got to his feet, shaking.

"I know you guys have radio equipment," she said. "And you're going to show me where it is."

He shook his head. "I don't have access."

For some reason, she believed him. The scribe was a coward, but he wasn't a liar. Lucky for him she had another idea. All she had to do was get to the bottom floor of the tower.

TWENTY

The next morning, the ship's mess hall was packed full of Cazador soldiers eating like starved animals. X sat by himself at one of the long tables, surprised they hadn't tossed him back into his cramped quarters.

He had proved himself in the sky arena and again in the wastes, but that didn't mean all the warriors had accepted him. Most of them hadn't fought by his side out there, and only two of those who had were still breathing.

Screw all these cannibalistic assholes, he thought as he took a bite of bread so hard it nearly cracked a tooth. He dipped the crust into the slop on his plate, trying to soften it while avoiding the flaky white meat that may or may not be fish.

The feeling of being watched didn't bother him, and he didn't need to look up to know that several of the hardened men and a few of the women were staring at him as they would an enemy.

X didn't care. All that mattered was filling his

belly after a decent night of sleep. His body still ached from head to toe, but at least he wasn't dog tired.

Footfalls sounded, and someone who smelled like sweat sat in front of X. He finally looked up to see a woman smiling at him. Sort of. He couldn't really tell whether she was grinning or frowning at him.

Most of her teeth were missing, bruises covered her neck, and she had one arm in a sling.

She was bigger than most of the men, and no youngster. On the left side, she had gray hair almost to her shoulders, but the right side of her head was clean-shaven, with the tattoo of a barracuda inked into her scalp.

"*Hola*," she said.

The voice sounded oddly familiar.

"Uh … hi," X replied.

Rhino walked over from the line of soldiers waiting for food. He set his plate down and sat beside the woman.

"Want to tell me why this lady is staring at me?" X asked.

Rhino glanced over at her and gave X a puzzled look. "Wendig?"

"No, this lady," X said.

Rhino laughed. "This lady *is* Wendig."

"Oh, shit," X said, nearly choking on the moistened bread in his mouth. He had never seen Wendig's face, and the breathing apparatus had always distorted her voice.

Wendig's grin turned to a frown when Rhino

explained what X had just asked. Then she gave a deep cackle and reached across the table with her good hand to clap X on his shoulder.

The gesture attracted the attention of the soldiers at the next table. Two of them walked over and said something to Rhino and Wendig. Judging by their eyes and gestures, he had a feeling they were talking about him.

Maybe going to his quarters would have been a better idea.

He had just taken another bite of bread when a hand reached in from behind him and yanked his plate away. X stood and faced three more Cazadores, all of them fair skinned and covered in tattoos.

"You don't belong here," said the middle guy, his blue eyes glaring at X. "I don't care how many of the deformed ones you killed. You're not one of us."

"Not going to argue with you there, pal. I didn't ask to come on this shit journey and fight with you." X held out his hand. "Now, I would appreciate it if you gave me my food back."

Rhino watched from his seat. Wendig also remained sitting.

"Not going to ask you again," X said.

The man looked at his buddies and then slowly held the plate out. Right before it was within X's reach, he tilted it, letting the slop fall onto the deck.

X sighed as Wendig and Rhino both stood. This wasn't going to end well.

"Back off, Sergeant Lurch," Rhino said.

The guy holding the plate directed his gaze at the lieutenant. "Rhino, me and the other boys don't like how you've warmed up to this skydiver."

"*Hell* Diver," X corrected.

Lurch cleared his throat and then spat a yellow glob on the plate.

"Here you go, *Hell Diver*," he said, handing it back to X.

A flash of motion came from the right. It happened so fast, X almost didn't see Wendig swinging her metal plate. She smashed it over Lurch's bald crown.

Slop dripped down his face, and he reached up and wiped away the muck from his eyes. Then he touched the bloody welt on the top of his head.

"You bitch!" he screamed.

He lunged at Wendig, but she sidestepped and he slammed into the table. The soldiers sitting there grabbed their plates and scrambled away, some of them laughing. X bent down and picked up his bread off the ground. He wasn't going to let good food go to waste.

"*¡Basta!*" Rhino shouted.

X had a feeling that meant "stop," but Wendig and the sergeant didn't seem concerned. Lurch threw a punch that sailed over Wendig as she ducked.

Moving backward, X bumped into someone, but the soldier was too busy yelling at the top of their lungs to notice X.

Wendig taunted Lurch by waving her broken arm and muttering something about a dog. That drove the spectators wild, and it worked on Lurch.

The soldier barreled toward her, screaming like a Siren. They slammed into each other, knocking Wendig backward. She let out a scream of her own and leaped onto Lurch, wrapping her legs around him.

X continued eating his bread, happy not to be the one getting his ass kicked, for once.

The brawling tangled mass slammed into a table, and Lurch bucked Wendig onto its splintery surface, knocking trays to the floor. She grabbed him with her good hand and pulled herself up by his shirt, biting his ear. Lurch screeched in agony and elbowed Wendig in her broken arm.

The two warriors fought for a few more seconds until Rhino finally grabbed Lurch by the scruff of the neck and yanked him off Wendig. Using only one hand, he lifted the sergeant a good two feet off the deck.

The other soldiers quieted down, and Rhino continued holding Lurch up, veins popping out on his massive arms while the man kicked in his grip.

Wendig got off the ground, cradling her broken arm. She bared her broken teeth like a dog.

"Get back," Rhino said.

She hesitated, then returned to her seat, throwing X a glance, and a grin. Rhino let go of Lurch as soon as Wendig was out of punching distance, and then dropped him in a heap on the deck, gasping for air.

"Give the Immortal your food," Rhino ordered.

Lurch glared at the lieutenant, rubbing his neck, his bloodshot eyes filled with rage. Getting up, he reached over to his table and handed his plate over.

X looked at the slop. "Is that human or monster meat? 'Cause if it is, I don't want any."

Rhino gave a half smile. "It's fish."

Shrugging a sore shoulder, X took the plate. He was hungry, exhausted, and hurting. Food would help him recover for the trip back to the Metal Islands.

Rhino said something to Wendig in Spanish, but she just shrugged and went back to her meal. So did the rest of the soldiers. The room again filled with casual conversations in several languages.

Sighing, Rhino sat beside X this time, keeping an eye on Lurch.

"He'll be doing a lot more of that now that Whale and Fuego are gone," Rhino said. "I'm going to miss those bastards. I fought with them for years."

X dabbed the rest of his bread into the fresh slop. "I know what it's like to lose friends," he said, "but here's what I don't get ..."

Rhino scooped up a hunk of the white fish but didn't bring it to his mouth. "What?" he asked.

"Why the hell do you guys waste precious ammo, supplies, and, most importantly, people to kill Sirens?"

"The deformed ones?" Rhino said. He put his spoon back down and leaned forward, as if not wanting anyone to overhear.

"El Pulpo believes the Sirens give us strength when we eat them," he said. "Normally, we don't lose this many on our expeditions."

Wendig looked over her shoulder at Lurch, who was talking quietly with his men. Unlike the sergeant, most of the soldiers seemed to really respect Rhino. Either that, or they feared him. X decided it was a bit of both.

You people are freaking demented, he thought.

"He will try to kill me soon," Rhino said, without a trace of fear in his voice.

"So kill him first." X glanced at Wendig, who was nursing her injuries. "Or maybe let her do it."

Rhino picked a fish bone out of his teeth. "I did the same thing to get to where I am," he said. "Killed my way to the top."

"I'm surprised you all haven't killed each other by now," X said.

Rhino chuckled. "It would take a very big army to take this one down. Lurch is just one of many who want someday to be general of the main force."

"Main force?" X asked.

The lieutenant set his spoon down and cracked his neck on one side, then the other. "You didn't think this was all of us, did you? We're just a platoon, Immortal."

X swallowed his food as the realization filled him with dread.

If there were more Cazadores he hadn't seen yet, then the Hell Divers wouldn't have a chance, even though they had better weapons. He tried to keep calm, but all he could think about were his friends.

"How long until we get back to the Metal Islands?" X asked.

Rhino shrugged. "Depends on how long it takes us to find the missing vessels."

"I thought we were going back to …"

"Not yet." Rhino's pierced nostrils flared, and he drew in a deep breath. "We're going to meet up with another platoon—or find them, rather."

X picked up his glass of water, trying to appear nonchalant while his mind raced with questions.

"One of our ships and some boats went missing," Rhino said, "and that doesn't happen very often. Not like this. Not without a trace. That's not how it works. We have communications and beacons like in your airships. One minute, they were there, and then they were gone."

X sipped his water and kept his poker face. This wasn't the work of some random storm. This was his friends. They were finally coming to the Metal Islands, and they had no idea what they were up against.

* * * * *

Katrina had waited her entire life for this moment. So why did she feel so nervous?

Lightning sliced through the soup outside the protective glass of the USS *Zion*'s command center. The scene transported her back to the final moments before a dive, when the glass floor of the launch bay revealed the storms raging beneath her boots.

In a few minutes, *Deliverance* would arrive over their location, and in a few hours, the *Hive* would also show up with the rest of their people.

The final moments before the beginning of

the end were finally upon her, and she felt that she was going to be sick. *Everything* was riding on the attack's success.

Just twenty miles east, the barrier between dark and light awaited her on the final leg of the journey to the Metal Islands.

She picked up the receiver and checked the coordinates they had used to contact Timothy Pepper of the *Sea Wolf.* Several days had passed since they last spoke to the AI, and they hadn't been able to reach him in the past several attempts.

The likelihood of Timothy sending another message was slim, but she had held on to the hope he would deliver more intel on what they were about to face. But now she feared he was disabled or worse. If he was compromised, he could doom them all.

A voice broke over the static. Eevi stood at the top of the ladder, holding a tablet that lit up her grim face.

"We're not picking up anything on radar out there," Eevi said. "No airships and no Cazador vessels."

"Copy that."

"There's something else, Captain."

Katrina waited for bad news.

"We lost one of the civilians from the container ship. A woman. She was too dehydrated … We couldn't save her."

"I'm sorry," Katrina said. She knew they wouldn't be able to save everyone, but the report stung nonetheless. Every life mattered now more than ever, and she had ordered her people to do everything they could to nurse those people back to health. "Once the airships arrive, we'll have better medical supplies for the survivors," she said. "Speaking of which, any update on what we salvaged from the container ship?"

Looking at her tablet, Eevi rattled off the new inventory.

"Ten assault rifles, two thousand rounds of ammunition, and a tank of gasoline with over five hundred gallons remaining," she said.

"Excellent," Katrina said.

Eevi continued, explaining the cache of frozen fish found in the belly of the ship that would last months if they could keep it cold. Even better, the ten captured Cazadores had jumped overboard when she aimed the MK-65 at the container ship's hull.

The sharks had gotten their fill of meat over the past few days, and after seeing the butcher shop aboard the container ship, Katrina didn't feel even a twinge of empathy.

Next on the chopping block was el Pulpo.

She planned to kill the bastard herself, just as she had Captain Leon Jordan. But first, she needed to sharpen the sword hanging from her belt.

The thought snapped her back to reality. She had much to do before she could hack off the cannibal king's head.

"Captain, we just picked up something on radar," Sandy said over the comms. "Looks like *Deliverance*. They're coming in from the southwest."

Katrina lifted her binos off the porthole sill and

pointed them to the southwest, using the night-vision optics to scan the clouds. She held them for several minutes until she saw the flames from the six thrusters appear through the clouds. The sight filled her with pride … and adrenaline.

"Let's go," she said to Eevi.

They climbed back down to the bridge, where Jaideep, Edgar, and Sandy sat patiently at their stations.

"Okay, people, this is it," Katrina said. "You all know what to do. You have the bridge, Eevi. I'll be in the cargo hold."

She moved through the USS *Zion* as fast as she could, going through the plan in her head. Everything that happened from here on out had to go smoothly, or the entire plan would derail.

When she got to the cargo bay, the door was already open. The wind outside was blowing the rain sideways.

Alexander, Trey, and Vish watched over the captives they had moved over from the container ship. There had been twenty-one new people, but a blanket covered the recently deceased woman, dropping the number to twenty. A grieving man knelt beside the body.

This was just the beginning.

Katrina took a quick inventory of the other newcomers. Only five men were in any sort of fighting condition. Victor was the leader, but he could speak only a few words of English, and communication was difficult. That would change, she hoped, when *Deliverance* showed up and she had Timothy to translate.

A draft of wind hit her as she made her way around the group. She put a hand to her bruised ribs. It still hurt like hell to breathe deeply.

Deliverance's turbofans whirred as the airship moved into position, its smooth black belly hovering five hundred feet above the stealth warship. One of the children pointed at the sky, and all the newly liberated people looked up in wonder, as if at an alien craft descending from the heavens.

Katrina smiled and nodded at all the new faces. Most of them looked at her with wrinkled brows, untrusting.

She couldn't blame them. This was only the second group of outsiders most of them had ever seen, and she didn't fully trust any of them yet, either.

She moved over to the open door as *Deliverance* rotated a few degrees to hover over the USS *Zion*. The cargo bay in the warship's belly opened. A rope dropped from the airship, and the blue glow of a battery unit came sliding down it. The moment the diver unclipped from the rope, another diver emerged from the airship and rappelled down into the cargo bay.

Footsteps clattered in the cargo bay as the captives from the container ship all got up for a better view of the two Hell Divers, one of whom was a good foot taller than the other.

Alexander and Vish remained standing guard, but Trey ran over to greet his father.

"Dad!" he yelled.

Les hurried over and hugged his boy.

"Captain," he said, nodding to Katrina.

"Good to see you again, Lieutenant," she said.

Layla took off her helmet, smiled, and went to give Katrina a hug, then stopped when she saw the thick bandage around her chest.

"That doesn't look good," Layla said.

"It's not a big deal," Katrina said. "How are you?"

Layla shrugged, and Katrina looked back up at the airship, sensing that her friend was worried about something besides the imminent battle.

"So where is Commander Everhart?" Katrina asked.

"Med bay, healing from his procedure," Layla said.

"Procedure?"

"He's got a surprise to show you," Les said.

"I guess I'm heading up to *Deliverance* for a bit," Katrina replied. "I'll go with these people once we work out a bucket system to get them up there."

Layla turned to look at the recently freed prisoners. "What are we going to do with them?" she asked.

Les and Layla took a long look at the haggard lot, who seemed to be studying them in return, as if they were alien creatures from another planet.

"I hope you have a plan," Les said.

"I do," Katrina said. "We're going to save these people. Just as we're going to save X, Magnolia, and Miles."

TWENTY-ONE

Michael moved the index finger of his new hand. That was the intention, anyway. He stared at the robotic fingers, willing them to move. One by one, he flexed them, curled them, wiggled them in the air. Then he clenched them into a titanium-alloy fist.

"How does it feel, Commander?" Timothy asked.

"Uh, it feels weird."

He sat up straighter, his back resting against the plastic frame of the bed in *Deliverance*'s medical ward. The spider had connected his nerve endings and muscles to the hyperalloy robotic arm from Red Sphere, and the nanotechnology was working to make the connections heal faster than normal— *much* faster.

Michael unclenched his robotic hand and moved the fingers, clumsily at first, but he already had them doing things that the real ones could not.

It was just Michael and the AI in the private quarters, but Michael could hear commotion outside.

The prisoners Katrina had freed on the container ship were being moved to the airship for medical treatment.

"This is really weird," Michael said.

"Sir, it will take some getting used to," Timothy said. "The nanotechnology will strengthen the connections between your nerves and muscles, and the wires from the robotic arm. You should be fully operational in a few days."

Operational, Michael thought. *Like a machine.*

Having robotic parts, especially parts that had belonged to Dr. Julio Diaz, was starting to freak him out. It wasn't until the spider finished the job and he woke up and saw his new arm that he really started thinking about what this would mean.

It means you can fight again. It means you can dive again.

"This was the only way," Michael murmured.

"Pardon me, sir," Timothy said. "I don't understand your question."

"Oh, nothing."

Timothy cupped his hands behind his back. "Are you in any discomfort, Commander?"

Michael raised the arm to look at the swollen flesh around the stump, where the robotic spider had connected him with the resized mechanical limb. The tender skin and muscle did burn, but he hardly felt any pain beyond the tingle of the nanotechnology gel that was busy working its magic.

"Not really, to be honest," Michael said.

"That's good, sir. The nanotechnology should

expedite the recovery process, but I must admit, I was a bit concerned about this operation." He paused and added, "I've never used a spider before."

"Thanks for keeping that to yourself earlier," Michael said with a hint of a smile.

"I didn't want to cause you any distress. Now that the mechanical parts have been connected to your nerves, you should no longer experience phantom pains."

Michael's grin widened. "I already feel better. Stronger."

He got up from the bed, but a wave of dizziness overtook him, and he stumbled several feet before reaching out with his robotic hand. The only thing within reach was a white medical cart.

His hyperalloy palm bashed in the side and sent the cart crashing into the wall. Drawers popped out, and supplies scattered over the deck.

"*Shit*," Michael growled.

The noise prompted a rap on the door. He closed his eyes and then opened them, blinking several times. When his vision returned, Layla stood in the open hatchway, with Captain DaVita behind her.

"Layla told me we could start calling you Tin again," Katrina said. "Now I see why."

Michael smirked. "This is a bit stronger than that flimsy tin hat," he said, raising the new arm. He slowly rotated it for the others to see.

Katrina walked over to his bedside and put her hand on his shoulder. "Good to see you, Commander."

"Likewise, Captain."

"It's also good to see that the trip to Red Sphere netted something positive."

"We also picked up another laser rifle," Michael said. He looked over at Layla. "You tell her about the nuke?"

"Nuke?" Katrina said. "I'm listening."

Layla shook her head.

"*Nuke?*" Katrina repeated.

"We dropped one on Red Sphere," Michael said. "Wiped that evil place off the map."

Katrina pursed her lips, frowning, but only for a moment.

"If it were up to me, I would have dropped them into the ocean a long time ago," Michael said. "But in this case, I agreed with Lieutenant Mitchells. Red Sphere was a stain on human history and remained a clear and present danger to humankind. It needed to be destroyed."

Katrina seemed to ponder his words for a few more seconds and then said, "I'll talk to Lieutenant Mitchells about this later. But right now we need to plan our attack on the Metal Islands. Are you good to go to the bridge for the strategic planning meeting?"

"Yes ma'am."

"Good. We're meeting there in an hour. In the meantime, enjoy some time together." Katrina stepped out of the room, closing the door behind her.

"A little privacy, Timothy?" Michael said.

The AI had already vanished, but his voice replied, "Roger, Commander."

Michael returned to the bed and sat, patting the mattress with his metal hand.

She sat down beside him, fingering the braid that lay over her shoulder. "How are you doing?"

"It feels odd, but it works." He drummed his fingers on the bed.

She watched and let out a sigh.

"Are you okay?" he asked.

"Yeah, just scared about the attack."

"I'd be lying if I told you I wasn't scared," he said. "But I'm ready to fight and see our friends again, and to see the sun."

Layla smiled. It was almost the smile he had fallen in love with all those years ago. But this time, her heart wasn't entirely in it. Something was bothering her.

"What is it?" he asked, brushing the braid away from her face and over her shoulder with his mechanical hand.

Her eyes flitted to the robotic fingers, but they didn't seem to bother her.

"There's something I want you to know," she said. "I wasn't going to tell you until this was all over, but if something happens, you deserve to know."

Michael lowered his hand.

"I think I'm pregnant," she said. Before he could respond, she added, "But that changes nothing as far as this fight is concerned. I'm still going to do my part. I'm still going to dive with you and the others."

"Layla," he said quietly. The thought of becoming a parent did change things. It changed everything.

"What?" she said when he didn't finish his thought. "Say something, Tin."

He turned so he could grab both her hands.

"I love you, Layla. You're my person, and you're all I've ever wanted. Adding another person to our team would be amazing, and that's exactly why you can't dive. It's too dangerous. I want you here on *Deliverance* during the attack."

"It's a bad time for this news, I know."

He held her gaze, staring into the eyes that he had loved since he was a kid. He and Layla had seen so much together, grown up together, and fought together to keep the airships in the sky.

"I want to dive with you," she said. "We should be together for this."

An emergency siren rang out, cutting her off. The rise and fall of the electronic whine echoed through the medical bay. Michael and Layla both stood and moved out to see what was happening.

He punched a comm button and connected to the bridge. "What the hell is going on?"

Ada Winslow responded a beat later. "We're picking up a ship on the radar."

"The *Hive*?"

"No," Ada replied. "This is on the surface, and it's headed our way. You'd better get to the bridge, Commander."

* * * * *

The horns ceased as the last of the Cazador boats vanished on the horizon, the red blinking lights swallowed by the darkness. The call to war was over, replaced by the chiming of some distant bell.

The *ding, ding, ding* reverberated through the capitol tower. Magnolia's heart quickened with the chime, and she took in a deep breath to try to calm down.

She knew what the bells meant.

They were a warning, like the emergency sirens on the airships. The lack of movement in the hallways proved that. Everything was on lockdown, which made escaping all the more difficult.

That was why she had taken refuge in the room that Inge and Sofia shared.

"There are too many guards," Inge said. "You can't escape."

"There is no way out of here even if you could get off this rig," Sofia said.

Magnolia pulled back the drape covering the windows. The *Sea Wolf* was still docked below, but she had no idea how the hell she was going to get twelve floors down.

She didn't even have a pair of shoes and was still dressed in a pair of shorts and a ripped T-shirt.

Magnolia turned back to the two women. Besides Rodger and Miles, they were the closest thing to friends she had on the Metal Islands.

"You attacked a scribe and killed two guards," Inge said. "El Pulpo will not forgive these sins. He will …"

Imulah mumbled into the ripped sleeve she had tied around his mouth. He sat in a chair, gripping his hand, which was still leaking blood onto the floor.

"That's why I have to try to escape," Magnolia replied. "You're welcome to come with me, but you've got about a minute to make up your mind."

Footfalls clanked in the hallway outside their locked door. Armed with only a knife, she had a feeling that things were about to get ugly. But she was more than ready to fight, even if it came down to using her teeth.

A rap sounded on the doorway across the hall, and then came the shouts.

"¡Abra!"

The Cazador yelled again, and more deep voices called out.

"Sofia, please, I just need some clothes and shoes," Magnolia whispered.

The voices continued as the door across from their quarters opened. A woman spoke rapidly, and Magnolia pointed her knife at Imulah to keep him quiet.

Sofia moved to a dresser and pulled out a pair of black pants and a black shirt, and then a black scarf.

Less than a minute later, Magnolia was clothed. Inge and Imulah looked on, but Sofia abruptly pulled off her shirt and brushed her long black hair over her shoulder, exposing the patchwork of raised scars.

"I'm leaving, too, Inge," she said. "I'm sorry, but I've decided I'd rather die than stay here any longer."

Inge sat on the left of the two beds and looked to the floor. A tear fell between her feet.

"You can come with us," Magnolia said.

"I … I can't." Inge kept her eyes on the floor—the gaze of a broken, terrified woman.

Magnolia knew then there was no changing Inge's mind. Fear had her paralyzed.

The locked door suddenly rattled, and a male voice boomed outside.

Magnolia tiptoed over to Imulah, pointing the knife at his lap. "Don't make a peep, or you're going to lose your peepee."

His eyes widened.

"You do have one of those, right?" *I already know you don't have any balls.*

He nodded.

Sofia replied in Spanish to the man in the hallway, and the door handle stopped shaking. She said something else, and the footfalls continued.

"What did you say to them?" Magnolia asked quietly.

Sofia flashed a pretty grin. "That I'm alone and naked and if they do come in and see me, their king will make them pay with their eyes."

Sofia put a necklace on, grabbed a book from the top of her dresser, and opened it up. The pages had been cut out, leaving room for a handgun.

She was full of surprises tonight.

"Where the hell did you get that?" Magnolia asked.

"My lover."

"Lover?" *I sure as hell know you're not talking about el Pulpo.*

"I'll tell you about him later."

"Maybe he can help us escape," Magnolia said.

Sofia stuffed the gun into the back of her waistband and covered the grip with her long black hair. "He's not here. He's off on a mission."

"Got it." Magnolia walked toward the door, but Sofia shook her head.

"Not that way."

"Where, then?"

Sofia moved to the glass doors that opened onto a balcony.

"Be careful, Sofia," Inge said. She got off the bed and walked over.

"Make sure Imulah doesn't rat us out, okay?" Magnolia said.

Inge nodded, but Magnolia didn't trust the redhead. She moved back to the scribe and said, "Sorry about this."

He tilted his head, puzzled. Then came the flash of realization in his eyes.

"Please, don't," he mumbled.

Before he could react, she swung, hammering the back of his head with the heel of her fist and the butt of the knife hilt, effectively knocking him out cold.

She almost felt bad as she walked away, but Imulah had made his choice, along with Inge. Now she and Sofia were making theirs, even if it ended in death.

"Hope you know how to climb," Sofia said as

she opened the doors. The chiming of the bell grew louder, and Magnolia felt an invigorating gust of fresh air.

She took a second to look out over the star-filled sky, and the moon's shimmery reflection on the water. The flowers growing in pots on the balcony moved in the salt breeze.

God, this really could have been paradise.

"Let's go," Sofia said. She swung her legs over the railing and bent down, then dropped to the next balcony. Magnolia looked over the edge and saw Sofia's grinning face about ten feet below.

"You coming, or what?" she asked.

Magnolia followed the younger, more agile woman down two floors. Sofia reminded her of a version of herself when she was still in her twenties.

At the third balcony down, two kids looked out from behind cracked glass doors. A well-built man in a tattered white T-shirt and dungarees emerged in the living space behind them, and Sofia put her finger against her lips.

The man nodded and vanished back into his quarters with both kids. That was when Magnolia saw the gun in Sofia's right hand. She tucked it back into her pants and went over the next railing.

They were on the fifteenth floor, not even halfway down.

A steady clanking sounded over the chiming bells as two elevator cages, one of which she had never seen before, cranked up toward the airship rooftop.

Magnolia looked down. The *Sea Wolf* bobbed in the torchlight. Still moored to the dock, it was there for the taking. All she had to do was get there and send out a transmission warning her friends not to come … And then get the hell out of this awful place.

They dropped to the next balcony, the next, then another. On the eleventh floor, Magnolia landed off-kilter on the foot she had bruised kicking the Cazador soldier in the jaw.

Sofia was already over the next railing. A shout rang out, and Magnolia limped over to check. On the balcony below, a husky Cazador soldier had Sofia by the throat. He pushed her against the railing, nearly knocking her over the side.

Magnolia moved to the right side of the railing and stuck her knife between her teeth. Then she swung her legs over and crouched down. Grabbing the bars, she lowered herself instead of dropping.

When she was a foot off the deck, she dropped silently and buried the knife in the man's right kidney.

Letting go of Sofia, he arched backward, in too much pain even to scream. Magnolia pulled the blade out and stabbed him again, this time under the jaw, pushing the blade deep into his brain.

The fat guy crumpled, jerked, and lay still. She bent down and relieved him of her knife and a handgun.

Sofia massaged her neck, gasping for air.

"¿Bien?" Magnolia asked.

"Sí."

Magnolia moved to the railing and took the lead. She made it down to the eighth floor before the pain in her foot stopped her.

Sofia, still breathing heavily, dropped down beside her.

"You good?" she asked.

Magnolia nodded, seeing motion through the glass door behind Sofia. Another kid stood watching them—a girl this time, no older than seven.

She raised a hand, and Magnolia raised hers to wave. But there was something else in the room.

Cazador soldiers stood in the hallway outside the open entrance door.

"Oh, shit," Magnolia said.

They dropped to the next balcony together this time, just as the glass window above exploded in a spray of gunfire. The next two balconies went by fast, Magnolia gritting her teeth with each impact.

At the sixth floor, a Cazador soldier stood waiting. He lunged with a spear, which Sofia avoided by jumping to the side. Magnolia grabbed the shaft and pulled, but the guy yanked back.

As Sofia raised her pistol, gunfire rang out several balconies above them. She moved away to avoid the rounds pinging off the rail. Jumping to the side, Magnolia moved under the roof for cover—right into the path of the man still holding the spear.

He jabbed at her head, then at Sofia, as more gunfire came from above. This time, Sofia grabbed the shaft and pulled so hard, the guy stumbled. Magnolia tripped him, and he sprawled near the railing, where gunfire ricocheted off the metal on both sides of his head.

When he got up, Magnolia used the eight feet of space to run and jump-kick him in the chest. The impact knocked him over the side.

A short yelp and a splash followed.

Magnolia and Sofia pulled their handguns and moved to opposite ends of the balcony. After a nod, they both maneuvered for shots and fired at the deck above them.

One of the Cazadores on Magnolia's side backed away, but the other, caught off guard, took a bullet to the head and slumped away from her view.

"I'm clear," Sofia said, still pointing her gun above them. "You go first."

Magnolia wasted no time. She swung down to the next balcony and covered Sofia while she climbed down. A head popped up above, and Magnolia closed one eye. The first shot missed, but the second took off his ear, forcing him back.

They had made it to the fourth floor when reinforcements showed up on balconies to the right and left. The pistol fire turned into automatic spray as the warriors busted out the big guns.

Magnolia and Sofia backed up to the glass door. Glancing over her shoulder, Magnolia looked inside the quarters. Going back inside would be a death sentence.

There was only one way out of this.

"We have to jump," she said.

Bullets pounded the railings around them and punched through the metal platform. Sofia gave a firm nod and drew in a breath. They tucked their weapons into their waistbands before bolting for the edge.

Sofia went over headfirst, but Magnolia hurdled the railing, narrowly clearing it. The fall lasted only a moment. The dark water rose up to meet her faster than she expected, and she slammed into the surface hard, clutching her weapons with one hand and holding her nose with the other.

The cool water was a jolt to her sweaty body. She kicked up toward the glow of the moon. Bullets lanced into the surface.

"Down!" Sofia yelled.

Magnolia ducked under the water and kept kicking. She couldn't see anything, and the horror of not knowing what else lurked in the depths filled her with adrenaline. She swam even harder when she realized she *did* know what lurked in these waters.

Bullets cut through from above, and it was just a matter of time before one ripped into her, sending her to the bottom, where the giant octopus these people worshipped would find her.

No. This isn't where your life comes to an end.

She kicked harder, pulled harder, swam faster.

For the moment, Magnolia was the woman she had been at Sofia's age, when she first dived to the surface and survived impossible situations because she did what it took to survive. That was what she had always done.

She would never be a slave again.

Kicking back to the surface for air, she glimpsed the docks ahead. Only a few more strokes. Sofia was already pulling herself up onto the dock.

The gunmen on the balconies had retreated into the building.

Magnolia took a moment to tread water and look around. The torches flickered in the breeze, creating shadows over the docks.

"Come on!" Sofia said, reaching out to her.

Magnolia kicked over toward the younger woman, but something seemed off ... As she swam, she felt for her pistol, but it was gone, lost in the fall. She pulled the sheath knife from her waist and put it between her teeth on the final kick to Sofia.

They locked hands, and Sofia pulled her out of the water. As she stood up, she saw the elevator clanking down from the decks thirty feet above.

"Run!" Magnolia said.

They sprinted down the dock toward the *Sea Wolf*, the clanking of the elevator urging them on. It hit the bottom and disgorged six soldiers.

Sofia fired over her shoulder on the run.

But these warriors did not return fire. Maybe they didn't want to damage one of el Pulpo's prized trophies. If that was the case, it gave the women an advantage.

Sofia was the first onto the *Sea Wolf*. She jumped over the gate leading to the starboard side and moved over to the motors. "Cut us free," she said.

Magnolia used her knife to saw through the bow rope, then moved back to the stern, where Sofia was still working. She pulled on a cord, and the motor choked to life.

The sound prompted more shouts from the men running up the dock. They were almost to the *Sea Wolf.*

Magnolia went to the pilothouse but stopped at the open hatch. Most of the dashboard was gone, the monitors stripped and cables sticking out of the gaps.

A new wheel and a throttle lever had been mounted to the dash. Replaced windows gave her a view of the men running onto the piers. She put the boat in reverse and pulled away from the dock as the young Cazador soldiers all made it to the edge. One brazen teenager jumped onto the stern of the boat and landed in the razor wire.

Sofia shot him in the chest, and he slumped back into the wire. Return fire lanced across the bow—a warning, forcing Magnolia down and out of view.

Over the crack of gunfire came a whistling noise, the same type she had heard the night of the banquet. From her hunched position, she saw that the radio she had used on the journey was also gone. The Cazadores had replaced it with what looked like an analog radio.

"No, no, no!" she shouted, slamming the dashboard with her palm. She had no idea how to use the radio, and the airships hardly ever monitored the old analog frequencies.

Magnolia's gut tightened with dread as she peered

out of the glass. The Cazador soldiers aimed their rifles at the boat, and muzzle flashes flickered across the docks. Apparently, they were less concerned now about damaging el Pulpo's property.

Sofia joined her, blowing into the shell whistle on her necklace.

"This better work," she said.

Magnolia reached up and pushed the lever down, burying the throttle in reverse. Another bullet broke through the windshield. The hole spiderwebbed, but the panel held firm.

The gunfire suddenly stopped, and for a moment there was only silence. A scream shattered the calm. This was not the angry shouting Magnolia had heard earlier. These were cries of pain and panic.

She slowly got up as three Cazador soldiers rose into the air, wrapped up in giant, slithering arms. The men twisted and howled as the beast pulled them off the docks as easily as a child playing with stuffed animals.

The body of the mutant creature surfaced—a slimy back covered in flaps and bumps. She couldn't see the eyes, but she already knew what they looked like after her close encounter on the open seas.

"It worked," Sofia said, holding the necklace. She grinned as a tentacle lined with suction cups snaked over the dock and snatched a fleeing soldier who had almost made it back into the elevator. Two others managed to flee before the giant arms could wrap them up.

Magnolia stood up, turned the boat around, and

pushed the throttle lever forward. By now, Sofia had the other two motors started, and the boat surged away from the capitol tower.

As they turned, a boneless pink limb slapped the front of the boat. It curled delicately around the corpse in the razor wire and plucked it away.

Magnolia shivered as the giant cephalopod slipped beneath the *Sea Wolf*'s wake. The thing could as easily have snatched her or Sofia instead of the dead soldier.

She turned her attention to the radio. "Do you know how to use that?"

"Yes," Sofia said, "but I think we have bigger problems right now."

"I need to get a message to my friends, send out an SOS, and warn them not to come here."

"Okay, I'll try," Sofia said.

While Sofia worked on the radio, Magnolia looked out over the waves. She had no idea where to go now that they had escaped. She also had no idea where either X or Miles was, and she didn't know how much gas she had in the tanks.

The only thing she knew for certain was Rodger's location. She had left him to the Cazadores once before, and she wasn't going to do it again.

She scanned the distant oil rigs, trying to remember their configuration from when she sailed past them a few hours earlier.

"I think I got it working," Sofia said. "We can send a message out on this frequency and hope someone who's monitoring analog dials us in."

something to fight with, but she couldn't even get up. This time, there was no escaping. No lucky break. She had played her cards and lost, and what came next would be worse than anything she could imagine.

Sofia crawled across the deck toward her, holding her gun in a shaky hand. Voices sounded outside, and the noise of boots slopping through water in the passage.

Magnolia pushed the hatch shut just as lights flickered into the command center. She managed to lock the hatch, then fell backward on a deck awash in seawater.

Sofia handed Magnolia the gun. "I've got seven bullets left," she said. "Make them count."

Magnolia took the pistol and trained it on the doorway at waist level.

"Save two bullets," Sofia said. "We can't let them take us alive."

TWENTY-TWO

"Clear a path!" Les shouted.

Everyone parted to make way for the thirty militia soldiers heading to *Deliverance* from the *Hive*. They tromped over the metal deck, cradling submachine guns—normally reserved for the Hell Divers due to the risk of an accidental discharge on the fragile ships.

But instead of yelling profanities or giving these men and women a hard time, the passengers on the way to their shelters moved aside to stand and pay their respects to the soldiers who would soon put their lives on the line for humanity.

The soldiers weren't the only people headed to war. Civilians who had spent their entire lives working on the ship trailed the militia soldiers. Rodger's dad, Cole, from the woodworking and clock shop; Marv from the Wingman; Dom from the Dragon; and dozens more: farmers, engineers, janitors, teachers, and even lower-deckers.

Les let them pass before taking the rigid passageway

connecting the two airships. The tunnel was packed full of passengers being reorganized under the updated disaster mitigation plan that Ensigns White, Winslow, and Connor had put together. During the attack on the Metal Islands, most of the civilians, including his family, would remain on the *Hive*.

He wasn't supposed to go to the *Hive*, but he had to see his girls before the ships uncoupled. Their shelter was already packed full when he got there. Fourteen passengers sat in the bucket seats, with red safety belts across their chests.

Seeing Phyl strapped into a child seat about melted his aching heart.

"Dad!" she shouted.

"Hey, sweetie." He knelt down in front of her. To his surprise, Katherine unbuckled herself and wrapped her arms around him.

"I'm so glad you came," she said. "I wanted to tell you something."

The emergency siren ceased for a moment, replaced by the kind, firm voice of Ensign Ada Winslow.

"T-minus ten minutes before the ships uncouple. Please report to your shelters or stations immediately."

As always, Les felt that he was running on a clock and that time was almost up.

Katherine tightened her grip around his neck and then pulled back to look him in the eyes.

"Now I understand why you became a Hell Diver and an officer," she said. "Everything you've done has been for your family."

He smiled. "I love you all too much to do less."

"I know," Katherine said. She looked up at the dented bulkheads of the shelter, then at the other people strapped inside. "This ship has carried us for long enough. It's time to find a new home, even if we have to fight for it."

"You're right, and that's exactly what I'm going to do."

Les kissed his wife on the lips and then kissed Phyl on her forehead.

"I'll see you both soon," he said.

"Look after Trey," Katherine said.

"I will."

He left the shelter and closed the hatch with a heavy but full heart. Knowing that his wife supported him gave him the energy to do what had to be done. After securing the hatch, he took off at a trot through the corridors.

Three engineers in red jumpsuits stood on the *Deliverance* side, waiting to retract the connecting walkway. He squeezed past them as the warning siren wailed.

When he reached the command center, the officers were finishing their final launch preps.

"Someone give me a sitrep," Les said.

"We've confirmed one enemy vessel on the water," Bronson reported.

Les stepped over to the porthole windows, but all he could see was darkness slashed by lightning. They were fifteen thousand feet above the ocean, far out of reach of any weapons the Cazadores could fire at them, and even if they did have some sort of missile, tracking the airships in the soup of electrical storms would be impossible, according to Timothy Pepper.

"Captain DaVita is moving into position," Dave said.

"Good," Les said, typing in his credentials. He eyed the empty captain's chair. *I sure hope you know what you're doing, Katrina.*

She had changed the plan at the last minute, and Les wasn't sure the new one was any better. The bridge doors whisked open and Layla entered, but to his surprise, she wasn't wearing her Hell Diver armor. Michael followed her inside.

"Commander," Les said.

"Lieutenant, Layla is going to stay on the bridge during both phases of the attack," Michael said.

Layla didn't look too happy about it, and Les wasn't going to ask questions. They didn't have time.

"Captain, all systems are a go," Ada said.

It took Les a moment to register that she was talking to him. With Katrina back on the USS *Zion*, he was in command of *Deliverance*. But if Layla wasn't diving, then perhaps she should be the one at the helm. He thought on it for a few seconds before giving the order to uncouple the ships.

Ada gave the order to the engineers.

A loud *clunk* reverberated through the ship. Using the turbofans, Les carefully backed up, and *Deliverance* peeled away from the *Hive* for the second time in as many weeks.

On the bridge, Les watched the main display and tried not to think about the precious cargo inside the *Hive*. *Deliverance* had its own precious cargo to protect: a cargo bay full of soldiers and Hell Divers to deliver.

"We're clear," Dave said.

Les nodded and did a systems scan, his eyes stopping on the display for the armaments. They had twenty cruise missiles ready to fly, and thirty bombs, including the remaining nuclear weapons.

He flipped the nukes offline. Red Sphere was one thing, but they weren't going to use any of them at the Metal Islands, even if they did lose the fight. Poisoning the one known habitable spot on earth would doom anyone else out there.

And now Les knew. There were more bunkers and more people hiding beneath the surface in multiple places.

Ada suddenly hurried away to her station, pausing near Les.

"Sir," she whispered, "I'm picking up something over an analog station that I think you might like to hear."

"What message?"

"It's really weak, sir, but I think it's Magnolia."

"Mags?" Les asked.

Michael and Layla both looked over at him.

"Yes," Ada replied.

"Well, what did she say?" Les asked, locking eyes with Michael.

"Sir …" Ada cleared her throat. "She said don't come to the Metal Islands. She said it's a fight we can't win."

* * * * *

"They found the missing ship," Rhino said. "Visibility is bad, but so far, it looks like no one's on board."

X rubbed his eyes. He had managed a few hours of sleep, but to feel human he needed another day.

"What time is it?" he asked.

"Time to get your dead ass up. Come on."

X got off his bunk and stood. His body felt a hundred years old.

"So, we're going to look for the missing crew?" he asked.

Rhino scratched his head and walked back into the gangway—his way of saying yes. X limped after him down the narrow, rusted passage. Water leaked from a pipe, dripping into a brown puddle on the deck ahead.

He passed the berthing area, where Wendig and several other wounded soldiers lay resting in their bunks. She sat up and grinned at him.

X forced a smile. He still couldn't believe the burly soldier had been a woman all along, and as much as he hated to admit it, he was starting to like her. Her aggressive personality, manners aside, reminded him of Katrina.

A part of him even felt bad about killing her cousin, Hammerhead. But the feeling passed. The guy had been trying to rip his head off, after all.

Rhino continued to the armory, where the other soldiers were already getting suited up and grabbing weapons under the Barracuda banner. X went to his locker and felt a little tug of nostalgia as, for a second, he was transported back to the launch bay of the *Hive*. He no longer remembered how many times he had suited up there with his brothers and sisters over the years. He missed those days.

But more than anything, he missed his dog.

He was anxious to get back to the Metal Islands. Maybe, his conduct during the fight would earn him a trip to see Miles.

The fleeting moment of wistfulness passed. The men and women inside this armory were not his brothers or his sisters.

They were his enemies—even Rhino, whom X had taken a liking to over the past few days. Wendig, too. He couldn't let his guard down against them. They would kill him if given the order.

He opened his locker and grabbed his armor, wondering whether his real friends had anything to do with the missing crews on the two Cazador vessels.

X finished suiting up and took the sword and pistol that Rhino handed him. They walked through the ship to the weather deck, where the rattle of chains greeted them. Dozens of Sirens, exposed to the elements, pulled on their restraints and kicked the bars of their cages.

X kept his hands on his weapons. He didn't pity the beasts, but he took no pleasure in antagonizing them.

Several of the children lay curled up in the corner of a cage, their eyeless faces keying on his battery unit. Shrieking through their gags, they sounded almost like birds.

X looked away to an island in the east. An orange river of lava poured into the ocean, raising a cloud of steam. To the west, the abandoned container ship drifted in the water. Beyond it, almost out of view, was a fishing boat with sails up.

He hurried to catch up with the other Cazadores gathering at the railing. Rhino gave quick orders, breaking a dozen soldiers into two groups. He led one group of four Cazadores plus X, and Sergeant Lurch led the other group of five. The men climbed down the rope boarding net to rowboats already in the water.

X grabbed the oars as Sergeant Lurch and his team veered off toward the fishing boat, which was much farther out. Instead of rowing, Lurch fired up the engine. Rhino cursed, and yelled after them, but Lurch didn't respond.

Rhino sat down and grabbed a pair of oars. The team started rowing, and X joined in, though his arms were already aching. He still wasn't fully awake, and fatigue made his movements sluggish. The other soldiers weren't in much better shape.

X glanced at the dark water slapping the starboard

side. Through the years, he had seen all sorts of mutant beasts, but the creatures that lived in the sea scared him more than those on land.

He looked up at the dark sky, exhausted and lost in his thoughts. The rowing became mechanical, and when he came out of his fugue, the container ship was just a few hundred feet out.

The rusting hulk towered over the little boat. Above the barnacles and red moss that encrusted the hull, bullets had pocked the steel plating. Flotsam drifted in the surrounding water, and several containers lay on their sides, on a deck blackened by an explosion.

This had to be *Deliverance*'s doing.

Trying to be discreet, X moved his helmet to scan a bit of sky with every pull of the oars. He had a feeling they were long gone after making a hit-and-run attack.

That was exactly what he would have done if he were trying to pick off the Cazador vessels. But where were the soldiers who had crewed this ship?

He shipped the oars as another soldier waited to tether the rowboat to the massive container ship.

Rhino raised a spear gun with a grappling hook and rope and fired it over the ship's rail. The smallest man on the team grabbed the rope, which was knotted every few feet, and pulled it snug. Then he started climbing. When he reached the top, he dropped two thin lines of nylon cord. A man sitting in front of X tethered the boat to one line, and the end of a rope ladder to the other. Then the climber hauled up the ladder and fixed it to the rail.

X was the next to last up the rope ladder and down into the dark hold. He bumped on his headlamp. Flashlight beams penetrated the inky darkness, revealing crates stacked four high, and a tracked vehicle like the one they had used to pull the wagonloads of captive Sirens.

Rhino grabbed X by the shoulder and spun him around.

"You listenin'?" he asked.

X shook his helmet. "I didn't hear you say anything."

"I said, you're with me and Stirling."

X nodded. He was out of it and needed to get his shit together.

The other three soldiers set off through the ship, and X tagged along behind Stirling and Rhino, his pistol locked and loaded. They made it about five minutes before finding the first sign of a battle. Several bullet-riddled corpses littered the narrow passage. But some of the wounds looked different from those left by a bullet.

He bent down to examine one.

"You ever seen somethin' like this?" X asked Rhino, who hovered over his shoulder.

"Yes, once before. Those are made by weapons we don't possess."

"What kind of weapons?"

Rhino glanced up at the overhead as a vibration rumbled through the vessel.

It sounded to X as if some gigantic monster had woken up angry. "What the hell is that?" he asked.

Stirling turned around, his submachine gun cradled over his armored chest plates. He said something in Spanish, but as Rhino replied, the tremor increased, making the spent bullet casings on the deck jitter audibly.

A whirring like the rush of wind came from above, and X knew exactly what was making the sound: a trap, set by his friends.

"Get out!" he yelled.

Before he could move, a violent quake shook the container ship, and the bulkhead behind him exploded in a wave of fire and shrapnel.

X hit the deck hard and crawled away, watching in horror as another explosion tore through the overhead behind him, crushing Stirling.

As the smoke cleared, X could see the pinned man's fingers swiping at the air.

"Leave him!" Rhino shouted. "He's done!"

The hand went limp under the flaming debris, and X stumbled after Rhino. Another blast rocked the ship, and he braced himself against a bulkhead. The vessel heeled steeply to port, and a loud gurgling followed. They were taking on water.

Keeping low, X moved through the smoke. His helmet gave him filtered air, but it did nothing to help him see through the dense cloud.

Rhino staggered through an open hatch and started up a ladder. X pounded up the rungs after him as the ship shuddered again. The impact knocked him down on the next landing and slammed Rhino into the handrail.

A soldier from the other team stood on the ladder overhead, his flashlight angled down at X and Rhino.

"Go!" X said, pushing on Rhino's wide shoulders.

Reaching the top, the soldier spun the wheel handle and opened the hatch just as an explosion rocked the weather deck. The blast sent him flying backward along with Rhino.

X flattened his body against the bulkhead and shielded his visor from the wave of flames. Heat washed over him in a scalding bath. When it passed, he opened his eyes and looked to the landing below. Rhino used the handrail to pull himself up.

The other man hadn't been so lucky. He had smashed into the bulkhead, where a steel strut impaled him through the chest.

Rhino gave his dead comrade a passing glance and started back up the ladder. "Keep going, Immortal," he said.

X led the way this time, bumping off his light as he stepped out onto a deck ablaze with burning debris. Turbofans whirred overhead, and he looked up at a beautiful and terrifying sight.

Deliverance hovered over the water just off the starboard hull.

He ducked as a missile streaked away and slammed into the side of the trawler. Sergeant Lurch and his crew were trying to escape in their boat, but the blast overtook them, lifting the bow into the air.

Tracer rounds ripped across the water, and X turned to see a warship heave into view around the island's peninsula, machine guns blazing. The rounds cut the men in Lurch's boat to pieces. One of them made it into the water but went under as more bullets pounded the surface.

Another missile streaked away from the airship and hit the other Cazador ship in the bow hull, opening a gaping rent in the heavy steel plate. On the deck, motion flickered in the barred cages.

X almost felt bad for the beasts trapped inside as they vanished in a fireball that cooked them alive.

Two of the ship's turrets were still active, and the Cazador soldiers inside cranked their machine guns up toward the airship. The bow turret exploded a second later as the attacking warship turned its guns on the Cazador vessel.

Fires burned all around X, but he couldn't tear his eyes away from the battle. His people had finally come, and they were slaughtering the Cazadores.

"Immortal, let's go!" Rhino yelled.

It was a reminder to X not to appear jubilant over the slaughter. Checking his enthusiasm, he finally forced his gaze away from the battle and ran after the lieutenant. Containers lay on their sides, the burning contents spilled onto the deck.

X jumped over a pile of boxes as the ship heeled farther over. They were taking on water fast.

Out of the corner of his eye, X watched *Deliverance* slowly rotating. Katrina, or whoever was in command, was preparing to finish the container ship. This wasn't the first time an airship captain had tried to kill him. This time, at least, they didn't know he was down here.

Rhino peeled his boots and armor off at the rail, and X followed his lead. He hated to lose the protection, but he didn't want to meet the Sirens' fate, as burnt meat on the deck.

"¡Rápido!" yelled the lieutenant.

A missile thumped away from *Deliverance* as X took off his helmet and breathed in smoky air. His eyes followed the streak to the ship's stern. The blast lifted him off his feet and slammed him into the rail, knocking the air from his lungs.

Another explosion rocked the vessel, this time knocking him over the side. He flailed for something to grab as he fell, but all he saw was the hull of the rusted ship, and *Deliverance* hovering overhead.

He smacked into the water, and darkness surrounded him. Swimming hard, he heard containers slide off the tilting deck and splash into the water behind him.

The ocean swallowed the Cazador ship. Rhino swam in a powerful front crawl, putting distance between his body and the suction, but X was too close.

Pulled down by the vortex, he panicked, clawing at the surface.

No! Not like this … Please, not like this!

As he was pulled down farther and farther, he forced himself to relax, as he would in a dive. Fighting would only waste the limited air in his lungs.

The cold, swirling water finally let him go, and he began kicking and pulling toward the sliver of light that seemed impossibly far away. Lungs burning, he fought the growing impulse to breathe while underwater.

At last, unable to fight it any longer, he let out the spent air in his lungs and breathed …

And breathed again. A wave slapped him in the face, and he coughed. The realization hit him: a drowned man didn't cough. He was alive and afloat—barely.

Above him, the blue flames of *Deliverance*'s thrusters faded up into the swirling dark clouds as his friends left the scene of devastation they had wrought.

Seeing the airship leave him brought back the painful memory of Hades over a decade earlier, when the *Hive*, instead of catching his helium balloon and pulling him in, had turned away and left him to the cold emptiness of the sky.

The memory filled him with anger. And it was happening again.

He kicked and pulled and kicked some more, using what strength he had left. If he must die, he would fight every inch of the way.

Gradually, he became aware of Rhino's voice over the ringing in his ears. The Cazador lieutenant was treading water and pointing at the trawler. The burning mass was still afloat.

Gasping for air, he swam after Rhino, who had almost reached the fishing boat.

But as X swam toward it, he saw that the trawler, too, was sinking. He looked around them for something they could hold on to, but there wasn't much of anything still afloat.

The Cazador ship they had taken from the Metal Islands had joined the container ship on the ocean floor. Several largish pieces of debris floated in the water, but without the NVGs, he couldn't make them out.

All he could see was the silhouette of the warship his people had used to ambush the Cazador vessels. Like the airship, it was sailing away from the destruction it had caused. Of the hundred-plus Cazador soldiers who had set out from the Metal Islands, only one remained.

But soon enough, he, too, would be gone, and so would X.

"Those were the sky gods," Rhino said between gasps.

X spat water and said, "My people. My friends."

To his surprise, Rhino laughed.

"Guess your people try to kill you, too," he said.

"My people didn't know I'm …" His words trailed off. His people hadn't known he was down here this time, but Captain Leon Jordan had certainly known and had left him on the surface to die.

Maybe the people in the sky had something in common with the people of the Metal Islands after all.

TWENTY-THREE

"What do you mean, 'don't come'?" Katrina said. She looked up from the radar monitor to read Eevi's face.

"Ma'am," she said, "the airships picked up something on analog from Magnolia Katib, and she's saying not to come to the Metal Islands."

Katrina swallowed. "I want to know exactly what she said."

Eevi played the transmission.

"This message is from Magnolia Katib. If anyone on Deliverance *or the* Hive *receives this, do not come to the Metal Islands. I repeat, do not come here. This is not the place we thought it was. There are too many soldiers to fight. Please, do not …"*

The words from her friend hit Katrina like a gut punch.

"How do we know she wasn't put up to it?" Eevi asked.

"We don't."

"Maybe we should think about postponing the mission, Captain."

Katrina walked back to the windows overlooking the western sea. She grabbed the binos and looked at the island, now just a flat speck on the horizon, with a weak reddish glow from the river of lava.

The two Cazador ships and the trawler had sunk, and the soldiers on them were dead or soon would be. Changing the plan at the last minute had worked well. Instead of dropping the militia and freed prisoners on the fishing boat and moving the passengers of the airships to the container ship, she had ambushed the Cazador ship and destroyed all three vessels.

She would save all remaining ammunition for the attack on the Metal Islands and just let the sharks pick off any survivors.

The first phase had been a huge success, with no lives lost except for the enemy and one of the prisoners freed from the container.

"Captain?" Eevi said.

"I'm thinking," Katrina said. The second phase of the attack was supposed to launch before dawn, but the message from Magnolia had her again reconsidering their plan.

"Thank you, Eevi, that will be all," Katrina said without turning from the window.

But Eevi didn't leave. Katrina could see her reflection in the glass.

"Ma'am, don't you want me to respond to *Deliverance*?" she asked.

"The message from Magnolia isn't anything we don't already know," Katrina said. "Just look out the window. We've already sunk three Cazador vessels with all hands. And we have two airships, one of them with a cargo bay full of troops, plus the *Zion* and a team of Hell Divers."

"So, do you want me to transmit?"

"Yes. Tell them the message changes nothing."

Eevi hesitated, then nodded and returned to the bridge.

Letting out a breath, Katrina held up her wrist computer to check the time. The mission clock ticked down.

One hour and five minutes to go …

Her nerves were stretched taut as a crossbow string. The very future of her people was at stake, and Magnolia's words were really starting to mess with her head.

Maybe that was what the enemy wanted. Maybe the Cazadores had put her up to it.

Katrina returned to the bridge, trying not to dwell on her friend's words. The members of her team who hadn't moved to *Deliverance* were at their stations, armed with rifles and handguns in case they were boarded.

She summoned her most confident and authoritative voice as Eevi, Sandy, Jaideep, and Edgar stood at attention.

"All right, everyone, we've got just over an hour," she said. "At go time, *Deliverance* will drop Trey, Vish, Alexander, Michael, and Les onto the capitol tower to rescue Magnolia, X, and Miles. They will also identify any aerial defenses that put the airship at risk.

Our job is to provide a distraction. We will punch through the barrier and take out any enemy vessels. *Deliverance* will target other defenses to buy the Hell Divers more time. The *Hive* will remain at a safe distance just in case the plan fails."

"Just the divers?" Edgar asked. "What about the militia and the prisoners we freed from the container ship?"

"*Deliverance* will drop them off as soon as any aerial defenses are taken out," Katrina replied.

"And what about the message from Magnolia?" Jaideep asked. "My brother is on *Deliverance*, and I don't want him diving into a trap."

"The message confirms that Magnolia is still alive, and that's it," Katrina said. "We already know they have warships, but neither of the ships we sank had antiaircraft weapons."

"So what?" Jaideep said. "None of us know what's waiting there."

"No, we don't. That's why I'm sending a Hell Diver team to the surface before *Deliverance* drops off our other soldiers."

The answer seemed to satisfy the rest of the group, but Jaideep shook his bandaged head.

"Any other questions?" Katrina asked.

"I don't have a question, but I do have something I want to say," Sandy said. She stepped away from her station and looked at each crew member.

"Take the wheel," Magnolia said. "We're heading to the rig where they're building a prison."

She bent down and grabbed the handset while Sofia took the helm.

"This message is from Magnolia Katib. If anyone on *Deliverance* or the *Hive* receives this, do not come to the Metal Islands. I repeat, do not come here. This is not the place we thought it was. There are too many soldiers to fight. Please, do not—"

"Oh, shit," Sofia said.

A bright light hit the windshield, and Sofia spun the wheel hard to port. Grabbing the back of a seat to keep from falling, Magnolia shielded her eyes from the bright glow.

She couldn't see anything, but she could hear the rhythmic cough of the exhaust pipes.

"Down!" Sofia yelled.

Before Magnolia could react, something slammed into the *Sea Wolf*. She lost her footing and went down hard, hitting her head on the cabin bulkhead. Water spurted from the passage outside the open hatch to the other quarters, and between blinks she saw a long, sharp spike that had punched through the hull and the little galley where she once cooked shark meat.

Blood trickled down her forehead, dripping into the seawater that poured in through the breached hull. Sofia tried to get up but fell back down.

The loud purr of idling motors surrounded the *Sea Wolf*, and bright lights glared through the broken windshield. Magnolia looked around her for

"With the loss of Jed, this journey has been heart-breaking for me, and while I don't know what's going to happen an hour from now, I know in my heart this is the right thing to do. Our people deserve a place to live, and from what I've seen, the Cazadores don't." She raised her chin. "Today, I fight for Jed. Today, I fight for those who can't fight for themselves."

The others all nodded.

"For Jed," Katrina said. "And for everyone on the *Hive* and *Deliverance*."

Thunder boomed outside, vibrating the metal shutters over the broken portholes. A moment later came the percussive white noise of more rain.

The storm had begun, and another, of a different sort, was imminent.

"Okay, everyone, let's get to it," Katrina said, clapping her hands together. They fanned out, and she returned to the command center.

Black storm clouds rolled over the dark water, blurring the boundary between ocean and sky. Not ten miles away to the east were the Metal Islands. In less than an hour, she would see the first habitable spot in her lifetime. Her heart skipped with excitement but also with an edge of fear.

She grabbed the assault rifle and threw on a vest over her uniform and Hell Diver armor. The armor was still tight around her chest even after pounding the dent out, but she could breathe, and the bruised rib was bearable.

Leaning down, she pulled magazines from the

duffel bag and stuffed them into the slots in her vest. Then she clipped the command sword of the *Hive* on her belt. She exhaled, ready to go. Ready to fight.

As the minutes ticked by, she used the time to check the radar and scan the sky with her binos. At thirty minutes till go time, she picked up the receiver and opened a line to the *Hive*, breaking radio silence.

"Captain, this is Samson. Go ahead, over."

She kept her voice low in case anyone on the bridge below could hear. She was more worried about that than about Cazadores listening in.

"How are things up there?"

"Good, Captain. We're at twenty-five thousand feet, at the location you gave us. Skies are clear of storms in this area. Don't worry about us."

She paused for a moment, lowering the receiver before bringing it back up to her lips. "If things go wrong, you will be all that's left of us. And if the worst does happen, you have your orders. Promise me you will follow them."

Static crackled. This time, Samson was the one to hesitate.

"I promise, but don't talk like that, ma'am. Everything is going to work out. I believe in you. Our *people* believe in you. Just do what you do best, Captain. Give 'em hell."

The line cut off, and Katrina checked her wrist monitor again.

Twenty minutes.

In fifteen, they would break through the barrier between darkness and light.

Her heart pounded even harder, and she took several deep, slow breaths. This wasn't like her. She had dived into the wastes dozens of times, fought monsters, survived the madman Leon Jordan.

So why did she feel that this was the end?

She rested her hand on the sword's pommel. It was a symbol of her people, and she would wear it proudly into battle.

A beep from the radar snapped her to instant alert.

She opened a line to the bridge.

"You see this contact, Eevi?" she asked.

"Copy that, ma'am. Looks like a single boat."

"Edgar, ready the MK-65," Katrina said.

"On it, ma'am."

Katrina stared through the binos. A hint of light appeared through the gloom. Was that the moon, or just her eyes playing tricks on her?

Another blip showed up on the radar. This one was much bigger than the others. It had to be one of the oil rigs.

Her eyes went from the monitor to the horizon. She didn't need the binos anymore. The darkness seemed to pale. The wall was becoming translucent, with a weak but visible white light showing through the other side.

In five minutes, they would be through the barrier. *Deliverance* would be moving into position now, and

Michael, Trey, Les, Alexander, and Vish would be preparing to dive.

Layla had taken over for Les as acting captain, and Katrina had full faith in her younger friend. She also had a sense of why Layla and Michael had decided that she not dive—something Katrina had suspected for a while now after a conversation with Layla in the locker room a month ago.

Their child would be the first born on earth to people of the sky.

The thought gave Katrina the reassurance she needed. Another blip appeared on the outer edge of the radar, then another.

Two minutes before breach.

She alternated her gaze from the radar, which now showed five contacts, to the view outside the porthole windows. The sky suddenly lightened, and a dot sparkled above.

The dot became two, and then twenty, and then a dazzling sky of stars.

She stared upward in awe as the mission clock hit sixty seconds.

"Are you seeing these?" Eevi asked over the comm.

"Yes," Katrina replied. "I never saw anything so beautiful."

"There are way too many," Edgar said over the comm channel.

Katrina brought her gaze back down to a view of an oil rig, and dozens of silhouetted shapes in the water. She switched the binos to night vision.

Dear God …

In the green hue of the NVGs, she saw dozens of vessels. An entire armada was spread in a long row across the water. Fishing boats, speedboats, armored boats, and WaveRunners mounted by one or two riders carrying weapons.

Beyond the fleet, three long speedboats waited.

"El Pulpo," she whispered.

A commotion on the nearest boat, a twin-hull vessel like the *Sea Wolf,* drew her attention. A sailor moved to the top deck and aimed binoculars at her. Then he waved wildly, and two men swung mounted machine guns toward the USS *Zion.*

"Captain, what are your orders?" Edgar asked over the comm.

She could hear the near panic in his voice, but there was none in her reply.

"Open fire, and give 'em hell."

The MK-65 fired a shell at the twin-hulled boat, and the man with the binos vanished in a puff of smoke and debris. The blast consumed two WaveRunners, setting the riders ablaze.

"Manual firing," Katrina ordered, keeping her voice calm. "Conserve ammo. Pick your targets wisely."

"Copy that," Edgar replied. His voice had calmed, too. "Firing on three, two …"

Another shell from the enclosed turret blew up a fishing boat with mounted machine guns. Orange flames spread across the dark water.

They had caught the armada flat-footed, but the

Cazador sailors were quickly moving their vessels into combat intervals. Small-arms and machine-gun fire from the armada pinged and ricocheted off the armored warship's deck and hull.

Katrina watched as one of the ships rotated a turret mounted with what looked like a rocket launcher. The barrel stopped, pointed right at the top of the island.

She grabbed her rifle and ducked as the glass shattered around her, raining onto the deck. Keeping low, she moved to the ladder. Just as she was about to duck into the opening, she glimpsed a missile streaking toward the command center.

* * * * *

Michael stood at the launch bay door on *Deliverance*, peering into a cloudless sky in the early morning hours. The half-moon was high overhead, shining through a sky so clear, he could see the oil rigs twenty thousand feet below.

But if he could see the surface, maybe the Cazadores could see him. That was where Katrina came in.

She had already started the attack. Miniature explosions flickered in the distance—shells and missiles exploding over the water.

He raised his prosthetic arm and turned to his team. They had already gone through their systems checks and were ready to dive.

Les, Trey, Vish, and Alexander stood behind him, carrying assault rifles, blasters, pistols, and one of the two laser rifles. Michael carried the other. They had covered their battery units with strips of black tape to hide the glow, and they all wore black jumpsuits under their dark armor.

All lights on the airship were turned off to conceal their approach. The light cloud cover passing below also helped.

Static crackled in his earpiece, followed by Layla's voice.

"Team Raptor, you are clear for launch," she said.

"Good luck," Timothy said. "I hope to see you all again very soon."

A private channel opened between Michael and Layla.

"Be careful, Tin. I love you."

"Copy that. I love you, too."

He had already promised her he would come home to her, and hearing her voice reminded him again of what was at stake.

He opened a channel to his team.

"Our target is the capitol tower below," he said. "The one with the saucer-shaped rooftop. We believe that Magnolia, X, and Miles are being held there. Look for aerial defenses on the way in. Our second objective is to identify those and report back so *Deliverance* can take them out with missiles."

The helmets all dipped in acknowledgment. He took a sip of water from the straw in his helmet. He wasn't well rested, and the flesh where his stump connected with the prosthesis throbbed despite the fresh application of nanotech gel, but he was ready for this.

Ready to dive into the first habitable drop zone in the history of Hell Diving. As he scanned the surface, he thought of all the divers who would have loved to see this.

"This is the moment we've all been waiting for," he said. "The moment that humanity has been waiting for. Hundreds of our brothers and sisters have dived so we could survive and find this new home. We just gotta dive one final time."

He stepped toward the edge, his gut tightening. The other divers stepped up behind him, getting their first view of the Metal Islands. Michael pointed his robotic hand at the capitol tower.

"Dive with me!" he yelled. "For X, and Mags, and Miles, and humanity!"

They all cheered as Michael leaped out of the cargo hold. The others followed, each of them shouting the Hell Diver motto as they stepped up to the edge and jumped.

"*We dive so humanity survives!*"

Michael dived headfirst, tucking his arms against his body. For the first few seconds, he felt the usual weightlessness as he speared through the clearest skies of his diving career. It didn't take long to work into an aerodynamic position. There were no crosswinds here, no turbulence threatening the stable fall. He checked his HUD for the other beacons. The other dots beeped on the minimap, and he watched the Metal Islands grow larger.

As he rocketed toward the ocean, he checked the naval battle raging to the east. Katrina was vastly outnumbered. Some forty boats were attacking her. But none of them were warships like the USS *Zion*.

The light from muzzle flashes and explosive detonations flickered over the water.

He stared down at the capitol tower, searching for any aerial defenses protruding from the tower's walls. He noted a platform about two thirds of the way up, but he saw no heavy weapons.

And why would they have them? They probably had never been attacked from the sky in all the history of their settlement here. They had probably never been attacked at all.

At ten thousand feet, he glanced over his shoulder. In the green backdrop of his NVGs, he identified the long frame of Les Mitchells cutting through the sky, head down, body straight as a spear. He had almost caught up to Michael.

Good to have you with me, Giraffe.

As Michael looked back down at the capitol tower, a flash of light broke through the darkness. Something streaked past him.

It took him a brief moment to realize that the Cazadores had fired something at the divers. The explosion came several seconds later, like the boom of nearby thunder. Another look behind him revealed that the shell wasn't meant for the divers after all.

The cannon, or whatever they had fired into the sky, was aimed at *Deliverance*. Bright orange flames bloomed by the airship's starboard hull.

Michael bumped on his comm channel. "Layla, get out of there!"

"What the hell was that?" she replied.

Another shot whistled past the divers, this one cutting right between Trey and Alexander. They rolled out of their nosedive, losing their angle and spinning away.

Michael flinched as *Deliverance* vanished in a blast of orange.

"NO-O-O-O-O-O-O!" he shouted.

He stared into the sky, not daring to blink.

"Layla!" he yelled. "Layla!"

The explosion faded away, and the shape of *Deliverance* returned. He remembered to breathe.

"Get out of there!" he yelled.

And the airship did appear to be moving.

"We've taken damage," Layla said. "Turbofans one and two are out."

"Use the thrusters!"

Static crackled over the channel, drowning out her response.

Michael's altitude was down to fifty-five hundred feet, with the top of the tower a few hundred feet closer. The fear of losing the airship and everyone on it terrified him.

He looked away from the altimeter reading, to something else that made his stomach knot.

The saucerlike roof of the capitol tower wasn't just any curved plate of metal. It was the remains of an airship.

He was wrong earlier. An airship had indeed come here, and if Layla didn't get *Deliverance* out of here, the Cazadores were going to have a second trophy to add to their collection.

Now he knew why Magnolia sent the message. Katrina had underestimated their enemy. *He* had underestimated them.

Michael shook off the tentacles of fear. The only way to survive was to fight. He scanned the forty-story capitol tower for the weapon that had fired on *Deliverance*.

"Does anyone have eyes on that cannon?" he yelled.

"Negative," Les replied.

So far, he didn't think Team Raptor had been spotted, but the moment they opened their chutes, they were going to be targets for small-arms fire. The tower had plenty of places to hide weapons, and hundreds of windows to shoot from. On the airship rooftop, a forest of trees surrounded a central amphitheater or stadium, but he didn't see any threats. He glanced back up at the sky.

Alexander and Trey had both managed to move back into stable position. Far above them, the airship was gaining altitude, using its thrusters to put some distance between it and the cannon below.

"I think I saw one of the shots come from the top of that tower!" Vish shouted over the comms.

At three thousand feet, he could see individual

trees growing around the perimeter of some sort of arena or ball field, but no weapons.

There was only one way to locate the cannon: watch the next shot. It came a beat later as a third shell streaked away. He had it.

The cannon was hidden by the tree cover. An explosion flashed overhead, but *Deliverance* was now safely out of range.

Michael bit down on his mouth guard, feeling the most dangerous emotion of all: hope.

All right, you sons of bitches. Team Raptor is coming for you.

A second ticked by as he prepared for the most important fight of his life. Now he saw that it was also going to be the most difficult fight of his life.

A small army crouched in the cover of the trees, waiting for the small fire team of Hell Divers. Michael was close enough that he could see them aiming rifles and pistols into the sky.

"Hostiles in the trees!" he barked over the comms.

"Copy that," Les replied.

The other beacons on Michael's HUD winked in acknowledgment. Flashes suddenly flickered across the canopy of trees.

Tracer rounds cut through the air, lighting the predawn skies up with the glow of war. Gunfire from a hidden .50-cal machine gun swept the air. Michael was close enough to hear the sharp cracking sound, and then a scream in his ear.

"Watch out!"

It was Les. He maneuvered right next to Michael, tilting his visor to look back at Trey. The green flashes raked back and forth.

"Fan out, fan out!" Michael yelled.

They were falling in stable position at two thousand feet now, slowing down before pulling their pilot chutes. As he checked his HUD, a beacon winked out above him.

Michael shot a glance back to see Vish spinning away, an arm and a leg blown off by the rounds.

Higher in the sky, *Deliverance* was crossing over the stars, like a black beetle walking over shiny bits of broken glass. A red spark streaked away from the belly of *Deliverance*.

Michael blinked, thinking at first that the ship had caught fire. But the spark turned into a projectile zipping toward him. A present for Team Raptor.

The missile cut through the sky, screaming past the divers and detonating in the middle of the forest, in the most beautiful explosion Michael had ever seen. The blast erased the gunfire and sent burning human shapes in all directions—some flying through the air, others running, others crawling.

Michael pulled his chute and ordered his team to do the same. The suspension lines drew taut, jerking him back into the sky, or so it always felt. Before grabbing the toggles, he pulled out a smoke grenade and dropped it in the dirt surrounding a sports arena like the one they had landed on in Florida.

"DZ is the smoke!" Michael said over the comms.

Cazador soldiers ran from the burning forest, several of them collapsing and rolling in the dirt. A husky man on fire jumped off the side of the tower—a big, slow meteor plummeting to the sea.

But the missile hadn't killed or maimed all of them. Several Cazadores had survived the inferno unscathed and stood their ground on the outer edges of the tree grove. They aimed weapons at the sky and opened fire on the divers.

Michael dropped another smoke grenade, then pulled the laser rifle from the sheath over his back, taking care not to tangle it in the suspension lines.

He pulled the right toggle to turn his canopy and give him a field of fire on the soldiers near the drop zone. His robotic trigger finger took the shot, and a single blue bolt flashed through the chest of a man crouching and firing into the air. He slumped over, smoke rising from the smoldering hole in his rib cage.

Michael moved to the next target: a soldier hiding behind a clump of red lilies. He sprawled in the foliage, a bright red tunnel glowing in his side. The next soldier lost an arm, just as Michael had.

With the drop zone mostly clear, he put the laser weapon back in its scabbard and checked his HUD.

Alexander, Trey, and Les had pulled their chutes and were coming in fast behind him. Les knew what to do, but both Alexander and Trey seemed wobbly.

Michael looked away, grabbing both toggles and steering toward the sunken stadium. He passed over more gardens and a pool of water, but he wasn't here to admire the beauty. He had come for one thing only: to kill these barbarians and save his friends and his people.

The arena of sand rose up to meet his boots, and he pulled the toggles to slow his decent. Flexing his knees slightly, he did a two-stage flare. He hit the dirt a little hard and ran out the momentum.

Gunfire lanced into the ground, kicking up dust. The two remaining shooters were running away from the burning forest, followed by at least ten more that Michael hadn't seen earlier.

He crouched down, released the collapsed chute, and pulled out his blaster, leveling it at the nearest Cazador. He waited for the sooty, half-naked enemy to get close. The man bared his sharp teeth like a wild animal and raised a pistol as Michael pulled the trigger.

The blast opened a hole in the barbarian's chest, and he fell on his face, raising a halo of dust around him. Return gunfire sounded, and a shot pinged off Michael's robotic arm. He shielded his face, deflecting another round. The soldiers ran at him, screaming and firing their archaic guns.

Michael fired the other shotgun shell into the gut of a man in armor, knocking him down. Then he drew the pistol at his hip and shot each of the other two soldiers.

They slumped to the dirt, giving Michael a moment to gather his gear and pull out the laser rifle. The other divers had landed on his left and right flanks, but both Trey and Alexander had come in crosswind, hit the dirt hard, and gotten wrapped in their chutes.

Les joined Michael, shouldering his assault rifle and laying down covering fire while the other two divers could get to their feet.

Michael came back to back with the lieutenant, shooting bolts at the Cazador soldiers who had taken cover behind the trees. In the glow of the burning missile crater, he could see dozens of them, mostly armed with spears and swords.

A shot kicked up dirt next to Michael's boot, and he fired a bolt through the tree and the shooter behind it. The man gripped his burning midsection and fell sideways into a bush.

It took the warriors only a minute to realize that whatever they hid behind was useless against his advanced weapon. One of them, a burly fellow with spiked hair, yelled commands in Spanish to the soldiers. Michael took off the crown of his head with a laser bolt.

Shouts came from behind the divers, and Michael turned to look for the source. Across the rooftop, men streamed out of a small building on the roof of the airship. Two hatches had swung open, disgorging silhouette after silhouette of Cazadores who had climbed the stairs from the tower.

"Don't let them flank us!" Michael shouted. He looked for cover, but the DZ was on bare ground between the trees and the building. The only place to run was the spectator booths above the recessed stadium.

The warriors still holding position in the forest seemed to hesitate, not knowing what to do now that their leader had fallen. And then, all at once, they screamed and ran out of the forest, straight at the divers.

Trey and Alexander were by now on their feet and firing their weapons, cutting down the charging Cazador warriors. The two divers backpedaled as they fired, nearly running into Michael and Les, who had turned to engage the soldiers piling out of the open hatch.

Team Raptor formed an armored phalanx, with enemies closing in from all directions. There was only one way off this airship roof.

"Kill them!" Michael shouted. "Kill 'em all!"

TWENTY-FOUR

After swimming to exhaustion, Rhino and X had made it to the remains of the fishing boat. Its wooden hull still burned, and one of the sails lay stretched out in the water, like a broken bird wing.

They searched in darkness through the debris field and found a bag and a few planks of wood, but nothing that would help them stay afloat.

At least, the sharks hadn't found them.

Yet.

X kept treading water. He was drained from swimming, and one calf was cramping. Though he didn't have his armor to weigh him down, he was struggling to keep his head above the surface.

It seemed that some monster was always trying to eat him, or some human was bent on killing him. All he wanted was a simple life and a place to settle down somewhere and live out his years with Miles.

Was that too freaking much to ask?

He kept searching through the flotsam for

anything that would help him get back to his dog and friends.

Some people in this world had an intense will to live, coupled with the skills to keep them alive. X knew he was one of them. What he didn't understand was *why* he continued to live.

What made him different?

Not some stupid prophecy, that much was certain. The fairy tale that Janga had preached for years on the *Hive* was nothing but bullshit. She wasn't much better than the woman from the trading post who had sold herbs to his wife when she was dying of cancer.

A destiny foretold wasn't the reason he had survived long enough to reach the Metal Islands in the *Sea Wolf*. Certainly, he wasn't any stronger or smarter than Cazador warriors like Fuego, Whale, or Wendig. He wasn't stronger or smarter than the Hell Divers who died before him, either. Not Commander Rick Weaver, Aaron Everhart, or Erin Jenkins.

Maybe he was just lucky. And maybe that luck was running out.

"Hey, you see that?" Rhino asked.

X brought his rambling mind back to the present and looked in the direction the Cazador lieutenant was pointing. It was a dark night with only a sliver of moon, but in the intermittent flashes of lightning, he saw the outline of what looked like one of the Cazador skiffs, and someone was standing inside.

"Shit, is that …"

Rhino was already swimming in a front crawl

toward the skiff. For a man of his size and dense muscularity, he was a damn good swimmer. X fell behind quickly, too tired to do anything faster than a breast stroke.

A voice called out at the halfway point.

"¡Hola, hola!" Rhino yelled.

The figure in the boat turned toward them. A Cazador soldier had survived after all.

But rather than respond to Rhino, the man ducked down in the stern near the motor. He was trying to start the engine, X realized.

X kicked harder, breaking into a crawl. Memories of the swamps back in Florida surfaced in his mind. Giant octopuses weren't the only monsters in the sea.

But he couldn't think about those beasts right now. Maybe that was why he continued to survive. He rarely gave in to fear, preferring anger as a motivating force.

"Hello!" Rhino called out. He swam the rest of the way to the boat and tried to climb inside, but the Cazador standing inside swung a cutlass, forcing him back into the water.

X didn't need to see a face to know that this was Sergeant Lurch. Why did everyone have to be such an asshole?

He sucked in a long breath, filling his lungs, and ducked under the water. Once he was down, he frog-kicked and breast-stroked for as long as he could hold his breath.

When he surfaced, Rhino had backed away from the boat, treading water.

"Don't do this, Lurch," he said. "We can all make it out of here."

"Fuck you!" The sergeant swung the cutlass downward and came within an inch of lopping off Rhino's ear.

X went back under the water, this time swimming under the boat and surfacing on the other side.

Lurch had his back to him, providing an opportunity, but X had nothing to fight with but his bare hands.

That'll have to do.

The sergeant swung at Rhino again, and X grabbed the side of the boat and shook it as hard as he could. It worked, knocking Lurch overboard.

X climbed over the side and slumped onto the deck. He couldn't see much in the darkness, but he did see a broken oar with a jagged end.

He could hear a lot of splashing and grunting in the water as the two Cazadores tried to drown each other. For a fleeting moment, he considered just leaving them to it, but there was something about Rhino that X respected—something he could relate to.

X picked up the broken oar. To his surprise, Lurch managed to push Rhino under the water and hold him there.

"Hey, numb-nuts!" X yelled.

Lurch glanced up, then cried out as X plunged the jagged end into the side of his neck. The splintered wood broke through gristle and took off a flap of skin that hung like a speared fish.

X stabbed again as the man thrashed with one hand and tried to clamp his neck wound with the other.

Rhino broke back through the surface, gasping for air.

X stuck the oar out, and Rhino grabbed on as X pulled him toward the boat, away from the thrashing sergeant.

Rhino got his hands on the gunwale, and X helped haul him in.

"Guess he won't be giving you problems anymore," X said.

Lurch reached up at the boat, but he was weakening fast. X locked eyes with the dying man, then turned away.

"*Gracias*," Rhino gasped.

X didn't respond. He was trying to start the motor. He had to get the hell out of here and back to the Metal Islands to help with the attack.

"How far out are we?" he asked.

Rhino looked over his shoulder.

"Twenty-five miles, maybe thirty—I'm not sure. Do you think you can fix it?"

"I've fixed worse," X replied. "The question is, do we have enough gas to get us there?" He had found at least part of the problem. The fuel injector was loose. He screwed it back in and then tried turning it on.

The motor coughed but didn't turn over.

As he moved around to check the back of the engine, something slammed into the boat, nearly pitching him over the side. He fell to the deck, where his hand closed on a screwdriver. Rhino moved from starboard to port, peering into the water.

"How is this asshole still alive?" X muttered. He went to look, when Rhino held a hand up. Then Rhino slowly picked up the broken oar.

A dorsal fin as tall as Miles rose out of the water before vanishing again. The dead sergeant had attracted the beast with the lure of fresh blood.

X quietly crouch-stepped back to the motor, holding the screw driver.

The screwdriver would make about as good a weapon as it would a fishing pole. X grunted as the shark slammed them a second time, knocking him down on all fours. Rhino held his stance and plunged the oar into the flesh as it moved under the boat. He yanked it out, blood dripping off the end, and moved to the other side of the boat.

"*Ven aquí, pinche cabrón!*" He raised the jagged oar like a lance.

X found a loose vacuum tube and reattached it, then pulled the cord again. The motor coughed twice. He pulled again and it turned over, billowing smoke out of the back.

"Hell yes!" X yelled.

He pushed the throttle lever hard forward, knocking Rhino on his butt. The dorsal fin pursued them but then went under the surface as the shark went for easier pickings in the debris field.

As they sped away, X looked over his shoulder and

couldn't help but chuckle, seeing the big man on his ass in the bottom of the boat.

"You good?" X asked.

"Yeah," Rhino said, pushing himself up. "You?"

"Depends."

Rhino stood. "Depends on what?"

"On what happens next," X replied. "I'm going to kill el Pulpo when we get back to the Metal Islands. If you have a problem with that, we should deal with it right now."

Rhino stepped up to the front, towering over X.

Great. I was afraid of this …

X still held the screwdriver he had used to fix the motor.

"I do have a problem with that, Immortal."

X had really hoped it wouldn't come to this. God damn it, why did everything have to be so hard?

He prepared to jam the screwdriver inside the Cazador's chin and up into his brain, killing the one man who stood between him and the Metal Islands.

"I have a problem with that, because *I'm* the one who's going to kill el Pulpo," Rhino said.

"Uh, *what?*" X relaxed a degree.

"Sofia has been his prisoner for too long," Rhino said. "It's time I set her free. She is my true love. I've known her since I was a child. The Cazadores took both of us from the same bunker in Texas. I was forced into the army, and she was forced into marrying the king."

X shook his head. "What the hell are you talking about, man?"

"I've fought all these years, enduring the loneliness and perils of a soldier's life, biding my time until the right moment. That moment is now." Rhino took a step back and looked into the distance.

X was surprised at how much they had in common. He, too, had spent years biding his time on the surface, staying alive and waiting for the right moment. At one point, he had even given up.

"I've always loved Sofia, and I always told her I would set her free. Your people have given me that opportunity, Immortal."

It hit X why he felt this bond with Rhino. They were the same breed of man. Both had been driven over the edge but somehow managed to come back from it and keep fighting.

Rhino reached out with a battered and bruised hand. "Let me kill him, and I will help you free your dog and your friends. I will fight with you, Immortal."

X was sick of killing, sick of trying so hard not to die, but he would happily fight one more time with this man.

He dropped the screwdriver and reached out his battered hand. And in an old-world tradition, they shook, sealing the deal.

* * * * *

Magnolia wasn't sure that Sofia was still alive. Her head was slumped against her chest, which didn't appear to be moving. But even if el Pulpo's favorite wife was still alive, her time, like Magnolia's, was running out.

You should have ended it when you could.

Back on the *Sea Wolf*, Magnolia had fired as the hatch broke open, but El Pulpo's men had overwhelmed her so fast, she didn't even have a chance to turn the gun on herself or Sofia.

But even given the opportunity, she wasn't sure she could have taken her own life or Sofia's, no matter how bad things were going to get for them. And things were getting bad.

Magnolia had woken up bound to one of the two windshield posts, each topped with a grinning human skull, on el Pulpo's war boat. Sofia was tied to the other, and she hadn't moved yet.

"Sofia ..." Magnolia tried to say. All that she could hear was a steady ringing. There was fluid in her ears that had to be blood.

Those weren't the only things that hurt.

She couldn't see out of her right eye after a fist had caught her there. The left eye wasn't all that much better, but it let her see the battle raging in the distance.

El Pulpo hung back from the rest of his armada, watching the fight. His thirty or so remaining boats were firing everything they had at the warship.

Apparently, Katrina either hadn't gotten the warning or had ignored it. Knowing the captain, it was probably the latter. But if that was the case, then where the hell were the airships?

She could understand keeping the fragile *Hive* at a safe distance, but *Deliverance*? She prayed it wasn't the source of the explosion a few minutes ago.

The blast was loud enough to carry over the rumble of the exhaust stack beside her, but her restraints had kept her from twisting around to see. They had trussed her up so tight, the rope cut into her bare flesh.

El Pulpo took his helmet off and set it on the seat beside Miles. He turned to look at Magnolia and Sofia. The glow from burning boats gave enough light for Magnolia to see the rage in his face.

His eye appeared to be bulging, and a vein stuck out in the center of his forehead, adding what looked like an extra arm to the octopus tattoo. She was going to take great pleasure in seeing her people kill him. If she lived that long.

After baring his teeth at the captured runaways, he went back to watching the battle. Another of his boats exploded in a cloud of debris. The *Zion* was on the run now, fleeing the armada of smaller vessels. Its wake heaved through the scrap yard of boats chewed up by its cannon and machine-gun fire. But the warship had taken some hits, too. Smoke fingered away from the deck and the top of the destroyed command center. Whoever was at the helm knew what they were doing.

Magnolia glanced over to see Sofia finally coming to. Her nose was broken, and some teeth had been knocked out. Blood streaked down her chin, neck, and breasts. With her looks destroyed, el Pulpo would be less likely to forgive her sins.

Now Magnolia understood why Sofia didn't want to be taken alive.

They both were as good as dead. Their only chance was to be saved by the only heroes left in this world. She looked back up at the jeweled sky, but there was no sign of the Hell Divers.

They couldn't be dead—not all of them … could they?

She twisted in the restraints, which cut into her hands and wrists. The pain didn't bother her, but Miles' sad gaze made her heart ache.

The dog cowered on the deck, quivering at the racket of explosions and gunfire. Magnolia fought harder, but there was nothing she could do. She was tied up too tight.

Her eyes flitted back to the star-filled sky.

All she could do was hope and pray that X had returned and that the Hell Divers would come for her. Not everyone believed in Janga's prophecy—certainly not X—but she did, and her gut told her that he was going to help end all this.

She just hoped she would live to see it.

TWENTY-FIVE

"Stay back until we can confirm there aren't more cannons!" Katrina yelled over the comm channel.

Gunfire and explosions in the distance made it difficult to hear the reply from *Deliverance*.

"You aren't going to last much longer if we don't get in this fight," Layla said.

There was no mistaking the frustration and panic in her voice. With the Hell Divers pinned down on the rooftop of the capitol tower, and the USS *Zion* on the run from the Cazador boats, they all had reason to panic.

"You stay back and let me take care of these assholes," Katrina shouted over the din of battle. "We can't afford to lose *Deliverance*."

The channel closed, and she went back to the monitors flashing reports of fires and system failures all across the ship. Despite massive damage, the engines were still running, the guns still fired, and the cameras still gave a panoramic view of the fight.

They were still very much in this.

She tabbed a screen to pull up the display on the starboard side, where a dozen enemy vessels, from speedboats to fishing trawlers, attacked with everything from handguns to rocket-propelled grenades.

Another grenade detonated against the warship's armored hull. Katrina braced herself against the monitor. Better the *Zion* than *Deliverance*.

"Captain, we can't take much more of this!" Eevi shouted.

On the port side, ten more boats mounted an assault. Katrina was drawing them away from the capitol tower to give the Hell Divers a chance to find the prisoners, and to give *Deliverance* an opportunity to come in and take out the fleet.

She just had to lead them outside the perimeter of the Metal Islands; then Layla could rain fire on them without being seen. So far, the plan was working.

The twenty-odd remaining boats pursued the warship toward the black void surrounding the Metal Islands. If she could get the Cazadores out there, they would be blind and wouldn't be able to track *Deliverance* through the cloud cover.

"Edgar, how are we on ammunition?" Katrina said over the comm.

"The fifty-cal on the stern is out, ma'am, the one on the bow is down to ten percent ammo, and our only MK-65 has five shells."

Katrina cursed at the report. Even if she did manage to draw the boats out there, she didn't have enough ammunition to destroy them. It would be on *Deliverance* to take them out.

"Full speed ahead," she ordered.

Sandy nodded, and the USS *Zion* picked up speed. It was much faster than anything the Cazadores had except the WaveRunners and the speedboats.

She heard chatter over the comms but couldn't make out much of it. And as soon as she passed into the electrical storms outside the border, the comms would receive only static.

What she could make out was something about Commander Everhart and the other Hell Divers being pinned down at the capitol tower, unable to advance.

And Vish was gone, dead before he even landed.

Katrina looked at his brother, hunkered on the floor at his station. He had heard the news, and it had dropped him to his knees. Since then, he had regained his composure, but she wasn't sure she could count on him once things got even dicier.

"Captain, look at this," Eevi said.

Katrina hurried over to her station.

They USS *Zion* passed an oil rig, and the images came online.

Lights flickered on each deck, providing a glow to the vertical slum these people called home. Metal shacks and flimsy partition walls separated one family from the next. Gardens grew out of trough planters, and drying fish and clothing hung from wires and ropes.

Hundreds of people watched from the safety of the oil rig, looking out over the battle.

They look just like us: scared and trying to survive.

Another voice crackled over the channel. It was Edgar.

"They're trying to board us!"

Katrina looked at the display of the starboard side, where six WaveRunners, carrying two riders each, sped alongside. They fired grappling hooks up over the rail.

She put on her helmet, switched on the comms system, and grabbed her laser rifle.

"Eevi, you have the bridge. Just keep us moving! Edgar, keep the boats away from us. I'll take care of these bastards."

Sandy got up from her station, gun in hand. "I'll help."

Katrina gave a nod, and the two women moved out to the deck.

The Cazador soldiers were already shinnying up their scaling ropes.

Katrina flashed a hand signal to Sandy, who moved behind the forward gun turret for cover. The moon and stars had vanished, leaving the deck in shadow. They were now crossing the threshold of light and dark.

She switched to night vision and shouldered her rifle as more boats came up along the starboard side. They had switched a high beam onto the warship.

"Down! Down!" she shouted.

Sandy hit the deck as tracer fire flashed across the water and pinged off the bulkhead behind them. Another RPG exploded harmlessly against the hull.

"Edgar," Katrina said, "port side, three hundred meters out, use the fifty on the twin-hull boat. They have an RPG, and if they get a lucky hit on the bridge, we'll have major problems."

She kept down and got the first Cazador soldier in her sights. Climbing over the starboard rail, long wet hair pulled back, glistening wet.

Closing one eye, she pulled the trigger.

The bolt flashed through him, and he peeled off the rail. Two more Cazadores took his place, one of them managing to get off a shot before Sandy caught them with short bursts from her assault rifle.

They both vanished over the other side.

Slinging the laser rifle, Katrina ran toward the grappling hooks, drawing her sword as she moved. Another soldier emerged over the rail, head poking out and eyes scanning for a target.

Her blade was there to greet him. A swift stroke opened his neck. He reached up to grab the spurting wound, then fell backward.

Not wasting any time, she leaned over the edge and saw several more men climbing knotted ropes. The closest looked up at her as she cut through the rope. He let out a yelp, his arms flailing air until he bounced off the motorboat he had just climbed out of.

Katrina sheathed the sword and unslung the laser rifle as the comm channel in her helmet crackled.

"Captain, half the boats are ending their pursuit!" Eevi shouted.

Katrina could see multiple lights heading away.

Maybe they had caught on to the trap she was laying. Or perhaps they were returning to the capitol tower to deal with Team Raptor.

"Layla, now's your chance," she said over the comm. "Take out those boats. Eevi, bring us about. We're going back in."

"Aye, aye, ma'am," Eevi replied.

There was no response from Layla.

"Layla," Katrina said. "Do you copy?"

The electrical storms were messing with the signal.

Katrina felt the ship begin banking to the left and heard the crunch of the hull obliterating a Cazador vessel. Ten boats were still out here, firing small arms at the warship.

The .50-cal on the bow blazed, riddling another twin-hull craft that was still trying to keep up with the *Zion*. Then the machine gun fell silent as the last spent casings rained onto the deck.

"That's all the fifty ammo we got," Edgar reported. "Three shells on the MK-65 remaining."

Katrina opened a channel to Layla again.

Please, kid, I need you.

Again her hails went unanswered.

She started back to the bridge with Sandy, keeping low and out of view of any hostile vessels. They were halfway across the deck when gunfire cracked behind them.

Sandy screamed and went sprawling.

Heart thumping, Katrina aimed the laser rifle at a team of four Cazador soldiers moving fast toward them. Before she could take them down, they opened fire, forcing her behind a bulkhead.

Sandy crawled toward Katrina, trailing a streak of blood.

"Captain," she said. "Captain, help …"

"Be still," Katrina said.

Gunfire ricocheted off the deck by Sandy, and Katrina moved her laser rifle around the corner to lay down suppressing bolts. Then, breaking cover, she dragged Sandy to safety.

As soon as Sandy was around the bulkhead, Katrina grabbed her laser rifle. She was about to fire again when something punched through the metal wall and slammed into her midsection.

The impact took the air from her lungs, and pain so overwhelmed her that she almost lost consciousness. There was no question the bullet had penetrated her flesh, even with the bulkhead and body armor to slow it down.

Gunfire pounded the deck to her left as she fell.

"Help," Katrina mumbled over the comm. "We need …"

She looked over at Sandy, who lay to her right. The bulkhead only barely covered both of them. Holes crowned outward as more gunfire ripped through. Someone was shooting armor-piercing rounds.

Katrina tried to speak, but all that came out was a croak. She gritted her teeth and reached out to Sandy. They laced their fingers together just as a round lanced through Sandy's helmet. Her fingers went limp.

"No …" Katrina choked. She crawled over to the hatch, leaning against it to sit up. Then she drew the sword and waited for the men.

When the first soldier rounded the bulkhead, she jabbed him through the groin and pushed upward. The pain from her abdominal wound was almost too much, but it didn't stop her. The man had killed her friend, and she wanted him to suffer.

Boots hit the deck, followed by shouts from the other Cazador soldiers. She prepared to meet her end, when the hatch behind her opened.

She fell backward and felt hands under her armpits. Jaideep looked down at her.

"Are you o—" His words cut off at the sight of Sandy's corpse.

"Where are they?" he asked, anger in his voice.

Katrina lifted her chin in the direction of the approaching enemies.

"Can you walk?"

With his help, she sat up gripping her gut, almost blacking out from the pain.

"I … maybe."

Jaideep helped her to her feet.

"Let's get you back inside," he said.

Katrina looked down at Sandy's body one more time and then left Jaideep.

"Take the laser rifle," she said, knowing that these were likely the last words she would ever speak to the courageous young Hell Diver.

Jaideep nodded. "Go, Cap," he said. "I've got this."

There was no trace of fear in his voice, only anger and confidence. With his brother dead, he had little to lose. The young diver had finally lived up to the family name.

Jaideep Abhaya raised the rifle, truly fearless.

Gunfire cracked behind her as Katrina shut the hatch.

"Come on, you animals!" she heard him yell. "I got a little somethin' for ya!"

Katrina limped through the passages back to the bridge and locked the hatch behind her. Eevi was standing at her station.

"Captain, you're …"

"I'm fine," Katrina lied.

Eevi hesitated as if too shocked to speak.

That makes two of us, Katrina thought.

"Stay with me, Eevi," she said. "I need a sitrep."

"We're almost back to the Metal Islands, and we still have four boats pursuing us, but they're quite a ways back."

Katrina brought up the comm line to the command center. "Edgar, fire the remaining MK-65 rounds at those boats. Make 'em count; then help Jaideep, to starboard. We've been boarded by at least four hostiles."

"Copy," he replied.

She slouched into the captain's chair and looked down at the blood leaking from around her gloves. Red encroached on both sides of her narrowing vision. She blinked and tried to manage her breathing. She just needed to stay conscious a little longer …

Gunfire cracked outside the bridge, snapping her alert.

An explosion rang off the port side, then the starboard side.

"Two boats down, two left," Edgar said. "I'll deal with them in a minute."

Katrina kept pressure on her wound, but the combination of bruised rib and gunshot wound made breathing a painful chore. Stars broke before her vision, and fear gripped her in that moment.

She had minutes before she lost consciousness.

Stay with it. Your people need you.

Katrina blinked and filled her lungs.

More gunfire cracked outside, followed by shouts.

Edgar returned to the bridge a moment later, assault rifle cradled across his chest. But Katrina wasn't deceived. She could see blood leaking down the armor over his upper chest.

"Jaideep?" she asked.

Edgar shook his dreadlocks.

"Just us three now," Katrina said. "Edgar, are you with me?"

He nodded. "Till the end, ma'am."

"Good. Keep them off the bridge. I just need a few minutes." She looked over at Eevi. "Go to the cargo hold and take the last Zodiac."

"Ma'am, no," Eevi said.

"That's an order. Your husband is still alive out there. Go find him."

Eevi stood up from her station, her face flushed. She hesitated, then threw up a salute.

"I won't forget this, ma'am. No one will," Eevi said. She stopped to give Edgar a hug before leaving the command center.

Katrina took another deep breath and stared at the metal hatches covering the broken port windows. She pushed a button, dropping them to give her a view of what lay ahead. They had crossed the barrier into darkness. The lights on the oil rigs blazed in the distance. Spotlight beams from the boats that had retreated earlier hit the USS *Zion*, making the weather deck bright as day.

There were still so many boats, and even more were coming from the oil rigs. Rowboats and fishing vessels filled with civilians. Everyone seemed to be rallying behind the octopus banner.

These people were ready to die for their home, just as her people were ready to die to take it from them.

She felt that familiar lump of dread in the pit of her stomach, but her heart knew that this was the right decision. El Pulpo was a cancer that had to be removed from the Metal Islands, just as Leon Jordan had been excised from the *Hive*. She would complete her mission even if it meant that some of her people, including her, had to die.

She heard pounding on the hatch to the deck.

The enemy was outside, trying to get in. Edgar leveled his rifle and took several steps back until he was beside Katrina.

She tabbed the monitor on her right, smearing blood on the screen as she set a course straight for the enemy fleet.

Magnolia had been right. There were too many to fight.

Katrina pushed the binos up to her failing eyes. Two larger ships like the container ship she had destroyed were out in front—a floating wall of rusty metal.

She swept the glasses back and forth until she found the shiny boat with two stacks, and …

"No," Katrina whispered. "That can't be."

Were her eyes playing tricks on her? Or was that really Magnolia?

Katrina coughed up blood and spat but kept the binos on the long boat. The woman tied to the windshield post looked just like her friend.

"I'm sorry I failed you, Mags," she said aloud, "but I won't fail our people."

Katrina tapped the screen again, plotting a course directly for the two big ships blocking the way to the capitol tower. Dozens of sailors were on deck, pointing their guns at the USS *Zion*.

She steered right at them.

"I'm so sorry, Magnolia," Katrina whispered. She opened a channel to Michael. "Raptor One, this is Captain DaVita, transmitting one final time. It's up to you and *Deliverance* now. I love you all, and I was proud to serve as your captain."

She closed the channel before anyone could respond.

Her body felt numb, the pain gone now. A bad sign. She was running out of time.

Please, just let me finish this …

Banging continued on the hatch, and a window shattered. Shouting came from inside the ship.

"They're inside," Edgar said.

"Hold 'em—" A loud whirring cut Katrina off. She unbuckled her harness to watch a massive object consume a swath of stars. *Deliverance* came in low over the water, and Katrina stood to watch.

Flashes of gunfire sparkled from the boats as the USS *Zion* plowed toward them. Bullets pounded the bridge. One punched through her armor, then another, her body jerking from the impacts.

Edgar dropped to the deck and reached up to pull Katrina down to safety, but she remained standing even as more bullets riddled her body. She took her final breath with a smile on her face, watching as *Deliverance* fired a salvo of missiles into the enemy armada.

* * * * *

Team Raptor had made it down to the thirtieth floor of the capitol tower. The central platform was lush with gardens, fruit trees, and a sparkling pool, but violence had torn the beauty asunder. Bushes still burned, tree limbs were broken, and fruit lay splattered on the ground.

"Coming in for another run in a few minutes," Layla said over the comms. "Got another package for el Pulpo. How you doing down there, Commander Everhart?"

Now *you use my formal name*, he thought.

"Holding strong," he replied. A white lie since the team was pinned down and running low on ammo. He looked through his binos at the field of burning debris on the water.

A massive wake rippled away from the zone of destruction. The USS *Zion* had plowed into two thin-skinned container ships, and both were sinking, one bow and one stern tilted upward and sliding under the dark water.

Reinforcements were coming from the other oil rigs as bells chimed, recruiting anyone who could fight. Not all the Cazadores were warriors, though. Breaking their way into the top floor of the tower, the team had even found some who spoke English, and this was where the man in the nice suit told him el Pulpo was keeping the "sky people."

But when Team Raptor arrived, they found empty cages under a statue of an octopus, and a dozen soldiers waiting for them. The team took cover behind a rock wall.

Michael looked at the cages. Where the hell were X, Mags, and Miles?

Katrina's message replayed in his mind, and now he knew that it was final. He had seen the USS *Zion* plow into burning ships as rockets streaked into its command center. Her last act as captain had been the most heroic he ever witnessed, providing a distraction so *Deliverance* could come in and take out most of the Cazador boats. The airship had retreated into the dark skies.

The sight of the USS *Zion* dead in the water, with Cazadores boarding it, filled him with rage.

If his friends weren't dead, they would be soon.

He wiped away a tear. This was not the time to grieve—it was the time to avenge the brave souls on the warship.

Screaming, he popped up over the stone wall and fired a bolt through a Cazador running toward them. The man splashed into the pool, sending up a puff of steam from the cool water.

Another soldier lay facedown, turning the pool pink with his blood. The brazen man had run right into their fire, screaming wildly, just as Michael was doing right now.

All the warriors seemed to enjoy fighting, and many, like this guy, were downright suicidal.

He checked his team. Les had survived a shot to his helmet that knocked him out cold, but he was back on his feet.

Alexander had taken a round to the fleshy part of his thigh. Trey had been shot in the ankle, and still hadn't stopped fighting. The father-son team continued to lay down a field of fire at the Cazador soldiers trying to storm their position.

Bullets zipped over the rock wall and broke

through branches of the trees just beyond the barrier. One bullet hit an orange hanging from a branch just above Michael's head. Citrus exploded all over his visor. He crouched down and checked on Les.

"We have to get out of here," he said.

Les nodded.

Michael waited for a respite in the gunfire chipping into the rock wall and popped up to knock down another soldier running at them. Trey did the same thing, dropping his man with a single round to the neck.

"Push 'em back!" Michael yelled.

Trey and Les continued to pick off any warriors who dared cross the stretch between the trees and the open door leading back into the tower. Alexander, with a bullet hole in his thigh, remained sitting with his back to the rock wall, helping reload weapons.

There were only three ways off this platform: over the railing to splatter on the dock below, down in the elevator cage, or through the very door where the Cazadores were coming out of the tower's interior.

He looked through his binos at the wakes of boats on their way to the capitol tower. Three long, narrow craft led the group, outpacing the others. He couldn't see the sailors clearly, but he could see the octopus on the shiny side of one of the boats.

"El Pulpo, you sack of shark shit," he muttered. Zooming in as far as he could, he saw two figures tied to the windshield posts.

That couldn't be X and Mags ... could it?

He stuffed the binos back into his vest.

"Team Raptor, we have to move!" he said. "Can't stay here any longer. I'll lay down suppressing fire with whatever laser bolts I have left."

Michael checked the battery by pushing a button under the barrel, ejecting the unit. It had 21 percent remaining. Maybe fifty or sixty shots. He popped the battery back into the gun and glanced over the wall. Bullets chewed into bark and chipped the stonework.

In that split-second glance, he identified four shooters lying in the dirt between the trees and the entrance back into the tower. They were crawling in the weak moonlight. More were behind them, and even more were inside the open door leading into the tower.

"Behind us!" Les shouted.

Grappling hooks fired over the railing, where reclining chairs were spread out on the platform. Les hunched down and moved toward the hooks but was forced back as rounds peppered the deck.

"Dad!" Trey yelled.

Michael grabbed Les and pulled him back. "You two lay down covering fire. I'll dislodge those grapnels. Alexander, shoot anything that comes over the rail."

Michael waited a beat, then sprinted for the railing. Halfway there, a head popped up, and he fired a laser bolt on the run, burning an apple-size hole where the man's nose and eyes had been. Alexander took down the next climber with his pistol.

Gunfire cracked behind them as Trey and his father picked out targets.

Michael knew he had to do something drastic to

get them out of here. But what? They would soon be taking fire on all sides.

There seemed only one option: use the ropes the Cazadores had shot up over the railing, and climb or rappel to a lower floor.

Just as he reached the grappling irons, another head popped up. With his robotic fist, he punched the soldier so hard that his face caved in. He fell away, dead before he hit the docks.

Looking down, Michael saw boats docked, and soldiers streaming out of a cargo ship. Fifty men, maybe more.

There was no escaping that way.

He took the grappling hook in his robotic fingers and yanked it loose. The men using ascenders to climb the rope screamed the entire thirty floors down.

As Michael grabbed the next hook, the highest climber looked up at him in terror. This man was no older than he. His mechanical fingers paused, resting on the hook.

"¡No, por Dios!" the man yelled.

Bullets slammed into the deck around him, and Michael ducked, seeing more Cazador soldiers rappelling down from the tower's airship rooftop. Some had already hit the deck and were running for the cover of the gardens.

Alexander popped up, but heavy fire forced him back down, one round nicking his shoulder armor.

"Alexand—" A powerful wind almost knocked Michael down. Above him, *Deliverance* lowered toward the dead airship mounted atop the capitol tower. A bright flash dazzled his eyes as a missile streaked away from *Deliverance* and into the water.

An explosion sounded, and Michael crawled over to the railing. A billowing fireball enveloped the dock thirty floors beneath the platform. The climbers on the rope fell away, some of them ablaze.

Michael retreated to the momentary safety of the rock wall.

Ropes dropped in the space between him and the other Hell Divers, and he hunkered down as militia soldiers and civilians in armor rappelled from the cargo hold of *Deliverance.*

One of them descended too fast and hit the deck hard, yowling in pain. Gusting wind slammed into Michael as the turbofans whipped vortices of wind across the platform, swaying the tree branches wildly. He vaulted the wall and checked on Alexander.

"I'm good!" he shouted over the noise.

Many boots hit the deck behind them. Sergeant Sloan led the militia soldiers, and Cole Mintel led the civilians.

A score of Cazadores ran toward them, brandishing spears, swords, and guns.

"For Rodger!" Cole yelled.

The two forces clashed, filling the garden with screams of pain and the clang of steel. Michael tried to pick targets, but he couldn't risk firing into the scrum. So he slung his rifle and ran into the skirmish. It was time to put his robotic arm to use.

A Cazador in full armor raised a sword over Michael's head. Titanium-alloy knuckles shot out and punched him in the throat, breaking his windpipe. The soldier let out a gagging noise and dropped to the dirt. Another took his place, jabbing with a spear.

Michael moved to the side and wrested the shaft from the warrior's grip. Then he broke it in half in his robotic hand and plunged the blade through the man's eye and into the tree behind him, pinning him there.

A female warrior swung a cutlass at his chest. She clicked her teeth together, taunting him. He had never hit a woman before, and in his hesitation, she swung low, glancing the blade off his shin armor.

Then she tilted forward, and he saw exposed brain tissue where hair had been.

He backed away as Sergeant Sloan lowered her blaster.

"Mustn't hesitate, Commander—" She screamed out in pain as a sword bit into her side armor. Michael pulled his handgun and shot the Cazador soldier twice in the chest, knocking him off his feet.

An explosion sounded behind them as he helped Sloan stand.

Deliverance had pulled away and was moving east over the water, firing more missiles at remaining boats. It didn't get far before taking return fire. Two explosions bloomed across the hull, and a third under the stern.

Michael raced back toward the railing, yelling into the comm.

"Layla!"

The airship fought for altitude, trailing smoke.

"We're going down," Layla said over the open channel. "Brace for impact."

The fear in her voice made his breath catch.

"Michael, I can't …"

Her voice cut off, replaced by white noise on the comm channel. He grabbed the railing, clenching it so hard, the metal bent like taffy in his robotic hand.

The airship crashed into the water, pushing out a high, rippling wave in all directions. The speedboats turned, arcing toward the downed airship. The rocket launcher that had brought the airship down rotated on the gleaming black boat with the octopus logo.

El Pulpo's boat.

Michael felt the fear and heartbreak turn into bubbling-hot anger.

He looked over the side, where the last grapnel rope hung. People with buckets of seawater had mostly put out the burning dock, and he spotted several WaveRunners bobbing in the water.

He turned back to the battle raging in the forest.

Cazador warriors with spears and cutlasses slashed through *Hive* militia and civilians. Dom, the owner of the noodle shop, went down with a spear through the chest. Cole Mintel and Sergeant Sloan were both injured but still in the fight. Trey and Les were side by side, firing single shots. A Cazador jumped on Trey and bit off some of his ear before Les shot the warrior in the head.

Two of the freed prisoners Katrina had conscripted were holding their own, but no one from the *Hive* was used to this type of hand-to-hand fighting. The Cazadores were winning the day, and with the airship down, Michael doubted his people could win the fight.

He drew his laser rifle again and began firing bolt after bolt, cutting down the Cazadores. Three of them went down in a row, and two more hit the deck before the barrel overheated.

More militia soldiers fell beside the dead Cazadores, their blood mixing and seeping into the fertile soil.

Les looked back at Michael. "Go, Commander!" he yelled. "Go help Layla, we'll be right behind you!"

Michael was waiting for his gun to cool when a strange light hit the platform. He turned to the horizon, which had turned pale apricot.

The first sunrise he had ever seen spread its weak glow over *Deliverance* as self-inflating rafts exploded out of the side, keeping the airship afloat.

He had to get down there before it was too late. He had to save Layla.

Michael swung his legs over the side of the railing, clipped the rope through his two carabiners, and looked at his friends for what could be the last time. Les and Trey, though wounded, were holding steady.

Good luck, Michael thought as he kicked off from the platform and started rappelling. His mind kept coming back to X. Where the hell was he?

I could really use your help right now, old man.

TWENTY-SIX

When X and Rhino finally made it back to the Metal Islands, the sun had risen over a scene of destruction. They motored through the field of floating debris. Patches of fuel burned on the surface. A neck and torso in a life vest floated amid the wreckage.

"Take over for me," X said. Ceding the pilot's seat to Rhino, he stood for a better view of the warship his people had commandeered.

Smaller Cazador vessels surrounded the ship like ants around a beetle. Soldiers climbed net ladders, and others moved freely across the deck. The Hell Divers had lost the ship.

"Shit," X muttered. Squinting into the sun, he could make out what looked like a massive shell floating in the water, surrounded by inflated red rafts.

It wasn't here before.

"Is that a sky ship?" Rhino asked.

X slumped against the windscreen. His heart sank

at the thought that this was the *Hive*, but as they drew closer, he saw that it was *Deliverance*.

"Hurry this tin pot up!" X shouted.

Was he already too late to help his friends?

His heart thumped at the prospect that his friends and his dog were already dead. He twisted to look at the Cazador lieutenant.

"We gotta move!"

Rhino pushed the throttle lever, nearly making X take a pratfall. He moved back to the bow, trying to get a sense of what the hell was happening.

Deliverance and the warship had caused plenty of damage before they were disabled. Smoke billowed from the top of the capitol tower, and the walls and dwellings on one of the oil rigs burned. Boats moved away from the structure, some of them carrying construction equipment, including a small crane.

It looked like the rig he blew up when he first arrived here. Then he remembered that the Cazadores were working to restore it, which explained the cranes, but he didn't recall seeing the prisonlike cages.

The breeze whipped his hair as he turned away and scanned the water. Most of the fighting seemed to have died down, but he could still hear sporadic gunfire. The action seemed to be moving to *Deliverance* as more boats sped away from the capitol tower, toward the downed airship.

"Where is el Pulpo?" he yelled to Rhino.

"Look for the shiniest speedboat with twin exhaust stacks! Two skulls on the windshield."

X scanned the vessels. His eyes burned, his stomach growled, and his whole body hurt, but he was used to fighting under these conditions. It just made him a meaner foe.

Rhino steered the craft toward the naval warship and the Cazador boats.

"What are you doing?" X yelled back.

"Getting us some weapons.

X settled back down in the bow. They were hurting and half naked and had nothing but a broken oar to use in a fight.

Not in the best position to fight an army of barbarians.

Rhino steered them toward a speedboat bobbing in the water on the margins of the battle. X reached out and grabbed the side and then climbed up onto the vessel. His boots slopped into pooled blood and crunched down on spent brass.

Three Cazadores lay sprawled on the deck and across one of the seats. Another man was slumped over the wheel, the windshield shattered by the same bullets that went through his chest.

X pushed him out of the way.

Rhino climbed into the better, faster boat and began scavenging for weapons and gear. In a few minutes, they had full Cazador armor, two rifles, two pistols, and three cutlasses.

"Get back," X said.

Rhino moved away, and X used a cutlass to break out the remaining shards of the windshield. Then he started the engine, grabbed the wheel, and pushed the throttle down.

The boat sped away from the battle scene. If any of X's people were still alive on the warship, they were in enemy hands now. The only way to end this was to kill el Pulpo.

Only then would this war end.

And X had a feeling he knew where the octopus king was heading.

He gunned the engine toward the downed airship. The bow thumped over waves as it picked up speed.

"Hand me those binos," X said.

He trained the glasses on the docks at the capitol tower. One was burned down to the pilings, but the others had survived, and people were moving out along them, boarding boats unscathed by the fires.

He zoomed in on what looked like militia soldiers.

How was that possible?

And then it hit him: Katrina had deployed the militia.

A few of the figures—maybe three among a group of twenty—wore Hell Diver armor. The Cazadores weren't far behind. Some rappelled off the side of the building; others were on the docks, firing guns and throwing spears at the departing boats.

"There!" Rhino shouted. He pointed at a long, sleek boat with shiny black paint, and the image of a purple octopus painted on the hull. Amidships, a glass windshield surrounded the single cabin and several seats. It bobbed in the water next to the airship, its stacks belching smoke into the air, and ropes hanging loose off the chromed windshield posts capped with human skulls.

X zoomed in on passengers climbing out of broken portholes to the flat top of the airship. A group huddled at the top, but Cazadores were also climbing up the ship's hull.

He wasn't sure what they would do to his people, but it couldn't be good.

He gave the boat more throttle, and it accelerated, thumping over sheets of burned plastic in the sheen of oil covering the surface. He checked his weapons: a rifle with a full magazine, a revolver with four bullets, and the sword.

"Remember our deal!" Rhino shouted.

"Don't worry, I remember!"

They were closing the gap between the airship and their bow when X saw dorsal fins cutting through the water on the port side. Rhino raised his rifle to fire, but X put his hand on the barrel.

"Those are not sharks," X said.

Rhino stared at gray creatures looping through the surface. A dozen dolphins were swimming next to the boat. One of them jumped out of the water and splashed back down.

They weren't the only spectators. A barge and several boats moved away from the oil rigs, carrying Cazador civilians wanting to see the battle firsthand now that both the airship and the warship were dead in the water.

"The sky people!" Rhino said, pointing to the flat rooftop. Several officers in white were on their knees, and a group of engineers in red suits and other civilians were clustered in groups.

Armored Cazador soldiers surrounded them, pointing spears at their backs. El Pulpo was also there, standing with a double-bitted axe in his hand. He pointed at the boats from the capitol tower that were starting to arrive. Militia soldiers, Hell Divers, and civilians jumped down onto the rafts.

This was it, the final battle for the Metal Islands, and the Hell Divers were outnumbered a hundred to one.

X slowed and came alongside the long speedboat with the octopus logo. A dolphin poked its head above the surface, gazing at him the way an old friend might. It was as if the creature knew he was a friend and wanted to wish him well in the fight against the monsters that ate its species.

Rhino jumped out of the boat.

"Come on!" he yelled.

X looked away from the dolphin and followed Rhino up the side of the airship, using a rope for support. At the top of *Deliverance*, the right flank of Cazador soldiers moved away from the prisoners to face the onslaught of militia and Hell Divers.

X climbed quickly, his wet bare feet slipping on the airship's curved hull. Portholes provided windows inside, but he didn't check for any people looking out. Screams sounded above, and when he finally summited the airship, he saw why.

El Pulpo brought a double-bitted axe down on Bronson White, splitting his head and spraying the deck with blood. Ensign Dave Connor was already dead from multiple stab wounds.

The bastard was killing the crew one by one.

"No!" Ada yelled.

Layla held the crying girl in her arms.

Other prisoners were here, too, including Magnolia and a woman X recognized from the banquet room. Both were in bad shape, their faces battered and swollen.

But where was Miles?

The Cazador soldiers looking in his direction started to step away from the group when they saw X and Rhino. One of them, not wearing a helmet, smiled a jagged grin.

"Sofia!" Rhino shouted.

The girl with Magnolia looked up.

The king turned, his axe dripping with blood. He moved away from the prisoners, dragging Miles on a leash. The dog wagged his tail, and his eyes brightened at the sight of his master. X almost shouted his furry friend's name.

"El Pulpo!" Rhino yelled, beating his chest once, then twice.

El Pulpo heaved the axe up over his shoulder and walked away from the prisoners. He grinned, but the ugly smile vanished when Rhino raised a sword and leveled it at the octopus logo on his chest armor.

It didn't take El Pulpo long to realize that his lieutenant hadn't returned to help kill the sky people. He had come to kill his king.

The raised sword wasn't a show of respect. It was a challenge.

X handed Rhino his sword. "You're going to need two," he said.

El Pulpo snorted, realization apparently setting in. Then he lifted his axe and turned it on Miles.

"NO!" X shouted.

Before the Cazador king could bring it down on the dog, someone burst through the cordon of soldiers and slammed into el Pulpo so hard, he fell down.

The man was wearing Hell Diver armor but no helmet. Long hair, pulled into a ponytail, hung to his shoulders.

X couldn't believe his eyes. It was Michael, and he had a robotic arm.

El Pulpo screamed from the deck, giving his soldiers orders. They all fanned out, but the Hell Diver wasn't alone. His small team and the militia soldiers and *Hive* civilians had taken down the soldiers on the other side of the ship and were making their way up to the top.

X pulled his pistol out and ran to join the fight, with Rhino by his side. Michael managed to get on top of el Pulpo and slugged him in the face, but the massive Cazador king slipped a hand around Michael's neck and lifted him into the air like a sack of potatoes.

X lost track of them in the scrum of armored

bodies and prisoners. He fired point-blank against a Cazador's skull, then swung the pistol into the next man's nose, smashing it. He followed up with a bullet to the chest as the guy went down on his knees.

A break in the chaos gave X a glimpse at Michael and el Pulpo. The octopus king still held Michael in the air in one hand. He used the other to smash him in the brow, opening a cut over his eye. He dropped Michael to the ground and went for his axe.

"Michael!" X shouted.

The disoriented diver staggered to his feet and put his fists up like an old-world boxer. He threw a wobbly punch with his robotic hand, which only drew a laugh from el Pulpo. He easily moved away from the blow and grabbed Michael by the ponytail.

He brought the axe up in his other hand and swung downward, only to have the blade deflected by Michael's robotic arm. The two men separated, and Michael threw an uppercut that knocked several of el Pulpo's teeth out and sent him stumbling backward.

Attaboy! X thought.

Again the crowd blocked X's view. He ducked under a spear and shot his last bullet into the belly of the man wielding it. Then he unslung his rifle and smashed the butt into the helmet of a Cazador soldier with his back turned.

The man dropped, providing X a window through the fighting. Michael was on his feet again, and so was el Pulpo.

X smashed another Cazador in the side of the

head, then jumped over a downed militiaman. The Cazador king drew a long knife from a sheath on his belt. He thrust it at Michael, who moved out of the way only to catch a glancing blow in the back of the head from a Cazador's hammer.

Michael sank to his knees.

"Tin!" Layla shouted. She tried to make her way over but went down in the melee.

The man with the hammer lifted it high to bring it down on Michael's head, but X darted over and swung the rifle butt, unhinging his jaw. Then he turned the other end on the man and shot him in the chest.

Bringing the muzzle around, he pointed it at el Pulpo, ready to finally end this. But before he could pull the trigger, another titan of a man grabbed the king.

X lowered the rifle, remembering his promise to Rhino. He moved over to Michael while the two behemoths went at it.

"You okay, kid?" X asked.

Michael held a hand to his bleeding scalp. "X … You came …"

As X helped Michael to his feet, he heard a bark. He looked for his furry best friend in the chaos but didn't see him. He watched Rhino throw his king to the deck. He brought an elbow down on el Pulpo's face, then went to work with his fists, pounding him over and over.

Blood splattered the deck and teeth rolled out. The octopus king twitched several times and then went limp as Rhino finally stopped the onslaught. He remained on top of his former master, chest heaving, sweat and blood dripping down his battered face.

X's and Rhino's eyes met, and the two men exchanged a nod of respect.

A flash of fur bounded over several corpses to reach X.

"Miles!" X shouted. He bent down to unfasten the collar with the inverted spikes and was rewarded by a wet tongue slapping his face. But X didn't have time to celebrate the reunion.

A guttural scream came from Rhino, who gripped the hilt of a knife that el Pulpo had jammed into his gut.

The sneaky bastard had played dead.

El Pulpo pushed the big man, and Rhino slumped on his side, eyes still locked on X. They exchanged another nod—weaker this time, but confirmation enough that it was now on X to kill the king of the Metal Islands.

X waved Miles back. "Stay, boy. I've got one last thing to do."

The dog barked as X waded through a group of militia soldiers battling Cazador soldiers. He pushed several soldiers out of the way before he saw their leader.

Just ahead, Cole Mintel raised the double-bitted axe that el Pulpo had dropped. His muscular, tattooed forearms flexed as he swung it and split open the back of a Cazador warrior.

X reached out, and Cole tossed him the axe. He

caught it in the air and gripped the shaft in his callused hands. A militiaman aimed a revolver at el Pulpo and pulled the trigger, but nothing happened.

The Cazador king grinned and grabbed the man by the head, turning him toward X. It was Monk, the bearded old guard who used to stand outside the armory. He tried to scream, but nothing came out as el Pulpo twisted his head and jerked it sideways, snapping his neck.

"Hey, *pendejo*!" X yelled. He ran forward with the axe raised.

El Pulpo grabbed Monk's revolver and turned the barrel on X.

This time, it fired.

A crack sounded, and a dark blur slammed into el Pulpo's side. X looked down at his chest, expecting to see a bleeding hole, but the bullet must have hit the axe head.

The Immortal had again been spared from death.

Growling, snarling sounds snapped him back to reality.

Miles had el Pulpo by the neck, tearing at his flesh. The dog pulled out a strand of gristle and bit it off.

"Miles, back!" X shouted.

The dog pulled another strip of flesh away.

El Pulpo looked up at X, a flash of fear in his eye as X brought the axe down, splitting in two the octopus engraving on the chest plate. He left the axe lodged there and backed away.

The fighting died down around them until only gurgling and gasping sounds could be heard. El Pulpo lay on his back, his muscular arms out by his sides, the axe in his chest rising and sinking as he struggled for air.

The soldiers on both sides paused, lowering their weapons as the rising sun beat down on the blood-stained rooftop.

It took X a moment to realize that the Cazador warriors and his people weren't looking at the fallen leader. They were looking at the sky.

A shadow passed over *Deliverance*, and a violent wind pressed down on the survivors. X looked up at the beetle shape descending from the heavens. An ancient speaker system on the bottom of the *Hive* blared a message audible over the whirring fans.

"Surrender or lose everything! We have bombs that will level your homes, sink your ships, and take the lives of everyone you hold dear!"

X felt Miles rub against his leg, and he patted the dog on the head, smiling as the message switched to Spanish from the Hive's databases.

"*¡El rey está muerto!*" someone yelled.

The Cazador soldiers all shifted their gaze to the king.

One by one, they laid down their rifles, spears, knives, and cutlasses.

"Grab their weapons!" shouted Cole Mintel.

Sergeant Sloan and her remaining soldiers went to work. X watched in shock. Only thirty-odd people were still standing on *Deliverance*'s bloody rooftop, and most of them were injured.

So this was what war looked like …

It was over now. Finally. But what happened next was anyone's guess. There were thousands of Cazador civilians, at least four hundred people on the *Hive*, and some probably hiding inside *Deliverance*.

X didn't have time to think about the future. Voices besieged him from all directions, and there were Cazadores to round up.

"Eevi!" shouted Alexander. He limped over to his wife, who had climbed the ladder up onto the airship's roof. More people followed her, including Rodger Mintel. Joining him was a group of filthy construction workers, all slaves who, apparently, had fought for their freedom. It explained the burning oil rig X had seen on the way in.

"Dad?" Rodger said. "Dad, is that you?"

Cole Mintel dropped the armload of weapons he was carrying. He brought up a hand to get the sun out of his eyes.

"Rodge?" he said. "Rodger, is that you?"

"Dad!"

They both ran to embrace.

X took a moment to bend down and hug his dog.

"I missed you, buddy," he said. "Missed you so much."

Miles licked his face and then followed him over to Rhino, who sat beside Sofia on the deck, with the knife still in his side. The massive warrior carefully got down on one knee and bowed his head as X approached.

"What are you doing?" X asked.

Looking around him, he saw all the Cazador soldiers going down on one knee. And not because the militia soldiers had guns pointed at them.

"*El rey Javier*," Rhino said. "The Immortal."

X shook his head. "I'm no king."

"You killed el Pulpo," Rhino said.

Michael limped over with Layla. "Guess that means you're in charge now," he said.

Layla wiped away a tear and looked out over the water. "I wish Katrina were here to see this."

X followed her gaze to the warship, realization setting in. He couldn't believe it, but then he could. Katrina had always been a fighter, and in the end, she had given everything.

"She sacrificed herself for us," Eevi said. "Gave me a chance to escape."

"She was the greatest of us," Layla said.

Michael slapped X on the shoulder and then looked up at the *Hive*.

"He doesn't really have bombs, does he?" X asked.

"Actually, Samson does have bombs," Michael said. "It was the contingency plan. The final order Katrina made before we started the attack, just in case this happened," he said, with a sweeping gesture that encompassed both *Deliverance* and the USS *Zion*.

Magnolia had worked her way over to Rodger and Cole.

"Good to see you, kid," X said. He gave Mags a gentle hug, then held her at arm's length. "You've looked better."

"You, too," she said, cracking a half smile.

"More scars, more stories."

Her smile broadened. "The life of a Hell Diver."

"I have the biggest scar of all," Rodger said, pulling up his shirt to reveal the wicked gash on his chest, then turning around to show where the blade went in.

The divers chuckled for a second before lapsing into silence.

"So what do we do now?" Magnolia asked, eyes on X.

All the divers looked to him.

He drew a breath of salt air and looked out over the ocean, where Cazador vessels floated and people watched from the oil rigs. Men, women, children. Grimy, needy, fearful people looking back at him.

He didn't see enemies this time. He saw people like those on the airship. His experience on his mission with the Barracudas had taught him that even enemy soldiers could change. Rhino and Wendig had proven it to him on his journey.

Finally, he looked at the warship where Katrina had given her life. His heart broke for her, but this was what she had always wanted for her people.

He saluted.

"Thank you, Katrina," he said. "For being the captain our people needed."

Janga's prophecy had ended up being more than a fairy tale. A man had led them to a home on the water, but he couldn't have done it without Katrina. Her bravery and sacrifice helped capture the Metal Islands from the Cazador king.

X turned back to Michael and clapped him on his robotic arm. He wasn't sure what would happen from here, or what the future held, but he knew that as long as there were Hell Divers, humanity would find a way to survive.

EPILOGUE

Zone 4, Sector 60

Year 1 of the New Light

Over two hundred and sixty years have passed since World War III left our earth poisoned and shrouded in darkness. For most of my life, I lived in the sky. But then my people discovered a habitable place to call home. A place where the sun shines and the water is crystal clear. A place where humanity has a second chance.

I left that home to help find you, the hidden survivors. People around the world who, like me, dream of living on the surface again. I know you're out there, hiding in the shadows and living in the darkness. Frightened of the monsters, machines, and even humans that want to wipe us out.

I have traveled the world, from the skies and sea to the poisoned soil, looking for survivors just like you. I have seen the nightmares on the surface. I have fought monsters and men who wanted to eat my flesh.

But I survived. My people survived. We built a new

home on the ocean, which we call the Vanguard Islands. My team has already rescued dozens of survivors from the poisoned darkness and brought them back to our colony.

We have farms, we have fish, and, most importantly, we have each other—a strong community governed by an executive council.

Things aren't perfect, but life is good here. Beautiful, even.

Beyond our dark walls, there are still threats everywhere. Mutant beasts and plants, radioactive dirt, electrical storms, and killer bots. The AI defectors that hunt and kill humans—the same machines that very nearly brought our species to extinction.

But as long as there are Hell Divers, we will fight. We will dive. And we will survive.

This is Commander Michael Everhart, transmitting from the airship Discovery, formerly known as ITC Deliverance. And if you're listening, don't be afraid. We are the last humans, and we are in the skies, looking for you. If you're out there, respond to this message. We will never stop diving for humanity. We dive so humanity survives.

COMING

NOVEMBER 2019

HELL DIVERS VI

The battle for the Metal Islands is over, but the threat of extinction continues as the machines wage their genocidal war on humanity. Alliances will be forged, and new Hell Divers will rise to fight the ancient threat and save their species.